The Best of

BETTY NEELS

A Matter Of Trust

Romance readers around the world were sad to note the passing of **Betty Neels** in June 2001. Her career spanned thirty years, and she continued to write into her ninetieth year. To her millions of fans, Betty epitomized the romance writer, and yet she began writing almost by accident. She had retired from nursing, but her inquiring mind still sought stimulation. Her new career was born when she heard a lady in her local library bemoaning the lack of good romance novels. Betty's first book, *Sister Peters in Amsterdam,* was published in 1969, and she eventually completed 134 books. Her novels offer a reassuring warmth that was very much a part of her own personality. She was a wonderful writer, and she will be greatly missed. Her spirit and genuine talent will live on in all her stories.

The Best of

BETTY NEELS

A Matter Of Trust

MILLS & BOON

YEAR'S HAPPY ENDING
© 1984 by Betty Neels
Australian Copyright 1984
New Zealand Copyright 1984

First Published 1984
First Australian Paperback Edition 2025
ISBN 978 1 038 94073 5

A VALENTINE FOR DAISY
© 1993 by Betty Neels
Australian Copyright 1993
New Zealand Copyright 1993

First Published 1993
Second Australian Paperback Edition 2025
ISBN 978 1 038 94073 5

Published by
Mills & Boon
An imprint of Harlequin Enterprises (Australia) Pty Limited (ABN 47 001 180 918), a subsidiary of HarperCollins Publishers Australia Pty Limited (ABN 36 009 913 517)
Level 19, 201 Elizabeth Street
SYDNEY NSW 2000
AUSTRALIA

Printed and bound in Australia by McPherson's Printing Group

CONTENTS

YEAR'S HAPPY ENDING 7

A VALENTINE FOR DAISY 193

Year's Happy Ending

CHAPTER ONE

THE SEPTEMBER SUN shone hazily on to the narrow garden. Its only occupant, who was busily weeding between the neat rows of vegetables, sat back on her knees and pushed her hair back from her forehead. Long hair, fine and straight and of a shade which could only be described as sandy. To go with the hair she had freckles, green eyes and long curling sandy lashes, startling in an otherwise ordinary face. She bent to her work once more, to be interrupted by her mother's voice from the open kitchen door: 'Your cousin Rachel wants you on the phone, Debby—she says it's important.'

Mrs Farley withdrew her head and Deborah dropped her trowel and ran up the garden, kicked off her sandals at the door and went into the hall. She picked up the receiver warily; Rachel was a dear and they were the best of friends, but she was frowned upon by the older members of the family, they didn't approve of her life. That she had held down a splendid job with some high powered executive was one thing, but her private goings on were something quite different. 'Hullo?' Deborah said, still wary, and her mother poked her head round the sitting room door to hiss:

'She can't come and stay—I have your Aunt Maud coming…'

But Rachel didn't want to come and stay, she spoke without preamble: 'Debby, you haven't got another job yet, have you? You're free…?'

'Yes, why?'

'You've heard me talk of Peggy Burns—you know, the girl who married some wealthy type with a house somewhere in Dorset? Well her mother's ill and she wants to go to her, only Bill—her husband—is in the Middle East or some such place and can't get back for a few weeks, and there are these kids—terrible twins, four years old, and the baby—just beginning to crawl. She's desperate for a nanny and I thought of you. Marvellous lolly, darling, and a gorgeous house. There's a housekeeper; rather elderly with bunions or housemaid's knee or something, and daily help from the village.'

'Where exactly does she live?' asked Deborah.

'Not far from you—Ashmore? Somewhere between Blandford and Shaftesbury. Do say you'll help out, Debby. Have you got your name down at an agency or something?'

'Well, yes—but I did say I intended to have a holiday before the next job.'

'Oh, good, so you can give them a ring and explain.' Rachel decided.

How like Rachel to skate over the bits she doesn't want to know about, thought Deborah; the phoning and explaining, the packing, the getting there… 'I haven't said I'll go,' she said a bit sharply.

Rachel's self-assured voice was very clear. 'Of course you'll go, Debby! Supposing it was your mother and no one would help you?'

'Why can't you go?' asked Deborah.

'I'm not a trained nanny, silly. Uncle Tom could run you over when he gets back from work; it's Coombe House, Ashmore, and here's the phone number so that you can ring and say you're coming.' Before Deborah could get her mouth open she went on 'I'm so grateful, darling, and so will Peggy be—bless you. I must fly—I've a new boy friend and he's taking me out this evening and I must wash my hair.'

'Rachel…' began Deborah, too late, her cousin had hung up.

Her mother said indignantly: 'But you've only been home a week darling, and the boys will be back for half term and you'll miss them. How like Rachel, arranging everything to suit herself without a thought…'

'Actually, she was trying to help,' said Deborah fairly, 'And I suppose I could go if its only for a week or two. I could ask the agency for a temporary job when I leave Ashmore and then be home for Christmas. I'd like that.'

Her mother brightened. 'That's true, love, and you haven't had a Christmas at home for a couple of years, have you? I don't know what your father will say…'

Deborah said gently, 'Mother, I'm twenty-three.'

'Yes, Debby I know, but your father always thinks of you as a little girl even though you're the eldest. He always will until you get married.'

'Mother,' said Deborah with faint exasperation. She would like to get married and have a husband and children and a home to run, but she considered her chances slight. She had plenty of friends for she had lived in Dorchester all her life, but most of them were married or thinking about it, and those who weren't, girl and man alike, tended to regard her as a well-liked sister to whom they could confide their amatory problems.

She sighed and went back to the phone.

The voice at the other end was pleasant, tinged with panic, but hopeful. 'Thank God,' said the voice fervently, 'Rachel said you'd ring, you've no idea...you're like a miracle, I'd absolutely no idea what to do. I'm not usually such a fool, but I seem to have gone to pieces...'

Deborah heard a watery sigh and said hastily, 'I'll come just as soon as I can, Mrs Burns—my father will drive me over as soon as he gets home, that'll be in about two hours. Can you go to your mother this evening?'

'Yes, oh yes. She lives in Bath so I can drive myself. I'll get all ready to leave shall I? And put the twins to bed and see to the baby. You're an angel. I don't know your name, at least I'm sure Rachel told me but I don't think I took it in.'

'Deborah Farley. Is your house easy to find Mrs Burns?'

'Yes, oh yes. Facing the village green. There is a green gate that runs up to the side of the house, if you drive in and turn off to the front door.'

'About half-past seven, Mrs Burns. Goodbye until then.'

Deborah hung up. She would have to pack; uniform and white aprons and sensible shoes. She decided to take some summer clothes with her as well, off duty seemed a little unlikely but she could change in the evenings when the children were in bed. She went and told her mother and then made tea for them both, glancing with regret at the half weeded border she wouldn't have the time to finish now.

'I daresay it won't be for long,' she observed philosophically, 'I mean, Mrs Burns' mother will either get better or die, I hope she gets better, Mrs Burns sounds nice.'

'I wonder what the children will be like?' Her mother wanted to know doubtfully.

'No worse than some I've had to deal with,' Deborah said cheerfully, 'and probably a good deal better. I'd better go and throw a few things into a bag.'

Her father wasn't best pleased, he had been looking forward to a quiet evening, reading the papers and watching the TV. He was a kind-hearted man inclined to be taciturn at his work, managing one of the banks in Dorchester, and good at his job, but at the end of the day he was glad enough to get home, potter in the garden if he felt like it, and enjoy the peace and quiet of the evening. He looked at his daughter with faint annoyance.

'Really, Debby you are supposed to be on holiday.'

'Father, dear, I know, but this Mrs Burns is desperate and as I explained to mother, I could take a temporary job after I leave there and then come home for Christmas.' She kissed his cheek and smiled at him.

So he got out the car again and she said goodbye to her mother and Thomas the cat and got in beside him. 'It's quickest if you go to Blandford,' she suggested. 'It's on the Shaftesbury road then you can turn off to the right—I looked it up.'

The village, when they reached it, was charming, with its duckpond and the nice old houses clustered around it. And the house was easy enough to find, across the green with the wide gate standing invitingly open.

Mr Farley parked the car precisely before the door and they both got out. The house was stone built, square and Georgian, sheltered by old trees, its sash windows open. Deborah, her father beside her with her case, thumped the big brass knocker, not too loudly in case the children were asleep, and the door was flung open.

The young woman who stood there wasn't much older than herself, a good deal taller and very slim, with a short mop of fair curly hair and a pretty face. 'Oh, golly,' she breathed, 'I could hug you—you are an angel. Come in…'

She looked at Mr Farley and Deborah said: 'This is my father, he drove me here.'

Mrs Burns smiled widely at him. She said earnestly: 'Nanny will be quite happy here, I do assure you Mr Farley, there's the housekeeper—she's getting supper actually, and there is plenty of daily help—it's just the children to look after. Come and have a drink...?'

Mr Farley, quite won over, said that no, he wouldn't as he had to drive back to Dorchester and his supper was to be waiting for him. He said goodbye to them both and got back into his car and drove off.

'He's nice,' observed Mrs Burns. 'My father died last year, he was nice too.' She wrinkled up her nose engagingly. 'You know—a bit fussy but always there. Of course, I've got Bill now, only he's not at home. He'll be back in a week or two though.'

She led the way across the hall into a comfortable room and waved Deborah to an easy chair. 'Do you mind if I don't stay for supper? I'll tell you as much as I can, then I'll be off... I'll leave my phone number so that you can ring every day. Mary—that's our housekeeper, will see to the house and the food and so on, she is a dear soul, but getting on a bit so the twins are a bit much for her. If you could cope with them and the baby she'll see to everything else.' She handed Deborah a glass of sherry and sat down herself. 'I'll tell you the routine...' She paused: 'Do you drive?'

'Oh, yes. Only I haven't a car.'

'Good. We all take it in turns to take the children to school. It's about a mile out of the village, mornings only; it won't be your turn until next week, anyway.'

'The baby's feeds?' prompted Deborah.

'Ah, yes.' Mrs Burns then dealt with them. 'And the baby's name is Deirdre, but we all call her Dee. The twins are

Suzanne and Simon.' She added, with devastating honesty, 'They're awful, but not all the time.'

'How long do you expect to be away?' asked Deborah.

'I haven't an idea. A week, two…it depends.' She looked so sad for a moment that Deborah said quickly: 'Well, a week here or there doesn't matter much. I'm between jobs.'

Mrs Burns cast her a grateful glance. 'I'll never be able to thank you enough. Now here's the twins' routine…'

Within half an hour Deborah had been told all she wanted to know, been introduced to Mary, toured the house, peeped in on the twins and the baby in the nursery and shown her room next to it. A very nice room it was too; pastel pinks and blues and a thick carpet with the sort of bathroom Deborah had so often admired in glossy magazines. But she didn't waste time examining it instead she went back downstairs to where Mrs Burns was talking to Mary. She smiled as Deborah joined them.

'I'm going now, Mary's got your supper ready. There's one thing I forgot, she's going to a wedding in two days' time and she'll be away all day. Mrs Twist will be up from the village in the morning—could you cope for the rest of the day?'

Mrs Burns was looking anxious again so Deborah said bracingly: 'Of course I can, Mrs Burns, everything will be fine. I hope you find your mother better.' She urged her companion gently to the door and into the Porsche parked in the drive. A lovely car but surely not quite the right thing for a mother with three young children. Her thought was answered as though she had uttered it aloud. 'This isn't mine—it's Bill's second car. I've got a small Daimler, it's safer for the children he says. But I'm in a hurry now and they're not with me!'

'Go carefully,' urged Deborah.

Mrs Burns nodded obediently and shot off with the speed of light. Deborah watched her skid round into the road and went indoors, hoping that her employer was a seasoned driver. She ate her supper presently in the panelled dining room at the back of the house and then helped Mary clear away the dishes and wash up, and by then it was time to give Deirdre her ten o'clock feed. She sat in the day nursery with the baby on her lap; she took her feed like an angel and dropped off to sleep again as Deborah was changing her. It would be too much to expect the twins to be as placid, thought Deborah, climbing into her comfortable bed.

It was. She went along, next morning dressed in her uniform and a nicely starched apron, to see if they were awake and found the pair of them out of their beds and on the night nursery floor, busy covering the hearth rug with a wild pattern, wielding their felt pens with enthusiasm. She knelt down beside them, wished them good-morning and admired their handiwork. They both peered at her, two small artful faces with the same bright blue eyes as their little sister.

'You're the new Nanny,' said Simon without enthusiasm.

'Yes, I am, and you're Simon,' she smiled at the little girl, 'and you're Suzanne.'

'Is Mummy coming back soon?' asked the moppet.

'Just as soon as your granny is better. Mummy's going to phone today so you'll be able to speak to her.'

'Where's Daddy?'

Deborah wasn't sure if she'd been told—was it China or Japan? Anyway it was some far flung spot which would take a day or two to get home from, even if he started that very minute. 'I don't know exactly, you could ask Mummy, but I'm sure he'll be home just as soon as he can. Will you start to dress while I change Deirdre?'

'No.'

'Then if you're going to stay in your nightclothes, you'd better go to bed, hadn't you?' said Deborah calmly, and went over to see if the baby was awake.

'Will you tell Mummy if we're naughty?' asked Simon.

'I don't tell tales,' Deborah told him cheerfully, 'that's a nasty thing to do.'

'We'll get dressed,' said Suzanne, 'but I can't do my hair but I can tie a bow knot in my laces.'

'Clever girl. I'll do your hair when I've seen to Deirdre.'

Breakfast, though noisy, was eaten in a friendly atmosphere, and as soon as it was finished the twins were collected by someone they called Aunty Doris and driven off to school, leaving Deborah to bath and dress Dee, put her in her pram and wheel it round to the back of the house into a sheltered corner while she nipped back indoors to make beds and tidy the nurseries.

Mary, watching her put a load of small garments into the washing machine, approved of her. 'Plain she may be,' she confided to Mrs Twist, 'but she's a lady, if you know what I mean, and the twins mind her as much as they mind anyone. Sitting there, telling them in that soft voice of hers to eat their breakfast and so sure she was they did too, like lambs! Pity we can't have her here permanent like.'

The twins returned with a great deal of untapped energy; Deborah combing hair and inspecting hands, decided that a walk was essential after their dinner. She left the twins playing while she saw to the baby and then, with the infant tucked up in the pram and the children armed with small baskets in case they found any blackberries, set out.

They went through the village, stopping at the stores to buy sweets and then took a lane beyond the last of the houses. It led uphill and gave them a view of rolling countryside when they reached the top. Deborah, hot from pushing the pram, sighed with relief to find a splendid hedge of blackberries, an excuse to find a shady spot for the pram and join the twins.

They got home in time for tea, nicely tired and went happily to bed after they had talked to their mother on the phone. There was no change in her mother's condition, Mrs Burns told Deborah, and she asked if everything was all right at home. Deborah said that everything was fine, that the children had been as good as gold and that Deirdre was a model baby, and would Mrs Burns like to talk to Mary?

A diplomatic gesture which earned her a pleased look, for Mary was delighted.

The next day followed the same pattern as the first, pleasant but filled with the many chores which went with three children. Deborah phoned her mother in the evening, assured her that she was completely happy and not in the least overworked and then went to bed early. The children had been very good, she thought sleepily as she curled up comfortably, and tomorrow there would be a respite because they were going to a friend's birthday party at the other end of the village. She would take them there, with Dee in the pram and then go back and have tea in the garden. Mary would be going to her wedding in the morning and once Mrs Twist had gone she would have the house to herself. Only for an hour or two but it would be a small pleasure to look forward to.

They had their dinner earlier than usual so that Mrs Twist could wash up the dishes before she went home. Deborah coaxed the children into fresh clothes, fed the baby and set off with her little party. There was a good deal of noise coming from the house as they approached it; the windows were wide open and there was a CD player belting out the latest pop music. Deborah handed the twins over to a rather harassed woman at the door, promised to collect them at six o'clock, and went off with the pram and the sleeping Deirdre. Simon had muttered a gruff goodbye as they went, but Suzanne had flung her arms round Deborah's neck and hugged her.

It was a glorious day; Deborah strolled along admiring the view, talking from time to time to Deirdre who chuckled and crowed and then dropped off to sleep. She was still sleeping when Deborah reached the house unlocked the door and carried her inside to finish her nap in her cot.

It was early for tea, but the prospect of half an hour in the garden under the open window of the nursery was very tempting. Deborah crossed the hall to go to the kitchen and put on the kettle and presently took her tray on to the patio under the nursery window. She could have spent the rest of the day there but the twins had to be fetched and Deirdre put back into her pram. Deborah whisked round the kitchen, getting things ready for the twins' supper; she could feed the baby while they ate it. It was still pleasantly warm as she went unhurriedly through the village, collected the twins and walked them back smartly. They were over excited, over tired and peevish. The next hour or so tried her patience and her temper, but at last they were all sleeping and she took off her apron, pushed the hair back from her hot face and went downstairs. Mary wouldn't be back until late and she had a key, mused Deborah, her mind pleasantly occupied with supper and the thought of an early night with a book as she reached the hall and started towards the kitchen. She was half-way there when the bell pealed, quite gently and only once. Not Mary, she would have let herself in, not any of Mrs Burns' friends; they knew she was away—her husband? Deborah, who had a romantic mind, pictured him hot footing it half-way round the world to be with his wife and children as she went to the door and opened it.

Not Mrs Burns' husband; she had seen a wedding photo, he was dark and not much above middle-height and had a moustache, the man on the doorstep was twice as tall and wide. Well, even allowing for exaggeration he was a very large man and solid with it. Besides, he had iron grey hair, bright blue eyes and no moustache. She said enquiringly, 'Yes,' in a severe voice, while a host of unpleasant ideas about thieves and robbers and kidnappers seeped into her head.

'My God,' observed the man softly, 'I thought the species was extinct.' And when she looked nonplussed, 'Nannies,' he explained kindly, 'that's what you are, isn't it? I thought you worthy aproned ladies had been swallowed whole by the au pair girls.'

Not only probably a thief thought Deborah, a trifle wildly, but also mentally unstable. 'Be good enough to go away,' she said in the firm no-nonsense voice she had been taught to use at the training college.

He leaned his elegantly clad person against the door frame and said equably: 'I haven't had a nanny for a long time; I never obeyed her anyway. I'm coming in.'

'You are not!' The two little terrors and baby Deirdre suddenly became very precious; he didn't know they were in the house, of course, but once inside he might go anywhere.

He changed his tactics. 'This is Peggy Burns' house?'

She nodded.

'Good, so I'll come in...'

'I don't know who you are,' she protested.

'I don't happen to have my birth certificate with me, would a passport do?' He was amused still but impatient now. 'You're alone in the house?'

She didn't answer and he tried again. 'Is Mrs Burns at home?'

'No.'

'Chatty little thing, aren't you? Where is she?'

Deborah was standing squarely in the doorway her small, rather plump person by no means filling it. 'At her mother's house.'

She watched his face change to become serious. 'Is she ill?'

'Her mother? Yes. Mrs Burns went yesterday—no the day before that. Now will you please go away?'

For answer she felt two large hands clasp her waist and she was lifted gently aside as he went past her and into the sitting room, where he picked up the phone. She closed the door and went after him, watching while he dialled a number, staring at the wall in front of him. He was a good looking man, in his mid-thirties perhaps. She wondered who he was; if he was an intruder she couldn't do much about it now, but he looked different suddenly, serious and worried, his voice was different too, no longer casual and so amused. He got the number and asked for Mrs Burns and then said: 'Peggy? what's wrong? I got back a couple of days early and came to see you. There's a small gorgon here, defending your children with her life's blood...'

He stood listening while Peggy talked. 'I'm coming over right away. No I didn't get your cable—I'd already left. I'll be with you in a couple of hours, maybe a good deal less.'

He listened again and turned to look at Deborah. 'Coping very well, I should have said; starched backbone and a mouth like a rat trap. I'd hate to be in her bad books.' And then 'Hang on love, I'll be with you in no time at all.'

He put the phone down. 'Any chance of a cup of coffee and a sandwich?' He smiled suddenly and she almost forgave him for calling her a gorgon, then she remembered the rat trap. 'Certainly Mr…' She gave him a steely look and he smiled again. 'Peggy's brother, Gideon Beaufort. And you?'

'Nanny,' said Deborah coldly and went away to the kitchen, where she made a pot of coffee and cut sandwiches, by now in a very nasty temper, not improved by his appearance through the door and the manner in which he wolfed the sandwiches as fast as she could cut them. She banged a mug and the coffee pot down in front of him, put milk and sugar within reach and said frostily: 'Excuse me, I'm going upstairs to the children.'

She crept into the night nursery and found them asleep, their small flushed faces looking angelic. She tucked in blankets, went to close one of the windows a little and let out a soundless squeak as a large hand came down on her shoulder. 'Nice, aren't they?' whispered their uncle. 'Little pests when they are awake of course.'

Deborah had got her breath back. 'I might have screamed,' she hissed almost soundlessly, 'frightening me like that, you should know better…' She glared up at him. 'I thought you were in a hurry to see your mother?'

He was serious again. 'I am, but I missed lunch and tea and jet lag was catching up on me. I'm going now. You're all right on your own?'

'Mary will be back later, thank you. Besides I have a definitely starched backbone and a mouth like a rat trap, haven't I? That should put the most hardened criminal off.'

'Did I say that? Next time we meet I'll apologise handsomely.'

They were in the hall, he gave her an encouraging pat on the shoulder and opened the door. He went without another word, not even goodbye. She heard a car start up outside but she didn't go to a window to see it. She never wanted to see the wretch again. Rude, arrogant, bent on scaring the hair off her head. She went to the dining room and gave herself a glass of sherry and then went round the house, locking the doors and shutting the windows. If anyone else rang the bell she had no intention of answering it. She got her supper, sitting over it reading a novel from the well-stocked bookshelves, and then fed Deirdre and settled her for the night. The twins were out cold, humped untidily in their beds. She tucked them in and dropped a kiss on their rosy cheeks and then went downstairs again to wait for Mary; somehow she didn't fancy going to bed until that lady was back.

Mary came home just after eleven o'clock. It had been a marvellous wedding, she told Deborah, the bride had looked beautiful and so had the bridesmaids; she didn't mention the bridegroom—a necessary but unnoticed cog in the matrimonial wheel. And lovely food she continued, accepting the coffee which Deborah thoughtfully put before her. The drink must have been lovely too; Mary was going to have a nasty head in the morning. It hardly seemed the time to tell her about Mr Beaufort, but Mary, revived by the hot drink, wanted to know what sort of a day she had had, and Deborah, skimming lightly over the gorgon and rat trap bits, told her.

'Such a nice gentleman,' observed Mary, still a bit muzzy, 'I've known him for a long time now, always so polite and so good with the children.'

She looked at Deborah and smiled and Deborah smiled

back; she would hardly have described Mr Beaufort's manners as polite although she was fair enough to hold back her judgment on his avuncular affability. She gave Mary another cup of coffee and then urged her to her bed. However much they might want to sleep late in the morning, there would be no chance; the twins would see to that, and Deirdre, although a placid baby, was unlikely to forego her morning feed.

The twins, bursting with energy, made sure that Deborah was up early. There was no sign of Mary as Deborah made herself a cup of tea and debated whether to take one to the housekeeper, but decided to wait for another hour and feed Deirdre while the twins got themselves dressed. She thanked heaven for Deirdre's placid disposition as she washed unwilling faces and squeezed toothpaste out on to brushes; the baby was already asleep again which would give her time to give the twins their breakfast, and with any luck, allow her to bolt a slice of toast herself. By some miracle they were ready when Aunty Doris arrived; Deborah handed them over clean, well fed and with shining faces and nipped indoors again to take a cup of tea to Mary.

'I have a headache,' said Mary predictably.

'I brought you a couple of aspirin, if you take them now and lie still for ten minutes or so, it'll go. Do you fancy breakfast? I'm going to make some toast presently, after I've bathed Dee and put her into the pram. I'll make you a slice.'

They sat down together presently in the kitchen with Dee in her pram, banging a saucepan lid with a spoon. Rather hard on Mary.

Mrs Burns rang during the morning. Her mother was better, she told Deborah, and it had been wonderful to see her brother, 'So unexpected—I mean I'd sent him a cable—I couldn't phone because I wasn't quite sure where he was, but I didn't think he'd get here for a few days. He's been marvellous; seen the doctors and found another nurse so that I don't have to stay up at night and he's going to stay until Mother's well enough to go to a Nursing Home, and by then Bill should be home, so I don't have to worry. You're all right, Nanny, no problems?'

I have problems, thought Deborah, one of them is having a rat trap for a mouth, but out loud she said, with her usual calm, 'No, none, Mrs Burns. The children are splendid and Dee is such an easy baby.' Then added for good measure, 'And Mary is super.'

'Oh, good. Gideon seemed to think that you were managing very well. I think I'll be here for at least a week, perhaps a little longer than that. Will you manage until then? Get anything you need at the village stores, I've an account there. Oh, and will you ask Mary to send on some undies and another dress? The grey cotton jersey will do—I've almost nothing with me.'

Deborah hung up and handed the message on, reflecting that it must be nice to have people to do things for you; she suspected that Mrs Burns had always had that from the moment she was born and kindly fate had handed her a doting husband who carried on the good work. Probably the horrible brother was her slave too, although, upon reflection, she couldn't imagine him being anyone's slave.

She had no time to reflect for long, however, Mary's headache had gone but she was still lethargic so that Deborah found it prudent to do as much around the house as she could. At least dinner was almost ready by the time the twins were brought back, both in furious tears and looking as though their clothes hadn't been changed for a couple of weeks. 'They had a little upset,' explained Aunty Doris with false sweetness, 'they're such lively little people.'

There was nothing for it but to be patient and put them into the bath, wheedle them into clean clothes and lastly load the washing machine once more, before sitting them down to a delayed dinner which they stubbornly refused to eat.

But after a long walk in the afternoon they cheered up, ate a splendid tea and went to their beds, looking too good to be true.

By the end of the next two days they had accepted Deborah as a great friend, a firm friend who didn't allow them to have their own way, but who nevertheless was good fun. The days had settled into a routine, a rather dull one for Deborah but busy with washing and ironing and feeding and keeping the twins happy and amused. It was at the end of the first week when the twins, bored with being indoors all the morning because of the rain, started playing up. Providentially, the rain stopped after their dinner and, although it was still damp underfoot, Deborah stuffed small feet into wellies, tucked Dee snugly into her pram and went into the garden. There was a good sized lawn behind the house. She put the pram in a patch of watery sunshine, made sure that the baby was asleep and fetched a ball. But half an hour of kicking that around wasn't enough for the twins, they demanded something else for a change. Deborah caught them in either hand and began to prance up and down the grass singing 'Here we come gathering nuts in May' and had them singing too, dancing to and fro with her.

Deborah didn't know what made her turn her head. Gideon Beaufort was leaning on the patio rail, watching them, and even at that distance she took instant exception to the smile on his face.

CHAPTER TWO

DEBORAH STOPPED HER singing and prancing so abruptly that the twins almost fell over. 'Good afternoon, Mr Beaufort,' she said in a cold way which was almost wholly swamped by the twins' ecstatic shrieks, although half-way across the grass Simon turned to shout: 'He's not a mister, he's a professor,' before flinging himself at his uncle.

'Very clearly put,' observed the professor, disentangling himself slowly. 'Now you can do the same for me and introduce Nanny.'

His nephew eyed him with impatience. 'Well, she's just Nanny...'

'No name?'

He looked at Deborah and she said unwillingly: 'Farley—Deborah Farley.'

'Charming—a popular name with the Puritans, I believe.' His voice was so bland that she decided to let that pass.

'What's a puritan?' asked Suzy.

'A sober person who thought it wrong to sing and dance and be happy.'

'Nanny's not one,' declared his niece. 'We've been singing and dancing,' she explained earnestly.

The professor nodded. 'Yes, and very nicely too.' He smiled at Deborah who gave him a cool look; the gorgon's rat trap still rankled.

'Is Mummy coming?' demanded Simon.

'Not today old fellow—Granny's better but not quite well yet. I thought I'd drop in and see how things are.' He strolled over to the pram and peered inside. 'Dee's asleep—I've never seen such a child for dozing off.' He glanced, at Deborah. 'She must be very easy to look after.'

'No trouble at all,' agreed Deborah airily.

'In that case perhaps I might stay for tea without straining your work load too much?' He smiled again with such charm that she only just stopped in time from smiling back in return.

'Certainly, Professor, the children will be delighted, won't you, my dears? Mary did some baking this morning, so there'll be a cake.'

Mary's welcome was warm and seemed even warmer by reason of Deborah's brisk efficiency. She wheeled the pram under the nursery window so that she might hear if Dee wakened; removed the twins to be tidied and washed for tea, sat them down at the table, one on each side of their uncle, and went to help carry in the tea tray, the plate of bread and butter and the cake Mary had so providentially baked.

The tea tray was taken from her as she entered the nursery by a disarmingly polite professor. What was more he remained so throughout the meal, talking nothings to her when not engaged in answering the twins' ceaseless questions. Deborah felt a certain reluctance when it was time to feed Deirdre, but she got up from the table, excused herself politely, cautioned the twins to behave and made to leave the room. At the door she hesitated: 'I get Dee ready for bed once she's been fed,' she explained, 'so I'll wish you good-bye, Professor, please tell Mrs Burns that everything is just as it should be.'

'Oh, I'm staying the night. Did I not tell you? I'm so sorry.' He sounded all concern, but all the same she knew that he was laughing silently. 'Mary said that she would get a room ready for me.' He added silkily: 'You don't mind?'

'I, mind? Certainly not. It is none of my business, Professor Beaufort. I daresay you've also asked Mary to cook extra…'

'No,' he told her gently, 'she suggested it. Should I have asked you?'

Deborah went pink; on the whole she was a good tempered girl but today her good nature was being tried severely; besides she had been rude.

'I'm only in charge of the children,' she told him, 'Mary runs the house. Besides I'm only temporary.'

As she dealt with the small Dee's needs, she could hear the twins giggling and shouting and the occasional rumble of their uncle's voice. 'They'll be quite out of hand—I'll never get them to bed,' she observed to the placid infant on her knee. 'He'll get them all worked up…'

But surprisingly, when she went to fetch the twins for their baths and bed, they went with her like lambs. Not so much as a peep out of them and so unnaturally good that Deborah wondered if they were sickening for something. She put a small capable hand on their foreheads and found them reassuringly cool and finally demanded to know what was the matter with them.

They exchanged glances and looked at her with round blue eyes, 'Uncle Gideon made us promise so we won't tell. Are we being good?'

'Yes—and I can't think why.' She gave them a close look. 'You're not up to mischief, are you?'

Meekly they assured her that they weren't. She tucked them into their beds, kissed them goodnight, and went to her room, where she did her face carefully, scraped her sandy hair back into a severe style becoming to a well-trained nanny, and went downstairs.

Professor Beaufort was stretched out on one of the outsize sofas in the sitting room, his eyes closed. She stood and looked at him; he was very good looking she conceded, and like that, asleep, he was nice; it was when he stared at her with bright blue eyes and spoke to her in that bland voice that she disliked him. She gave a faint yelp when he spoke.

'You don't look in the least like a nanny should.' He observed and got to his feet in one swift movement, to tower over her, beaming.

She fought against his charm; saying severely: 'I assure you that I am fully qualified.'

'Oh, I can see that, you handle the twins like a veteran. Tell me—what is your ambition? To get a post with some blue-blooded family and stay with them all your life and then retire to an estate cottage?'

She felt rage bubble inside her. 'I might possibly marry,' she pointed out sweetly and choked at his bland: 'He will be a brave man… Shall we have a drink? Mary told me that dinner would be ready in ten minutes or so.'

She accepted a sherry and wished that she had asked for something dashing like whisky or even gin and tonic. Just so that he would see that she wasn't the prim, dedicated nanny that he had decided she was. But she did the next best thing; she asked for a second drink and he poured it without comment, only his eyebrows lifted in an amused arc which she didn't see. She tossed it off smartly so that she was able to face their tête à tête meal with equanimity and a chattiness quite unlike her usual quiet manner.

Professor Beaufort quite shamelessly led her on, his grave face offering no hint of his amusement. She told him about her three brothers, her home in Dorchester, cousin Rachel and only just stopped herself in time from regaling him with some of the foibles she had had to put up with from various parents whose children she had taken care of. Finally, vaguely aware that she was talking too much, she asked: 'And is your work very interesting, Professor? I'm not quite sure what you do…'

He passed his plate for a second helping of Mary's delicious apple pie. 'I study the production and distribution of money and goods.'

'Yes, but don't you work?'

'Er—yes. I have an office and I travel a good deal as well as lecturing regularly.'

'Oh—do people want to know—about money and goods, I mean?'

'It helps if they do. The management of public affairs, the disposition of affairs of state or government departments, the judicious use of public money—someone has to know about such things.'

'And do you?' she queried.

'One might say that I have a basic knowledge…'

'It sounds dull. I'd rather have the children,' said Deborah, still rather lively from the sherry.

He said slowly: 'I think that possibly you are right, Nanny. I hadn't given the matter much thought, but now that you mention it, I shall look into it. Do you suppose that Mary would give us our coffee on the patio? It's a delightful evening.'

Somehow being called 'Nanny' brought her down to earth with a bump. She poured their coffee almost in silence and when she had drunk hers excused herself with the plea that Dee would be waking for her feed very shortly. She wished him goodnight, every inch the children's nurse, and went upstairs. It was too early to feed Dee; she pottered round her room for half an hour, aware that she would have liked to have stayed and talked, and aware too that she had said too much anyway.

She gave the baby her bottle presently, turned the twins up the right way and tucked them in once more, and got herself ready for bed. It was very warm and she had taken too hot a bath; she sat by the open window for quite some time, brushing her hair and thinking about her future. The professor had been joking, supposing her to be content with a lifelong job with the same family and an old age in some cottage, but it held more than a grain of truth. She didn't relish the idea in the least. She got up and went to look at herself in the triple mirror. No one—no man—was likely to fall for her; sandy hair was bad enough, sandy eyelashes were the utter end; the lovely green eyes she ignored and studied the rest of her face; the small straight nose and much too wide mouth above a determined chin; there was nothing there to enchant a man. She overlooked the fact that she had a pretty figure and nice hands and legs, all she could think of was curly blonde hair and bright blue eyes fringed by dark curling lashes. Her own lashes curled, but being sandy they were almost invisible. 'I could of course dye them,' she told her image, but perhaps that would make the rest of her face look odd. She got into bed, fretting about the eyelashes and fell asleep almost at once.

She awoke to pitch darkness and a whimper, thin as a kitten's protest; by the time she was sitting up in bed to listen, the whimper had become a furious roar. One of the twins was having a nightmare; she shot out of bed and went on bare feet through the day nursery and into the adjoining room where the pair of them slept. It was Suzanne, half awake and bellowing with fright. Deborah plucked her gently from her bed, gathered her into her arms and sat down in the little arm chair by the window, half strangled by the child's arms. It took a few moments to wake her up completely and twice as long to get her to stop crying. Deborah had soothed the sobbing to a series of sniffs and gulps when Simon woke, sat up in bed and demanded to know why Suzy was crying. The two of them were very close; he got out of his bed and came to join them, perching on the arm of the chair, demanding to know in a loud voice what the matter was.

'Well, that's what we are going to find out,' said Deborah reasonably, 'I expect it was a nasty dream, wasn't it? But you are wide awake now and dreams aren't real you know. You shall tell me about it and then you'll forget it and when you've had a nice drink of warm milk, you'll go to sleep again and wake up in the morning quite happy again. Now tell Nanny what made you cry, darling?'

Simon slid off the chair and she turned her head to see why. The professor was leaning in the doorway, huge and magnificent in a dazzlingly-striped dressing-gown. The little boy hurled himself at him and was swung into his arms, to be carried to his bed and sat on his uncle's knee.

Deborah, her hair hanging in a clean, shining curtain on

her shoulders and down her back, bare feet digging into the thick rug, gave the professor a passing glance, and turned her attention to Suzy; she had forgotten that she hadn't bothered to put on her dressing-gown and there was nothing in his face to remind her of that fact. She bent her head to hear the child's tearful whispering, tossing back her sandy tresses with an impatient hand. The telling took some time with a good deal of sniffing and gulping but she listened patiently and finally when the child had come to a halt said hearteningly: 'There now—it's all right again, isn't it? You've told us all about it and although it was a nasty dream, you've forgotten it because we all know about it, don't we? Now I'm going to get you some milk and then I'll sit here until you've gone to sleep again…'

'Let me have her here,' suggested the professor, who went on: 'I should put your dressing-gown on before you go downstairs.' His voice was quite impersonal but she gave a horrified squeak and pattered out of the room without another word. Bundled into her useful saxe-blue robe, buttoned from neck to ankle, she was glad of the few minutes it took in which to heat the milk. What must he have thought? She was no prude, after all she had three brothers, but children's nurses to the best of her knowledge didn't go prancing round in the dead of night in cotton nighties and nothing else when there were strangers around. And the professor was a stranger, and although she didn't care a jot for his opinion of her, she squirmed at the idea of giving him something to snigger about… snigger wasn't the right word, she conceded, give him his due, he wasn't like that. All the same she dared say that he would have no hesitation in remarking on her dishabille if he felt like it.

She removed the milk from the Aga, poured it into two

mugs, put them on a tray and bore it upstairs with a stiff dignity which caused the professor's fine mouth to twitch, although he said nothing, merely took the mug she offered Simon while she sat Suzy on her lap and coaxed her to drink. The pair of them were sleepy now; the milk finished, she tucked them back into bed, refused the professor's offer to sit with them until they were well and truly asleep and bade him a dismissive goodnight. Only he wouldn't be dismissed. 'I'm going to make us a hot drink,' he informed her, 'I'll be in the kitchen when you are ready.'

He cast an eye over the two drowsy children. 'Ten minutes at the outside, I should imagine.'

'I don't want…' began Deborah and was stopped by the steely look he bent upon her. 'You will have to be up soon after six o'clock for Dee—it is now a little after two in the morning; you will need to sleep as quickly as possible, a hot drink helps.'

He was right, of course, although it wouldn't be the first time she had gone short of sleep, and he was right about the twins too, they were asleep within minutes of being tucked in. She waited for a good five minutes and then went downstairs to the kitchen, cosy and magnificently equipped, to find the professor pouring steaming milk into two mugs.

'Cocoa,' he said, barely glancing at her, and handed her one.

She sat down at the table and drank it as obediently as Suzy had done, and tried to think of something to say; but small talk didn't come easily at the dead of night and anyway, her companion seemed unworried by the silence. She had almost finished when he observed: 'It's the twins' birthday in two weeks' time—I'm giving them a dog—a golden labrador puppy—he'll keep them busy and sleep in their room, that should stop the nightmares.'

'You approve of animals in bedrooms?'

He gave her a surprised look and then smiled thinly. 'I suppose you have been trained to discourage it?'

'Well yes, but personally I think there's no harm in it. Our cat always sleeps on my bed when I'm at home.' She drank the last of her cocoa. 'We haven't got a dog—at least he died last year… I don't suppose you have much time for one?'

'Very little, but I have three. Two labradors and a Jack Russell—there are cats too—my housekeeper has two and a constant supply of kittens.' He put down his mug. 'You had better go to bed Nanny.'

He had spoken so abruptly that she opened her green eyes wide, just for only a few moments she had forgotten that he didn't much like her. She put her cup in the sink, said 'Goodnight' in a quiet little voice and went back upstairs. The twins were sound asleep, so was Dee; she got into bed and was asleep within two minutes.

She had fed Dee and was dressed and ready for her day before the twins woke, their disturbed night forgotten and bounding with energy, but she was used to them by now; they were sitting down to their breakfast no more than five minutes late, shovelling corn flakes into their small mouths by the time their uncle appeared, Mary hard on his heels with fresh coffee and toast. He bade the room a general good-morning, gave it as his intention to drive the twins to school and ate a huge breakfast with no more than a quick look at Deborah, sitting behind the coffee pot, clean and starched and severe. 'In that case,' she remarked, 'I'd better phone Aunty Doris and ask her not to come.'

'For God's sake, do—that garrulous woman…'

'Little pitchers have long ears,' said Deborah sternly and then blushed because she had sounded like a prig.

'What's a pitcher?' asked Suzy.

'Doesn't God like Aunty Doris?' asked Simon.

'You see what you've done?' snapped Deborah and was answered by a great bellow of laughter.

The house seemed very quiet after they had gone, the three of them. Deborah bathed and dressed Dee and put her out in the garden in the pram before racing round making beds and tidying up.

'It'll be a nice roast chicken for lunch,' said Mary. 'Mister Gideon says he must go this afternoon—he's partial to my trifle too.'

Deborah tried to think of something suitable to say to this; it was evident that Mary doted on the man and there was no point in offending the dear soul by saying what she thought about the professor; after all, she was unlikely to meet him again. She would forget him, just as she had forgotten a number of people she had met and disliked during the last few years.

Mary was looking at her, waiting for her to make some comment. She said brightly: 'I'm sure he'll love that—men like sweet things, don't they?'

The housekeeper gave a rich chuckle. 'That they do—never grow up, they don't, not in some ways. Now Mr Burns, he likes a nice chocolate pudding.'

She watched Deborah collect an armful of small garments ready for the washing machine, and added comfortably: 'Well, I'll be off to my kitchen. I must say you're a real help around the house, Nanny, not like some of those toffee-nosed au pairs Mrs Burns has tried out. Not a success they weren't.'

Deborah looked up briefly. 'I'm only here for a short time, Mary. I expect Mrs Burns will have other plans.'

'Ah, well as long as they speak English,' she sighed.

The professor appeared suddenly and almost silently, just as Deborah was settling Dee back in her pram after her morning feed. 'Any coffee?' he wanted to know.

'Mary will have it ready, I expect.' Deborah kicked the brake off, and began to wheel the pram across the lawn towards the drive. She usually had her coffee with Mary, this morning she would go for a walk first and leave the housekeeper to enjoy their visitor's company.

But it seemed that the professor had other ideas. He laid a large hand on the pram's handle so that she was forced to stop. He said smoothly: 'You don't have to run away you know, I don't bite; we've had no chance to get to know each other.'

'What would be the point?' she wanted to know matter-of-factly. 'We're most unlikely to meet again; I go all over the place.'

He had steered the pram towards the patio, anchored it there and put his head through the open french window to shout to Mary. When he emerged he observed in a friendly way: 'You must see quite a lot of life,' and spoilt it by adding: 'From the wings as it were.'

She said in a decidedly acid voice: 'I daresay that's more fun than being buried alive in economics.'

'Ah, but when I've reduced high powered chaos to orderly statistics, I er—I enjoy myself.'

Mary came with the coffee and the three of them sat drinking it in the bright sunshine while the talk eddied to and fro between Mary and the professor, with Deborah not saying much. She was in truth, very occupied in wondering just how he enjoyed himself. In a room full of computers, perhaps? catching up on a little light reading in the Financial Times? entertaining some pretty girl to dinner, spending the evening—the night, with her? more than likely.

'A penny for them,' said the professor suddenly so that she went a bright and becoming pink. She mumbled something and Mary said comfortably: 'Thinking about where she'll go next, I'll be bound. Isn't that right, Nanny? For all you know it'll be one of those Arab countries with gold bath taps and a horde of servants—much in demand our nannies are in that part of the world. Would you love to go there, dear?'

'No, I don't think so.' It was a great relief that she hadn't had to answer Professor Beaufort's question.

'But you do travel?'

'Well, yes, but I've only been to the south of France and Brussels and Scotland. I'm quite happy to stay in England.'

'But you don't object to going abroad?' The professor's voice was very casual.

'Not in the least. Children are the same anywhere.' She put down her coffee cup and got to her feet. 'I'll take Dee for her walk.' She glanced at her watch, but before she could speak: 'I'll fetch the twins, Nanny. Mary, may we have lunch just a little early so that I can get away in good time?'

As she wheeled the pram away Deborah took time to tell herself how pleasant it would be when he'd gone—quite quiet and a bit dull perhaps, but pleasant; he was a disturbing person to have around the house. 'He may be your uncle,' she told the sleeping Dee, 'but I don't like him. Him and his economics, indeed.' She tossed her sandy head and marched smartly through the village and up the hill on the other side where presently she sat down with her back against a tree until it was time to go back and give Dee her orange juice.

Lunch was a boisterous affair which petered out into tears and tantrums from the twins because their uncle was going away again.

He swung them in the air in turn and hugged them briefly. 'If you are very good and don't howl in that frightful fashion and do exactly what Nanny tells you and eat your dinners without fuss, I'll give you each a real bicycle. It had better be before Christmas otherwise I might get in Father Christmas's way. Let's see, shall we say the first of December?'

He left them with a brief nod to Deborah and a much warmer leave taking from Mary. If she hadn't been kept so busy all the afternoon counting days on the calendar for the twins' benefit, she might have had the time to feel annoyed about that. Although in all fairness she herself had pointed out that they were most unlikely to see each other again, and as far as she could see they had absolutely nothing in common.

There was no point in thinking about him; she dismissed him from her mind and bent to the task of keeping the twins occupied in a suitable fashion, making sure that they ate their food and acting as mediator when they quarrelled—which was often. What with the pair of them and baby Dee, who although no trouble at all, needed her attentions more or less round the clock, the next few days passed rapidly enough. But Mrs Burns gave no indication as to when she would return although she telephoned each day.

It was four days since the professor had left, just as they were about to start a picnic tea on the lawn, that Mrs Burn's racy sports car turned into the drive and stopped with a squealing of brakes before her front door.

The children had seen of course, and were already racing to meet her as she got out of the car. They closed in on her and for a moment there was pandemonium; laughing and shrieks of delight and Mrs Burns explaining that she had come home, Granny was well enough to leave and Daddy was on his way back too. She crossed the lawn to where Deborah sat with Dee on her lap, beginning to explain all over again long before she reached her.

'I should have phoned, Nanny, but I wanted to make sure that Doctor Wyatt was perfectly satisfied with my mother's progress. There's a nurse with her of course, but when he said that she was quite out of danger and that I need stay no longer, I just threw my things into a bag and came racing home. And Bill's on his way back too; it's all so exciting!'

She held out her arms for the baby who smiled contentedly showing a good deal of gum. Her mother kissed the top of her head: 'They all look marvellous. Have they been good? I know you said each day that they were giving no trouble, but I daresay you were driven out of your mind…'

Deborah laughed. 'No, indeed, I wasn't—and they were good, really they were. Would you like tea here, or indoors?' She got to her feet. 'I'll go and tell Mary…'

'No need, Nanny. I'm going to have tea here with you. I'll borrow Simon's mug and he can share with Suzy.' She settled gracefully on the garden seat and patted it. 'Come and sit beside me and tell me what you think of my family.' She tucked Dee under her arm, told the twins to sit on the grass beside her, and watched Deborah pouring the tea, handing round mugs of milk and plates of bread and butter.

'Gideon came?' she said and there was a question behind the remark. 'Yes,' said Deborah equably, 'The twins loved it—he took them to school…'

'God doesn't like Aunty Doris,' shrilled Simon.

Mrs Burns said calmly: 'I suspect you've got it wrong,

darling; Uncle Gideon's been using grown up language and it doesn't quite mean the same as the things we talk about.'

'Nanny frowned at him…'

Mrs Burns looked at Deborah. 'He may be a professor, but he has his lighter moments—he can be very tiresome—I'm always telling him so, aren't I, darlings?'

With no effect at all, thought Deborah.

Later, with the children in bed, over dinner with Mrs Burns Deborah gave a blow by blow account of her days. 'So you see, they've been very good, and great fun too.'

'Splendid. Don't go rushing off, will you?' Mrs Burns turned persuasive eyes on to Deborah. 'Bill will be home late tomorrow; the children will go berserk, they always do, and they'll need someone to make them eat and go to bed and so on, so please stay for a little longer—unless you've another job waiting?'

'Well, I haven't actually—and of course I'll stay until you don't need me.'

'Oh, good! What a relief. My mother wants to see the children, I thought we might drive over after Bill gets home and let her see them for a few minutes. She dotes on them and it'll do her good.'

Mrs Burns suddenly looked very young and sad. 'Oh, Nanny I was so frightened. I thought Mother wasn't going to get better. Thank heaven Gideon came, he's so sensible and always knows what to do, just like Bill, I mean he'd got everything organised within an hour of his getting there and he was so sure that Mother was going to get better that I believed him—he was calm and certain about it. He is such a dear, don't you agree?'

'He's a marvellous uncle,' said Deborah guardedly and

Mrs Burns looked at her, a flicker of amusement in her eyes although she didn't say anything.

It was difficult to keep the children even moderately quiet the next day, by the time their father arrived they were in bed, wide awake, and since it was quite obvious that they had no intention of going to sleep until he had got home, Deborah sat between their beds, reading soothingly from Little Grey Rabbit and very relieved when at last they heard a car turn into the drive and stop before the house. There was no holding the twins; she got them into their dressing gowns, thrust wriggling impatient feet into slippers and led them downstairs. They broke free of her restraining hands once they reached the hall and flung themselves at their father standing in the drawing room doorway. Deborah waited where she was, not sure what to do; the children should have been in their beds, on the other hand they hadn't seen their father for some weeks and from the look of it, he was delighted to see them again. He scooped them up and swung them round laughing and turned to smile at his wife. They all looked so happy that Deborah felt a pang of loneliness, instantly forgotten when Mrs Burns caught sight of her and said: 'Bill, here's Nanny, she's been marvellous—I don't know what I would have done without her—and she's promised to stay a little longer.'

Mr Burns smiled across at her. 'Hullo Nanny—I'm glad to meet you and very grateful too. Once we've got these little horrors in bed again, come down and have a drink.'

Deborah was on the point of making some excuse, but Mrs Burns said: 'Yes, do—I know you've had the hell of a day with the children, but just come for a little while, please.'

It was surprisingly easy to get the twins to bed now that they were satisfied that their father was really home; they were asleep at once and it wasn't quite time for Dee's last feed. Deborah tidied her hair, powdered her flushed and rather tired face and went downstairs.

Mr Burns was sitting in an armchair, his wife perched beside him but he got up as Deborah went into the room, offered her sherry and poured it, and then waved her to a chair. 'I can't tell you what a relief it was to hear how well you've been coping—Gideon sent me a most reassuring cable—it made all the difference, I can tell you—all those miles away and unable to get home to poor Peggy. We thought we might go over to Bath tomorrow—we'll take the children of course and if you would come too...?'

'Of course,' said Deborah in a quiet voice.

'Good, just a brief visit, you know. I'm very fond of my mother-in-law,' he smiled at his wife as he spoke, 'I'm glad and relieved that she's recovered. She wants to see the children and I want to see her, so if you could take charge of them for half an hour? There's a nice garden there—Dee can stay in her Moses basket.'

He was quite different from the professor, thought Deborah, listening to him; unassuming and reserved with a nice open face and kind eyes. 'We'll be quite all right, Mr Burns,' she assured him: 'Dee's such a good baby and I'll take something to amuse the twins. Shall we be going in the morning or later in the day?'

'An early lunch?' suggested Mr Burns to his wife and she nodded. 'We can have tea there, and be back in good time for the twins to be put to bed.'

Deborah put down her glass and stood up. 'It's time for Dee's feed. Thank you for my drink, goodnight Mrs Burns, goodnight Mr Burns.'

The twins naturally enough were enchanted at the idea

of going to see Granny in Daddy's car, but they were still more delighted to hear that since lunch was to be early they wouldn't be going to school. Deborah took them for a walk; protesting loudly, rebellious hands holding on to the pram as she wheeled Dee off for the morning airing. 'Just for an hour,' coaxed Deborah. 'So that your father can get the car ready for this afternoon.'

They travelled in Mr Burns' estate car, roomy enough to take them all with the twins strapped into their seats and Deborah sitting between them with Dee on her lap. The weather was warm and sunny although the trees were showing the first early signs of autumn, although she was kept much too occupied to look around her.

Mrs Burns' mother lived in a nice old house a mile or two outside Bath and when they arrived Mrs Burns went in alone to make sure that her mother was feeling up to seeing them, then her husband joined her, leaving Deborah in the garden with the twins and Dee in her carry-cot. Luckily not for long, for they were impatient to see the invalid, and under dire threat not to so much as raise their voices, they were led inside with Deborah, Dee tucked under her arm, bringing up the rear.

Mrs Burns' mother was an elderly edition of her daughter and although she looked ill, she was still pretty in a faded way, but her eyes were bright and missed nothing. She was kissed carefully by the twins, admired Dee, and then turned her attention to Deborah. Not that she said much, but Deborah had the distinct impression that she was being closely examined, although she couldn't think why. If she could have stayed behind instead of taking the children back into the garden she would have found out…

'She'll do very well,' said Mrs Beaufort. 'Have you said anything?'

'Nothing, Mother—we thought we'd see what you thought, first, after all, you'll see quite a lot of her for several weeks.' She added, 'Bill likes her...'

'And Gideon,' said her mother. 'Which surprised me very much—you know what he's like and she's hardly his type. He says she unnerves him—probably all that sandy hair and those eyes. They are absolutely beautiful.'

'She's super with the kids.' Mrs Burns stopped to kiss her parent. 'Bill will talk to her tomorrow and get things settled. The doctors say another two weeks before you are fit to travel, that gives us time to get organised. Is Eleanor coming too?'

'Yes,' Mrs Beaufort was looking tired but interested. 'But for some reason best known to him, Gideon asks us not to mention that.'

She and her daughter stared at each other for a long moment. 'You don't say,' observed Mrs Burns, and then: 'We'll see, won't we?'

Deborah was under the trees at the end of the garden, making daisy chains for the twins while Dee slept. She would have liked a cup of tea and as if in answer to her thought, a stout woman came out of the house with a tray, and a moment or two later Mr and Mrs Burns came out too. They picnicked at leisure and presently Mr Burns carried the tray back indoors and they all got into the car once more and drove home. The children were sleepy by now and Deborah had a chance to mull over the afternoon; it was strange but she was unable to rid herself of the feeling that she had been on some sort of trial; perhaps they would tell her that she wasn't needed any more. It seemed more than likely when

Mr Burns said over his shoulder as they stopped before the door: 'Nanny, I'd like to talk to you sometime. Tomorrow? Or perhaps this evening when you have some time to yourself?' He smiled at her kindly. 'After dinner if that suits you.'

She agreed calmly, already composing a letter to the agency in her head as she bore Dee off to the nursery and bedtime.

CHAPTER THREE

DEBORAH HAD IMAGINED that she would be summoned to the study during the evening, but the three of them had dinner without any mention of the talk Mr Burns had suggested, it was only after they had had their coffee in the drawing room that he glanced at his wife and said: 'We should like to talk to you, Nanny. We hope that you haven't another job lined up because we would be very glad if you could come with us on holiday in a couple of weeks' time. We plan to take Mrs Beaufort away—a villa in the Algarve—where she can laze around in the sun and get really well again. Of course we shall take the children with us and we hope that you will come too. Three weeks or a month, and in the meantime if you would like to go home? Now that I am here, we can cope with the twins for a couple of weeks, but without you on holiday with us, I don't think that we could manage. Will you think about it and let us know? It won't be much of a holiday for you although we'll see that you get time to have to yourself each day...'

'We would be back in England about the end of October?' asked Deborah.

'Yes, but I can't give you the exact dates just yet.'

Deborah sounded matter-of-fact, but she was excited too. She liked the twins and Dee; compared with some of the children she had cared for, they were like angels. Besides, even though she would have her hands full all day, it would make a pleasant change. She didn't give herself time to weigh the pros and cons; she said in her calm way: 'Yes, I'll come with you, Mr Burns. I should like to go home first as you suggest, but I can be ready whenever you want. I've nothing in view at the moment, and I only have to let the agency know.'

'That calls for another drink,' declared Mr Burns and presently, nicely glowing from a second sherry, Deborah went up to bed. She didn't go to sleep at once; her usually sensible head was full of pleasant, excited thoughts. New clothes, suitable for the undoubtedly warm weather they would enjoy, a respite from going back to the agency and deciding which job she would take, there were usually several to choose from, and few of them so far, had been even bordering on perfection. Besides she had to admit to a feeling of faint discontent, not at all her usual self and as far as she could discover it came for no reason at all. She lay pondering this and since she couldn't find an answer, sensibly went to sleep.

She went home three days later, with the twins screaming goodbyes and come back soons at her, and with strict instructions to prepare herself for the journey. They were to travel in ten days' time, flying from Bristol they would then stay in the villa Mr Burns had hired for three weeks. She was to go to Bristol Airport and meet them there not later than ten o'clock in the morning. Mr Burns drove her home, staying briefly to have coffee with her mother before he went again.

'Such a nice man,' observed Mrs Farley, 'everything's turned out very nicely hasn't it darling? Let me see, it's almost the end of September, you'll be back home at the end of October, if you could get a temporary job until just before Christmas…then in the New Year you could find a nice permanent post!'

'Yes, Mother,' agreed Deborah, with no desire at all to do any such thing. She would have to, of course, a girl had to be independent, her brothers were costing a lot and, although she was barely twenty-three, no one had asked her to marry. She had friends enough, cheerful young men who called her Debby, poured out their problems about girl friends into her sympathetic ear and teased her in a kindly, offhand way. They all liked her, indeed, were fond of her, but not one of them had had the idea of marrying her. And why should they, she would tell her reflection as she wound her sandy hair into a tidy coil, she had no looks to speak of. All the same it would be nice to have a proposal…

The faint, unsettled feeling was partly drowned in the fun of buying clothes; a couple of pretty cotton dresses, some skirts and tops, sandals and a swim suit and bikinis. No uniform, Mrs Burns had said, they so wanted to be in sun dresses or swim suits all day; even though she would be looking after the children, Deborah felt as though she was going on holiday. She packed with her usual neatness and wearing a sensible uncrushable two-piece, short sleeved, round necked and easy on the eye, she got into the car very early in the morning and settled herself beside her father, who hadn't needed much persuading to take a day off from the Bank and drive her to the Airport. It was a glorious morning with a faint autumnal chill which would presently give way to the sun's warmth. 'You'll come back as brown as a coffee bean,' declared her father.

'I go red, Father, and get covered in freckles—I shall have to wear a sun hat. I've packed lashings of Ambre Solaire though.'

'As long as you enjoy yourself, my dear.'

They had half an hour to spare at the airport, they drank a quick cup of coffee and then went to the reception area to look for the Burns family. They were already there, the twins sternly controlled by their father, Mrs Burns carrying Dee and Mrs Beaufort in a wheel chair. They all looked a little gloomy, but when they saw Deborah the gloom lifted as if by magic.

'Thank God!' said Mr Burns, and meant it. 'We should have fetched you over yesterday—we bit off rather more than we could chew. Still we're here now.' He beamed at her, shook hands with Mr Farley and edged away so that they might say goodbye. Mr Farley didn't linger, Deborah was a sensible girl, quite able to cope with any situation and quite unruffled. He turned to wave once and she waved back and then took Dee under one arm, attached the twins (holding hands) to her free hand and watched while Mrs Burns picked up her overnight bag and Mr Burns gave orders about the luggage before leading the little party briskly to the end of the reception hall. It didn't seem to be the same direction as everyone else was going but Mrs Burns and her mother, still in the chair being pushed by an airport attendant, looked quite unworried. Deborah, trailing the twins, brought up the rear.

It took her a minute or two to realise that they were flying by charter plane. A sensible, if expensive way of getting an invalid lady, two boisterous children and a baby, not to mention the Burns and herself, to their destination. They embarked smoothly, with Deborah settled between the twins and with Dee on her lap; Mrs Beaufort on her own now, stretched out on the opposite seat; and the Burns sitting in front. The twins were ominously quiet, Deborah gave them each a book to look at, saw with relief that Dee had dropped off, and prayed silently for at least half an hour's peace.

The children took no notice of take-off, immersed in their picture books they flicked over the pages with the blasé air of big businessmen flying the Atlantic for the hundredth time. Deborah, anxious not to disturb the peace, sat quietly; she didn't care for flying, but since her work took her among people who accepted it as a matter of course, she accepted it too. All the same, she was glad when they were airborne.

The unnatural quiet came to an end, of course, Deborah handed out drinks and biscuits, played endless games designed to keep the children in their seats, fed Dee and then handed her over to a refreshed Mrs Burns while she had a drink herself. Mrs Beaufort had gone to sleep and Deborah envied her; it was by far the best way to fly she considered; wiping sticky little fingers, changing Dee and settling her to sleep again, beginning an endless story which lasted until they touched down at Faro Airport.

There were two cars waiting for them, a large estate car and a small Fiat. Deborah, the children, the luggage and Mr Burns travelled in the first, Mrs Burns followed them with her mother comfortably installed in the back of the Fiat. The party took some time to get settled and it was by now the hottest part of the day and they had an hour's drive before them; but so far everything had gone smoothly and the clear blue sky and the sunshine gave promise of pleasant times ahead. As an added bonus the twins fell asleep as soon as they started, curled up against Deborah. What with their small warm bodies pressed to hers, and Dee on her lap, she grew hot and rather sticky. Probably her nose was shining and her hair a mess but at least her dress looked fresh and cool. She sat very still, and since Mr Burns spoke only occasionally, admired the scenery.

There were mountains in the distance, tree covered, sweeping down to orange groves and vineyards and fields of stunted olive trees, and every few miles a village—a narrow street lined with small square houses with shuttered windows and when a door was open she could glimpse inside, black emptiness. Of course, there would be furniture there and people, but they weren't visible. There were dogs too, lying round in the dust, taking no notice of anyone, sensibly asleep like everyone else. The sea was on their left but it was some miles away although there were frequent signposts pointing seawards, but for the moment Deborah was quite content to marvel at the oranges and lemons and the brilliance of the flowers. There was a good deal of traffic on the road, but they travelled fast, Mr Burns explaining over one shoulder that once they had arrived everyone must have a rest before unpacking. Deborah agreed cheerfully, well aware that the twins, refreshed by their nap, would want to be up and doing, and since she had been hired as their nanny it would be her duty to keep them from disturbing everyone. She began to plan various forms of entertainment calculated to keep them as quiet as possible.

'We're almost there,' said Mr Burns suddenly and turned the car off the road on to a narrow winding lane leading to the sea. Sure enough, she could see the coast now, high cliffs and sparkling water and here and there a red roofed white painted villa tucked away behind the trees growing thicker on either side of them. They drove past them all though and didn't stop until the sea was only a few hundred yards away down below, and they turned into a sandy drive leading to a handsome villa surrounded by a garden stuffed to choking point with flowers.

'We've been here before,' explained Mr Burns, 'there's a swimming pool round the back and steps down to the beach.' He stopped before the wide porch and got out. 'I'll carry these two in first—nice if they stay asleep for a bit longer. Can you manage Dee?'

She, following him inside, had Dee under one arm and wondered whose car it was parked beside the house and then forgot it while she admired the cool splendour of the hall; terra cotta tiles and white plastered walls and beautiful rugs and some rather uncomfortable looking chairs around the walls. She followed Mr Burns upstairs and discovered that there was a small dark woman ahead of them, leading the way. 'You'll be here,' Mr Burns told her and went in in front of her into a high-ceilinged room with closed shutters and a bed with an ornately carved head board; there were doors on either side, a bathroom and the children's room, shuttered against the heat. He lowered the still sleeping twins on to one of the beds and rubbed his arms. 'They are getting heavy,' he observed and glanced at Dee. 'She's due for a feed, isn't she? There's some made up in the car in the freezer bag, isn't there? I'll fetch it for you and ask Maria to send you up a tray of tea and something cold for the children when they wake. With luck you'll have time to shower and change before they rouse. Can you cope? Peggy will see to Mrs Beaufort and have a rest and we can have dinner when the children are in bed.'

Deborah said that of course she could manage, in her serene voice and added: 'If the children wake can we go into the garden? We'll stay in the shade and they can make more noise outside.'

'A good idea. Mrs Beaufort will rest I expect, but Peggy and I will be around in a couple of hours.'

Deborah inspected the room while she waited for her tea; it was pleasantly cool and dim and the furniture was of dark wood and very simple. There were a few rugs on the tiled floor and a gaily coloured bedspread. She approved of what she saw, just as she approved of the bathroom and the simply furnished room the children were in. She unpacked her overnight bag and called a quiet 'come in' when someone knocked on the door. It was Maria, unsmiling and polite, bearing a tray with a welcome teapot and a plate of little cakes and following hard on her heels, Mrs Burns.

'Nanny, can you manage for a bit? I'm putting Mother to bed and I'm going to lie down for an hour. This evening we'll work out some kind of time table between us.'

'Everything is fine, Mrs Burns. I expect Mrs Beaufort's pretty tired—let me know if I can help in any way. I expect we'll go outside once the twins wake. I'll get Dee fed and changed and take her with us in the carry-cot.'

Mrs Burns disappeared looking relieved and Deborah drank the teapot dry and then, with one eye on the twins, had a quick shower and changed into a cotton dress. Just in time, they woke together, demanded drinks and wanted to know where they were and what they were going to do. Deborah told them while she fed Deirdre, put them into cotton shirts and shorts, rubbed their small plump persons with lotion and suggested that they should creep downstairs and into the garden. It was cooler now and she opened the shutters and then, with Dee asleep in her carry-cot and the twins trotting behind her, went downstairs. She had slapped lotion on as much of her as she could reach and tied her hair back with a ribbon. They crossed the hall silently and went out through the open door. The first thing she saw was Professor Beaufort, leaning up against an orange tree, one arm flung round the thin shoulders of a girl of ten years or so.

She stood gaping at him, her gentle mouth a little open, while the twins made a concerted rush to wind their arms round his legs, their voices shrill with delight.

'Hush,' she whispered fiercely, 'don't disturb everyone.' He said 'Hullo Nanny. Not that you look in the least like one at the moment. Did we surprise you? Shock is perhaps the better word… This is my daughter Eleanor, we arrived yesterday.'

Deborah smiled, said hullo and wondered why she suddenly felt depressed. Eleanor, giving her a rather shy smile, looked at her with her father's blue eyes. She was a pale child and later on she would be pretty with all that fair curly hair tumbling around her shoulders. She said in a voice as shy as her smile: 'Shall I show you the garden and the way down the steps to the beach?'

'Would you? Simon and Suzy can't wait to see everything,' Deborah grinned. 'Me too,' she added honestly. She supposed that Eleanor would join the nursery party and leave the professor and his wife free, and after all one more child didn't make all that difference and she was old enough to help with the twins if they became too boisterous.

The professor waved them a casual goodbye and went to the house and she found that her depression was strongly mingled with pleasure at seeing him again, which, considering she didn't like him in the very least, seemed strange. She wondered what his wife would be like and then pushed all thought of that to the back of her head so that she could give her attention to the children, capering along each side of Eleanor; they liked her, that was obvious. Deborah, with Dee awake for once and peering contentedly from her basket, followed them along a path bordered by a tangle of flowers and shrubs, which ended at a vast expanse of lawn and at one side a swimming pool. The twins instantly demanded to get into it and indeed Deborah eyed its cool blue water with longing, but she pointed out with cunning that she had nothing with her no towels, no swim suits…

'We don't need swim suits,' declared Simon.

'No, love but I do,' she pointed out reasonably, 'and you can't go in without me. Look, it's getting on for bedtime anyway. Shall we put everything ready for the morning and come here before breakfast?' She glanced at Eleanor and smiled, and the girl said: 'I'll come too, please, Nanny.'

'Of course. I'll ask Mummy if she will have Dee for half an hour.' She pretended not to see Simon's turned down mouth, and said briskly: 'Now what about that path down to the beach? Is it close by, Eleanor?'

The path was really a gentle zigzag of easy steps, ending on warm yellow sand; a small cove, sheltered by rocks on either side and no one else in sight. 'May we paddle?' asked Eleanor, 'I'll take care of the twins. It's quite safe here; Daddy and I went swimming this morning…'

Deborah perched on a handy rock by the water's edge, her hand on Dee's basket, and watched them with envy. The water was a clear, bright blue, she would have liked to have torn off her clothes and swum for hours. Perhaps, when they had settled in, Mrs Burns would tell her when she could be free, so that she could spend her leisure here, swimming and lolling around; wearing a sunhat, of course, and even that wouldn't stop the freckles. Not that anyone was likely to notice them.

They all wandered back presently, the twins quite content after their paddle, Dee asleep again and Eleanor, now that she had got over her shyness, full of plans for picnics and outings and a trip along the coast in one of the fishermen's boats. Deborah, listening with only half an ear, knowing her role from previous experience. Dee was too small to take on such trips; she remembered the countless times she had been left at home with a baby or a toddler while everyone else made off joyfully, intent on a day out. After all, she reminded herself, it was her job, that was what she was paid for.

They found the others on the patio, lounging in comfortable chairs, with a tray of iced drinks on the table between them. Mrs Burns beamed at them all: 'There you are my dears. Have they been good, Nanny? Now it's supper for you and then bed, we've had a long day.'

Deborah looked away from the tempting contents of the glass jugs on the table; she longed for a cool drink but if the children were to have their supper it was unlikely that she would get one.

'Nanny needs a drink,' observed the professor, and got up out of his lounger. 'I'm going to take the children to see the kittens in the garage while she has it.'

He collected the three of them, picked up Dee out of her basket and deposited her on her mother's lap, and waved Deborah to a seat, while Mr Burns got up and poured a drink for her. She sat down, feeling awkward, like a gatecrasher, and watched the professor wandering off with his party.

'He's marvellous with the children,' declared Mrs Burns,

'and Eleanor gets on so well with the twins—you won't mind if she tags along with you, Nanny?'

'Not in the least, Mrs Burns—she's a sweet little girl and the twins adore her don't they? What a heavenly place this is.'

'Mmm we've been coming here for years. Have you all you want in your room? Do say if you need anything else. There's Maria, who housekeeps for us and two girls who come in each day—they'll see to the rooms and the beds and the washing. Mother will have to take things easily for a bit, but we'll get into a routine in a day or two. Once the children are in bed and we've had dinner, we'll put our heads together and work something out.' She turned her head to watch her brother and the children coming through the garden and Deborah got up, picked up Dee from her mother's lap and stood waiting for them.

'Supper's in the dining room,' said Mrs Burns, 'and there's plenty of hot water for baths, you'll be all right with Dee? She can sit on your lap...'

The professor had handed over the children unfussily, now he took the baby from Deborah and tucked her under one arm. 'Dee hasn't spoken to me yet—she shall sit with me until the children have finished their supper.' And he sat down with the infant, leaving Deborah to shepherd her charges into the house, sit them at table in the richly dark oak and leather dining room, and serve them their suppers. Eleanor sat with them explaining that when she was on holiday with her father she usually had her supper with him, but if Deborah didn't mind, she'd have it now and help her with the twins. 'Then perhaps I can help you to unpack,' she suggested.

Deborah smiled at her; she was a nice child and perhaps

not quite as happy as she should be, she was too quiet for a start. Deborah wondered about her mother and hoped that someone would tell her sooner or later where she was, or if she were alive. No one had mentioned her.

She was to know soon enough. Two hours later, with the twins fast asleep, Dee fed and tucked up and herself in an Indian cotton dress and wearing a little more make-up than usual, she went downstairs. Mrs Burns had said dinner at half-past eight and it wanted five minutes to that hour. In the hall she paused, not quite sure where to go; she couldn't hear voices, only the faint clash of pots and pans from the kitchen part of the house. Perhaps it would be better if she went back to her room and waited for a gong. She turned on her heel and the professor said from somewhere behind her: 'No, don't go back to your room. The others aren't down yet—come and have a drink.'

He led the way outside, offered her a chair and went to the tray of drinks set ready. 'Something long and cool?' he suggested. 'I do hope Eleanor hasn't been a nuisance…'

'Of course not,' Deborah heard her voice a bit too loud and indignant, 'she's such a nice child and a great help with the twins. When they were in bed she helped me unpack. She's in bed herself now, reading.'

'Yes, I know, I've been up to see her.' He gave her a long considered glance over his glass. 'I'm glad that you get on well together. You have been wondering about her mother?'

'Yes,' said Deborah baldly.

'She died six years ago; she left us a year previously. Eleanor doesn't remember her. She has a governess; a nice old fashioned maiden lady who conceals a clever brain under a mild exterior, her name is Miss Timmis.'

'She's not here?'

'No, she's having a well earned holiday. Which is what we are all having with the exception of yourself Deborah.'

She overlooked the Deborah and said a little tartly: 'I take my holidays between jobs, Professor Beaufort.'

'You must have the constitution of an ox and the temper of an angel.'

She looked away from him. 'What a curious mixture you must find me, professor, a gorgon with a mouth like a rat trap, and ox—a strong ox—with an angelic temper.'

He said blandly: 'You forget the sandy hair and the green eyes, they all add up to something quite out of the ordinary.'

She looked at him then and found him smiling. 'They add up to a children's nurse,' she told him soberly.

They dined presently in a leisurely fashion on melon soaked in port wine, *lulas recheadas* (which after she had eaten it Deborah discovered was squid embellished with egg yolk and tomatoes), ham and onion, a salad and *pudim fla* which she had no difficulty in recognising as egg custard. There was little time to talk before it was time to give Dee her feed; over coffee Mrs Burns suggested a flexible routine to be gone into thoroughly later on. 'Meals all together,' she suggested, 'but the children will wake early, Nanny, perhaps you could let them play in the garden—the nursery's overlooking the lawn isn't it? You could keep an eye on them while you see to Dee?'

Deborah had reservations about that, the twins needed two eyes on them all the time, that was something she would have to work out for herself. She murmured politely and Mrs Burns went on: 'Breakfast at half-past eight; Mother will have hers in her room, then we can all do our own thing until lunch time. Lunch at half-past twelve and the children must rest for a couple of hours unless we're picnicking, of course. You must have some free time—perhaps after tea for an hour or two? If the children have their supper at half-past six, that would give you time to go for a swim or write those letters or something. I daresay we shall go out quite a lot once we're rested—we won't always be able to take Dee—you won't mind being here with her? Maria will look after you, of course.' Mrs Burns smiled suddenly: 'It'll give you a break from the twins—isn't it a blessing that Dee's such a placid child?'

Deborah smiled and agreed, 'But if I don't give her a feed, she won't be placid at all,' she observed, and made a quiet exit, rather surprised when the professor got up and opened the door for her. Without saying anything though.

Dee was an easy baby; Deborah popped her back into her cot, undressed and showered, wrote a brief letter to her mother, took a final look at the twins and Eleanor in the little room across the passage, and then got into bed. A busy day, she reflected, and probably all the other days to come would be just as busy. It had been thoughtful of the professor to take the children off her hands for a few minutes; she still didn't like him of course, but perhaps she didn't dislike him quite as much, and she was sorry for him, poor man, with no wife and a child to bring up. She wondered about his wife and why she had left him and Eleanor—perhaps he was a tyrant in his own home…she slept on the thought.

She awoke to warm sunshine and the sound of a nearby church bell chiming six o'clock. The twins were still asleep but Dee was waking. Deborah fed her, changed her and put her back in her cot and got dressed herself. A swim in the pool would be heaven—but quite impossible. She tied her hair back, slipped bare feet into sandals and found the twins awake and demanding to go out at once. They had the same idea that she had: to get into the pool and she had to explain why they couldn't, but no amount of explaining helped! She wrestled them into shorts and cotton tops and was brushing two tousled heads when the door was opened and Eleanor put her head round. 'I heard you,' she said. 'May I come with you?'

Deborah beamed at her, 'Of course. The twins want to go in the pool but they'll have to wait until after breakfast, I can't leave Dee...'

The door behind Eleanor was pushed wide and the professor, looking huge in a towelling robe, flung an arm round his daughter. He wished them good morning, dared them to utter a squeak and suggested—in a voice which commanded more than suggested—that there was no reason why they shouldn't all go to the pool. The twins opened their mouths to shout delightedly, 'Quiet!' He told them firmly then went on: 'Eleanor, help them into their swim suits or whatever they wear; Deborah, go and put on your bikini and put Dee in her basket, we'll take it in turns to mind her. Now look sharp everyone.'

Deborah found herself doing exactly as she had been bidden; it took only a couple of minutes to get out of her few garments and in to the newest of the bikinis she had brought with her. She snatched up Dee's basket, popped her in and went into the children's room. 'Towels?' she asked.

'In the changing room at the pool.' He looked at her briefly: 'Don't ever expect me to call you Nanny again,' he observed silkily. 'Shall we go?'

It was already warm and the garden smelled delicious. They ran over the lawn, the professor with a twin on each hand, Deborah with Dee and Eleanor skipping between them, all of them in silence. 'If anyone wakes up and hears us they might get cross, so mum's the word, especially you Simon.' The professor turned to grin at Deborah before he slid into the pool, helped the children in and began swimming up and down its length with first one then the other of them. Eleanor, Deborah noticed, could swim well, and between them she and her father ferried the little ones to and from each side with a lot of suppressed laughter and splashing.

'Now it's your turn,' the professor had heaved himself out and was sitting beside her, 'In you go, do you swim?'

She gave him a cold look. 'All Nannys swim,' she told him and slid in at the deep end to shoot down the pool to where Eleanor was playing with the twins. The water was warm; this would be where she would spend her precious free time, she decided as she joined the others in a watery game of ring o'roses.

The professor sat like Buddha with Dee cradled on his crossed legs. He watched the twins with tolerant amusement, his daughter with tender affection and then turned his gaze on to Deborah, bounding around like a twelve-year-old. He watched her for so long and so intently that a casual observer might have been forgiven for scenting a romance, but there was no romance in his face only a kind of intense speculation.

They all scrambled out presently and went in to dress for breakfast, leaving him there by the pool. It was half an hour before they met again at table, the twins in shorts and cotton tops and Eleanor and Deborah in sun dresses.

'A heavenly morning,' declared Mrs Burns from behind the coffee pot, 'who's for the beach?'

It seemed that they all were, although Mrs Burns stayed behind for a little while to settle Mrs Beaufort in a shady corner of the garden. Half way through the morning, when everybody was tired from being in the water and the twins had turned their energies to making sand castles, Deborah was asked—very nicely—if she would go back to the house and make sure that the old lady was all right. 'And don't bother to come down again,' said Mrs Burns, 'we'll be up for lunch in less than an hour, so I'll look after the children.'

Her husband and brother exchanged amused glances; Peggy was a good mother and a loving one but she had long ago devised a system of delegating maternal authority to whoever happened to be handy. She smiled at them both: 'I'm quite exhausted with all this heat, will you two keep an eye on them while I snatch a few minutes' peace?' She added generously: 'You can leave Dee here in her basket.'

Easily done since Dee was asleep. 'You're a humbug,' declared the professor equably, 'I pity Bill from the bottom of my heart.'

'Wait until you marry,' said Peggy. 'No don't answer that, I'm asleep.'

Eleanor had listened. 'If you ever marry again, Daddy, can it be someone just like Deborah, I do like her.'

'You mean, Nanny, darling?' asked Mrs Burns.

'She said I could call her Deborah: I'm too old to say nanny.'

'So you are love.' The professor had got to his feet. 'You and I are going for a short walk—we haven't had a talk for a long time have we?'

Eleanor took his hand. When they were well away from the others she asked: 'What about, Daddy?'

He flung an arm round her small shoulders. 'I've had a rather nice idea,' he began and started to explain it to her.

Back in the garden, Deborah fetched another jug of lemonade for Mrs Beaufort, walked her gently up and down in the shade for a short time, and then sat down on the grass at her feet. The sun was really warm now and despite the sun hat and sitting in the shade, her freckles were making a splendid show. They made her look very young and Mrs Beaufort said suddenly: 'You're nothing more than a child…'

'I'm twenty-three, Mrs Beaufort, and I've been trained for more than three years now.'

'Indeed? And no boy-friends?'

'No, I've lots of friends though. I think perhaps I'm not the kind of girl a man wants to marry.' She turned her head, her ordinary face lighted by a smile. 'Isn't it lucky that I like my job. After Christmas I shall look for a permanent post—you know, with some county family with hordes of children, so that I can stay with them forever.'

'You'd like that?'

'It's the next best thing to being married and having children of my own, isn't it?'

'I daresay it is. Peggy has been very lucky in her marriage; her husband adores her and the children are charming, which is a fortunate thing for I am sure she would have made a deplorable mess of a job and being single. As for Gideon—well, at least he has Eleanor—his wife left him when Eleanor was three years old. An American millionaire I think he was, it's a terrible thing to confess, but I was glad when she died in an accident a year later. There was no love left between them but it has changed him.' She gave a little chuckle: 'He's not quite a misogynist but he has cultivated an amused tolerance toward women. Some girl will come along one day and crack it wide open, and the sooner the better.'

They had lunch out of doors under the orange trees before Deborah took a sleepy pair of children up to their beds and set about feeding Dee. There were small chores to do after that, and she was hot and tired by the time they were done. She got on to her own bed and dozed until Simon came pattering in, asking for a drink, and while he had it she told him a story.

They went to the beach again before tea but this time Deborah didn't go into the water; Mrs Burns hadn't joined them and she sat with Dee while Mr Burns splashed around with the twins. They trooped up to the house presently and found the others sitting in the garden round a table laden with a teapot and plates of sandwiches and cake. It was the professor who observed presently: 'Isn't it about time Nanny had an hour to herself. It's cool enough now to play ball with the children.'

'I'll come with you,' said Eleanor eagerly as Deborah got up and before her father could say anything Deborah said cheerfully: 'Yes, do—we'll go for another swim shall we?' Although she longed to be alone just for an hour. All the same Eleanor was good company, they swam for a while and then strolled along the beach, letting the warm water wash round their feet, until Deborah glanced at her watch. 'Time to feed Dee,' she cried, 'my goodness I almost forgot.' She took the hand Eleanor held out. 'It's been fun, hasn't it?'

The twins didn't want to have their supper, neither did they want to go to bed, it took all Deborah's powers of persuasion to settle them for the night and by the time she had tidied the room and put out clean clothes for the morning, she had to rush through a shower and change of clothes, not wasting much time over her hair or her face. The freckles looked worse than ever, she decided, dabbing on powder and then washing it off again because they weren't to be disguised. She got downstairs with a couple of minutes to spare, and accepted the glass Mr Burns offered her.

'A lovely day,' observed Mrs Burns happily. 'I say, Nanny, you have caught the sun—have you something to put on your face? Those freckles...'

Everyone looked at her as she said quietly: 'Aren't they awful? I get them every summer and it makes no difference what I put on them.' It vexed her very much that she blushed as she spoke and that made the wretched things even more noticeable.

The professor started to talk about something else, turning attention away from her and she was grateful for that. He could be kind, she had discovered. After dinner, making the excuse that she was tired so that she wouldn't be the odd man out in the family, he had gone to the door with her. 'I hope Eleanor didn't spoil your free time,' he said quietly, 'that wasn't intended.' Then he added: 'We must make amends.'

CHAPTER FOUR

THERE WAS NO sign of the professor making amends during the next few days, not that Deborah was at all sure what he had meant. Amends for what? Did he think that she expected to be free for hours on end? Or that she had minded having Eleanor for company when she was free? She dismissed the subject as being too trivial to think about, in any case she hadn't all that much time to sit about thinking. The days fell quickly into a pleasant pattern, if a hard working one, for the children were here there and everywhere; eating their meals out of doors, up at first light and never wanting to go to bed. Nonetheless, Deborah heard without rancour Mrs Burns' suggestion that they should drive along the coast to Cape St Vincent and have lunch out: 'That nice place at Sagres…'

'*Pousade do infante*,' murmured the professor.

Mrs Burns nodded. 'That's the one. Nanny you won't mind staying here with Dee, will you?' She smiled charmingly, 'you'll be glad of a nice quiet day with her. Maria will look after you and we'll be back in good time for the children to go to bed.'

Deborah agreed with ready cheerfulness, forbearing to mention that Dee was cutting a tooth and had had a restless night so would probably have a restless day too. Perhaps it was just as well that everyone was going out so that she could give her her whole attention. At least for the moment the infant was sleeping which gave Deborah the chance to get the twins ready for their outing.

'I wish you were coming too,' said Eleanor softly as the party assembled at the front of the house. 'There's heaps of room because Daddy's taking his car and there is only me with him.'

'Another time, love,' promised Deborah and went to settle Mrs Beaufort in the front seat of the Burns' car, and then arranged the twins one each side of their mother in the back. 'We shall be very hot,' said Mrs Burns worriedly, and then: 'You're sure you'll be all right, Nanny?'

'Quite sure. Have a lovely day.' Deborah dropped a kiss on each twin's cheek, 'Bring me back some seaweed.'

Mr Burns drove off and she turned to the professor's car. 'Have a nice day,' she repeated and was engulfed in Eleanor's hug.

The professor was leaning against the bonnet: 'I heard Dee grizzling dreadfully during the night. Teething?'

He didn't look the kind of man to bother about childish ailments. Deborah said shortly: 'That's right, yes,' and then, 'I hope you have a lovely day.'

'You said that just now. When do you have your day off?'

She flushed slowly, 'Mrs Burns hasn't had time to discuss it with me,' she told him shortly. 'In any case…'

'It's none of my business,' he finished for her smoothly. 'Jump in, Eleanor and let us sample the delights of Cape St Vincent and Sagres.'

He drove off with a careless wave of the hand and Deborah waved back, not to him but to Eleanor, standing watching the little Fiat until it had reached the lane and disappeared. It was still early and the day stretched before her; she went indoors and changed into a bikini and put the sun hat and sun glasses on and carried the still sleeping Dee out into the garden setting her basket against one of the orange trees. It was pleasantly cool and shady and she sat, doing nothing until Dee woke and began to cry. Deborah took her out of the basket and sat her on her lap giving her a teething ring, but she went on wailing. It was too early for her feed so Deborah tucked her under her arm and wandered round the garden with her until presently the sobbing stopped. Fed and changed and for the moment content, Dee slept again and Deborah lay back, idly day-dreaming. To be married to a man who could provide luxurious villas for holidays and charter planes to get one there would be quite something. She wasn't envious of Mrs Burns, she was too sensible for that, but there was no harm in letting her imagination run riot for a bit. She wouldn't want a husband like Mr Burns though; he was a dear, kind and thoughtful and good natured and he spoilt Mrs Burns outrageously. Deborah thought that a man like him would get on her nerves after a time, but neither would she want to be bullied. The professor came near to doing that from time to time, perhaps not bullying, but certainly overriding anyone who didn't fall in with his suggestions. She was aware that she wasn't being quite fair but she busied herself thinking up all his faults and failings so that she could prove to herself that she was right.

The day wore on slowly with Dee getting more fractious as it became warmer, Deborah was walking up and down in the shade with her over one shoulder, longing for the tea which she saw no chance of getting, when the Fiat raced up the drive and stopped by the house. Eleanor and her father reached her at the same time. The professor stretched out an arm, transferred Dee to his own shoulder and patted the small back with a large hand.

'Take Deborah into the house and see that she gets some tea,' he told Eleanor. His eye lighted on Deborah's face which was all ready to refuse. 'And you do as I say Debby.' His eyes skimmed the bikini. 'Since you're dressed for a swim, I suggest that you have one as soon as you've had tea.'

He marched off with Dee, and Eleanor tugged at Deborah's hand. 'Come on, Daddy's awfully good with babies and children—he frightens grown ups sometimes, but that's all.'

Quite enough too, thought Deborah, allowing herself to be led indoors to fall gratefully upon a plate of sandwiches and drain the teapot.

'Did you have a nice day?' She offered a sandwich to her companion.

'Lovely. We went to Prince Henry's Fort and watched the fishermen and went swimming at Sagres. Has Dee been crying all day?'

'Well, on and off, yes. The tooth's nearly through though. I daresay she'll be happier tomorrow, the poor poppet.'

'Aren't you tired, Deborah?'

She swallowed the rest of her tea and got up. 'Only a very little bit—that tea was lovely, I was beginning to think that I wouldn't get any.'

'Daddy drove back very fast because he said perhaps you'd need a break. Wasn't it lucky that we got home early?'

'Very, and I'm most grateful. Now I'm going back to Dee...'

'You haven't had your swim, Daddy said you had to have a swim.' Eleanor took her hand as they went back into the garden. 'There's heaps of time, the others hadn't even started when we left.'

There was no sign of the professor and Dee, Deborah stood uncertainly for a moment, and then, urged on by Eleanor, followed her down the path to the beach. The water was warm; she swam lazily, keeping an eye on Eleanor and left the sea reluctantly. They went back into the house and ten minutes later were back in the garden, both rather damp about the head but cool in sundresses.

The professor was lying under the trees, his niece spread over his chest asleep. He opened an eye as they reached him. 'The tooth's through, thank God. How nice and clean and cool you look.'

'The water was heaven and so was the tea. Thank you very much, Professor.'

'The pleasure was mine. I do hope that my sister hasn't any plans for this evening, I'm for early bed.' He glanced at his watch. 'They'll be here shortly. The twins have had a busy day I can tell you, with luck they'll gobble their supper and fall into bed.'

'They said they never wanted to go home again,' said Eleanor.

'Then we must remind them that the puppy will be waiting for them. Here they are now. I'll stay with Dee while you deal with the twins, Deborah.'

She collected them without loss of time, pausing only long enough to murmur sympathetically at Mrs Burns' rather plaintive remark that she was exhausted. Mrs Beaufort looked exhausted too, but the quicker the twins were fed and put to bed the sooner everyone could relax. For once they were angelic; eating their suppers with no fuss at all, submitting to lightning showers and pyjamas with the minimum of complaints, indeed they chattered happily about their day, only stopping when Deborah popped them into their beds and tucked them up. She went along to her own room then, made sure that she was presentable and then went downstairs. Mrs Burns was lying on one of the sofas in the sitting room. 'Bill's gone to see to something in the car and Dee's still asleep with Gideon; Eleanor's with them. I'm very weary, Nanny, will you be an angel and help Mother to bed? I think she should rest at once and have her dinner there, don't you?'

Mrs Burns was undoubtedly tired, Deborah told herself going back upstairs and tapping on Mrs Beaufort's door. She was tired herself, but she forgot that when she saw Mrs Beaufort sitting in a chair by the window.

'I've had such a lovely day,' she told Deborah, 'but you know, I'm too tired to get undressed! Isn't that silly?'

'It was a long day,' observed Deborah, 'and of course you're tired. Mrs Burns asked me to give you a hand and I'll tell Maria to bring you up a tray and you can have it sitting up in bed. That way you can go to sleep just whenever you feel like it. Now let's get you to bed…'

It took quite a while; Mrs Beaufort wasn't to be hurried and she wanted to talk about her day, so it was well past the time for Dee's feed by the time Deborah had been to the kitchen to arrange for Mrs Beaufort's supper and Dee still had to be got ready for bed. Of course, Mrs Burns might have started…

She hadn't. The professor came in from the garden with Dee draped tearfully over one shoulder just as Deborah came into the room.

'Aren't you a bit late, Nanny?' asked Mrs Burns pleasantly. 'Did you get Mother into bed and see to her supper?'

The professor spoke before she could. 'Do I understand that Deborah has fed the twins, put them to bed, put Mother to bed too and now has to feed Dee and get her into bed as well? Isn't that a bit much, even for a highly trained nanny, my dear?'

'But you're so capable, aren't you, Nanny? And you've had all day without any of us…'

The professor shook his head at her. 'Deborah's been up half the night with Dee—she's cut a tooth, and I'll wager she's had a long hard day of it.'

Deborah stood between them, feeling a fool. She snapped: 'I'm perfectly all right, Professor.' And whisked Dee away from him and out of the room, leaving him laughing softly and Mrs Burns bewildered. 'She's a girl in a thousand,' she observed, 'but it is her job and I pay her well.'

The professor stopped laughing. 'And make the fullest use of her, just as you do of Bill and me and anyone else who happens to be around. Look, love, let her have the day off tomorrow—heaven knows she's earned it. I've got to go back to Lagos, I'll be happy to give her a lift there and back.'

Mrs Burns gave him a quick look. 'What a splendid idea—do you suppose Eleanor would stay here with us? She's so marvellous with the twins—we could go on the beach…'

'I'm sure she'll be delighted.' She watched him stroll away, out into the garden. Mrs Burns broached the subject of a day off during dinner: 'And as Gideon has to go into Lagos tomorrow he can give you a lift.'

Deborah opened her mouth to refuse and then closed it again when she saw the faint, knowing smile on the professor's lips. 'Thank you,' she agreed sedately, 'that would be very convenient, I should like to explore the town and do some shopping—presents you know.'

'embroidery and pottery,' said Mrs Burns rather vaguely, 'the shops shut in the afternoon, but I daresay you'll find something to do…'

She smiled kindly at Deborah; she was a dear girl and so good with the children, and she had quite forgotten that until Gideon had mentioned it she had overlooked the fact that Deborah, with the exception of the brief hour or so after tea, had had no time to herself. She added: 'You go and enjoy yourself Nanny, I'll be able to manage—Bill's here to help and Eleanor…'

They left directly after breakfast while it was still cool. Deborah wore a sundress with a little jacket and had her swim suit packed in the roomy straw bag Mrs Burns had lent her. She had rammed her sun hat on top of her piled up hair and put on her sun glasses, then spent a few moments regretfully examining her freckles which seemed worse than ever. The rest of her was nicely tanned, as the professor pointed out to her as they drove off. 'I like the freckles too,' he added with casual friendliness. He talked easily as they drove, pointing out various things which might interest her but never once mentioning the children or her work so that after a while Deborah began to feel that she too was on holiday without a care in the world—no teething baby, no rumbustious twins; she sniffed the warm air and relaxed.

The professor slowed down as they reached the town, pointing out the fish market, the fort and the bus station on the boulevard by the river. When he stopped at a car park Deborah asked: 'Shall I meet you here when you are going back, or shall I catch a bus?'

'Let's talk about that over coffee,' he invited, 'but first

we'll go to the bank, if you don't mind—they close at noon and only open for a couple of hours in the afternoon.'

The town was still fairly full with tourists and the narrow streets were crowded. Once the business at the bank was attended to he then turned up a narrow lane and ushered her into a shop selling pottery and embroidery, but he didn't stop there going on, down a passage into a coffee shop.

Over their coffee she said again: 'If you'd tell me what bus to catch?'

He leaned back in the narrow cane chair which creaked abominably.

'Oh, I'm having a day off too, I was hoping we might do some sightseeing and I've some things to buy—I could do with your advice.' He watched her face. 'If you don't care for the idea, don't mind saying so.'

She stared at him across the small table. 'Won't I bore you?'

'No.' He beckoned the waiter for more coffee. 'Shall we do the shopping first and put it in the car? We can lunch at one of the local restaurants, they are very simple but the food is usually good. Everything shuts until four o'clock so we could drive to Rocha, it's not far, and have a swim.'

'That sounds heavenly if you are sure?'

'I'm sure. Finished? You'd better use the loo here, some of them are a bit primitive, but Eleanor's given this one the okay.'

Deborah went meekly and presently found him in the pottery shop. 'The trouble is,' he observed, 'these things tend to break on the way home. I want something for my housekeeper. What do you suggest?'

Deborah started to poke round the embroidery. 'Is she house proud?' she wanted to know.

'Oh God, yes.'

'This then,' decided Deborah, picking out an exquisitely embroidered teacloth. 'Aren't they gorgeous? I think I'll have one for Mother.'

They wandered out to the street, stopping to look in shop windows while the professor patiently worked out the prices into pounds and pence. After an hour, laden now with odds and ends which had caught her fancy, they sat down in the tiny square in the centre of the town to drink orange juice before strolling back to the car. Empty handed once more, they went back into the town and went into a small rather bare restaurant in one of the main streets.

'You've been here before, of course,' said Deborah. 'I expect you know all the restaurants and cafés.'

'Most of them. This one's plain but the food's good and the fish is excellent. What about grilled sea bream and a salad? And Vinho Verde to go with it?'

They sat idly, not talking much but at ease with each other, drinking their wine and watching their lunch being cooked at the back of the restaurant.

'You may find dessert rather sweet—I should have an ice,' counselled the professor. 'I shall have *cabeiro*—that's goat's milk cheese.'

It was hot when they went into the street again and got into the car to drive the short distance to Rocha.

'Just look at that beach!' exclaimed Deborah as they drove slowly along the boulevard. It wasn't very wide nor very long, but there were shops facing the sea, smart boutiques and coffee shops and newspaper kiosks.

The professor turned the car into the car park behind a large hotel built on the very edge of the beach then took Deborah's hand and led her inside.

'Sit there while I have a word,' he said and went over to the desk. He came back very shortly with two keys. 'There are changing rooms at the bottom of the steps leading to the beach. Here's your key—let the desk have it before we go on to the beach, now stay here while I fetch our things.'

The beach wasn't crowded just nicely filled and the water was warm and very clear. Deborah, free from keeping an eye on the children, swam happily out to sea only vaguely aware that the professor was beside her. Presently she turned on to her back and found him idling close by.

'It must be very hot in the summer,' she observed, her eyes closed.

'Very—this is the best time of the year—and spring, of course, but it's not quite as warm.' He rolled over. 'Race you back?'

He allowed her to win and they lay on the sand under a canvas awning, presently Deborah went to sleep. When she woke up the professor was sitting beside her, watching her. She wondered why he looked so intent, as though he was trying to decide something and then forgot all about it when he suggested that they should have another swim before tea.

They sat on the verandah and drank a surprisingly English tea, and ate little, very sweet cakes, then walked along the wide sand in the late afternoon cool.

'Oughtn't I to be going back?' asked Deborah.

'Only if you would like to, you're not expected. I said we'd be back around midnight.'

'Midnight?' She turned surprised green eyes on his bland face.

'They dine late here you know. We could go back now and sit over a drink.'

She stood still facing him. 'You spent the whole day taking me around. I'm most grateful but there was no need—I'm quite used to getting along on my own, and I expect you've done all this before.'

'I'm not going to make the obvious answer to that. Just reflect that I could have left you at the car park this morning.' He took her arm. 'I need a drink.'

Sitting outside a wine bar on the boulevard he asked suddenly 'What do you think of Eleanor?'

'Nice,' said Deborah promptly. 'Shy at first but so—so loving if you know what I mean. Is she like her mother?'

She wished she hadn't said that. The professor's face froze into an inscrutable mask. 'No.' She hoped that he would say something else, but he didn't so she went on hurriedly: 'Oh, well anyway—she's a darling. The twins adore her and she's good company—rather grown up for ten years old.'

'That is probably because she has no mother; Miss Timmis is elderly—more like a kindly aunt, my housekeeper is no longer in her first youth either, and nor for that matter am I. Which is perhaps the reason why Eleanor is less of a child than she should be.'

'But she is quite happy?'

'She could be happier—it's rather on my conscience. That's why we came here with Peggy and Bill and the children—they're a family.'

He sounded bitter and she wanted to say something sympathetic, but she had no chance for he went on in his usual casual way: 'Let's stroll back to the hotel and have dinner.'

The meal was excellent and very leisurely, so it was well after ten o'clock by the time they got back into the car. The evening had darkened and the sea glittered under a full moon. A night for romance, thought Deborah sleepily and wished, just for a moment, that she was sitting beside some young man who was hopelessly in love with her, with the promise of a delightful future and undying devotion before her... She gasped when the professor said silkily: 'The night's wasted on us, isn't it? It's a night for lovers; not a not-so-young widower and a dedicated nanny!'

'I am not dedicated!' declared Deborah quickly, her voice tart.

'There's hope for me yet,' said the professor, the silk back in his voice.

'Don't spoil my lovely day making silly jokes.'

He shot the car up the drive and stopped silently before the villa. Before he got out he said gently: 'I'm sorry, Debby. It was a lovely day—I've enjoyed every minute of it, thank you for your company.'

She got out and stood beside him. 'I enjoyed it too, thank you for taking me.' She smiled up at him and he swept her close and kissed her gently but thoroughly too. She stared at him in utter surprise before she ran indoors.

The twins, refreshed by a sound night's sleep, welcomed her enthusiastically when she got up to feed Dee at six o'clock. They climbed into her bed and sat telling her in a chorus of yesterday's pleasure. She responded suitably, saw to Dee's comfort then washed and dressed before going into the garden.

Eleanor usually joined them at their early morning games, but there was no sign of her and it wasn't until they were all sitting at breakfast that Mrs Burns remarked casually that Eleanor and her father had gone off at five o'clock, long before anyone else was stirring, to go fishing. 'Gideon persuaded one of the local fishermen to let them go with him—they drove into Lagos and planned to go on board there—they won't be back until this evening. Nanny, we're going into Portimao before lunch, I must get my hair done. If we're not back before twelve go ahead and have yours and settle the children for their rest, will you?'

Deborah hadn't really expected the Burns and Mrs Beaufort back for lunch and she was quite right, she coaxed the twins into their beds, saw to Dee and went to sit in the garden. It was hot and airless, and although the sky was blue she had the nasty feeling that there would be a storm before long. The sunlight became more and more brassy and the birds stopped singing. She watched the skies darken and pretended not to mind when she heard the first rumble of thunder. She made herself stay where she was until the next rumble, but then her calm deserted her and she scampered for the house. There was no one about; the two girls who came to help every day had long since gone home and Maria went to her own little house down the lane each afternoon and wouldn't be back until it was time to prepare the evening meal. Deborah peered into the kitchen just to make sure that she had gone; the tea tray was ready on the table but there was no sign of Maria, she hadn't expected to find her anyway. She went upstairs, flinching at a flash of lightning, and found the children still sound asleep. It would have been nice if they woke up, she thought wistfully, the house seemed very silent and getting darker every minute. She went back downstairs and then tore back up again as there was a vivid flash of lightning and the children woke, screaming with fright, rivalling the thunder and waking Dee.

Deborah picked up Dee, popped Suzy on to Simon's bed and sat down on its edge. It was far too warm with the twins wrapped round her as close as they could get and the baby on her lap, but just for the moment it was impossible to budge them; they bellowed at each flash and she could hardly blame them—she would have liked to bellow herself.

It started to rain, bucketing down, crashing on to the roof, overflowing the gutters, adding to the noise. Deborah gave up trying to speak, for there was no way of making herself heard. The storm was right overhead now, crashing and banging round the house with hardly a pause. She hoped that Mr and Mrs Burns were still in Portimao or had at least taken shelter. Only a madman would drive through in such weather. She hadn't allowed herself to think about the professor and Eleanor; out at sea the storm would surely be quite terrifying. She worried about it for a few minutes and found that she was worrying just as much about the professor as his daughter, which would never do. She mustn't allow a pleasant day with him to change her opinion of him; he could turn on the charm, she knew that now, but he could be just as beastly if he felt like it.

Somewhere close-by a tree crashed down and Suzy screamed, burying her head against Deborah and at the same time she saw the car lights coming up the drive. The Burns, she thought thankfully and then: supposing it wasn't? Supposing it was someone wanting shelter? Or just someone? She swallowed her fright and listened in vain for sounds other than the storm. The front door bell, and oh lord, she had left the door open when she came in. Surely the Burns would call out as they came into the house? And it couldn't be the professor and Eleanor because they were being tossed around somewhere at sea.

She had left the door open when she had come into the children's room and in the brief pause between the thunder and the lightning she heard steps on the stairs.

She was so frightened that she could hardly breathe; the

storm didn't matter any more, only the steps drowned now in celestial noise. She had gone very white, clutching the children close to her, not knowing what to do.

When the professor loomed in the doorway, his clothes plastered to him, water forming pools round his feet, she could only stare speechlessly.

His hullo was laconic, although his sharp glance had taken in Deborah's ashy face. He squelched across the floor, picked up the twins and said: 'Let's go down to the kitchen, shall we?' And he waited while she got to her feet with Dee under her arm before shooing her gently downstairs.

Eleanor was in the kitchen, taking off her wringing wet clothes. She grinned at Deborah over her shoulder and said in an excited voice: 'Isn't this simply super? You should have been there Deborah, you'd have loved it!'

Deborah smiled with a shaking mouth and felt the professor's large wet hand on her shoulder, pressing her gently into a chair. 'I frightened you—very thoughtless of me, I'm sorry. Sit there and we'll all have a cup of tea. But first of all I'd better get out of these wet things. I'll take the twins with me, and Eleanor can stay here with you. There's a towel she can wrap herself in; I'll bring down her dressing gown.'

He loomed over Deborah and for once his face was full of concern and kindness, but she hardly noticed; she was busy enough struggling to regain her usual calm. She was almost back to normal, despite several violent thunder claps and the vivid lightning, when he returned clad in slacks and a shirt, carrying Eleanor's dressing gown and trailed by the twins.

The electricity had been cut off soon after the storm began but he went through the cupboards until he found an old primus stove and lit it, filled a kettle and got out the tea pot. And all the while he kept up a rumbling monologue about nothing much, making the children laugh while Deborah sat as stiff as a board with fright, clutching Dee and hardly speaking, furious with herself for allowing her feelings to show but quite unable to do anything about it. She avoided the professor's eye, drank her tea and almost dropped the mug when another tree came crashing down close to the house. The professor sat opposite her at the table, a twin on each knee with Eleanor close to him; she found herself wishing that she could be close to him too, he gave the impression, probably erroneous, that while he was there nothing awful was going to happen. She watched his face, wondering what he had to laugh about when she was straining every nerve not to burst into tears along with the children, but she didn't look away quickly enough and he caught her eye. The smile he gave her was kind, but just sufficiently mocking to make her sit up and lift her chin. She remembered that he had called her a gorgon; the memory helped enormously and she felt her courage creeping back, after all the storm couldn't last much longer. She flinched as the room was filled by vivid blue lightning and the thunder tumbled and crashed around the house. In the quiet pause before the next deafening din he observed: 'I think the storm is moving away.' And he was right; surprisingly fifteen minutes later the sun was shining from a blue sky and the ground was steaming. The children, their fright forgotten, demanded to go down to the beach. 'And why not?' asked their uncle. 'That is if Nanny permits it?'

What a stuffy creature he must think her. Deborah said quietly: 'I think it's a marvellous idea. I'll get Dee's basket and the swim suits.' She paused: 'If you wouldn't mind keeping an eye on the twins for a minute?'

He reached out and took Dee from her. 'Eleanor's got to

put on something—it's too late for the children to go into the water. I'm afraid you've missed your time off Deborah.'

'It doesn't matter. I'd have been petrified if I'd been on my own, anyway.' She looked up at him gravely. 'I'm a coward about storms, I'm sorry.'

He lifted an eyebrow. 'You don't have to apologise to me, my dear. We all have our Achilles' heel.'

He hardly spoke to her again, but ran races with the children at the water's edge while she sat with Dee. They were returning to the house when Mr and Mrs Burns and Mrs Beaufort returned and the next ten minutes were taken up with rather excited talk on the part of Mrs Burns, and very exaggerated accounts of bravery on behalf of the twins. Deborah led them away presently, gave them their supper, saw to the baby and put them to bed. She had been afraid that after all the afternoon's excitement they wouldn't take kindly to the idea of sleep, but they gave her no more than ten minutes of tantrums before falling asleep with welcome suddenness, leaving her free to go as quickly as she could to her room, at last free to change her dress and do things to her face and hair. It hadn't been much of a day she reflected, pinning her sandy tresses back rather severely, the storm had been bad enough, but having to admit to near panic in front of the professor was far worse. He must think her a spineless creature. Not that that mattered in the least; she couldn't care less what he thought of her, although she had to admit to a strong desire to do something which would take that tolerant, faintly mocking smile off his handsome face.

She went downstairs presently and found everyone on the patio sitting in the cool of the evening over their drinks. She accepted Mr Burns' offer of a long, cool drink without enquiring as to what he intended to put into it, and sat down in the chair Mrs Burns was patting.

'Such a dreadful afternoon,' said that lady, 'I've never been so terrified in all my life. I'm still shaking…'

Deborah took a look; her employer looked as cool and unruffled as a newly scooped ice cream, moreover she looked very pretty in a vividly patterned cotton dress that Deborah hadn't seen before.

'How lucky for you that you were here,' went on Peggy Burns. 'Nice and safe in the house and the children seemed to have behaved splendidly. Sorry about your free time though—we'll have to make it up to you…'

The professor, lolling back in a wide cane chair, spoke: 'I don't know about Deborah, but I thought I'd stroll along as far as the village after dinner; there's a café there where someone sings *fado*, perhaps she'll come with me.' He added dryly: 'The children are all tucked up and sleeping, so she can leave them with a clear conscience.'

'Splendid!' cried his sister not giving Deborah a chance to say a word. 'A lovely little outing for her and, as you say, the children won't disturb me—I really am too exhausted to cope with them until I've had a good night's sleep…'

No one, Deborah reflected, had asked her if she wished to go out with the professor. She felt like a hungry dog offered a bone, but unlike the dog, not over keen to take it. The matter was decided for her: 'We can walk along the beach path,' said Professor Beaufort, 'enjoy the *fado* and come back along the lane.' He yawned, 'Or the other way round. It doesn't really matter.'

This stung Deborah into speech. 'So kind of you to suggest it,' she said with slight waspishness, 'but I think I'm too tired…'

She was overruled; even Mr Burns, who seldom took part in any argument, was against her. She ate her dinner meekly while inwardly fuming.

It was a splendid night when they set out to walk along the beach path; a romantic night, with a full moon slowly turning everything to a silvery day, and the faintest of breezes stirring the warm air.

They discussed the storm at some length, with the professor going into rather boring details about weather and so on—deliberately she thought. Well, it made something to talk about anyway. But once they were sitting at a small table at the *casa de fado* everything was different. Deborah hadn't been sure what to expect, but the black clad *fadista* pouring out her melancholy song of regrets and sadness, absorbed her whole attention. She drank whatever the professor ordered, ate the bits and pieces he offered her from time to time and sat enraptured, her melancholy almost as deep as the singer's, but somehow more pleasurable.

The singer went away presently and the professor asked mildly: 'Enjoying it Debby?'

'Oh, yes, very much. I've never heard anything like it before, though I suppose you have. Is it a kind of folk song?'

'Yes, and very old. There are two kinds—the traditional, which you hear in and around Lisbon and this one, the Coimbra *Fado*—I suppose you would call it regional.'

They stayed late, with Deborah unaware of the time and the professor watching her with a faint, amused smile. When at last she glanced at her watch he answered her horrified squeak of surprise with a reasonable: 'Well, there's no need to fuss—Peggy's quite able to feed Dee for once and I imagine that the twins won't stir until morning. You don't have to look so guilty, you spend long hours with the children and never complain.'

'But it's my job.'

'So you have reminded me on several occasions. Would you like to be free, Debby?'

She had had a little too much to drink and her tongue was running riot. 'Yes, oh, yes. To do what I want to do—have a huge garden and dogs and cats running in and out and buy lovely clothes just whenever I wanted to and travel.' She stopped suddenly 'That's just pipe dreaming—I expect everyone has those, but that's not real life, is it?'

He didn't say anything but got up when she did and walked beside her out of the café and into the village street, taking her arm, which, actually, she was glad of because the fresh air after the stuffiness of the café and all the wine she had drunk, was making her a little dizzy.

'We'll go back the way we came,' he said. 'It's much prettier and the moon is still up.'

They walked in silence for some time until Deborah, finding it awkward, said the first thing which came into her head: 'The moon makes it very romantic, doesn't it?'

'Indeed, yes. Are you romantic, Deborah?'

'Only sometimes, mostly I'm too busy… My last reference said that I was a sensible, level-headed girl with a realistic attitude to life. That's not romantic, is it?' She sighed, 'And I daresay it's quite true too!'

Their stroll had come to a halt and he turned her round to face him.

'Will you marry me, Deborah?' asked the professor. And at her look of utter astonishment: 'Oh, there's no question of romance and love. I like you enormously, for your reference is correct, you know and over and above that you're kind and serene and quiet and Eleanor is very fond of you; in time I think that she could love you. She needs someone like you—Miss Timmis is all that a governess should be, but she's no longer young and she has never aspired to the maternal. She'll remain with us, of course, probably for the rest of her life in some capacity or another, but she will be the first to agree that Eleanor needs a mother—you are a little young perhaps, but all the same you have become very dear to her. I am away from home from time to time, but life won't be dull for you—you will have your garden and your dogs and cats—a couple of donkeys and a pony too, and I can promise you that you may buy all the clothes you want. The question is: what should I be depriving you of? Perhaps there is someone who wants to marry you?'

She shook her head silently.

'Or you might wish to wait for a more romantic proposal?'

She shook her head again. 'That's not very likely.'

'You would like children of your own, and not other people's?'

She looked away from him, to the smooth moonlit sea with the lights from the fishing boats reflected in the water. 'Yes, it would have to be a very special reason for me to—to accept. I'm sorry, it's very kind of you to ask me.' She added slowly: 'I didn't know you liked me even.'

'I've already said that I do.' His voice was pleasantly bland with no sign of what he really thought. 'Do you like me, Deborah?'

'It's a funny thing; I didn't at first—you called me a gorgon, you know and you laughed at me a lot, but then when we came here and I met Eleanor, I began to like you—yes, I suppose I like you now.'

'Well, that's something. All the same, you are refusing me?'

Deep down inside her she felt regret. 'Yes, you see I'd like to have a husband who loved me and whom I loved, otherwise I'd just as soon stay as I am.'

He turned her round and took her arm again. 'Well, at least you're honest. I'm sorry, Debby—I really believe that you would have made life very happy for Eleanor. I can't pretend to love you, or even hold out the hope that I could do so in the future—you see, I'm being as honest as you. I think I've forgotten how to love, and I'm not sure that I want to fall in love again—there are plenty of girls around who come easily and go just as easily—perhaps I'm getting too old.'

'You're not even middle aged. Perhaps if you go on looking, you'll find someone.'

'Oh, very likely.' His voice was light; she felt that he was already putting the whole episode behind him and presently would forget it completely. For some reason that annoyed her. The idea of all those girls rankled too. She dismissed it smartly and asked: 'Will Eleanor go back with you—to your home, I mean or does Miss Timmis fetch her?'

'I'll take her back. I have to attend several meetings, all of them in Europe.' He stopped again. 'I suppose that you wouldn't consider going to see Eleanor once she's home again? It would give her something to look forward to?'

'I could go on my way home from Mrs Burns if it's not too out of the way.'

'Tollard Royal—the other side of Shaftesbury, quite close to Peggy, as it happens. Someone can come over and fetch you from Peggy's—perhaps you could stay for the night?'

'Perhaps,' said Deborah cautiously, not to be hurried into an answer. 'I'd like to see her again.'

'Good we can talk about that later.' He took her arm once more and they walked up the drive to the villa, quiet and gleaming in the moonlight. He opened the door and she went past him into the hall which was dimly lit by a candle lamp.

She waited while he locked the door. 'Thank you for a lovely evening. I'm sorry about—about not feeling I can marry you…'

'Don't give it another thought, Debby.' He had come to stand by her, now he bent his head and kissed her gently. 'Sleep well, I enjoyed the evening too.'

CHAPTER FIVE

DEBORAH DIDN'T SLEEP WELL; no man had ever asked her to marry him before and even though she had refused, it was something to mull over at great length. Just before she finally dropped off she wondered if she should have given such an important matter more thought. She had said no without hesitation…anyway, she thought sleepily, it was too late to do anything about it now, only meeting him in the morning was going to be a bit awkward.

She need not have worried; when she and the children got down to breakfast it was to find him casually friendly, offhand almost, giving her the faint, half-mocking smile she so disliked. He stayed that way and the days slipped by in a carefree routine of beach, picnics, bathing and pleasant evenings doing nothing on the patio after dinner, and, although Deborah had another day off at the end of the week, there was no offer to take her into Lagos—anywhere else for that matter. Not that the professor didn't remain friendly; but he was aloof too. Only to be expected, she supposed, probably his pride was hurt, but since he had solemnly assured her with what she considered with hindsight was rather brutal honesty, his feelings weren't involved in the very least, so that left her with the unwelcome thought that he had already dismissed the whole episode from his mind.

Eleanor, on the other hand, hardly let her out of her sight; and when, at the beginning of the third week, the professor announced that he would have to return on the following day to attend some important meeting and that she would be going with him, the child burst into tears and cried so hard that Deborah found herself promising to go and see her before she went home from the Burns family. She felt reluctant about it, for it seemed to her that the sooner she ceased to see the professor, the better it would be. She found him disquieting; she never quite knew what he was thinking or what he would say next; he could be unexpectedly charming and kind and without warning say something cutting. She hoped, quite passionately, that he would be away from home when she went to see Eleanor.

It seemed quiet when they had gone the next day. The twins bereft of a playmate, were peevish and almost unmanageable by turns, Mrs Beaufort without her son's company was plainly miserable, even Mrs Burns, not one to notice anything amiss, remarked on his absence, and confessed herself upset, then persuaded her husband to drive her along the coast to Albufeira, leaving Deborah to mind the children and keep Mrs Beaufort company. That lady, nicely recovered by now, spent the day with them reminiscing about the professor at great length, so that Deborah got to know quite a lot about him. 'Such a clever boy,' Mrs Beaufort confided. 'Brilliant in fact, just like his father. A great pity that his marriage was such a disaster. Too young of course. He needs to marry again for Eleanor's sake.' She shot a glance at Deborah but her face was almost hidden under the sun hat. 'He's still young enough to enjoy life again—family life—I mean. All this travelling is so unsettling…' She gave Deborah a second look. 'What will you do when you leave us, my dear?'

'Go home for a week or two, then go back to the agency and get another job, Mrs Beaufort. I've enjoyed being here though; the twins are darlings and so is Dee; It's been a marvellous holiday.'

Mrs Beaufort gave a delicate snort. 'Hardly a holiday for you, Deborah—three children to care for and precious little time to yourself! but there, I suppose you will tell me that's why you are here.'

Packing up was a sad business even though Deborah did a little here and there so that the children wouldn't notice too much, and on the last day she got up extra early and they went down to the beach in the cool of the morning, parking Dee in her basket where she could see her, and romping in the water with the twins before hurrying back to the house to get ready for breakfast. They left immediately after the meal, and drove to the airport to board their chartered plane and Deborah had no chance to take a last look round, which was perhaps just as well.

They drove back to Ashmore in Mr Burns' car, rather squashed, what with the luggage, Deborah, the twins and Dee on the back seat and Mrs Burns squashed in with them, so that Mrs Beaufort could sit in comfort in front. It was a cool, overcast day and Mrs Burns, usually the most good natured of young women, was disposed to find fault with everything. It was a relief to get into the house and whisk the children up to the nursery to give them their tea and then get them to bed early. Deborah, busy seeing to Dee and then starting on the unpacking, was grateful for the tray of tea Mary brought up to her. She sat drinking it wishing she was back once more by the sea. A silly waste of time, she reminded herself; it had been marvellous but there was no reason to mope about it. She went back to her unpacking.

At dinner, with Mrs Burns cheerful once more, Mr Burns interrupted himself during a rambling résumé of their holiday to ask: 'You'll stay for a day or two, Nanny? Three or four days just while Peggy adjusts and we get the twins back to Nursery School and everything back in place once more. I'll be home for several months and Mary has a niece in the village who will come every afternoon and take over the children for a couple of hours. It's just a question of getting them settled in again.'

She wanted to go home and tell her mother about the villa and the children and Mrs Beaufort—she might even mention the professor, but she saw that she would have to postpone that for a little longer.

'Yes, of course I'll stay—would four days do? If I could leave on Friday...?'

'I'll drive you back, shall we say directly after lunch?'

The four days went quickly; besides coping with the twins: getting them to school each morning, taking them walking in the afternoon with Dee, helping Mary in the evenings after the girl from the village had gone home, Deborah had a mass of small garments to wash, iron, and lay tidily away and since Mrs Burns had the reins of the household to pick up once more, and Mr Burns had to spend a day at the head office of his firm, she spent what free time she had (which wasn't much), by herself. Inevitably, she passed the time mulling over her stay in the villa, wondering about Eleanor, and unwillingly wondering about the professor too. He would be deep in his economics, she supposed, offering other learned men the benefit of his expert advice.

On her last day before leaving Mr and Mrs Burns had gone to dinner with friends and she had her supper on a tray and had then gone to sit in the nursery to finish the mending before she went to bed. She had packed, washed her hair and slapped a face mask guaranteed to turn her into a beauty overnight, on to her freckled face; so now she sat with her hair in shining tresses hanging down her back, her beautiful face unmade-up, plying her needle and thinking. She hadn't meant to think about the professor, but somehow sooner or later he seemed to take over in her head. He would be in Brussels perhaps, or the middle East or America. She bit off the thread only half hearing a car stop in front of the house. Where else did high powered economists go?

Apparently to their niece's nursery, for there he was, standing in the doorway watching her.

Deborah pricked her finger, muttered under her breath and said with studied coolness: 'Good evening, Professor Beaufort.'

He leaned against the wall, looking at her. 'Nanny back in her safe little nest,' he observed blandly.

'I'm leaving tomorrow,' she told him sharply.

He came a little further into the room. 'Anything in view?' he wanted to know.

'I hope to have a week or two at home. In peace and quiet,' she added.

'If that's what you think you'll be old before your time—who wants peace and quiet until they're knocking eighty?'

She chose to ignore that. 'How is Eleanor?'

He was all at once serious. 'Missing you. She's downstairs now with Mary, handing over the apples we picked for her. Be kind to her, Deborah, she's not happy.'

Deborah put down her sewing. 'Why not? Does she miss the twins and the fun we had?'

He shook his head. 'No, she misses you—she'd rather set her heart on having you for a mother you know. I expect you thought my wish to marry you was for purely selfish reasons, in fact I wanted to make Eleanor happy.'

He shrugged. 'That's water under the bridge, isn't it? But if ever you should change your mind, the offer still stands. In the meanwhile, I hope you'll spend the day with us to-morrow?'

Deborah was on the point of saying that no, she didn't think she could, when Eleanor came in, her small serious face at once alight with joy at the sight of Deborah. It would have been cruel to have refused in the face of the child's pleasure in seeing her again. Deborah returned her hugs and said yes, she'd love to spend the day with them. 'Only you'll have to tell me how to get there,' she pointed out.

'You will be fetched directly after breakfast,' said the professor with faint smugness at having got his own way. 'I'll leave you two to have a gossip.' He added belatedly: 'You ought to be in bed Eleanor.' His daughter took no notice of him, too busy telling Deborah about the four kittens the family cat had produced only that morning.

Deborah was up betimes finishing the rest of her packing, coaxing the twins from their beds and feeding Dee. She had phoned her mother before she had gone to bed and explained that she wouldn't be home until later in the day, cleverly skirting round her mother's searching questions, and now, breakfast over, the twins kissed good-bye and, Dee given a final cuddle, she stood watching the professor's Bentley coming up the drive. It was a vintage car, beautifully kept and probably worth its weight in gold. Eleanor was beside him on the front seat and after a brief flurry of goodbyes, Deborah was shoved in beside them, clutching a large paper-wrapped box Mrs Burns had pressed upon her. Her cases had been stowed in the back by Mr Burns and the professor had turned the car and sailed back down the drive before she had had time to do more than wave.

'What's in that box?' asked Eleanor, squashed by her closely, her hand tucked into Deborah's arm.

'I've no idea, we'll have to open it when we get to your home, won't we?'

'Yes, please. You will stay all day won't you?'

'I'll drive you home after Eleanor is in bed.' He spoke so decisively that Deborah, her mouth open to dispute this, changed her mind and said thank you so meekly that he glanced at her sideways and then, very much to her annoyance, laughed.

It was a short drive through country lanes and then up a steep hair pin bended hill. 'Quite rightly named Zigzag Hill,' commented the professor, 'And the view from the top is magnificent, only we won't stop now, Mrs Buckle will be brooding over the coffee pot.'

They came down the hill through a leafy lane with here and there glimpses of the country around them, and came upon Tollard Royal with unexpected suddenness. It was a small village but very beautiful, with a nice old pub, a church, several cottages and skirted by the grounds of a big house where horses were bred, Deborah was informed by Eleanor. There was a scattering of larger houses, well spaced out, but they had gone through the village for perhaps a quarter of a mile before the professor turned the car through an open gateway and slowed along a curved drive bordered by shrubs and trees. The house at the end of the curve was old, red bricked and of a respectable size. It was long and low, with gables, tall twisted chimneys and mullioned windows set in stone frames and its solid, wooden front door stood open.

'Home,' said the professor and got out and went round to open their door. 'Eleanor, take Deborah somewhere where she can tidy herself—we'll have coffee in the sitting room when you're ready.'

A very large buxom woman with boot button eyes in a round cheerful face met them in the hall. 'There you are, dearie, and the young lady with you.' And when Eleanor introduced her to Deborah, with a very correct, 'Deborah this is Mrs Buckle our housekeeper, Mrs Buckle this is Miss Farley!' Mrs Buckle beamed at them both. 'Now isn't that nice?' she asked of no one in particular. 'Just you take Miss Farley up to the Chintz Room, love and I'll take the coffee in.'

She sailed away through a baize door at the back of the panelled hall and Deborah followed Eleanor up the uncarpeted oak staircase, along a gallery and into a room at the back of the house; a charming room, furnished in mahogany decorated with marquetry and living up to its name by reason of the faded chintz curtains at the latticed windows and the matching bedspread. It was a comfortable, luxurious room with an easy chair or two and the glimpse of a bathroom through a half-open door. There were fresh flowers too. Deborah wondered if all the bedrooms had those as a matter of course or whether the professor had been so sure of her coming that he had ordered them to be put there. She bent to sniff at them and then sat down before the dressing table to comb her hair. Eleanor, perched on the bed, watched her.

'It's super having you here—couldn't you stay for a few

days? I thought—I wanted you to marry Daddy—I still do. I suppose you couldn't change your mind?'

Deborah turned to look at the child. 'Your father did ask me,' she said, 'but I—I couldn't accept...'

'Don't you like him?'

'Oh, yes. Yes I do, but I'm not clever and he is, and I'm not used to all this.' She waved a hand at the elegant furniture around them, 'Besides, I think that people should love each other if they're going to marry.' She paused because after all, Eleanor was only a child still; what would she know about love?

She was surprised when Eleanor said at once: 'Oh, I know about that; Daddy explained, but he said that a lot of people got on very well together without it; he said sensible people like you and him. My mother didn't love Daddy, you know, at least she thought she did at first but she went away with someone else... Miss Timmis told me because I asked her one day.' She added matter-of-factly: 'I couldn't ask Daddy, could I?'

'No,' agreed Deborah. And then to change a conversation which was getting a little out of control: 'Is Miss Timmis here?'

'Yes, she's dying to meet you; she says she's longing to be just a governess and not a surrogate mother—she didn't tell me that, I heard her telling Daddy.'

Eleanor slipped off the bed and came to stand by Deborah, 'But if you marry Daddy you'll be a real mother won't you? A nice young one—we could have such fun and I'd help you look after your babies.' The child sounded so wistful that Deborah felt a lump in her throat. If I go on like this I'll be in a fine pickle, she told herself and got up briskly. 'Let's go down,' she invited, 'I'd love to meet Miss Timmis.'

The sitting room was long, low ceilinged and panelled like the hall. There were comfortable chairs and sofas scattered around, several small tables bearing reading lamps and two walls held bow fronted cabinets, but there was still plenty of space. The Professor was standing at the end of the room at an open french window with a black labrador beside him gazing out, and sitting nearby was a small, compact lady, very neat with grey hair in an old fashioned bun and wearing gold rimmed glasses fastened by a chain to a pin on her dress. She was so exactly what Deborah had imagined a governess to look like that she smiled involuntarily and Miss Timmis smiled back and got up.

The professor turned round. 'There you are.' His tone implied that they had been a long time away. 'Deborah, this is our Miss Timmis, prop and mainstay of both Eleanor and myself.' He glanced across and smiled at the governess: 'Miss Timmis, this is Deborah Farley, whom I hope to marry sooner or later—preferably sooner.'

He ignored Deborah's indrawn breath and Miss Timmis, taking her heightened colour for shyness, said at once: 'How splendid that will be—such a delightful young wife and mother.' She added in sentimental tones: 'How happy we shall all be.'

Deborah was strongly inclined to point out that she wasn't at all happy and wished for nothing but to be excluded from Miss Timmis's romantic musings, but she held her tongue, largely because the professor was watching her, waiting with wicked anticipation for her to speak.

She smiled and murmured at Miss Timmis, bent to pat the dog's head and observed that the garden looked delightful. A mistake because she was barely given time to swallow her coffee before the professor whisked her outside with the bland observation that, since she found the garden delightful, he would give himself the pleasure of showing her the whole of it. 'While you have your music lesson, Eleanor,' he added and allowed the lid of one eye to drop as he said it. Deborah was quite taken aback with Eleanor's instant agreement; she wasn't looking at Miss Timmis or she might have wondered at that lady's bewilderment.

Contrary to her forebodings, the professor uttered not one word concerning themselves, instead he dwelt at great length on the various shrubs, trees and flowers which made up the very large garden, explaining their Latin names in a kindly fashion which set her teeth on edge. Then, when she felt that the subject should be exhausted, he began on the weeds.

Deborah stopped on a narrow path between beech hedges, instantly vexed with herself for not waiting for a more roomy spot, for her companion, politely stopping as well, was a great deal too close. 'Look,' she said severely, 'I like gardens very much, but I thought I came to spend the day with Eleanor.'

'Oh dear, oh dear, I haven't made much headway, have I? You know—absence makes the heart grow fonder—such a comforting theory. Ah, well. There was no harm in hoping that you'd changed your mind…'

'I cannot think,' said Deborah in a carefully matter-of-fact voice, 'why you wish to marry me?'

'I didn't make myself clear? Eleanor needs a mother and you fill the bill, and the only way to bring that about is to marry you, isn't it? We shall get on very well together—you're hardly the sentimental type are you? And I'm not in the least in love with you, although I like you well enough to want to marry you. But it will be a marriage without the romance—I hope I make myself clear?'

'Oh very,' said Deborah in a smouldering voice. 'I wonder if there's a girl in this world who has received a proposal...'

'A second proposal,' he reminded her.

'A proposal,' she continued taking no notice, 'so very candid and business-like. I doubt it.' She started to walk on again, 'And the answer is *no*.'

'I felt that it might be. Nonetheless, if you should change your mind will you come to me and tell me so? And I promise you that I won't ask your reasons?' He put a hand on her shoulder so that she had to stand still again and turn to face him. 'Promise?' he repeated.

She studied his face; there was no trace of mockery now, like that she could imagine that he would make a good friend. 'I promise,' she said.

Eleanor came running to meet them as they turned into the drive. She got between them, taking an arm of each. 'Miss Timmis likes you,' she told Deborah and peeped at her father who shook his head slightly. 'She's nice, isn't she?'

'Very. You are lucky to have someone like that to teach you.'

'Yes, aren't I. Will you come and see my room?' She glanced at her father again. 'You don't have to go away Daddy?'

'No, love, but I've got some work to do until lunch time. Shall we meet in the drawing room at half-past twelve? You've a lot to show Deborah!'

He made not another attempt to talk to her alone all the rest of the day and during the drive back to Dorchester he kept up a gentle flow of small talk which left her feeling vaguely resentful.

When they arrived at her home she invited him in, in a polite voice which expected a refusal, but he accepted at once. Instantly at ease with her mother and father, sitting there, she thought crossly, like an old family friend, drinking her father's beer. He was clever at parrying her mother's questions, not evading them merely turning them aside with polite vagueness. He got up to go at length and since it was expected of her, she saw him to the door.

'Thank you for a delightful day,' she told him. 'It was super seeing Eleanor again.'

He paused in the open doorway, put a finger under her chin and lifted it. He didn't say anything at all, only bent and kissed her cheek.

She went on standing there for quite some time after the car had slid smoothly into the evening dark.

It surprised her when she got back to the sitting room, that her mother had no questions; instead she suggested that Deborah might like to go to bed after such a long day. 'And you'll have a few days at home before you start looking for another job, won't you, darling? Professor Beaufort said you'd had a busy time of it even though it was in such a lovely place.'

Deborah had been home a week and had made up her mind to ring the agency the following morning when the agency clerk phoned her.

'I know you were thinking of a permanent post somewhere, sometime after Christmas, but it's only just November and one of our nannies has just phoned to say that she has to go home for a week—her mother's died, poor dear, and she wants to know if there is anyone to replace her just for that time. It's in London—Belgravia—nice house, three children under ten years old and sole charge. To be honest they are a bit of a handful, she says, but it's only for a week...'

Deborah, feeling unaccountably restless, didn't give herself time to think about it; she said yes, as long as it was only for a week, and went to tell her Mother. 'I might as well stay at home until Christmas, Mother, if that's all right with you? That will give me time to look around for a permanent post, somewhere where I can stay for a really long time…'

'Yes, dear,' her mother looked as though she wanted to say a good deal more than that, but she didn't.

Deborah left for London the next day, she would have liked a few more days at home, even though she had planned to ring the agency; looking out at the city's suburbs crowding in on either side of the train, she had to admit that she didn't know what she did want.

The agency had been quite right, the house was indeed nice—a quite inadequate adjective thought Deborah, getting out of the taxi and looking at its imposing front. Georgian London at its best, three storeys of it gleaming with paint and window boxes. She noticed the bars on the top floor windows—the nursery, well out of the way. She hoped it wasn't the kind of family where the children were kept out of sight all day then allowed downstairs for an hour after tea. She mounted the steps—anyway it was only for a week…

She was admitted by a butler with an expressionless face who answered her civil greeting with a voice chilly enough to make her shudder. He led her upstairs to a vast drawing room where the lady of the house was lying on a sofa reading. A quite beautiful woman, beautifully dressed. She glanced up at Deborah, put down her book and said: 'Ah, the temporary nanny. I expect you'd like to go upstairs straight away. The children know that you are coming. Bring them down at half-past five will you? They go to bed at seven o'clock and you will be free after that—they usually sleep all night. Bennett will see that you get your meals in the schoolroom.' She added, not unkindly but with a complete lack of interest, 'I hope you'll be happy while you are with us.'

Deborah, going up more stairs behind Bennett's poker like back, doubted that.

Not only had the agency been right about the house, they were right about the children too; they were just about as difficult as she had ever encountered. At the end of the first day, she wondered if she would be able to stick it out for the rest of the week; she was fond of children but it was hard to like these three: spoilt and rude and ill mannered. Through no fault of their own, she guessed, for they saw their mother for barely an hour each day, and for the entire week Deborah never set eyes on their father. He was in the house all right, his voice often to be heard, even from the fastness of the top floor, but he never came to the nursery. No wonder the children were such little toughs; she hoped that the nanny she was replacing was kind to them.

The week dragged along; Deborah, who found London, even in the bright autumn weather, not a patch on the wide horizons of Dorset, walked the children to the park each afternoon, saw them to school in the mornings, and kept them amused indoors. No one had mentioned off duty to her; she supposed that since she was only there for a week, none was considered necessary.

It was the last afternoon, in the morning she would be leaving the moment the other nanny got back, and she had taken the children to Green Park, wheeling the four-year-old in his old fashioned pushchair, although in her opinion he was perfectly capable of using his own legs. They were waiting to cross Piccadilly when a taxi passed them with the professor sitting in the back. It stopped a few yards further on and he got out, paid off the driver and strode back to where Deborah was still standing.

'The last place I expected to see you,' he observed. 'Rather far from home aren't you?'

He glanced at the children who stared back at him. Deborah was staring at him too. 'So are you,' she said. She found her voice with difficulty, and then went pink because she had sounded rude. 'I mean,' she explained carefully, 'I am surprised to see you here.'

'I get around.' He glanced at the children again. 'These the permanent lot you were so keen on acquiring?'

She said with dignity, 'I am filling in for their nanny; she'll be back tomorrow. I must go—it's time for the children's tea.'

'I'll walk with you.' And he did, the whole way, firing questions at her as she went. 'You'll go back by train I suppose?' And when she said yes: 'The morning, I believe you said?' And when she said yes again: 'Remember it takes the best part of half an hour in the rush hour.' Which led her quite naturally to tell him that she had arranged for a taxi already, 'And it won't be the rush hour; I asked at the cab rank and they said that twenty minutes was heaps of time, besides the eleven-forty's never full and I've got my ticket.'

'A sensible precaution.' He bent his gaze on the child in the push chair. 'Can't this little chap walk?'

'Of course he can. He is four years old; his mother prefers him to be wheeled around.' She spoke in a neutral voice which said a great deal.

'This is where the children live. Good-bye, Professor Beaufort. Please give my love to Eleanor.'

He nodded. 'I certainly will do that. Good-bye, Deborah.' He stood on the pavement and watched until she had ushered her small party indoors. She was filled with vague sadness that he hadn't said a word about seeing her again, although there was no reason why he should, was there?

Naturally, when she took the children down to the drawing room after tea, they told their mother about the man who'd got out of a taxi and walked home with Nanny in an excited chorus. Their mother looked across the room to where Deborah was sitting. 'I should have made it clear, Nanny, that I don't allow followers unless you have a free day.'

Deborah clasped her hands tightly together. She said very evenly: 'Professor Beaufort is the brother of Mrs Burns, whose children I've been looking after, he was kind to enquire why I was in London. And I have no followers.'

If the coldness of her tone was noticed, it wasn't remarked upon, but: 'Professor Gideon Beaufort? A charming man, I met him recently at some party or other. Such a pity—he could have come in for a drink. Oh, well—you can take the children, Nanny. Nanny Masters is back in the morning, isn't she? Come and see me before you go and you can collect your wages.'

How could anyone so beautiful to look at be so rude, thought Deborah, herding the three children back to the nursery, supper and bed.

Nanny Masters arrived soon after breakfast, a thin stern woman in her forties, who waved away Deborah's tentative sympathy and wanted to know if anyone had remembered to make appointments with the dentist for all three children.

'Well, I haven't for nobody asked me to,' said Deborah, her usually mild temper slowly inflaming at Nanny Master's pointed remarks about hair needing cutting and why was the four year old wearing grey socks with blue knickers.

'Unless you want to talk about anything else, Miss Masters, I'll go—I have a train to catch.'

She said good-bye to the children which was a waste of time, and as for Nanny Masters her lips parted in an even thinner smile. 'I daresay you'll be quite good at your job when you've had my experience.'

Deborah bit back rude words, muttered and went to her room. She was still in uniform and there was no time to change. She buttoned herself into her uniform coat, planted the no-nonsense hat on her sandy head, and went to collect her wages, handed over with a casual good-bye and no thanks.

Well, it didn't matter, she could forget her unpleasant week and the money was welcome. She picked up the case one of the maids had carried down to the hall, and since there was no one about, opened the door and hurried down the steps.

The professor, sitting in his vintage Bentley, leaned over and opened the door and then got out and took her case, throwing it on to the back seat he shoved her gently into the front seat.

'I'm going by train,' protested Deborah. She had been unable to put up any kind of resistance to his large hand in the small of her back, but she sat upright, looking ready to spring out of the car at any moment.

'No,' said the professor, 'I'm driving you down to Dorchester. I'm on my way home.'

'Not if you go to Dorchester, you're not.'

'What I like about you, Debby, is your habit of not mincing your words. Now just relax and put up with the inevitable.'

He drove in silence for some minutes. 'Was it very bad?' he wanted to know.

'Pretty awful. I think that the children weren't loved enough. I never saw their father although he was often in the house—he didn't come near the nursery and they spent an hour with their mother after tea each day. No wonder they were so anti.'

'Poor little blighters. What is the nanny like?'

'Stern and unbending, she disapproved of me. Isn't Eleanor with you?'

'No, I'd like to have her with me, but what would the child do all day while I'm tied up with work. If we were married of course, it would be different, you would come too and that would solve the problem.'

Deborah said faintly: 'There is Miss Timmis…'

'Who has no interest in window shopping or Madame Tussaud's or standing for hours outside a church were there a wedding to see. I can't say I blame her at her age. Now you—you're younger and would enjoy such things.'

'You don't give up, do you?' observed Deborah in her severest voice.

'No I am glad you realise that. Let's stop for coffee.'

They had their coffee in a wayside pub and drove on. 'We should be back in nice time for lunch, that is if your mother lunches at half-past one.'

'One o'clock. Would you like to stop at a phone box and I'll ask her to wait until we get there.' She added belatedly: 'Will you stay for lunch?'

'I was beginning to think that I wasn't going to be asked.'

Whatever Mrs Farley's plans had been for the meal she had done wonders in the short time she had had. The cold joint had been ruthlessly minced, and was now a mouth watering cottage pie, Mr Farley's early sprouts, just ready, lay piled in a dish and when he caught sight of them and opened an indignant mouth, he was silenced by a fierce look from his wife. Even the last of the cherished greenhouse tomatoes were on the table. Later he would have something to say about that, but now he greeted their guest politely, offered him a drink, engaged him in conversation and presently sat down to table.

The professor enjoyed his meal and complimented Mrs Farley with such charm that she blushed. 'Do have some more sprouts,' she urged him, 'my husband grows them you know—he's a keen gardener.'

Which gave him the happy cue to discuss gardening in all its aspects with his host. Deborah, almost silent, watched her father's carefully concealed annoyance evaporate and winked at her mother, who gave her a little smile and a nod. When there was a pause in the conversation she asked: 'You'll stay home for a little while, love? You haven't said much about these last people, but I don't think you enjoyed it much, did you?'

'Not really. Yes, I'd like to stay at home for a bit.' She looked defiantly at the professor, who smiled gently and raised his eyebrows. She looked away quickly and he said: 'I really must be going; I promised Eleanor I'd be home for tea. A delightful meal, Mrs Farley.'

He shook hands, leaving Deborah to last, and letting her hand go almost before he had clasped it. She stood at the porch watching him get into the car and fought a fierce desire to nip into the seat beside him. She wanted to go with him, more—she wanted to stay with him. She never wanted to let him out of her sight again, and if this was love it was simply terrible, swamping one at a most awkward moment when it was quite impossible to do anything about it. The sensible thing to do would be to call him back and tell him that she'd changed her mind, but for one thing she was having difficulty with her breathing, and for another, one simply didn't do things like that. Why couldn't she have discovered it on their drive down? She could have brought the conversation round to marrying him in a cool and collected way, and never let him know that she had fallen in love with him. One thing she knew: she would marry him. It would be difficult but not impossible to be the kind of wife he wanted, and surely she could be happy even if she did have to hide her love?

She followed her parents indoors and did the washing up in a dream, hardly conscious of her mother's cheerful talk; and presently, when she went upstairs to unpack, she sat on the bed instead and allowed dreams, quite impossible dreams, to take over.

CHAPTER SIX

DEBORAH REMAINED IN a state of euphoria for the rest of the day, but with morning came common sense. She hadn't changed her mind about marrying Gideon Beaufort—indeed her wish to do so was stronger than ever, but there was no use in pretending to herself that there was going to be any romance about it; that didn't mean to say that she wouldn't make a success of it. He wanted a mother for Eleanor and someone to fill the place of a wife even if he had no wish to get involved romantically. She dared to think that they might become good friends; he had said that he liked her and that was important and she loved him enough to want him to be content and free of worry about Eleanor. And miracles did happen. Who knew? He might, in time, fall a little in love with her.

She thought about it all the next day, presenting a *distraite* manner to her puzzled parents and then, in the evening, asked her father if she might borrow the car.

'Why?' asked Mr Farley.

It was as good a time to explain as any. 'Well, Gideon has asked me to marry him—several times, and I've always said no, but I've changed my mind, and I promised him that if I ever did so I would go and tell him. So I thought I'd drive over to Tollard Royal tomorrow.'

'Can't you phone him?' asked her father.

Mrs Farley said sharply: 'Really, Tom, that would be most unsuitable. You're quite sure, darling? He's a good deal older than you are, though I must admit that he is a remarkably handsome man, and should make a good husband.' She added by way of explanation: 'Nice manners, you know.'

Deborah didn't say anything and her mother went on: 'You haven't known each other very long, have you? Not that that matters; one can fall in love at first sight, and no one need tell me otherwise.'

Neither of her companions contradicted her and presently Mr Farley said: 'You would live at Tollard Royal, I suppose?'

'Yes, Father, but Gideon would like us—Eleanor and me—to go with him sometimes when he has to attend these conferences.'

'H'm—well, Debby, you are old enough to know your own mind and you've shown you're sensible enough to know what you want. Go and talk to Beaufort, but I hope that he'll come and see me.'

'I'm sure he will, Father. And may I take the car?'

'Yes, certainly.' He hesitated. 'You'll be happy with him, Debby?'

She turned a suddenly happy face towards him. 'Oh, yes, Father. I'm very sure of that.'

She left soon after breakfast and drove without hurry, taking the smaller country roads. She had dressed with care in a dark green velvet jacket, a tweed pleated skirt and a cream silk shirt with a pie-frill collar. Her high heeled shoes were on the seat beside her because she couldn't drive in them, but she would change the elderly lace-ups she was wearing when she reached the house.

It was a crisp day, but the sun shone and the country was at its autumnal best; her spirits rose as she drove, she was going to see Gideon again and that was all that mattered.

The village looked charming as she drove through it and presently turned in to the grounds of his house. The brickwork glowed in the hazy sunlight and there were a great many windows open, but the front door was closed. Deborah drew up carefully before it, got out and pulled the old fashioned bell. Mrs Buckle answered it almost at once.

'Well, I never—Miss Farley. What a surprise. Eleanor's at her lessons but the professor's in his study working. Come in and I'll let him know you're here. Lucky that you came when you did, for he told Buckle he wanted the car after lunch.'

She steamed across the hall with Deborah at her heels, but before she could tap on the study door Deborah said diffidently: 'Mrs Buckle, would you mind very much if I surprised him? I…'

The boot button eyes twinkled at her. 'Of course not. It'll be just the thing, he's been sitting over his papers far too long for the last day or two.'

Deborah waited until the housekeeper's vast form had disappeared kitchenwards, then knocked on the door and went in.

'I don't wish to be disturbed,' observed the professor without bothering to look up.

'Well, yes—suppose I should have phoned you first but if I had you would have wanted to know why I should want to see you and I couldn't explain over the telephone.'

He put down his pen and got slowly to his feet. 'Forgive me, Deborah—I wasn't expecting you. What can I do for you?'

His voice sounded friendly but hardly encouraging, only she had made up her mind and she wasn't a girl to change it again. 'I don't think you can do anything for me,' she told him. 'It's me that can do something for you. You asked me to promise to come and see you if I ever changed my mind. Well, I have, but if you don't want to marry me I'll quite understand...'

'Why should I not want to marry you?' He was quiet, smiling a little.

'Well, people get fed up with waiting for answers, don't they? And I've said no several times.'

'Indeed. And why have you said yes now, Deborah?'

'You said you'd not ask me my reasons.' The fright in her face sent his eyebrows up, but all he said was: 'You're quite right, I did say that. I won't ask a single question and I still want to marry you.' He added lightly. 'Shall I propose again, just to make sure?'

She said seriously: 'Oh, no there's no need. There's just one thing—I'm not marrying you because you're rich, I mean I'd still marry you if you were poor. I've thought about it and I expect having a lot of money will make it much easier, won't it?—you'll be able to go off to wherever you go and leave Eleanor and me here.' She stopped when she saw the thunderous look on his face, drew a breath and finished bravely: 'That's what you intended wasn't it? For me to look after her while you were away?'

'A masterly summing up, Deborah. You have the situation in a nutshell. Eleanor will be delighted, and so for that matter, am I.' His mouth twisted in a wry smile, 'I should have said that sooner, shouldn't I?'

She said in her sensible way: 'No, why should you? If we're to be friends then we mustn't pretend, must we?' She blushed brightly as she spoke because, of course, her whole life was going to be one long pretence from that moment.

'Most sensibly spoken. When shall we marry? There's no reason to hang around is there? I don't suppose you want to glide down the aisle in white satin, do you?' His eyes were fixed on her sandy locks and then studied her face, and the blush which was beginning to die down took fresh fire.

She lied in a firm voice. 'Oh no, nothing like that, but I would like to marry in church and I'd like my family and some of my friends to be there.'

He said carelessly: 'Why not? I'll get a special licence—shall we say in three weeks' time? Two weeks if you could manage it; I have to go to the Hague and we could take Eleanor with us—you two can amuse yourselves while I am working.'

She tried to make her voice as businesslike as his and succeeded very well. 'What a splendid idea. Two weeks will be ample time. Will you make the arrangements—we go to the parish church...'

'We had better go together, hadn't we? We'll settle the details presently, I think. In the mean time shall we tell Eleanor?'

She was sure of one thing, Eleanor was happy which helped to warm the rather chilly feeling she had inside her; it was going to take a great effort to remain as cool and offhand as Gideon, but she promised herself that she would cope. If she had patience he might discover that he loved her—she was a great believer in miracles. In the mean while she returned Eleanor's ecstatic hugs warmly, received Miss Timmis's delighted good wishes and accompanied Gideon to the kitchen, so that he could tell the Buckles.

By then it was lunchtime and it was while they were having their drinks that Gideon observed it might be a good idea to phone her mother. 'I should of course, like to have a talk with your father,' he pointed out, and picked up the phone on a side table.

'I told Mother and Father why I was coming here,' said Deborah quietly, 'I said I'd be home around tea time.'

He smiled at her. 'I'll drive back with you in my own car.' He dialled and in a moment said: 'Mrs Farley—Deborah is here to speak to you,' and held out the phone.

Mrs Farley took the news with considerable calm, expressed her delight, agreed to tell her husband when he got home for lunch and invited Gideon to supper. 'You'll have a good deal to talk about,' she declared, 'and two weeks isn't long.'

'No, Mother,' said Deborah, 'we'll talk about that when I get home. Here's Gideon.'

She had to admit that he said exactly the right things; she pictured her Mother's pleased satisfaction as she rang off, she had known for some time that although her mother loved her dearly, she had never entertained much hope of Deborah getting married. She had been told bracingly so many times that she would make a splendid wife, and she thought, without conceit, that she would, but men liked a wife, however splendid, to have a modicum of good looks too. A good hairdresser, thought Deborah and she would splash out on one of the expensive brands of make-up. But what to wear? It was an awkward time of year…

'What's worrying you?' enquired Gideon. It was a casual question and she answered just as casually: 'Nothing important,' smiling carefully. 'Clothes and things.'

She saw his faintly mocking smile and said quickly to

Eleanor: 'What would you like to wear at the wedding, Eleanor?'

'May I be a bridesmaid? And wear a blue dress…oh, please…'

'I'd love that if your father allows it?'

'Of course she may—make whatever arrangements you like, I'll have to leave a lot to you, I've two or three important meetings coming up. Get what you need and send the bills to me.' He sounded impatient, and Miss Timmis, who had been basking in the reflected rays of a romance right under her nose, looked taken aback. But of course, the dear professor was a very busy and important man and couldn't be expected to waste his time bothering about the details of the wedding. She said in her precise voice, 'I think a navy blue dress and jacket—so useful during the winter months, too.' She caught Deborah's surprised eye: 'For myself you know.'

Deborah was about to enlarge on the interesting subject of weddings when she glanced at Gideon and saw the faint boredom on his face. She said briskly: 'What a good idea; we must have a talk about that sometime!' And then: 'I interrupted your work, Gideon, I expect you want to be left in peace to get on with it when we've had lunch.'

She met the annoyed blue eyes squarely and after a moment was relieved to see him smile. 'I see that you will make me an excellent wife, Deborah,' he observed. 'Shall we have lunch now? I'll join you for tea and then we can drive back to Dorchester?'

The dining room was charming and the table beautifully appointed; Deborah ate her lunch, trying to stifle the excitement that in a few weeks' time she would be sitting opposite Gideon at that very table—probably she would have arranged the flowers… She was a little *distraite* throughout the meal but Eleanor was too excited to notice, Miss Timmis put it down to being in love and the professor, having got things all his own way, didn't notice either, not because he was excited but because he wasn't all that interested. He had attained his objective; Deborah would make an excellent surrogate mother for Eleanor, run his house with no fuss, be capable of dealing with any small crisis which might arise during his absence from home, and be a pleasant companion without becoming tiresomely starry eyed. He made a mental note to get her a ring and studied her across the table. A nice little thing, no beauty, but a good hairdresser could do things to that sandy hair and she had lovely eyes. He made another mental note to arrange for her to have a generous allowance.

He went back to his study after lunch and became immersed in his work and didn't think of her once.

Deborah being taken on a second and more detailed tour of the house by Eleanor, was unaware of his thoughts, of course, although she was sensible enough to know that to him this marriage was to be a strictly business-like arrangement. It was a little daunting, she mused, stopping to admire some ancestral portraits on the upstairs landing, but she was quite sure in her own mind that loving him as she did would be sufficient to overcome that in time. In the mean time, living with him in his home was the next best thing; she had every intention of being a good wife and she could see no reason why she wouldn't be.

Tea was a pleasant meal, and Miss Timmis listening to the light hearted talk, beamed approval; young love, she thought, disregarding the fact that the professor was no longer a young man, and presently she stood with Eleanor waving to the happy pair as they drove off, Gideon in the Bentley, Deborah in her father's car.

They stopped for coffee at Sturminster Newton and Deborah, naturally dying to talk about their wedding, didn't mention it. A sensible decision which reaped its own reward, for presently Gideon asked: 'You are happy about the arrangements? I'll put a notice in the Telegraph and you had better invite whoever you want to come. We shall go straight over to Holland, so see that you wear something you can travel in. Eleanor seems bent on being a bridesmaid, but I suppose she can cover her dress with a coat.'

Deborah refrained from pointing out that it was already November and the child would wear a coat in any case. As for herself, if he thought she was going to turn up for her own wedding in sensible tweeds, then he was sadly mistaken. She murmured an agreement and sat looking at his hands on the table: large, well cared for and very capable. Her eyes slid up to his face, very good looking although the mouth was firm to the point of hardness, but she liked his faintly beaky nose and his grey hair. Very distinguished, they would make an odd pair she reflected.

Presently they got back into their respective cars, the Bentley held in check behind Deborah's steady pace. She could imagine Gideon's suppressed impatience but there was nothing she could do about it; it was a narrow, winding road and her father would never forgive her if she so much as scratched the paint.

She stopped at length outside her home and the Bentley purred to a halt behind her. Gideon got out and came to open her door. 'You drive well,' he observed. 'I must get you a car of your own.'

She lifted her green eyes to his. 'Really? How super—

something small… I drive faster than this you know, but it's Father's car.' And then: 'You mustn't feel that you have to give me things, you know.'

His blue eyes were very cool. 'Allow me to be the best judge of what I give you, Deborah.' He turned away as the door opened and her mother came out to meet them.

She had been feeling nervous about the evening, but her fears had been groundless. Gideon didn't put a foot wrong; after he had gone home, with the three of them sitting over a pot of tea, Mr Farley pronounced himself quite content with his future son-in-law. 'A sound man, and clever, not boastful thank heaven, but very sure of himself. He'll make you a good husband, Debby.'

'So good looking,' murmured Mrs Farley. 'I'm glad he's bringing Eleanor over to see us, he's obviously very fond of her. You've not had time to talk about the wedding, I suppose? I know we've talked it over this evening, but only in general terms. Two weeks' time—that isn't long—clothes, and we must have a reception even if it's to be very quiet. I wonder if we'd better hire a room?'

'Gideon suggested that we keep the guests to a minimum—we could manage twenty or a couple of dozen people here, couldn't we? We have to leave very soon after the wedding, anyway, he has to go to *den Haag* and Eleanor and I will go with him.'

'Eleanor?' began her mother and then changed it to: 'He's a busy man, I'm sure, it'll be nice for you to have company while he's at these meetings.'

Two weeks was very little time in which to organise even the quietest of weddings, Deborah spent most of the next day making neat lists of things to buy and people to invite. Then in the evening, unexpectedly, Gideon arrived.

'We might go out to dinner,' he suggested, 'there's still a good deal to talk over and while you are getting ready I'll see if your parents are free to come over and spend the day on Sunday. I'd like them to meet Eleanor. Will you stay for a day or two? I have to go up to London for a few days and it would give you the chance to get used to the place and arrange about Eleanor's clothes. Miss Timmis has a friend who makes Eleanor's things, perhaps if you bought whatever you want for her, she could make it up.'

He glanced rather impatiently at her sensible grey flannel skirt and matching sweater. 'I daresay she would be only to glad to make something for you, or perhaps you'd prefer to buy… There are some decent shops in Salisbury, or so Miss Timmis tells me.'

She gave him a smouldering look. 'Perhaps you have some suggestions about the colour I should wear?' Her voice was sweet with a nasty edge to it.

'Oh, lord—have I upset you? But since you ask me—how about a rich clotted cream—a fine wool dress and a matching coat. If you have your hair decently dressed and some sort of a hat you'll be quite attractive.'

She said in a voice which trembled: 'You seem to know a great deal about it, but I think I should warn you that I'm not a doormat by nature and you may find it harder than you think to change the ways of a rat trapped gorgon. I like to make up my own mind, especially about clothes.'

They were standing by his car, for she had been in the garden when he had arrived, now he took her by the shoulders and made her face him.

'Oh Debby, I'm sorry. And your mouth isn't a rat trap; it's a kind, generous mouth. As for being a gorgon, you certainly don't turn me to stone; you give me a nice, warm friendly feeling when I'm with you. I think that with a little give and take, we shall get along very well together.'

Deborah registered a silent promise to wear cream-wool. 'I shall do my very best,' she assured him and was surprised when he bent and kissed her quite hard. 'Friendship sealed with a kiss,' he informed her gravely and put his hand into his pocket. 'I hope this fits—it was my mother's. It's old fashioned because it was my grandmother's too. Try it on.'

He took the ring out of its box and slipped it on her finger, and she stared at it with delight; it fitted perfectly—that must be a good omen. It was a sapphire surrounded by diamonds and set in gold; she touched it gently. 'It's beautiful Gideon. Thank you very much.' She would have liked to have cried, but she made her voice friendly and nothing else.

They went indoors and the ring was duly admired before she went to change; she stood for quite some moments in front of her small wardrobe, wondering which dress Gideon would like. In the end she settled for a russet wool, by no means the height of fashion but the colour suited her. Not that it mattered, she told herself, applying make-up with care, he had a low opinion of her dress sense. She would have liked to have experimented with her hair, but there wasn't enough time. 'If only I had some sort of a hat,' she told her reflection and giggled.

They went to the Old Market House in Cerne Abbas, and ate the delicious food at leisure. Deborah had never been sure if she liked champagne, but now she decided she did; perhaps because she was given more than one glass and the champagne was a good one. She remarked that it was a very pleasant drink and Gideon smiled slowly. 'In the right company there's nothing like it.' He waited while she was served pears cooked in red wine and smothered in cream. 'Now, as to the details of the wedding—shall we get them settled?'

It had been a very pleasant evening, she thought sleepily, getting ready for bed; she had, she considered, matched his casual friendliness very well; discussing the wedding as coolly as though it were not her own, but some acquaintance's. They had agreed on almost everything, and she had accepted the life he had outlined for her without demur. A pleasant enough prospect, most of it at Tollard Royal—the quiet country life she enjoyed, with occasional visits to Shaftesbury or Salisbury, his friends to entertain, and the house to run with Mrs Buckle to guide her. He would be home for the most part of the time, he had told her, but occasionally he had to stay in London and whenever possible there was no reason why she and Eleanor shouldn't be with him. And when he had to go to Brussels or *den Haag* or any other European capital not too far away, there was no reason why she, and perhaps Eleanor too, shouldn't accompany him. He had been very matter-of-fact about it and even for a few moments she had wondered if she would be able to go through with it, but of course she could; she loved him and that was surely the best reason in the world for marrying him. And having settled this she closed her eyes and slept.

She had told Gideon that two weeks would be ample time in which to get everything arranged for the wedding, but she hadn't reckoned on the time taken up by his surprisingly frequent visits, the dinner party he gave at his home, with the Burns and Mrs Beaufort, and they in their turn giving a dinner party in return. Besides, the boys were home for half term, hindering her at every turn, talking excitedly about the wedding. And then there was Eleanor's dress to see—the pair of them spent the day in Salisbury searching for exactly the right material—sapphire blue velvet and a matching tweed coat to go on top of it. That done and safely delivered to the dressmaker, she at last got down to the task of finding something to wear for herself. She found it in Sherborne, in a small, expensive boutique where normally she wouldn't have dreamed of going. But just for once, and quite forgetting that when she was married she would be able to buy all the clothes she wanted, within reason, she felt justified in being extravagant. It was not only the exact shade of cream she had in mind, it also fitted perfectly; a simply cut dress in fine wool with a top coat of thicker tweed. The price paled her cheeks, but didn't prevent her from buying a little blue velvet hat the colour of Eleanor's dress and then adding shoes, gloves and a handbag. She was just about flat broke by the time she got home, but she had what she wanted.

They were to be married at half-past eleven, have a buffet lunch at her home, and leave directly afterwards for Holland. Since Gideon had the car with him they would cross by Hovercraft and drive up through Belgium along the coast road, to reach *den Haag* in good time for dinner.

Mrs Farley, happily immersed in plans for the reception, deplored the fact that it had to be such a quiet affair, although, as she assured Deborah, that didn't mean to say that it wasn't going to be an extremely elegant one. As for Deborah, all she could think of was that in a few days' time, she would be Gideon's wife.

She was up early on the morning of the wedding, contrary to custom pottering round the house, helping her mother get breakfast, arranging flowers, polishing glasses, and finally going back to her room to get herself dressed. She was sitting before her dressing table mirror, carefully doing her hair in the style the hairdresser had suggested, when she heard Eleanor's excited voice. A moment later there was a tap on the door and the child came in.

'Deborah... Oh, don't you look nice, and your hair's different, is my dress all right? Daddy liked it. He's gone to the church, but he left your flowers. They are downstairs...'

Deborah gave her a hug. 'You look smashing, and see, I found a hat which matches your dress. Just sit still on the bed while I put it on.' And when she had done so: 'How do I look?'

'You're beautiful,' declared Eleanor and she meant it. Deborah thanked her soberly; it would be marvellous if Gideon thought the same, and still more marvellous if he were to say so.

There was, of course, no opportunity for him to say anything at all when they met, but the long look he gave her as she joined him at the end of the aisle gave her a pleasant glow; at least he approved of her appearance, and since she had taken a considerable time to achieve it, she was satisfied. The glow lasted all through the short service and turned her into what Mrs Buckle, there with Buckle, described as a radiant bride. Mrs Buckle was a sentimental lady and saw the occasion through rose coloured spectacles, but the same Deborah bore all the outward signs, at least, of a very happy young woman. The dear professor looked happy too, she declared, though happy wasn't perhaps the right word; his handsome features bore an expression of satisfaction—he had got what he wanted; a mother for his small daughter, and a wife who gave every indication that she would fall in with his lifestyle and refrain from indulging in romantic ideas. What was more, he liked her; she was a good companion and she had a mind of her own. No looks, although he had to admit that there was something about her which caught the eye…

Deborah, sitting beside him in the Bentley being whisked off to the Hovercraft, admitted to herself that he had behaved beautifully, he had the easy good manners which made him liked by everyone and he had called her his dear wife when he had made a brief speech after they had cut the cake. She believed him, he might not love her, but she was sure in her bones that he thought of her as a companion and a friend.

She peeped sideways at his profile, impassive and silent and had her thoughts interrupted by Eleanor's excited voice from the back seat, still intent on discussing every aspect of the wedding. A topic which kept them fully occupied for the greater part of the journey.

Neither Deborah nor Eleanor had been on a Hovercraft before. Gideon, who had, answered their endless questions with good humour and patience and once they had landed, kept up a casual running commentary of the country they were passing through. Once over the border, he turned off the motorway and stopped at an hotel in Rosendaal where they had tea and fragile little biscuits. Deborah, who had hardly eaten any breakfast and almost nothing at the reception, would gladly have gobbled up a plateful. As it was, she nibbled at them daintily and hoped that no one could hear her insides rumbling.

The professor, watching her, smiled faintly. 'I think that when we get to the hotel, Eleanor had better go straight to bed and have her supper there, otherwise she will not enjoy your morning together.'

She was an obedient child and agreed placidly. 'Will you be working all the time?' she asked her father.

'A good deal of it, I'm afraid. But I'm sure the pair of you will find more than enough to do. The conference I have to attend is being held near the hotel though I doubt if I shall get back for lunch, but I think we might all go to the puppet theatre one evening, and to Scheveningen for Sunday lunch. There's a splendid zoo and an ice skating rink if you skate, Deborah?' And when she nodded: 'Good, I can see that you will both be amply amused. And, Eleanor, sometimes I shall take Deborah out in the evening and you will have your supper in bed and one of the chamber maids will look after you. Okay?'

Eleanor nodded. 'Will you go dancing?'

'I daresay we shall. We shall certainly tell you all about it afterwards.'

He signalled the waiter. 'Shall we go? It's not much further now.'

Deborah found *den Haag* to be a very elegant place, she admired the broad, tree lined avenues, and the solid houses lining them. Then as they neared the heart of the city, the brightly lit shop windows and old fashioned trams and the crowded streets. Gideon drove without hesitation, finally turning into Lange Voorhout, and parking before the Hotel des Indes. Its foyer was comfortable and a little old fashioned, but the service was instant and unobtrusive. She knew very little about hotels, but she guessed that this one was in the luxury class and when they reached their rooms she found this to be right, each elegantly furnished and with a splendidly appointed bathroom too, with communicating doors so that Eleanor, who was in the middle, could go into either room if she wanted to.

Deborah unpacked for them both and when Eleanor went to see her father, she went to her own room and tidied herself. Presumably they wouldn't be going out that evening, so there was no need for her to change her dress. Presently Eleanor came back and Gideon with her.

'Shall we go down and have a drink, and get a menu so that Eleanor can decide what she wants for her supper, then she might go to bed, don't you think? When she's settled perhaps you will join me in the bar again?'

The three of them went downstairs and found the bar crowded, but Gideon sat them down at a table near one of the windows, and ordered lemonade for Eleanor and drinks for Deborah and himself, then laid himself out to be entertaining. It wasn't until Eleanor had finished her drink and decided what she wanted for her supper that Deborah suggested the two of them might go back to their rooms to which the child agreed readily. It had, after all, been a long and exciting day.

It was half an hour or more before she was in bed, her supper tray on the bed table. 'I'll come back to see that you've eaten it,' promised Deborah, 'and tuck you up.'

Eleanor beamed at her. 'It's so nice to have a mother. Will you tuck me up every night?'

'Well, of course, darling, I expect that Daddy will too when he is at home.'

She watched Eleanor start off on the food and then went down to the bar, feeling shy. She found Gideon standing with several men, deep in talk, but when she came in and he saw her, he broke off what he was saying and came to meet her.

'Eleanor settled?' He wanted to know. 'Most of the commission seem to be staying here, come and meet some of them.'

He took her arm and steered her through the crowded room and introduced her to a handful of men, all older than he, some Dutch, some English. They were charming to her and although she felt a little out of her depth she did her best and was rewarded presently by Gideon's: 'Well, you did very well, Debby. You look so pretty in that dress too.'

'Not pretty,' she told him sharply, 'you know I'm not that.'

He said frankly: 'I've never thought of you as pretty, but I see that I was mistaken—you've done something to your hair…'

She looked away. 'The hairdresser showed me how to arrange it.' She glanced around her. 'And the light's dim in here.'

He laughed then, not unkindly, but all the same it hurt. He went on: 'Shall we have dinner—we can dance if you like.'

'That would be nice. I'll just see if Eleanor's all right, I promised I would tuck her up.'

'How easily you have fallen into your new role,' he smiled and got up with her. 'I'll come too.'

Eleanor had eaten her supper and was sitting up in bed reading. 'Bedtime,' said Deborah firmly and took the book away with a smile. 'You can wake me up in the morning if you like…'

'Ah, yes, I'll arrange for morning tea. Half-past seven? We don't start until ten o'clock, but I've some notes to make first—if we could have breakfast at half-past eight?'

They said good-night and went downstairs once more to the restaurant and were led to a table in the window, not too near the small dance floor. Deborah studied the menu. 'I could eat everything on it,' she observed, 'I'm famished.'

'Me too. Let's see—shall we have lobster soup? I think I'll settle for a steak, but I'm told the *poulet l'estragon* is excellent—would you care to try it?'

The sharp edge of their appetites blunted by these delicious foods, they danced before going back to their table to enjoy soufflé Harlequin and then they danced again. Deborah was a good dancer, shedding her rather prim appearance once the music started, and Gideon, who for years had only danced when it had been unavoidable, was agreeably surprised.

'For an ex-nanny, your dancing is quite astonishing. Did you dance for one of those TV dance groups on your days off?'

She said severely: 'Certainly not, when would I have had the time?' She added thoughtfully: 'It would have been fun, though, I do like dancing.'

'I am rapidly coming to the conclusion that I like dancing too. We must indulge our liking as often as possible, Deborah.'

They lingered over their coffee and it was almost midnight when Deborah went up to bed. Their goodnight was formal as they were in the restaurant, and she was glad of that, anything else would have had her on the verge of tears. 'And what else did you expect,' she muttered to herself as she undressed. 'Be thankful for what you have got and make the most of it.'

She frowned at her forlorn face in the mirror and got into bed. She had often dreamed of her wedding day, what girl didn't? But she had never imagined that it would be like this. 'It doesn't matter,' she mumbled to herself, her head buried in the pillows. 'I love him—I have to remember that, and I've got years ahead of me to make him love me.' She closed her eyes and presently two tears squeezed their way down her cheeks. It was all very well to have years and years in which to do that, but she couldn't think how to set about it. She had no beauty with which to charm him, she would learn to dress well in time, but at present there was nothing about her to catch the eye. She considered herself rather a dull companion, especially for a man such as Gideon. Really all that she was fit for was to be a mother to Eleanor, and that after all was why he had married her. He had never minced matters over that.

But she felt better about it in the morning; Eleanor and her early morning tea arrived together and a few minutes later, Gideon joined her, sitting on the side of the bed and eating the tiny sweet biscuits which had arrived with the tea. It was all very cosy and domestic and a splendid start to the day. And what a day; at the end of it, with a tired but happy Eleanor tucked up in bed, Deborah lay there in the bath and thought about it. They had seen very little of Gideon, but then they hadn't expected to; he had left them soon after breakfast but not before giving her a street plan, a phone number to ring if anything went amiss, and a fat roll of notes. Her eyes had almost popped out of her head when she had counted them.

The shopping streets were close by the hotel, the two of them had made their way there as soon as Gideon had left them and wandered up and down the arcades, looking in all the windows and finally going into La Bonnetiere to find a dress for Eleanor; dark red taffeta and just the thing for Christmas. After that it became imperative that Deborah should buy herself something too, and since the roll of notes was still comfortably thick, she bought a pleated chiffon dress over a silk slip, it had long tight sleeves and a deep V neckline, so it showed off her pretty figure to advantage. 'Shoes,' prompted Eleanor so that slippers had to be searched for and bought, plus a purse which matched exactly added to the parcels.

They had stopped for coffee, purchased a bead necklace Eleanor fancied and then taken a tram towards Scheveningen, got off at Madurodam and spent a fascinating hour touring that miniature city watching the tiny cars and buses travelling through its streets, the ferries in the harbour and listening to the music coming from the church and the opera house. Deborah was just as entranced as her companion and since they had spent far longer there than they had intended, they took a tram back to the city centre and had lunch in a coffee shop; giant pancakes, glasses of milk and enormous cream cakes. Deborah had thought that had Gideon been with them he would have had something to say about unsuitable diets, but it was exactly what they had both fancied and had revitalised them sufficiently for them to pay a visit to the Ridderzaal, where they trailed behind a guide and a dozen or so other people, trying to take in all that they were being told.

'I liked the morning best, shopping,' Eleanor had said as they went back through the Binnenhof, past the Vijver pond and made for the hotel. It was almost tea time and Gideon said that he would be back to have tea with them.

He was there, waiting for them and she had been relieved to see that he did no more than raise an amused eyebrow at their parcels and ask if she needed more money for the next day. She had assured him that she had plenty to spend still and sat quietly while Eleanor had poured out the excitements of the day. Only when she had finished did she ask: 'And you, Gideon, have you had a good day?'

She had been taken aback at his abrupt answer; he didn't want to discuss his work, or perhaps he thought that she wasn't interested, for he started a lively argument with Eleanor about the evening's programme; bed, he said firmly, there was another day tomorrow and he would book seats for the puppet theatre. 'You can amuse yourself this evening?' he asked Deborah, 'I've quite an amount of work to do and one or two people I've promised to meet.'

She had said quietly that yes, of course—she had letters to write and a book she had bought that morning and was dying to read. The hope that they might have been going out somewhere that evening where she could have worn the new dress, she buried deep inside her. He hadn't wanted to know what was inside their parcels and probably her lovely dress would never be worn. Tomorrow she decided, applying careful make-up, they would go to the Mauritshuis because it was one of the places he had suggested they visit, and then they would go shopping again, this time for an outfit which she could wear each and every day and they would dash back to La Bonnetiere and get the fur lined gloves Eleanor had wanted.

She had been surprised when there was a knock on the door and Gideon walked in. 'Eleanor's settled? You've arranged for her to have supper up here?'

Deborah laid down her powder puff. 'Yes, I did wonder if we might have dinner together, just the two of us, but I thought you might not like that. But I shan't be long over dinner and I've promised her I'll read to her when I get back.'

He leaned against the dressing table, looking down at her. 'My dear Deborah, do I detect reproach in that remark? I explained to Eleanor before we came that she would only stay up for dinner on one or two occasions. Now if you are ready, shall we go down?'

She had put on one of the dresses she had bought before they married; not particularly fashionable but pretty. She stood up now, hoping that he would at least notice that she was wearing something different, but he went to the door and held it open for her without a word.

She drank her sherry talking nothings to the same men she had met the previous evening and ate her dinner without appetite. As soon as she had finished her coffee, she said in a cool voice: 'I will go back to my room now, you must be wanting to—to do whatever you want to do. Goodnight, Gideon.'

He got up with her and followed her out of the restaurant and walked through the foyer to the stairs. He halted there while she teetered, on the lowest tread, not wishing to be impolite but wanting to go.

'You haven't told me about your day,' he observed blandly. 'Did you buy anything interesting?'

'Eleanor told you about her dress.'

'And you?'

'Oh, I bought a dress too.'

'And lunch—where did you go?'

She gave him a guilty look. 'Well, it was quite late by the time we'd looked round Madurodam. We went to one of those coffee shops in the arcades—we had pancakes with bacon in them, milk to drink and chocolate cakes with whipped cream.'

He gave a subdued shout of laughter, bent his head and kissed her hard and suddenly, wishing her goodnight he walked away, leaving her looking guiltily round to see if anyone had noticed. The foyer was almost empty and nobody was looking her way. Perhaps he'd had too much to drink, she mused going slowly upstairs, but upon reflection she knew that to be absurd. She reflected with satisfaction that she hadn't kissed him back although the temptation had been great. The less she thought about the whole episode the better; she hurried to Eleanor's room and began to read the 'Wind in the Willows' in a calm, quiet voice.

CHAPTER SEVEN

THE SECOND DAY was as good as the first, better in fact, for Deborah found a wool jersey separates outfit in a green which exactly matched her eyes. The price made her shudder, but trying it on she was instantly aware that it did something for her. Her hair lost its sandy colour and became pale auburn, her eyes shone like emeralds and the cut of it turned her from mundane dowdiness into instant chic. She and Eleanor marched out of the shop their hearts light, and her purse even lighter. Not so light, however, that she wasn't able to purchase a hat to go with the new outfit, and in an exactly matching shade of green; a ridiculous trifle which when perched on her neat head transformed it immediately to the very pinnacle of fashion.

They had their elevenses, bought the gloves and a fur cap for Eleanor and then mindful of Gideon's instructions once more, went to the Mauritshuis where they gazed at the Rembrandts, Vermeers, Jan Steen and an enormous canvas by Paulus Potter—the bull—they retraced their steps to study it for a second and third time, bewitched by its size and its lifelike style.

Eventually Deborah said with reluctance. 'We really must

go,' and added: 'We'd better have lunch at the hotel, your father didn't quite approve of our meal yesterday.' She blushed as she said it, remembering how he had kissed her. 'At least I don't think he did.'

They had their lunch and then went to Deborah's room, where she tried on the green outfit and the hat while Eleanor sat on the bed watching her, her fur cap on her head, the new gloves in her hand. Deborah was rotating slowly and a little anxiously, craning her neck to see the back.

'Is it a bit tight?' she wanted to know and heard Eleanor giggle and then Gideon's:

'Certainly not—it's er—a most pleasing fit.' And when she whisked round to stare at him: 'I didn't startle you? this afternoon's meeting has been adjourned and I came back here on the chance of finding you.'

He came further into the room and deliberately turned her this way and that. 'Delightful—who would have thought… Keep it on, Deborah, such an attractive outfit deserves a new top coat.' He turned to his daughter. 'Get your coat, love, we'll go shopping.'

'We've been shopping most of the morning,' said Deborah faintly. 'At least we did go to the Mauritshuis…'

'Splendid, that leaves us all the more time to shop now.'

He bustled them out of the hotel and towards the shops, where presently in the cathedral calm of a very select boutique, Deborah found herself trying on coats in tweeds, fine wools, cashmere…she chose a rich chocolate brown cashmere. She had tried to see the price on its label but Gideon said softly: 'No, Deborah, there is no need for that.' A remark which made her blush rosily. She supposed that in time she would buy things without bothering to look at their price and with female logic she chose a beret thrust through with a quill, which the saleslady assured her was intended to be worn with the coat. She stared at her reflection in the large mirror finding her image almost unrecognisable; this highly fashionable woman staring back at her didn't seem to be her at all, she looked, well, not pretty but certainly worth a second glance.

But Gideon merely glanced once, his 'very nice', was to her ears, decidedly tepid. She swallowed disappointment and said in a bright voice: 'May we buy Eleanor a dressing gown? We saw such a pretty one this morning—it was in one of the arcades…'

So they went in search of that before having tea in an elegant little tea shop and then going back to the hotel to dine early and go to the Puppet Theatre. Eleanor sat entranced and so did Deborah; Gideon hardly looked at the stage but watched their faces, his own was impassive.

They stayed for two more days, into which they crammed enough sight seeing to satisfy the most seasoned of tourists. Indeed they enjoyed the tour of the city's canals so much that they went a second time, this time with Gideon for company, and on their last day Deborah took Eleanor to the Costume Museum, where they inspected bygone fashions and spent a great deal of time poring over the dolls houses before shopping for presents to take home. Eleanor was allowed to stay up for dinner on their last evening and pronounced it to be the best holiday she had ever had, didn't Deborah agree?

Deborah said serenely: 'By far the best—it's been wonderful, though I'm sorry that your father had to work so hard.'

'No need to waste pity on me,' declared Gideon carelessly, 'I daresay I should have been bored with nothing to do.' A remark which left his daughter quite unmoved and to which Deborah took the greatest exception.

She said chattily: 'I expect you'll be glad to get home again?'

'Yes, although I shall have to be in London for several days at a time.' He was watching her narrowly. 'But I'm sure that you will be able to fill your days.'

Deborah didn't answer, but Eleanor said at once: 'Oh, yes Daddy, there's heaps to do—I'll never be lonely again now we've got Deborah. Miss Timmis said how nice it will be just to be a governess and concentrate on teaching me things. She doesn't like long walks you know, or swimming or going shopping…'

Her father laughed. 'I can see that Deborah is going to lead a strenuous life. Now how about going to bed, love?'

Deborah got up at once and an attentive waiter pulled back her chair as Gideon got to his feet too. 'I'll come up with you,' she began and was interrupted by his: 'But come down again, won't you? I thought we might dance for a while?'

They danced for a long time and when Deborah suggested that she would go to bed she had been reminded with gentle blandness that they were, after all, on their honeymoon.

He had looked at her with a small mocking smile as he spoke and she wasn't sure if she wanted to hit him or burst into tears, instead she said brightly, '*Den haag* is such a lovely place for a holiday, though I expect you know it well.'

'Next time we come we must go further afield; I've had several invitations for us both to visit associates here—some of the old country houses are charming.'

The band paused so they went back to their table where Gideon ordered another bottle of wine. 'Miss Timmis had a talk with me last week—she has an older sister who is a semi-invalid and she very much wants to visit her. Could you cope with Eleanor for a few weeks on your own? She has no intention of leaving us, but she also suggested that Eleanor might like to go to school now that she has a more secure background, and that she might stay on as a general factotum, sewing and so on,' he added vaguely.

'Of course I can cope,' said Deborah briskly. 'Is there a good school nearby?'

'Oh, yes. If you could drive her there and fetch her… I thought that perhaps after Christmas…'

'Will she like that?'

'I think so—of course we'll talk to her about it. There will be people coming to stay during the next week or so—old friends, people I meet at work, now that I have a wife it will be easy to entertain them at home. I shall bring them back with me at the weekends.'

'I see, will you be gone all the week?'

'Not every week.' He gave her a thoughtful look. 'Debby, are you happy?'

She said instantly, 'Oh yes, indeed I am. It's all a bit strange, of course. I mean, all this…' she waved a hand vaguely around her, 'but I do my best, Gideon and I'll get better.'

'My dear, you're everything I could wish for in a wife and Eleanor loves you.'

But you don't, thought Deborah silently, and if I were clever I'd know how to make you love me, only I'm not clever and I'll just have to hope that you will or that something happens to make you.

They travelled home the next day, a smooth journey that went without a hitch, to be met by the Buckles' welcoming faces, great log fires in all the rooms and an elegant dinner. Eleanor, who had chattered away unceasingly all day, was almost asleep by the time they had finished and Deborah whisked her off to bed. 'Miss Timmis will be here in the morning,' she pointed out, 'wanting to hear all about our holiday and you don't want to fall asleep in the middle of telling her.'

Gideon got up and opened the door for them. 'Come down again Deborah,' he said, 'we must have a talk.'

Now what, thought Deborah as she urged Eleanor into her bed and tucked her up, half throttled by the child's arms.

When she joined Gideon in the drawing room, Buckle had brought in the coffee tray and put it on a small table by a chair drawn up to the fire opposite Gideon. It looked cosy in a grand way, and she thought sadly how delightful it would have been if Gideon had leapt to his feet and kissed her, just as a newly wedded husband would. He certainly got to his feet but he showed no signs of kissing her, merely invited her to sit down and pour the coffee.

'I'll have to go to town tomorrow,' he observed as she handed him his cup, 'and I probably shan't be back for a couple of days—it's hardly worth the journey home since I have to attend another conference on the second day. I thought we might have our first guests next weekend; they can drive down with me on Friday evening—I'll let you know who and how many, and we might give a dinner party before Christmas, don't you think? You'll need some clothes—you might leave Eleanor with Miss Timmis and come up to town with me—let me see—' he frowned a little. 'If I drive down on the day after tomorrow you could go back with me in the morning, but you may have to take a train home—you'll go to Salisbury and Buckle can pick you up there.'

She murmured her agreement; there wasn't much point in doing anything else, he had obviously decided it all for himself. He went on: 'That will give you a day in which to make sure that everything is all right for the weekend.' He glanced at her: 'Mrs Buckle will help you; she knows where everything is and Miss Timmis is a tower of strength.' He smiled suddenly: 'Although I imagine that you are quite capable of arranging a weekend for any number of people without turning a sandy hair.'

He hadn't meant to be unkind she told herself, but she, who had been enjoying rising self assurance engendered by her new wardrobe, became instantly aware of that same sandy hair and ordinary face. She said soberly: 'I expect I can manage. I'll come up to town with you if you wish... what shall I need? That is—are your friends smart?'

'The women? Well yes, not outrageously I suppose, but good, well cut clothes and pretty dresses in the evening—you know?'

She wasn't sure that she did, but she nodded. It was very humiliating that he so obviously didn't consider that the clothes she had were good enough. Why on earth had he married her? She knew the answer, of course, because he loved Eleanor and wanted the child to be happy; all the same, it was a pity that he couldn't have settled upon a chic beauty who combined a high sense of fashion with affection for Eleanor. She sighed without knowing it, and he said sharply: 'You're tired, go to bed it's been a long day.' He got up and opened the door and as she went past him touched her lightly on the shoulder. She paused and smiled at him and wished him good-night, crossed the hall and went upstairs. He watched her go...she was a graceful girl. He waited until she was out of sight before going back to the drawing room, reminding himself that he would have to go to his study and go through his post, but he went on sitting there, staring into the fire, his thoughts unaccountably given over to Deborah; he wasn't thinking of her suitability as a wife but of her wide green eyes and her sandy hair—beautiful hair actually—shining with cleanliness and good health; in her new green outfit she was quite something. He realised suddenly that given time to acquire poise and in the right clothes, she would be a knock-out. And of course, she was splendid for Eleanor; he had chosen wisely. He got up presently and went along to his study, to sit down at his desk. He found it quite an effort to start on his letters, but of course, once he did, he dismissed her from his mind.

The next morning, sitting opposite her at breakfast, he hardly looked at her and when he did, it was with the tolerant eye of a friend; certainly there was no vestige of glamour about her at eight o'clock in the morning. She was wearing a sweater and a skirt and her hair had been brushed smoothly back and pinned up quite ruthlessly. She looked fresh and wholesome and very young. He put down his post and asked mildly: 'What are you two going to do today?'

'Well, Miss Timmis comes back after lunch and Eleanor's got such a lot to tell her so if you don't mind, since it's so early, I thought we might drive over to Dorchester...'

'A good idea, take the Mini. Give my love to your mother. We must arrange a visit very soon.' He smiled at her. 'I must be off; I'll be home tomorrow early evening. Don't forget you are driving back with me.'

He got up and came round the table, stopping to kiss Eleanor on the way. At Deborah's chair he stopped again. 'Why do you screw your hair up like that?'

'It's quick.'

He leaned forward and pulled the pins out of her hair so that it fell loose round her shoulders. 'That's even quicker, and much prettier.'

He kissed her slightly open mouth and went away, leaving her a little pink and Eleanor giggling.

She wore the new green outfit and the coat Gideon had bought her, when they left presently in the Mini; her mother's surprise at her new image gave her deflated ego quite a boost. 'Darling!' declared her parent, 'you're positively pretty—and your hair…does it take ages?'

Deborah nodded, 'But once it's up it stays that way.' She plunged into an account of their trip to *den Haag*, handed over the presents she had brought with her and then sat quietly while Eleanor babbled excitedly.

Just before they left Mrs Farley asked: 'You're happy, darling?'

'Yes, Mother,' Deborah kissed her and added, 'Very.'

Miss Timmis arrived after lunch and Deborah left Eleanor and her together while she went to the kitchen to talk to Mrs Buckle. She didn't know how many guests Gideon would invite, but she could at least talk things over with the housekeeper. They spent an hour or more deciding on which rooms to get ready and possible menus, by then it was tea time. She spent the evening with Miss Timmis, finding that lady's gentle talk very soothing. All the same she was glad to go to bed; the house without Gideon seemed very large and empty, even the dogs were subdued.

Eleanor had lessons in the morning and Deborah spent it in inspecting the various bedrooms and then making a list, with Mrs Buckle's help, of food they might need to get in. There was a well stocked, large larder and a freezer too; Buckle knew all about the wines and the greenhouses were nicely full of chrysanthemums and pot plants. There wasn't much more that she could do, so she spent a pleasant afternoon in the library while Eleanor had her music lesson then the three of them had tea round the schoolroom fire with Deborah glancing every five minutes at the clock. Gideon would be coming soon, the dogs knew it too sitting in a heap on the hearth rug.

Five o'clock struck and after what seemed like a very long time indeed, six o'clock. It was half an hour after that when the phone rang and Deborah went to answer it on the schoolroom extension before Buckle could get to the phone in the study. Gideon's voice, casual to the point of coolness, came very clearly over the line.

'I'll not be home until about eleven o'clock,' he told her. 'Old friends have asked me to dine—don't wait up for me, I'll see you at breakfast. Let me speak to Eleanor will you?'

Deborah said nothing at all, she put down the receiver and called to Eleanor, then went to sit down again by Miss Timmis and started to talk rather loudly so that she wouldn't be able to hear what Eleanor was saying. The child came back presently, she looked resigned. 'Daddy says he met Auntie Barbara while he was having lunch—he asked her to come for the weekend, but she isn't sure so he is taking her out to dinner instead.'

'Lady Barbara Inge,' murmured Miss Timmis. 'Married one of the professor's friends—they are divorced now. A very beautiful young woman. She has been in America I believe.' She glanced at Eleanor's downcast face: 'You'll see your father in the morning, Eleanor.'

Deborah made an effort. 'Yes, of course, love. I'm sorry you are disappointed, we all are. Shall we have a game of cards then you can have your supper and Miss Timmis and I will have dinner at the usual time. I'd better let Mrs Buckle know.'

Why, she pondered on the way to the kitchen, should Gideon tell her that he had been asked to dine with old friends and yet be doing nothing of the sort? He must be feeling guilty or surely he could have told her the truth—or perhaps he thought it was none of her business? It was a lowering thought.

They had their game of cards and while Eleanor ate her supper with Miss Timmis for company, she took the dogs for a walk. It was a cold, dark evening, exactly suited to her mood and she walked fast, trying to get away from her thoughts. But it didn't help; she went down to the village and back again, took the dogs into the kitchen for their supper and went back to the schoolroom. Eleanor had just finished her supper and Deborah said cheerfully: 'Since Miss Timmis will have you all day tomorrow, how about me seeing you to bed?' She smiled at the little lady, 'Do go down to the drawing room and give yourself a drink: I'll be with you shortly.'

She pottered round the child's room while Eleanor undressed and then went to run her bath. 'It's a pity that Daddy's not here,' said Eleanor, 'I wanted to tell him about my history; Miss Timmis says I'm very good at it—I wanted to surprise him.'

'Think what a nice surprise it will be in the morning,' observed Deborah, 'and I'll tell you what, you shall stay up for supper tomorrow evening—I'll ask Miss Timmis to get you all ready for bed and you can wear your new dressing gown!'

A happy thought which sent the little girl to bed content.

Miss Timmis went to bed happy too; dear little Mrs Beaufort had listened with sympathy when she had explained about visiting her sister, indeed, she offered help if it should be needed and expressed pleasure in knowing that Miss Timmis would return in the role of a family companion. Miss Timmis's small frame swelled with pride at the nice things which had been said to her. The professor was a very lucky man to have such a sweet natured girl for a wife.

Deborah, neither happy nor in bed, sat by her bedroom window with the lights out staring out into the dark. She had never imagined that being married to Gideon was going to be easy, but she hadn't expected him to be so indifferent; it would have been better if she irritated him or made him angry, as it was she did neither. She would have to do something startling; go blonde perhaps? buy some really way out clothes that even he couldn't ignore? develop a semi-invalid condition which would allow her to lie around all day in frilly negligees—go home to mother?

She giggled and then choked on the tears crowding her throat. Sitting and moping wouldn't do any good at all; she had married Gideon with her eyes open and she would make a success of their marriage although just at that moment she couldn't think how. She sat by the window until she saw the car's lights as it came from the village and then got into bed, still in the dark.

She was her calm, serene self in the morning, chattering gaily to Eleanor about her shopping, promising to bring her a present, letting her sit on the bed, which she enjoyed, while she did her hair and face. She had decided to wear the green again and the new coat and beret, they went down to breakfast in good time with Eleanor still talking nineteen to the dozen.

Gideon was already there reading his mail, his breakfast pushed to one side. He pushed his chair back as they went in, but Deborah said quickly: 'No don't get up, Gideon. I hope you don't mind, I told Miss Timmis to come down later.' She served Eleanor and herself and started to sit down, while the little girl went to kiss her father. He looked over his daughter's fair head: 'Why?'

'Well, it's early, isn't it? and she will have Eleanor all day. She'll be here by the time we go.'

He ruffled Eleanor's hair. 'What a good idea,' he sounded absent minded, thinking of other things. Aunt Barbara perhaps, wondered Deborah and bit savagely into her toast.

She said with careful casualness. 'I hope you had a pleasant evening with your friends,' and hurried on before he could reply: 'We played cards and Eleanor won—she's good you know, Miss Timmis and I never have a chance.'

He wasn't in the mood for small talk. 'You'll be all right if I drop you off at Harrods? Take a taxi to Waterloo when you've finished your shopping. I suggest that you phone Buckle from there and he'll meet you. Don't stint yourself, Deborah—your allowance is in the bank, and if you go over it ask for the bill to be sent to me.' He mentioned a sum which sent her pale eyebrows up into her hair.

'All that?' she asked incredulously.

He said smoothly: 'You can fit yourself out for the next month or so.'

She thanked him, she certainly would do that; she would let herself go, and outshine his women friends.

The drive to London was totally taken up with details as to the guests they might expect that weekend. 'We don't do much; walk the dogs, and perhaps ride if the weather's good, sit around and chat. I'm sure you will be able to lay on a good dinner each evening; Mrs Buckle is a first rate cook and is always complaining that she has no chance to show her talents to the world. Miss Timmis will help you with the flowers and the linen and so on.'

He was driving fast, looking ahead, and Deborah, seething silently at his assumption that she was quite out of her depth, said nothing.

'Well?' His voice was impatient and faintly annoyed.

'I'm sure that everything will be all right. You must tell me if I do anything wrong or fall down on my duties, but I don't imagine that your friends will expect a polished hostess, considering the circumstances in which we married.'

He made an explosive sound which she took to be a swear word she wasn't familiar with. 'Do you imagine that I broadcast my—our—personal lives to every Tom, Dick and Harry I meet? I have no doubt at all that you will be an excellent hostess.' He added to surprise her: 'I'm sorry if I was overbearing.'

'Not at all. If there's anything special about your guests will you tell me? So that I know what to talk about.'

'A pity we can't meet for lunch—I have a previous engagement and I can't get home this evening either. I shall bring two of our guests with me—he's something in the EU, very quiet and easy to talk to, so is his wife. Then there will be another married couple; he works with me a good deal, rather learned and withdrawn, his wife is just the opposite—they're a devoted pair. Then there is another guest—a last minute one—which makes us an odd number but that can't be helped. An old friend just back from the States…'

'Aunt Barbara,' murmured Deborah.

He drove in silence for a few moments. 'Eleanor told you?'

'That's right,' her voice was matter-of-fact although her heart was pounding with a mixture of quite murderous feelings. 'Did you think that she wouldn't? And you could just as well have said so to me in the first place; why should I mind about your friends? After all I know almost nothing about you, do I?' She took a breath, 'And I'm not a bit interested.'

He didn't reply, although when she peeped at him she could see his profile was taut and severe; she had annoyed him and she was glad. After that they didn't speak again. He stopped outside Harrods and she thanked him for the lift, smiled emptily at his chin because she didn't feel quite able to look him in the eye, and walked jauntily into the store.

The jauntiness dropped off her like a cloak once she was inside and she shook so much that she went first to have a cup of coffee. She hadn't done well, in fact she had behaved badly. How easy it would be, she thought, if they could talk—really talk, about themselves. He had put her into a compartment; she was a small part of his life, a convenience not meant to mingle with his own way of living, but to live in his home, run it to his liking and love his daughter. In all fairness, she had known that when she had married him, and if she hadn't loved him so much she might have thought the situation through and backed out.

She finished her coffee and got out her list. Well, she wasn't beaten yet and she would change her tactics...

Having money yourself to spend was a great help; she chose greens and browns and rich tawny shades—tweed suits beautifully cut, cashmere sweaters, silk blouses, an armful of fine wool and silk dresses and three evening gowns, all very much in the fashion. Six months ago she wouldn't have dreamed of even trying them on even if she had had the money. There was plenty of money still, she found shoes which cost the earth, leather handbags and belts, gloves and undies and, true to her promise, a splendidly dressed doll for Eleanor and a mohair stole for Miss Timmis. She had shopped steadily without stopping for lunch and she was finished by three o'clock. She arranged to collect her parcels presently and went in search of a tea room. She wasn't hungry but a pot of tea was what she needed. She would find somewhere quiet and sit for half an hour, her train didn't go until five o'clock so there was time enough. There was a tea room across the street; she had a foot off the kerb when she saw Gideon and a tall, handsome young woman crossing towards her. She had time to compose her features into a casual smile which almost killed her before they came face to face. Gideon's face was a blank mask. He stopped and the young woman stopped too. 'Deborah…'

She managed a beam. 'Hullo—can't stop—I've a train to catch.' She switched the beam on to the girl and nipped across the street, dying to look back, but instead she went to the tea room and resolutely took a table well away from the window. She sat there drinking cup after cup of tea until she felt better and then went back and collected her packages, got into a taxi and caught her train in comfort, sitting alone surrounded by all the clothes she had bought. They won't be a waste, she told herself fiercely, they'll help, I know they will. They'd better; the girl had been lovely and her clothes quite something. Deborah, her green eyes glowing, marshalled her new outfits in a mental parade like soldiers going into battle and when she had done that to her satisfaction made a note to call the hairdresser in the morning.

Buckle was waiting for her; he loaded her mass of boxes and packages into the car, expressed the hope that she had had a good day, and drove her home. 'The professor phoned just before I came away, Madam, wanted to know if you were back and said he'd try and ring again later.'

She received the news with mixed feelings; if he was going to try and explain over the phone then she wasn't going to listen, on the other hand if she didn't answer when he rang he might think that she was annoyed. Annoyed—she was so angry that she could have burst into flames.

She doused her temper for Eleanor and Miss Timmis's sake; they seemed so glad to see her and so happy with the presents she had brought them. They had supper together and then Deborah undid her boxes and tried everything on before an admiring audience. She was twirling round and round in the finest of her evening gowns when Buckle came to tell her that the professor was on the phone and she went to the extension by the bed. Strangely, she felt quite light hearted, largely because the dress she was wearing had turned her from an ugly duckling into a swan. As Miss Timmis had remarked primly, it was a ravishing dress, even if rather revealing. 'Although as you are a married lady, an exposed bosom is quite allowable,' she had observed.

Deborah perched on the side of the bed with a great rustle of wide skirts. 'Hullo there,' she greeted him and allowed her gaze to sweep over the lovely things spilling over the chairs and bed.

Gideon's voice sounded so cool that she shivered. 'Deborah? I shall be home tomorrow at about six o'clock, Dr and Mrs Wallis and Barbara Inge will be with me, John and Joyce Morris will be arriving half an hour later. We could perhaps dine at eight o'clock. Eleanor had better be ready for bed and I expect Miss Timmis to join us.'

She said airily: 'Okay, Gideon. Eleanor's here, she wants to say good-night.'

'You enjoyed your day?'

'I had a marvellous time, here's Eleanor.'

Deborah was dressed and ready for Gideon and their guests by half-past five. She had spent the day making sure that everything was just so, taken the dogs for a walk so that they wouldn't bother Gideon the moment he came in, and now, dressed in a green crepe dress the exact colour of her eyes, she was sitting in an upright chair, terrified of disarranging the artlessly simple style the hairdresser had created with her sandy hair. Eleanor was with Miss Timmis, getting into her blue velvet dress under that lady's eye, for Deborah had decided that even if the child couldn't stay up for dinner, there was no reason why she shouldn't be downstairs to greet her father, besides that would give Miss Timmis time to get into the navy blue dress.

Eleanor came into the room presently, her fair hair beautifully brushed, her small face beaming with excitement. She walked all round Deborah taking in every exact detail and finally pronounced her to be utterly super.

'Thank you, darling, and remember when I say so, go upstairs, have your supper and get ready for bed. I'll pop up to say goodnight. Dinner's not till eight o'clock, so I can nip along while everyone is in their rooms.'

Eleanor asked wistfully: 'Do you think Daddy will come too? He always does when he is at home.'

'Then he'll come this evening.'

'I like it better when there's just you and Daddy and me, and Miss Timmis, of course.'

'Yes, love, but Daddy has to entertain his friends and they won't be coming very often at the weekends.'

It was a little after the hour when the Bentley swept up to the door closely followed by a Mercedes. Deborah went into the hall with Eleanor just as Buckle opened the door, she would have much preferred to have run upstairs and shut herself in the fastness of her room, as it was she went forward looking, she devoutly hoped, welcoming. Gideon had stood aside to usher the others in and when he did turn round she was pleased to see the look of astonishment on his face, it was only there for a moment, but it satisfied her; the wildly expensive dress and the hair do had served their purpose. He had really looked at her, he had discovered, she was sure, that she wasn't 'Nanny' any more.

She said in her pleasant voice: 'Hullo, Gideon, did you have a good journey down?' She smiled at him and then at the others.

He crossed the hall and bent to kiss her cheek. For the sake of appearances, she told herself silently as he introduced Dr and Mrs Wallis and then John and Joyce Morris who had come with him after all. 'And this is Barbara Inge—an old friend, just back from America.'

'And utterly devastated to find Gideon married,' said that young lady. 'You see what happens the moment my back is turned?' She looked at everyone, gathering laughs. 'I never was more surprised…' She kissed the air an inch from Deborah's cheek. 'He's quite a handful, my dear, but I daresay you'll cope.'

Deborah said sweetly: 'I shall do my best. It's delightful to meet his friends. Do please come in, I expect you would like a drink before going to your rooms?'

Eleanor was talking to Gideon and she led the way to the drawing room as Buckle took coats and hats, and Gideon followed with Eleanor. And from then on a kind of magic mantle fell on Deborah; she had been terrified of entertaining Gideon's friends because she knew nothing about them, come to that, she didn't know much about him, either. But a kind of recklessness had seized her and that, coupled with the knowledge that she really looked rather nice, had the effect of turning her into the perfect hostess, laughing and chatting and what was better, listening more than talking, so that the two men, finding her such a good listener, would have monpolised her if she had allowed it. But she won over their wives just as easily, while Eleanor kept close to her, sipping her lemonade and every now and then tucking a hand into Deborah's. Of course, that left Gideon with Barbara which in a way was very satisfactory, for Barbara was a young woman who liked an audience and the only person attending to her was Gideon, while Deborah, stealing a look at him from time to time, thought that he was bored.

Eleanor said her goodnights presently and after a while everyone went to their rooms leaving Deborah and Gideon together. She sat herself down by the fire.

'I'd love another sherry before you go,' she told him.

'I like your friends, Gideon, are they all as nice?'

He brought her the sherry and stood looking down at her. 'I believe so. You look different, Deborah.'

She said kindly, 'I'm still me, only without the cap and apron.' And then, because he looked suddenly ferocious. 'I didn't want you to be ashamed of me.'

'That is a very silly remark, you must know that you look delightful and that Ben Wallis and John are falling over themselves to get at you. I feel as though I've married a quite different girl…'

'Don't you like me?'

He said silkily: 'Oh, indeed I do—I am enchanted—but it would hardly do for me to behave like John and Ben, would it. I am—surprised…'

'I am a bit surprised myself, I mean, feeling quite different just because I'm wearing a model dress and have had my hair done differently. But I'm still me.'

She finished her sherry and he took the glass from her and drew her to her feet. 'I think that there is a lot more to you than I imagined,' he observed slowly, 'and I don't mean new dresses and elaborate hairstyles.'

He bent suddenly and kissed her, but this time it wasn't a light peck on her cheek. 'I'm going to change.'

CHAPTER EIGHT

THE WEEKEND WAS a success, indeed Miss Timmis pronounced it a social triumph for Deborah; nothing had gone wrong—the food had been above reproach, the weather had been fine for the time of year, so that everyone could get out of doors and for those who were disinclined to do that, there were cheerful fires, plenty of books to read and of course, the TV. Deborah playing her part, avoided Gideon as much as possible, electing to stay at home with Joyce Morris when everyone else went walking on Saturday morning and then offering to show Ben and Mary Wallis the church after lunch. 'And I'll take Eleanor with us,' she said cheerfully to Gideon, 'then if you want to play bridge you won't be interrupted.'

This had been naughty of her; Gideon loathed bridge. When she got back rosy cheeked from the cold, a Gucci scarf exactly matching her beautifully cut tweeds tied under her chin, she sensed a distinct atmosphere at the card table. Gideon looked impassive, the Morrises tolerantly amused and Barbara Inge furious. She turned towards them as they trooped in and said peevishly: 'There you are—I hope you had a better time than I have—Gideon doesn't even bother to play…' She flung the cards down and went over to the fire.

'It's cold and lovely outside,' said Deborah lightly: 'We enjoyed it. Just give us time to take our outdoor things off and we'll have tea.'

Sitting behind the teapot presently, Deborah looked around her: The Wallises were enjoying themselves, so were the Morrises, tucking into buttered muffins and one of Mrs Buckle's fruit cakes, so was Eleanor with Miss Timmis sitting beside her. She had personally settled them there so that it was left to Gideon to sit with Lady Barbara.

That evening, after an excellent dinner, she had suggested dancing in the drawing room and the lovely silk rugs had been rolled aside while she selected a few tapes. She was sure that Gideon hadn't wanted to dance, but he had agreed pleasantly enough, filling glasses and joining in the light hearted talk and when she had switched on the tape she had excused herself, explaining that she wanted to say goodnight to Eleanor. Gideon opened the door for her and then went straight across the room to Joyce Morris and started to dance. Deborah, out of the corner of her eye, saw Barbara's cross face, and felt a pleasantly wicked wave of pleasure at the sight.

Everyone left after lunch on Sunday and Gideon had taken Eleanor and the dogs for a walk, suggesting smoothly that Deborah might like to rest. A remark she took instant exception to, although Miss Timmis, going thankfully to her room to put her feet up, remarked upon her employer's thoughtfulness. Left to herself Deborah mooned around the house, picking up the Sunday papers and putting them down again, moving vases of flowers from here to there and back again, finally putting on her old mac and the thick shoes she kept for pottering about in the garden, she let herself out of the back door. She wandered round for a bit and finally took herself off to the shed where Willy the gardener stored the apples. It was cold but fragrant inside, she perched on a pile of old sacks and selected one of his best Cox and bit into it. The weekend had been a success, she felt sure, but Gideon hadn't said a word and yet he had appeared to have enjoyed himself. They had all gone to the village church that morning and she had sat with Eleanor between them in the family pew, and he had smiled at her several times during the service. Probably for the benefit of the congregation, she thought sourly, biting into another of Willy's apples.

She was roused from her thoughts by Gideon's voice on the other side of the house and a moment later all three dogs had hurled the shed door open and were scrambling all over her, just as though she had been away for years.

She felt quite guilty when Gideon and Eleanor poked their heads round the door to look at her. She nibbled the last of the apple core and got up.

'Did you have a pleasant walk?'

'Lovely. Deborah, Daddy says you're a super hostess and there's no reason why we shouldn't have people staying each weekend, only we are not going to because he likes peace and quiet.' Eleanor came close to Deborah and put an arm round her neck. 'I do too, just us. May we play Scrabble after tea?'

'If your father would like that…'

'Her father will be delighted, it will make a nice change from bridge.'

'Oh, well yes. Though I should have thought that you would have liked that—I mean you have to be clever to play, don't you?'

He said silkily: 'There are a great many games one can play where cleverness doesn't count, only low cunning and guile.'

She had the grace to blush and jumped to her feet. 'Let's go indoors and have tea. The Buckles have the afternoon off so I'll get it.'

In the hall Gideon said: 'Eleanor, will you go and ask Miss Timmis if she would like tea in her room—I'm sure she would like a good rest.' And when the child had skipped upstairs: 'I'll give you a hand with the tea things.'

'Please don't bother, Buckle will have left everything ready.'

She need not have spoken for he took no notice but followed her along the stone passage to the large, cosy room with its scrubbed table and old fashioned dresser and the kettle simmering on the Aga. The tray was indeed ready but he made no effort to carry it away, instead he sat on the edge of the table and watched Deborah warm the pot and put the muffins to toast.

He leaned across and cut himself a slice of cake. 'A very successful weekend,' he observed, 'we must find time to do it again one day. We can, of course, have Barbara down on her own…'

Deborah, measuring tea into the pot, spilt some of it on to the table. 'Is—is she a great friend of yours?'

'No, but from your behaviour I can only assume that you wish her to be just that.'

She fetched the kettle and made the tea. 'I don't know what you mean…'

He took the kettle from her and put it back on the stove. 'Now, now, Debby, I'm sure that you have always impressed upon your little charges the necessity for speaking the truth; you should practice what you preach.'

She turned on him. 'How very unfair, and here have I been leaning over backwards, being understanding and tolerant—and not m-minding…'

She stopped just in time, indeed, she had said too much and she could have bitten off her tongue with chagrin. She said airily, not looking at him: 'I think Barbara is very lovely and very witty—she made you laugh a great deal—well she made us all laugh—she's great fun.'

She glanced at him and although he looked poker faced, she was sure that he was amused about something. 'Well, we must have her as a frequent guest, mustn't we, Deborah, since you would like that?'

'I never said…' she began and interrupted herself to see to the muffins. It seemed prudent not to add to that; she busied herself with them, and then leading the way went to the drawing room where Eleanor was stretched on the rug before the fire, with the dogs leaning against her.

She jumped up as they went in. 'Miss Timmis said she'd love to have her tea upstairs but that she'd come down to collect it.'

'Run and fetch a tray love, and we'll get it ready for her and I'll take it up.' Deborah started to cut cake. 'I'll make a little pot of tea for her.'

Miss Timmis was almost embarrassingly grateful. 'Really, Mrs Beaufort, you shouldn't—I could have got tea for myself. I must say it's very pleasant sitting here with a book.'

'Visitors are fine, but tiring,' observed Deborah. 'We're going to loll round the fire and Eleanor's to stay up for dinner, so don't bother with anything until you hear the gong.'

Tea round the fire was a cheerful meal and if Deborah was a little quiet it passed unnoticed in Eleanor's happy chatter, and afterwards they played Scrabble until Deborah heard the Buckles' elderly Morris 1000 chug round the house and excused herself with the plea that she must go to the kitchen and make sure that everything was as it should be for the evening. She bore Eleanor upstairs presently to tidy herself for dinner and went to her own room to do her hair once more and add a little more make-up. She felt sick at the very idea of Barbara becoming a frequent visitor, that had been her own silly fault, too; she hadn't started off with such high ideals…

She called to Eleanor and went downstairs, to sit opposite Gideon, sipping her sherry, carrying on an empty conversation until Miss Timmis joined them, and the talk, centering round her forthcoming visit to her sister, became easier.

It surprised Deborah very much when Gideon stayed at home for the next two days, he worked in his study, writing a great deal and spending a lot of time telephoning so that they saw very little of him. All the same, it was nice to have him in the house, and at the end of the second day, he drove Miss Timmis to Salisbury to catch her train and when he got home, came straight to the drawing room where he showed Eleanor the rudiments of chess until Deborah carried her off for supper and bed. He was still there when she got back and laid himself out to be a charming companion for the rest of that evening. Deborah, in another new dress, aware that she looked her best, felt her hopes rising; he hadn't mentioned having weekend visitors, perhaps he found her a satisfying companion after all.

She might have known that it was nothing of the sort; they had watched the nine o'clock news together over their coffee and she had put aside her cup and picked up her sewing. Gideon asked her idly what she was making.

'Clothes for a doll I've got for Eleanor's Christmas present.'

'Ah—yes Christmas. We had better decide what we intend to do—rather short notice to invite friends, but I've no doubt they'll accept. I expect you want to see something of your family. Decide what you want to do, will you and let me know? I'm going up to town tomorrow and I have a dinner date I don't care to break, but I'll give you a ring early the following morning. I must get seats for a Pantomime too, Eleanor's old enough to go to an evening performance so we'll make an occasion of it. That will give you a chance to wear a new dress...'

Deborah put down her sewing. There had been mockery in his voice and she couldn't bear that, it was as though he found it amusing that she should be trying to shake off her former staid image. She said quietly: 'I think it would make no difference what I wore. Not to you, at any rate; you think of me in nanny's uniform, don't you, Gideon? But I expected that.' She added fiercely. 'What else was there to expect?'

He was sitting back in his chair, staring at her with a calm face. 'Are you happy, Deborah?' He waved a large hand. 'Here? Do you find it too quiet? Peggy was asking me a day or so ago if you would like to take Eleanor for a visit; the twins would love to see you again and Eleanor likes being with them.'

She said in a wooden voice: 'That sounds delightful. If you're going to be in London, she won't miss you so much.'

'And you, Debby? Would you miss me?'

She eyed him stonily. 'I really don't think that my feelings come into it, nor do you have the least interest in them.'

She got up quickly and whisked out of the room and flew up the stairs, as she reached her room she heard the drawing room door open and Gideon's voice calling her, but she shut her door firmly on the sound.

Things were going from bad to worse and what a very good thing that he was going to London in the morning; she would have a headache and not go down until he had left and perhaps by the time he phoned… Perhaps what? she thought in a panic, and in the mean time he would have spent the evening with Barbara Inge. She ran a hot bath and lay in it until the water was cool, her thoughts whizzing round and round inside her head until the headache she was going to pretend to have in the morning was really there.

Indeed, it was still there when she woke after a brief, heavy nap towards morning so that she was able to tell Eleanor when the child came to her room, that she wouldn't be down to breakfast and would she see her father off. 'And I've taken something for my headache, love, so tell Daddy not to come up; I shall be asleep.'

To be on the safe side, she kept her eyes shut until she heard the car going down the drive.

Peggy Burns telephoned during the morning. 'Come for lunch,' she suggested when Deborah told her that Gideon wouldn't be home until the next day. 'And why not leave Eleanor here for the night—I'll drive her over in the morning—that'll give you time to get your plans laid for Christmas. I don't suppose you are doing much this year—you've not had the time—have you? But I expect there will be the usual family gatherings and so on.'

It was nice to have something to do; Deborah drove over later in the morning with Eleanor beside her. It was a cold grey day and she wondered if it was going to snow as she took the car the short distance; the day suited her mood, although she was cheered by Peggy's greeting of: 'Deborah, don't you look marvellous? That heavenly suit, and your hair is different!'

They had a boisterous lunch, with the twins allowed to sit at the table and Dee sleeping peacefully as usual. 'It isn't just you, Deborah, who looks smashing, it's Eleanor as well—she's plump and such a lovely healthy colour and so very happy. How's Gideon?'

'He is fine,' said Deborah. 'He works too hard, but he enjoys that, doesn't he? We had people for the weekend—he's a marvellous host…'

'Who came?'

Deborah told her, keeping her voice casual.

'Oh, is she still around?' asked Peggy Burns. 'The ghastly Barbara—always getting her talons in someone else's husband.' She gave Deborah a lightning glance. 'She's pretty good to look at, isn't she?'

'Fabulous, and such gorgeous clothes…'

'Well, as to that, you're not doing too badly yourself. Gideon must be so proud of you.'

Deborah couldn't think of an answer to this and Peggy went on kindly: 'Gideon's not always as busy as this; he tends to work in fits and starts; he's got a TV interview coming up—he's told you, of course, and that means making notes, but you'll be going to Brussels with him in the New Year, won't you? When is Miss Timmis coming back?'

Happily a question Deborah could answer: 'After Christmas; Gideon wants to send Eleanor to school—a day pupil of course—and I think she might like it, we're going to discuss it when he comes home.'

She left shortly after lunch. 'The Buckles have the afternoon off and the dogs will need a run before tea. Will you come to lunch tomorrow?'

'Tea, if I may. Can we all come?'

'Well of course; I'll get Mrs Buckle to make a chocolate

cake. Please give my love to Mrs Beaufort when you see her.' Deborah began a round of hugs and kisses, ending with Eleanor who wanted to know anxiously if she would be lonely.

'I shall miss you, love, but I promise I won't be lonely—I've letters to write and I want to phone Granny Farley.'

The afternoon was melting rapidly into twilight by the time she got back to be welcomed rapturously by the dogs, their barks sounding hollowly in the empty house. She went indoors, changed into stout shoes, and went out of the back door, locking it behind her; the Buckles might be back before she returned but they had a key. With the dogs circling round her, she took the path which skirted the wood beyond the grounds at the back of the house. It was slippery with frost but she knew it well. It circled round the trees as it climbed the hill and came down the other side to join the lane to the village; half an hour's walk at the most, she would be back home before it grew dark.

She went fast, trying to outrun her unhappy thoughts and she was beginning the downhill rutted path on the other side of the wood when she noticed the Jack Russell, Benjy, was missing. She stopped and whistled and Jack and Prince whined. She hushed them and whistled and called again and this time she heard a faint bark, coming from somewhere within the wood. She had never penetrated its sombre depths but she did know that somewhere in its heart, towards the bottom of the hill, there was a pond. She whistled again, listened for Benjy's bark and then walked back a little way to where a narrow path led down into the trees. Jack and Prince came with her, walking sedately now, keeping to her heels as she began to slip and slide, barely able to see her way.

It seemed a very long way down and she stopped from

time to time and called, to be answered by a whimper which sent her hurrying on once more.

The path ended at last, abruptly terminated by a pool of sluggish water, thinly coated with ice. Ice through which the unfortunate Benjy had fallen; she could see his small head turning desperately this way and that as he paddled in the broken ice, unable to get out because of the sheer sides of the pool. Jack and Prince barked and then went to the edge and whined, Deborah said: 'No, you don't. Stay, both of you.'

It was barely light by now, she cast around for some means of help and thankfully laid hands on a broken off branch, it was stout enough and there were any number of smaller branches on it, leafless now, but that was all to the good. She knelt down on the muddy ground and pushed the branch cautiously on to the water as near to Benjy's head as she could reach. He was a bright little dog and she prayed and hoped that he would have the sense to allow her to drag him to the edge…

'Get on the branches, love,' she begged him gently, 'just hang on and I'll pull you inside.'

For a few moments she thought that she must fail, but suddenly she felt his weight on the twigs as she scooped him up and then began to drag the branch back towards her. He fell off at once, and they had to start all over again but at last she had him at the pond's edge, but still out of reach. She shuffled backwards, hampered by Jack and Prince trying to help, and lifted the branch slowly, terrified that Benjy might drop off into the water again. But he didn't; with a yelp of delight he fell into her lap and shook himself, completing the ruin of her new suit. Not that she cared; she hugged him with relief while his friends nosed happily at them both. She didn't dare stay longer; she had moved round the pond and now she wasn't sure which path to take, there were several, barely discernible now, and anxious to get away from the pool she started up the first one she blundered into. It led uphill but twisted away after a few yards and presently, to her horror, it came to an abrupt end, barred by a towering thicket. She had Benjy in her arms, small and shivering and wet, and the other dogs crowded close to her. There was no help for it; they would have to go back—but not to the pond. She had seen a narrow track a short distance back, they would take that and hope for the best.

She found the track, but by now it was so dark that she could see nothing at all. Fighting panic, she stood still, deciding what was the best thing to do—the answer seemed to be to stay where she was. It was bitter cold and would get much colder as the night advanced, but surely if she and the dogs kept close together they would have a modicum of warmth. She felt around her and found a tree stump, icily cold but better than the damp, frosty ground. She perched on it, tucked Benjy under one arm and dragged Prince and Jack close on either side. They whined anxiously, but as they leaned against her their warmth was comforting.

Gideon had had a busy morning, indeed it was early afternoon before he stopped for sandwiches and beer eaten at his desk while he added a few more notes to the lecture he was to give later on in the week. These finished he sat back, not thinking of lectures at all, but of Deborah. He had expected to see her at breakfast that morning and when she hadn't come down he had felt a keen sense of disappointment, followed by an increasing desire to shake her until her teeth rattled for filling her head with such silly ideas, and an even greater desire to discover if she meant what she said. The more he considered this the more urgent it became to find out. He pushed his papers aside, asked his secretary to ring his home and when there was no answer, told her to try his sister's house, remembering that Eleanor and Deborah had been invited there.

Peggy answered the phone. 'Deborah? She left a couple of hours ago, Gideon, said she was going to take the dogs out and of course there's no one at home, she told me that she had given the Buckles the afternoon off since you weren't coming home and she would be on her own. Eleanor's here... She wants to talk to you.'

No one listening would have found the professor's manner anything but his usual urbane self. He talked to his small daughter for several minutes and then rang off.

'Cancel everything there is for the rest of the day, and that goes for my dinner date. I'm going home at once.'

His secretary had been with him for a long time. 'But sir—the rest of the afternoon appointments are easily postponed, but not this evening's—it's the Ministry...'

'I know, I know. Ring through and see if I can have a half an hour of someone's time now—explain—oh, say anything you can think of...'

She earned every penny of her excellent salary; within minutes he was in the Bentley driving down Whitehall.

The half hour stretched over an hour, only his promise that he would return the following day made it possible for him to get away even then.

The evening rush hour was already under way as he crawled out of the city, showing no signs of impatience at the hold ups, but once on the M3 he kept up a steady seventy until he reached Salisbury and changed to the A30. In less than half an hour he was turning in through his own gates, to see lights shining from the house. Deborah was home.

She wasn't. The Buckles, delighted to see him, assured him that Mrs Beaufort hadn't returned from Mrs Burns, and when he rang Peggy it was only to hear her repeat what she had already said. 'And where are the dogs?' He wanted to know from Buckle.

'Possibly with Mrs Beaufort, sir. Although it's a little late…and dark…'

The professor grunted, shrugged himself into his sheepskin jacket, pulled on rubber boots, took the torch Buckle handed him, and left the house.

'Do you wish me to inform the police, sir?' asked Buckle at the door.

'I'll look round first; if the dogs are with Mrs Beaufort, she shouldn't be too hard to find.'

He tried the lane to the village first, with no success; then the grounds round the house, whistling for the dogs; half an hour had gone by by the time he started up the path by the wood, and it had begun to rain, a freezing downpour which made the going doubly difficult. He was at the top of the hill, circumventing the wood when he heard the dogs bark, and when he whistled, bark again.

Deborah was numb with cold and very frightened, even with the dogs for company the wood was giving her the creeps with its vague small rustlings and the steady drip of the rain. She had cried a little but since crying wasn't going to help, she had made herself stop and now sat huddled against the dogs' warm hairiness, sniffing and gulping and talking to them from time to time. When they barked she had let out a small yelp at the unexpectedness of it and it wasn't until they barked again, joyfully this time, that she heard the whistle. Gideon, come home by some miracle. She allowed herself the luxury of a few tears and forgot to wipe them away as the whistling grew louder and before very long gave way to the steady tramp of Gideon's feet. She could see the torch now and called out, but what with cold and fright her voice came out a useless squeak, lost among the rustling and dripping round her.

The torch's powerful light came to rest on her face, making her blink.

'You little fool,' said Gideon in such a rough voice that she winced. And then: 'Which one of you fell into the pool?'

She found a voice of sorts. 'Benjy.'

'You're soaked…'

'Well, I had to get him out.' She started to get to her feet and discovered to her embarrassment that her numbed legs wouldn't obey her. Gideon bent down and hauled her to her feet and bidding the dogs stay still, he began to rub her legs with hard hands. The pain of returning feeling brought the tears to her eyes again, and a small sob secretly escaped her. But it was only one; his, 'For God's sake, don't start snivelling,' was enough to choke back any desire to weep; if she could have laid hands on something suitable and heavy she might have been tempted to bang him over the head. To have spent the night in the miserable cold wetness of the wood could have been no worse than Gideon's even colder anger. His, 'Come along now,' was uttered so harshly that she gibbered with rage, but silently; if she said all the things on the tip of her tongue then he might turn round and walk away and leave her there. At the back of her head she knew quite well that he would never do such a thing, but it suited her at that moment to think so. She allowed herself to be led up an overgrown track, almost hidden by rough undergrowth, with Benjy tucked firmly under one arm and the glad dogs, their noses at Gideon's heels, crowding her on either side. Gideon didn't speak but went steadily ahead, holding fast to her hand and once or twice she felt sure that he must have lost the way, for the track seemed to go on for ever. And when they at last emerged at the top of the hill there wasn't much difference; the icy rain was still falling and the dark was stygian.

'Can you walk?' asked Gideon.

'Of course.' She strove to make her voice haughty and spoilt it with a sniff.

He hadn't let go of her hand but now he walked beside her, shining the torch ahead of them, highlighting the icy slipperyness of the path. She could see the lights from the house now and since there was no one to see allowed herself to weep from sheer thankfulness. By the time they reached the house she would be so wet that the tears would be unnoticed. She still had to explain exactly what had happened to Gideon even if he was in a rage. The bad temper could be accounted for, of course, Barbara had stood him up and he'd come home instead of spending the evening—or more than the evening?—with her. Well he could spend it alone as far as she was concerned. Deborah sniffed again; she had every intention of having a hot bath and going to bed.

The Buckles' reception made up to a large extent for Gideon's terse greeting and lack of sympathy. Mrs Buckle bore her upstairs, tut-tutting all the way. A hot bath, hot soup, a glass of brandy and then a good hot dinner would soon put madam right, what a shame that the suit was a ruin, covered in mud and slime and smelling very nasty too. Deborah, soothed by the housekeeper's soft, country bred voice, turned to look down into the hall. Gideon, who had flung his jacket down, was examining Benjy, walking at the same time to the kitchen with Prince, Jack and Buckle behind him.

He hadn't spoken to her, not even to ask if she was all right. He had behaved abominably; the hero in a romantic novel would have wrapped her in his sheepskin jacket and carried her all the way home, breathing easily too. Gideon had been breathing like a man under great stress and she had to admit, being a sensible girl, that if he had wrapped his jacket around her she would have dropped to the ground with the sheer weight of it. Besides, despite his size and strength, she and the jacket would have gravely impeded his way through the wood. She giggled and then burst into tears, something which Mrs Buckle saw with satisfaction. 'You'll feel better after a nice little cry, madam. You just sit down while I get these shoes off, and that suit.'

Deborah found herself in a hot bath, drinking brandy from the glass Mrs Buckle was proffering. 'I didn't have any tea, I shall be tight…'

Mrs Buckle urged her to drink it all. 'You get yourself dried, madam dear, and I'll fetch up a tray of tea at once. You can have it before you go down stairs. Dinner is put back half an hour so that the professor can change his clothes and see to the dogs.'

The brandy had set up a pleasant glow and, moreover, given her a lovely don't-care feeling. Deborah did as she was told, and buttoned cosily into a russet velvet housecoat, emptied the teapot, and then, urged on by Mrs Buckle, went down stairs to the drawing room.

Gideon was standing in front of the fire with the dogs lying on the rug. He looked at her without speaking when she went in and she stopped just inside the door.

'I wouldn't have come down like this, but Mrs Buckle said you expected me… I—I won't stay.'

He smiled thinly. 'Afraid of me, Deborah?'

'Certainly not. I'd have stayed upstairs if I was. I expect you want to read me a lecture, so do get it off your chest, I don't expect it'll make much impression on me because I've drunk rather a lot of brandy and I feel a little light headed.' She was finding it much easier than she had expected thanks to the brandy and she added airily: 'I'm sorry your evening has been spoilt but I expect you can arrange another one; although she must be very much in demand.'

A kind of spasm swept over the professor's handsome features. 'Oh undoubtedly,' he agreed quietly.

'Well, it must be a bore for you having to come home instead of having an evening out,' went on Deborah kindly, egged on by the brandy, 'but I'm glad you did because I don't know what would have happened to the dogs.'

She came a little further into the room and sat down. 'I'm ready.'

Gideon bit back a laugh. 'I have no intention of blaming you, Deborah. I'm sorry I wasn't more sympathetic when I found you—I was—er—worried.'

'I expect you were; a whole evening spoilt.'

He let that pass. 'You were very brave to stay there with the dogs—did it not enter your head to try and find a way out of the wood alone?'

'Alone? Without the dogs? Don't be silly, Gideon.'

He went over to the sofa table and filled a glass and gave it to her.

'You're right—I am silly—so silly that I haven't seen something right under my nose these past weeks.'

She said hastily: 'Oh, you're not all that silly really—I shouldn't have said that. I think you must be a very clever man—Peggy said so, besides you have so many friends.' She added for good measure, 'And they like you.'

'Do you like me, Deborah?'

She took a sip from her glass. 'Well, you know I do.' She was pleased to hear how coolly friendly her voice sounded. 'I wouldn't have married you if I hadn't liked you.'

'But the first time I asked you, you refused me out of hand. What made you change your mind I wonder?'

Her eyes flew to his face. 'You said you wouldn't ask me that.'

'Ah yes, I was forgetting. I phoned Eleanor while you were upstairs; she sent her love—she misses you.'

'She misses you too when you are not at home.'

He turned away to put his glass on the table. 'But that's why I married you, wasn't it, Deborah?' She didn't answer and he said briskly: 'Well, shall we have dinner?'

She had no appetite but she did her best, and made conversation when Buckle was in the room, lapsing into silence the moment he was out of it. Over coffee she asked: 'Are you staying tonight, Gideon?'

'But of course. I'll have to be in town tomorrow afternoon, but I'll go over to Peggy's and fetch Eleanor back for lunch, Peggy can come some other day.'

She nodded, thinking how delightful it was, sitting opposite him by the fire. She put down her coffee cup and sat back comfortably, feeling drowsy. A little too full of brandy and sherry and the glass of wine she had had with her dinner, she allowed her careful pretence to slip and smiled at Gideon, her face made beautiful by love. The next moment she was almost asleep. Gideon sat watching her; Buckle came in, removed the tray soundlessly and crept out again; an hour later he returned, it was, after all, almost eleven o'clock and time to lock up for the night.

'Come back in ten minutes, Buckle,' the professor said quietly, 'I'll carry Mrs Beaufort upstairs—she's tired out.'

'Mrs Buckle wanted to know if madam would want anything for the night?' whispered Buckle, 'she's in the kitchen...'

'Very kind of her, but I fancy sleep is the only thing my wife needs.'

He sat a little longer after Buckle had gone and then got up, scooped Deborah up gently and carried her upstairs and into her room. He stood for a minute looking down at her, her sandy hair spread over her shoulder, still deeply asleep, indeed snoring in a faint ladylike manner.

She didn't stir as he laid her on the bed and pulled the quilt over her, arranging her hair neatly on the pillow and then stooping to kiss her gently. She looked enchanting and he paused to admire her curling eyelashes before he went quietly to the door, turning out all the lights except the small lamps on either side of the bed. He went back again and poured water into a glass and left it within reach; she would probably wake with a blinding headache.

CHAPTER NINE

DEBORAH WOKE IN the very early hours of the morning with a mild headache and a raging thirst. Still half asleep, she sat up in bed, drank the water Gideon had so thoughtfully left for her, wondered for about fifty seconds why she was still in her housecoat and then turned over and went to sleep again. When she woke again it was to find Molly, the daily housemaid, drawing back the curtains, and her tea tray on the bedside table. Her headache had gone and as she drank her tea she recalled the previous evening. Someone had carried her up to bed and since neither Mrs Buckle nor Buckle were physically capable of that, it must have been Gideon. She sighed; no wonder he stayed in London if she had so little to offer in the way of companionship. Just how unglamorous can I get? she asked herself crossly, snoring my head off in a dressing gown. The thought sent her out of bed, to shower and dress in a dashing pleated skirt with a matching waistcoat over a silk shirt which had cost the earth and was worth every penny. And because she wanted to get down to breakfast quickly she tied her hair back with a ribbon and hurried downstairs.

Gideon was standing with his back to the fire, the dogs

at his feet. His good-morning was affable and when she thanked him rather diffidently for seeing her safely into her bed, he shrugged. 'Think nothing of it,' he told her lightly. Over breakfast he asked her if she had any plans for the next few days.

'Why no—well, shopping for Christmas, but nothing arranged.'

'Good. I'm taking a few days off. I'll be back tonight—but late—don't wait up. If you like we could drive over and see Mother tomorrow and leave Eleanor for a couple of days. She likes to stay with her Granny and do her shopping.'

'Yes, of course. Does she know?'

'I'll tell her this morning—have you any messages for Peggy?'

'Only my love and thanks for having Eleanor.'

He was back with Eleanor before lunch, a meal he didn't stay for. 'No time,' he observed, 'I must be at the office by half-past two and it's already well past eleven o'clock.' He kissed Eleanor and then crossed the room to touch Deborah's cheek briefly. 'We'll leave after breakfast in the morning—will you pack a few things for Eleanor? Oh, and if you take the dogs for a walk this evening, take a torch and keep to the lanes.'

She heard him come home very late that evening, entering the house very quietly, pausing in the hall where Buckle had put a tray with a thermos jug of coffee on the side table, and then going to his study. She stayed awake until she heard him come upstairs twenty minutes later; only then did she curl up and go to sleep.

The dogs went with them in the morning, crowding into the back of the Bentley with Eleanor while Deborah sat beside Gideon. The little girl did most of the talking; planning her shopping, excited that she was to visit Mrs Beaufort, describing the shops in Milsom Street and what she intended to buy. She and Deborah were still deep in a friendly argument as to the best colour to choose for a scarf for Mrs Buckle when they reached Mrs Beaufort's house.

They received a warm welcome. 'Never felt better in my life!' declared Mrs Beaufort in answer to Deborah's enquiries. 'Let's have coffee first then you shall go to your room, Eleanor—the same one as usual. I daresay Deborah will help you to unpack.'

Presently, when the unpacking was done, they went downstairs again. Deborah saw that mother and son were deep in conversation, so she suggested at once that she and Eleanor should take the dogs into the garden. It was a cold morning but brightened by thin sunshine, she put on her brown top coat, tied a scarf round her head, buttoned Eleanor into her coat, and went outdoors, where they threw twigs for the dogs and ran races over the grass.

Gideon, sitting facing the windows, watched the distant figures and presently his mother stopped in mid-sentence and smiled because he didn't notice her silence. 'It is delightful to see little Eleanor so happy,' she remarked in a mild voice. 'Such a change in the child—she loves her stepmother, doesn't she?' She picked up her embroidery from the table beside her chair. There were other questions she would have liked to have asked, but a quick glance at her son's expressionless face stopped her. 'What are your plans for Christmas?' she asked cheerfully, 'I hear that you had friends for the weekend—perhaps you plan a houseparty?'

He shook his head, not looking away from the window. 'No—I don't know, Mother...'

And that, thought Mrs Beaufort, was so unlike Gideon's well ordered life, something, or someone, must have thrown him off balance. She followed his gaze out of the window, to where Deborah and Eleanor were standing arm in arm, laughing their heads off about something or other, and smiled gently.

They left the little girl with her grandmother after lunch, and started on the drive back to Tollard Royal. The short day was losing its brightness already and there was a nip in the air. Deborah, snug in her coat, settled back beside Gideon. It had been a pleasant lunch and they had all laughed a lot and Gideon had teased Eleanor gently and she had giggled and cheeked him back; it was hard to think of her as the rather solemn little girl she had first known, and her grandmother had noticed it too, for she had said as she kissed Deborah good-bye: 'What miracles you have done for that child, Deborah—she's really happy. I do hope you're just as happy, dear.'

Deborah thought about that as they drove along. It seemed impossible to be happy and unhappy at the same time, but she was; happy to be with Gideon, however briefly, happy to be his wife, even if she wasn't, happy to have Eleanor and a lovely home. And unhappy because she meant so little to him. Oh, he liked her all right, he had even once or twice since she had started to dress well, looked at her with a look of surprise on his face, as though he'd never really seen her before. Not that she could ever hope to compete with Lady Barbara's beauty. But that didn't mean that she wouldn't try; she had enough money, that thanks to Gideon's generosity. She heaved a small sigh and he said gently: 'What's the matter, Deborah?'

'Nothing,' she spoke too quickly.

'Would you like to stop for tea, or wait until we're home?'

'Oh, home, I think—besides Mrs Buckle made you a fruit cake when I told her you'd be home for a day or two.' She hesitated, 'But perhaps you've plans...'

He said very evenly: 'Why do you imagine that I find your company so boring that I should wish to leave the house the moment I get back into it?'

'I don't—I mean... That is, you've lots of friends, people you've known for years—shared interests, and—and that sort of thing.'

'And so, do we have no shared interests?' His voice was placid but he was driving too fast.

'Eleanor,' said Deborah promptly and thought what an awkward conversation they were having. 'And you love your home and so do I—and the dogs and...'

'Yes?' he prompted.

'I can't think of anything else at the moment.'

'A mutual liking?' He asked blandly.

'Well, naturally.'

'Nothing more?' She mistrusted the silkiness of his voice. She gazed out of the window and wondered what he would say if she told him that she loved him. 'Nothing more,' she told him steadily.

After that they didn't exchange more than a few words, and those quite impersonal. They talked like two strangers over their tea and then the phone rang and he went away to answer it, not coming back. Deborah, anxious to occupy her mind, sat down at the desk in the drawing room and addressed Christmas cards, rang her mother and then went upstairs to tidy herself for the evening. She got back to the drawing room to find Gideon already there with Buckle. They were in their shirt sleeves, erecting a large Christmas tree in the wide bay window at the end of the room and just for the moment she forgot that they weren't on the best of terms and hurried over to admire it. 'Oh, how super—shall we decorate it this evening?'

'Eleanor and I have done it together ever since she was a toddler.'

He spoke pleasantly but she felt her cheeks redden at the snub. All the same she said quickly: 'Oh, of course—it'll be ready for her to help you when she gets home. It's a magnificent tree.'

'We have left our plans for Christmas rather late this year, but the tree is something we can't overlook.'

Buckle murmured something and Gideon replied with a cheerful: 'Well, since I'm at home for a couple of days, I daresay we can get organized. We'll have to have some friends in for drinks.' He glanced across to where Deborah was standing uncertainly, watching them. 'There are half a dozen invitations in today's post—they are on my desk if you would like to look through them?'

He stood back, surveying his handiwork with Buckle beside him. 'We're just about finished here—I'll be back to pour our drinks in ten minutes or so.'

She went along to the study, feeling like a child who'd been dismissed back to the schoolroom. And yet Gideon hadn't actually said anything unkind; merely put her where she supposed she belonged—in the outer perimeter of his life. She went over to his desk and picked up the little pile of cards and looked at the first one, not seeing a word because her eyes were full of tears. She hadn't thought it would be like this, being held at arm's length, reminded, oh, so politely, that he had married her for Eleanor's sake and for no other reason. She even doubted now if he liked her; hadn't he called her a fool that evening when she had got lost in the wood—his voice had been rough, and he'd been angry although later he had been kind enough.

She was shaken out of her dreary, depressing thoughts by the opening of the door, and before she had time to wipe away her tears, Gideon was beside her.

He had seen them, of course, although she had turned away her head. He took the cards from her and laid them on the desk. 'Now why should a handful of invitations make you cry?' he wanted to know.

Because she wasn't looking at him she didn't see the gleam in his eyes and since his voice was calmly deliberate and nothing more she was filled with icy despair. 'Nothing,' she mumbled, and then, like a child, 'I should like to go to Dorchester...'

She didn't see his bitter little smile, either. 'Running home to mother, dear?'

He had never called her that. She wished with all her heart that she was his dear. 'No, Gideon—only if you wanted me to go...'

The gleam in his eyes turned into a blaze. 'How long have we been married?' he wanted to know, 'A couple of weeks—not much more...'

She didn't answer although she could have told him down to the last minute.

'And you think that I am regretting our marriage already?'

Deborah had mastered the tears except for an odd sniff or so. 'Perhaps. You see, in theory it was a splendid idea, and I know that Eleanor is happy now, and that's what you wanted, didn't you? But in practice I don't fit in, do I? Your friends... They're clever and witty and I don't know them.' She sighed. 'I can't compete.'

'With what or whom?' He interrupted.

'Everything,' she said simply. 'This!' She swept an arm around the handsome, solidly furnished room. 'Money, comfort, your lovely house, driving around in a Bentley,' and because she was an honest girl 'and Lady Barbara Inge...'

The professor said 'Ha!' in a fierce voice, 'and now we come to the root of the matter. Could it possibly be that you are jealous, Debby?'

She made an instant denial, not looking at him. 'That's ridiculous, how could I be jealous when I don't—that is—there has to be a reason...'

'You're very mealy mouthed all of a sudden. What you haven't the nerve to say is that one has to love someone to be jealous of them.' His voice was silky. 'I'm sure you must agree with me.'

'Yes—no, I don't know.' She could feel the tears crowding into her throat again. She whispered: 'Please could we not talk about it any more?' And fate for once gave her a helping hand in the shape of Buckle, coming to warn them that dinner had been ready to serve for the last ten minutes, adding reproachfully: 'I sounded the gong madam.'

'Oh, Buckle, we're so sorry—we just didn't hear it.' She slipped past him and into the dining room with Gideon silent beside her and nibbled at Mrs Buckle's excellent dinner without really eating anything, carrying on a half witted conversation at the same time. She was only vaguely aware of what she was talking about, but anything was better than silence. True, after a while Gideon responded, egging her on gently, the corners of his rather grim mouth twitching. She was quite worn out by the time they left the table, her head empty of words, for the life of her she was unable to stop the relieved sigh when he told her that he had some work to do and would go to the study. He heard it and stopped on his way from the room saying curtly: 'I shall be working late—we shall see each other at breakfast. Goodnight, Deborah.'

She mumbled her own goodnight and sat down by the fire, looking composed. She even smiled, but too late, he'd already closed the door behind him.

Then she sat there, doing nothing, although there were still a few presents to wrap, and even last minute Christmas cards to do. She had forgotten them entirely while she tried to decide what to do. Obviously the matter couldn't rest; she and Gideon would have to have a talk. Something could be worked out and in a sensible fashion; she didn't think that he wanted to be rid of her, he had wanted a mother for Eleanor and she knew without conceit that she had more than come up to his expectations. On the other hand, if she hadn't fallen in love with him, she would have taken Barbara as a matter of course and not minded over much, although he should have told her that he was in love with her, she frowned, but when they had married, he hadn't known about Barbara's return from America, had he?

She went upstairs to her room and got ready for bed. She had made a fine mess of everything, now how to put it right? No amount of thinking helped; she slept at length, her head a kaleidoscope of highly colourful fancies.

Morning brought common sense and pride to the rescue, as well as a nagging fear at the back of her mind that Gideon might have wondered why she had suddenly become such a weepy, waspish young woman, quite unlike her most normal calm, quiet self. Something which must be nipped in the bud at once.

He was coming into the hall from the kitchen, the dogs at his heels, as she got downstairs and she didn't waste a moment in putting her resolution into effect. Her good-morning was cheerful, friendly and brisk; she followed it up with a remark about the weather, a grey stormy morning which didn't merit mention, anyway, and then sat herself down to breakfast.

Gideon had wished her good-morning, accepted his cup of coffee and begun on his post. She began on her own breakfast in silence, thinking sadly that she might just as well not have been there and then telling herself bracingly that self pity wasn't going to do her a ha'p'orth of good, so she opened her own letters and read them through several times until he put the last of his mail down and passed her several cards.

'More invitations—we had better accept these, I think, and give a party after Christmas.'

'So I'll accept them all?'

'Yes, if you will. And we still have to decide about Christmas. Eleanor has always stayed either with Peggy or my mother and I've joined her for a few days, but we shall have to change that, shan't we?'

Here was an opportunity for her to let him see that she was still the sensible, undemanding girl that he had married. 'I expect you took the opportunity to visit your friends—well, I'll be here with Eleanor—I mean, she need not stay with Mrs Beaufort or Peggy and I expect you'll be here for some of the time…' Her voice trailed away under his ferocious stare.

'You talk arrant nonsense Deborah.' He gathered up his letters and got up and stalked out of the room, leaving her to stare at her plate. She discovered that she wasn't only angry, but that she was very unhappy too. After a few minutes' thought she got up quickly and marched across the hall and flung the study door open without knocking.

Gideon was standing at the french window, staring out into the garden. He looked over his shoulder with a frown and then raised his brows in surprise, but before he could speak, Deborah said very flatly: 'I'm going to see Mother, I'll take the presents and stay for lunch.'

She flew out again and galloped up the stairs, fearful that he might come after her, but he didn't and she felt quite irrational disappointment.

She put on her splendid coat, found scarf, handbag and gloves then went almost stealthily downstairs, anxious not to meet Gideon. But before she went she would have to see Mrs Buckle and arrange for his lunch; she went to the kitchen and Mrs Buckle, asked to produce lunch for her master, nodded uncertainly. 'So he won't be going with you madam?'

'Well, no, Mrs Buckle—he has some work he wants to finish.'

'I see madam—and Christmas? What will the arrangements be? There's not much time?'

Deborah said hastily: 'Yes, I know—I'm sorry Mrs Buckle, but we'll let you know this evening—I'll be back this afternoon and we'll talk about it then.'

'Right, madam,' said Mrs Buckle and glanced out of the window. 'Nasty weather blowing up if you ask me, will you be driving the Mini?'

'Yes it's quite a short trip and I know the road very well.'

She smiled and went through the door into the back lobby of the house where everyone kept their macs and wellies and dog leads hung on the wall; out of sight were the keys for the Mini and the Buckles' car.

Deborah stretched out a hand. There was only one set of keys and they weren't for the Mini. They were not on the floor either, she got down on her knees to make sure.

'They are in my pocket, Deborah,' said Gideon behind her, and she scrambled to her feet, furious at being found grovelling. She put out a hand wordlessly, but he didn't give her the keys, instead he caught her hand in his and held it fast. 'I'll drive you, Debby. There's bad weather on the way, and even if the sun were blazing from a blue sky, I would still drive you.'

'Why?' asked Deborah and seeing his face, caught her breath, closed her beautiful eyes and opened them again just to make sure. He was looking at her as though she were something precious to be cherished; there was no mockery in his face now only an intentness and a question. Suddenly all the things she had longed to say and had kept bottled up, came pouring out; she didn't care any more what he might think or say, if only he would go on looking like that for ever.

'I've made a fine hash of things,' the words tripped off her tongue and she made no attempt to stop them. 'I truly didn't mean to, you know and it would have been all right if I hadn't fallen in love with you, I mean I wouldn't have minded about you always being away and looking at me as though I wasn't there and Lady Barbara Inge…'

She choked to a stop because Gideon's great chest was heaving with laughter. 'Oh, you…' she cried and thumped him with her free hand, to have it caught and gently held. He had both her hands now, she tugged at them, but he pulled her close and put his arms around her, holding her very tightly.

'Hush,' he said in a voice as gentle as his hands had been. 'Listen to me, my dearest girl. I don't know when I first discovered that I loved you; I suppose it must have been from the first moment we met, only I didn't realise—you grew on me, slowly, until you were with me all the time, wherever I was. Most disconcerting it was, I can tell you. And the more

I loved you the more difficult I found it to say so; I tried teasing you to be met with your most nannyish airs, I tried telling myself that I would get over what was no more than an infatuation, only my God it wasn't—it isn't. I've never loved anyone in my life as I love you, darling, my darling. There isn't a woman who can hold a candle to you.'

He bent and kissed her hard and then gently, and Deborah slid her arms round his neck and kissed him back. When she had her breath she started: 'Lady Ba…'

'Oh, lord, not her again,' declared Gideon, 'unwitting bait, sweetheart, to try and trap you into letting me see your real feelings.'

'You never guessed?'

He shook his head. 'No, but just once or twice I hoped…' He kissed her again and Mrs Buckle opened the door, gave a surprised squawk and began to retreat. Gideon didn't loosen his hold on Deborah. 'Ah, Mrs Buckle—we shall both be out for lunch, and while we are gone, you may start making plans for Christmas and don't tell me that there isn't enough time. Spend what you want to. My wife and I will arrange the details while we are at her mother's and let you know this evening.'

Mrs Buckle nodded speechlessly and disappeared as Deborah said: 'But Gideon, darling, how can we at the last minute…'

'Say that again my love.'

'At the last minute…'

'Quite easily. Say that again, darling.'

'At the last minute?'

'Not that bit…'

'Gideon, darling,' said Deborah and was kissed for her pains.

* * * * *

A Valentine For Daisy

CHAPTER ONE

THE HAZY SUNSHINE of a late July afternoon highlighted the steady stream of small children issuing from one of the solid Victorian houses in the quiet road. It was an orderly exit; Mrs Gower-Jones, who owned the nursery school and prided herself upon its genteel reputation, frowned upon noisy children. As their mothers and nannies, driving smart little Fiats, larger Mercedes and Rovers, arrived, the children gathered in the hall, and were released under the eye of whoever was seeing them off the premises.

Today this was a small, rather plump girl whose pale brown hair was pinned back into a plaited knot, a style which did nothing for her looks: too wide a mouth, a small pert nose and a determined chin, the whole redeemed from plainness by a pair of grey eyes fringed with curling mousy lashes. As Mrs Gower-Jones so often complained to the senior of her assistants, the girl had no style although there was no gainsaying the fact that the children liked her; moreover even the most tiresome child could be coaxed by her to obedience.

The last child seen safely into maternal care, the girl closed the door and crossed the wide hall to the first of the rooms on either side of it. There were two girls there, clearing away the results of the children's activities. They were too young for lessons but they spent their day modelling clay, painting, playing simple games and being read to, and the mess at the end of the afternoon was considerable.

They both looked up as the girl joined them. 'Thank heaven for Saturday tomorrow!' exclaimed the older of the girls. 'Pay day too. Ron's driving me to Dover this evening; we're going over to Boulogne to do some shopping.' She swept an armful of coloured bricks into a plastic bucket. 'What about you, Mandy?'

The other girl was wiping a small table clean. 'I'm going down to Bournemouth—six of us—it'll be a bit of a squeeze in the car but who cares? There's dancing at the Winter Gardens.'

They both looked at the girl who had just joined them. 'What about you, Daisy?'

They asked her every Friday, she thought, not really wanting to know, but not wanting to be unfriendly. She said now, as she almost always did, 'Oh, I don't know,' and smiled at them, aware that though they liked her they thought her rather dull and pitied her for the lack of excitement in her life. Well, it wasn't exciting but, as she told herself shortly from time to time, she was perfectly content with it.

It took an hour or more to restore the several play-rooms to the state of perfection required by Mrs Gower-Jones; only then, after she had inspected them, did she hand over their pay packets, reminding them, quite unnecessarily, to be at their posts by half-past eight on Monday morning.

Mandy and the older girl, Joyce, hurried away to catch the minibus which would take them to Old Sarum where they both lived, and Daisy went round the back of the house to the shed where she parked her bike. It was three miles to Wilton from Salisbury and main road all the way; she didn't much like the journey, though, for the traffic was always heavy, especially at this time of the year with the tourist season not yet over even though the schools had returned. She cycled down the quiet road and presently circled the roundabout and joined the stream of homegoing traffic, thinking of the weekend ahead of her. She went over the various duties awaiting her without self-pity; she had shouldered them cheerfully several years earlier when her father had died and her mother, cosseted all her married life, had been completely lost, unable to cope with the bills, income tax and household expenses with which he had always dealt. Daisy had watched her mother become more and more depressed and muddled and finally she had taken over, dealing tidily with the household finances and shielding her mother from business worries.

In this she had been considerably helped by her young sister. Pamela was still at school, fifteen years old, clever and bent on making a name for herself but understanding that her mother had led a sheltered life which made it impossible for her to stand on her own two feet. She knew that it was hard luck on Daisy, although they never discussed it, but she had the good sense to see that there was nothing much to be done about it. Daisy was a darling but she had never had a boyfriend and it had to be faced—she had no looks to speak of. Pamela, determined to get as many A levels as possible, go to college and take up the scientific career she had decided upon, none the less intended to marry someone rich who would solve all their problems. She had no doubts about this since she was a very pretty girl and knew exactly what she wanted from life.

Daisy wove her careful way through the fast-flowing traffic, past the emerging tourists from Wilton House, and turned left at the centre of the crossroads in the middle of the little town. Her father had worked in the offices of the Wilton estate and she had been born and lived all her life in the small cottage, the end one of a row backing the high walls surrounding the park, on the edge of the town. She wheeled her bike through the gate beside the house, parked it in the shed in the back garden and went indoors.

Her mother was in the kitchen, sitting at the table, stringing beans. She was small like Daisy, her hair still only faintly streaked with grey, her pretty face marred by a worried frown.

'Darling, it's lamb chops for supper but I forgot to buy them…'

Daisy dropped a kiss on her parent's cheek. 'I'll go for them now, Mother, while you make the tea. Pam will lay the table when she gets in.'

She went back to the shed and got out her bike and cycled back to the crossroads again. The butcher was halfway down the row of shops on the other side but as she reached the traffic-lights they turned red and she put a foot down, impatient to get across. The traffic was heavy now and the light was tantalisingly slow. A car drew up beside her and she turned to look at it. A dark grey Rolls-Royce. She eyed it appreciatively, starting at the back and allowing her eyes to roam to its bonnet until she became aware of the driver watching her.

She stared back, feeling for some reason foolish, frowning a little at the thin smile on his handsome face. He appeared to be a big man, his hair as dark as his heavy-lidded eyes…it was a pity that the lights changed then and the big car had slid silently away before she was back in the saddle, leaving her with the feeling that something important to her had just happened. 'Ridiculous,' she said so loudly that a passer-by on the pavement looked at her oddly.

Pamela was home when she got back and together they set about preparing their supper before sitting down in the pleasant little sitting-room to drink the tea Mrs Pelham had made.

'Been a nice day; have you enjoyed it?' asked Pamela, gobbling biscuits.

'It's not been too bad. The new children seem all right. I've got four this term—that makes fifteen. Two of the new ones are twins, a girl and a boy, and I suspect that they're going to be difficult…'

'I thought Mrs Gower-Jones only took children from suitable families.' Mrs Pelham smiled across at her daughter.

'Oh, they're suitable—their father's a baronet or something,' said Daisy vaguely. 'They're almost four years old and I think they'll drive me mad by the end of the term.'

Pamela laughed. 'And it's only just begun…'

They talked about something else then and after supper Daisy sat down at the table, doling out the housekeeping money, school bus fares, pocket money, and then she put what was over—and there wasn't much—into the old biscuit tin on the kitchen mantelpiece. They managed—just—on her wages and her mother's pension; just for a while after her father's death they had got into difficulties and her mother had appealed to her for help, and ever since then Daisy sat down every Friday evening, making a point of asking her mother's advice about the spending of their income. Mrs Pelham always told her to do whatever was best, but all the same Daisy always asked. She loved her mother dearly, realising that she had had a sheltered girlhood and marriage and needed to be taken care of—something which she and Pamela did to the best of their ability, although Daisy was aware that within a few years Pamela would leave home for a university and almost certainly she would marry. About her own future Daisy didn't allow herself to bother overmuch. She had friends, of course, but none of the young men she knew had evinced the slightest desire to fall in love with her and, studying her ordinary face in her dressing-table mirror, she wasn't surprised. It was a pity she had no chance to train for something; her job was pleasant enough, not well paid but near her home and there were holidays when she could catch up on household chores and see to the garden.

She was a sensible girl, not given to discontent, although she dreamed of meeting a man who would fall in love with her, marry her and take over the small burdens of her life. He would need to have money, of course, and a pleasant house with a large garden where the children would be able to play. It was a dream she didn't allow herself to dwell upon too often.

The weekend went far too quickly as it always did. She took her mother shopping and stopped for coffee in the little town while Pam stayed at home studying, and after lunch Daisy went into the quite big garden and grubbed up weeds, hindered by Razor the family cat, a dignified middle-aged beast who was as devoted to them all as they were to him. On Sunday they went to church and, since it was a sultry day, spent the rest of the day in the garden.

Daisy left home first on Monday morning; Mrs Gower-Jones liked her assistants to be ready and waiting when the first of the children arrived at half-past eight, which meant that Daisy had to leave home an hour earlier than that. The sultriness had given way to thundery rain and the roads were wet and slippery. She was rounding the corner by Wilton House when she skidded and a car braked to a sudden halt inches from her back wheel.

She put a foot to the ground to balance herself and looked over her shoulder. It was the Rolls-Royce, and the same man was driving it; in other circumstances she would have been delighted to see him again, for she had thought of him several times during the weekend, but now her feelings towards him were anything but friendly.

'You are driving much too fast,' she told him severely. 'You might have killed me.'

'Thirty miles an hour,' he told her unsmilingly, 'and you appear alive to me.' His rather cool gaze flickered over her plastic mac with its unbecoming hood framing her ordinary features. She chose to ignore it.

'Well, drive more carefully in future,' she advised him in the voice she used to quell the more recalcitrant of the children at Mrs Gower-Jones's.

She didn't wait for his answer but got on her bike and set off once more, and when the big car slid gently past her she didn't look at its driver, although she was sorely tempted to do so.

She was the first to arrive and Mrs Gower-Jones was already there, poking her rather sharp nose into the various rooms. As soon as she saw Daisy she started to speak. The play-rooms were a disgrace, she had found several broken crayons on the floor and there were splodges of Play-Doh under one of the tables. 'And here it is, half-past eight, and all of you late again.'

'I'm here,' Daisy reminded her in a matter-of-fact voice, and, since her employer sounded rather more bad-tempered than usual, she added mendaciously, 'and I passed Mandy and Joyce as I came along the road.'

'It is a fortunate thing for you girls that I'm a tolerant employer,' observed Mrs Gower-Jones peevishly. 'I see that you'll have to make the place fit to be seen before the children get here.'

She swept away to the nicely appointed room where she interviewed parents and spent a good deal of the day 'doing the paperwork', as she called it, but Daisy, going in hurriedly one day over some minor emergency, had been in time to see the *Tatler* lying open on the desk, and she was of the opinion that the paperwork didn't amount to much.

The children started to arrive, a thin trickle at first with time to bid a leisurely goodbye to mothers or nannies and later, almost late, barely stopping to bid farewell to their guardians, running into the cloakroom, tossing their small garments and satchels all over the place and bickering with each other. Mondays were never good days, thought Daisy, coaxing a furious small boy to hand over an even smaller girl's satchel.

The morning began badly and the day got worse. The cook, a local girl who saw to the dinners for the children, didn't turn up. Instead her mother telephoned to say that she had appendicitis and was to go into hospital at once.

Daisy, patiently superintending the messy pleasures of Play-Doh, was surprised when Mrs Gower-Jones came unexpectedly through the door and demanded her attention.

'Can you cook, Miss Pelham?' she wanted to know urgently.

'Well, yes—nothing fancy, though, Mrs Gower-Jones.' Daisy removed a lump of dough from a small girl's hair and returned it to the bowl.

'Mandy and Joyce say they can't,' observed Mrs Gower-Jones, crossly, 'so it will have to be you. The cook's had to go to hospital—I must say it's most inconsiderate of her. The children must have their dinners.'

'You want me to cook it?' asked Daisy calmly. 'But who is to look after the children? I can't be in two places at once.'

'I'll stay with them. For heaven's sake go along to the kitchen and get started; the daily girl's there, and she can do the potatoes and so on…'

Daisy reflected that if she were her employer she would very much prefer to cook the dinner than oversee a bunch of rather naughty children, but she didn't voice her thought, merely handed Mrs Gower-Jones her apron, advised her that the children would need to be cleaned up before their dinners and took herself off to the kitchen.

Marlene, the daily help, was standing by the kitchen table, doing nothing. Daisy wished her good morning, suggested that she might put the kettle on and make a cup of tea and said that she had come to cook the dinner. Marlene, roused from daydreaming, did as she was asked, volunteered to peel the potatoes and the carrots and then observed that the minced meat had just been delivered.

'Beefburgers,' said Daisy; mince, offered as such, never went down well—perhaps the beefburgers would. Marlene, brought to life by a mug of tea, saw to the potatoes and carrots and began to collect cutlery ready to lay the tables. Daisy, her small nose in and out of store cupboards, added this and that to the mince, thumped it into shape, rolled it out and cut it into circles with one of Mrs Gower-Jones's best wine glasses, since there was nothing else handy. She would have liked to do chips but there wasn't time, so she puréed the potatoes with a generous dollop of butter and glazed the carrots. By half-past twelve she was ready to dish up.

Mrs Gower-Jones took over then, drawing hissing breaths at the nicely browned beefburgers and the mounds of buttery potatoes. 'And really,' she protested crossly, 'there is no need to put parsley on the carrots, Miss Pelham.'

Which was all the thanks Daisy got.

There was a temporary cook the next day, an older woman who spoke little English, and who, in Daisy's opinion, didn't look quite clean. She served up fish fingers and chips with tinned peas. Daisy thought that she wasn't a cook at all but probably all Mrs Gower-Jones could get at a moment's notice.

When she went into the kitchen the next morning to fetch the children's mid-morning milk the sight of the woman preparing dinner in a muddle of dirty saucepans, potato peelings and unwashed dishes made her glad that Mrs Gower-Jones's meanness stipulated that her assistants should bring their own lunches. Unwilling to disparage a fellow worker, all the same she went in search of her employer.

'The new cook seems to be in a bit of a muddle,' she ventured. 'The kitchen...'

'Attend to your own work,' commanded Mrs Gower-Jones. 'She is perfectly capable of attending to hers.'

The children ate their dinner—what Mrs Gower-Jones described as a wholesome stew made from the best ingredients, followed by ice-cream—and Daisy, Mandy and Joyce took it in turns to eat their own sandwiches before arranging the children on their little camp beds for their afternoon nap, a peaceful hour during which they prepared for the hour or so still left before the children were collected. Only it wasn't peaceful; before the hour was up every child—and there were forty of them—was screaming his or her head off, clasping their small stomachs in pain and being sick into the bargain.

Daisy, rousing Mrs Gower-Jones from the little nap she took after lunch while the children were quiet, didn't mince her words. 'All the children are vomiting and worse—something they've eaten. They'll have to go to hospital. I'll phone…'

She sped away to dial 999 and then to join the hard-pressed Mandy and Joyce. The place was a shambles by now and some of the children looked very ill. They wiped hands and faces and comforted their wailing charges and had no time for Mrs Gower-Jones, who had taken a look and fled with her hands over her mouth, but she appeared again when the first of the ambulances arrived, asserting her authority in a shrinking fashion.

'I shall have to notify the parents,' she uttered to no one in particular. 'Miss Pelham, go to the hospital and let me know immediately how the children are. Mandy, Joyce, you can stay here and clear up.'

It took some time to get all the children away; Daisy, squashed in with the last of them, looked down at herself. She smelt nasty for a start and the state of her overall bore witness to that fact; she felt hot and dirty and very worried. Food poisoning—she had no doubt that was what it was—was no light matter with small children; she remembered the new cook and shuddered.

Casualty was full of screaming children although some of them were too quiet. Daisy, making herself known without fuss, was led away to wash herself and remove the overall and then she was given a plastic apron to take its place. Feeling cleaner, she was handed over to a brisk young woman with an armful of admission slips and asked to name the children. It took quite a while for she stopped to comfort those who weren't feeling too bad and bawled to her to be taken home. The brisk young woman got a little impatient but Daisy, her kind heart torn by the miserable little white faces, wasn't to be hurried. The last two children were the twins, no longer difficult but greenish-white and lackadaisical, staring up at her in a manner so unlike their boisterous selves that she had a pang of fear. Disregarding her brisk companion's demand for their names, she bent over the trolley where they lay one at each end.

'You'll be all right very soon,' she assured them, and took limp little hands in hers. 'The doctor will come and make you well again…'

Two large hands calmly clasped her waist and lifted her to one side. 'He's here now,' said a voice in her ear and she looked up into the face of the owner of the Rolls-Royce.

Katie and Josh spoke as one. 'Uncle Valentine, my tummy hurts,' and Katie went even greener and gave an ominous heave. Daisy, a practical girl, held out her plastic apron and the man beside her said,

'Ah, sensible as well as sharp-tongued.' He looked over his shoulder. 'Staff Nurse, these two are dehydrated; get a drip up, will you? Dr Sims will see to it. Where's the child you told me couldn't stop vomiting? I'll see him next.' He patted the twins on their sweaty little heads, advised Daisy in a kindly voice to dispose of her apron as quickly as possible and, accompanied by one of the casualty sisters, went away, to disappear into the ordered chaos.

The brisk young woman showed her where to dump the apron, took a look at her overall and found her another plastic pinny. 'If I could have their names,' she said urgently. 'They called Dr Seymour Uncle Valentine…'

'Thorley, Katie and Josh, twins, almost four years old,' Daisy told her. 'They live along the Wylye valley—Steeple Langford, I believe. If I could see one of the sisters just for a minute perhaps she could let me know if any of the children are causing worry. Mrs Gower-Jones told me to phone her as soon as possible so that she can warn the parents.'

Her companion gave a snort. 'I should have thought it was Mrs whoever-it-is who should have come here with the children. Still, I'll see if I can find someone for you.'

A nurse and a young doctor had arrived as they talked and they began to set up the saline drips, no easy task for the twins took exception to this, screaming with rage and kicking and rolling round the trolley.

'Well, hold them still, will you?' begged the doctor impatiently. 'What a pair of little horrors…'

'Well, they don't feel well,' said Daisy with some spirit, 'and they're very small.' She leaned over the trolley, holding the wriggling children to her, talking to them in her quiet voice.

Dr Seymour, coming back to take another look, paused for a moment to admire the length of leg—Daisy had such nice legs, although no one had ever told her so. He said breezily, 'They need a ball and chain, although I have no doubt they prefer to have this young lady.' As Daisy resumed a more dignified position, he added, 'Thanks for your help—my nephew and niece are handfuls, are they not?' He ignored the young doctor's stare. 'You work at the nursery school? You may telephone the headmistress or whatever she is called and assure her that none of the children is in danger. I shall keep in some of the children for the night—Sister will give you their names. Run along now…'

Daisy, mild by nature, went pink. He had spoken to her as though she were one of the children and she gave him a cross look. If she had known how to toss her head she would have tossed it; as it was she said with a dignity which sat ill on her dishevelled appearance, 'I'm not at all surprised to know that the twins are your nephew and niece, Doctor.'

She gave him a small nod, smiled at the children and walked away; fortunately she didn't see his wide grin.

She was kept busy for quite some time; first getting a list of the children who would be staying for the night and then phoning Mrs Gower-Jones. That lady was in a cold rage; the nursery school would have to be closed down for the time being at least—her reputation would suffer—'and you will be out of a job,' she told Daisy nastily.

Daisy realised that her employer was battling with strong emotions. 'Yes, of course,' she said soothingly, 'but if you would just tell me what you want me to do next. Shall I stay until the children are collected?'

'Well of course,' said Mrs Gower-Jones ungratefully, 'I've enough to do here and Mandy and Joyce are still clearing up. I have never seen such a frightful mess; really, I should have thought you girls could have controlled the children.'

A remark which Daisy thought best not to answer.

She phoned her mother then went back to organise the children who would be fetched as soon as their parents had been told. Anxious mothers and nannies began arriving and in the ensuing chaos of handing over the children fit to go home Daisy lost count of time. They all, naturally enough, wanted to see Mrs Gower-Jones, and since she wasn't there several of them gave vent to their strong feelings, bombarding Daisy with questions and complaints. No matter that they had already had reassuring talks with Sister; they could hardly blame her for their children's discomfiture, but Daisy, unassuming and polite, was a splendid target for their indignation. She was battling patiently with the last of the mothers, a belligerent lady who appeared to think that Daisy was responsible for the entire unfortunate affair, when Dr Seymour loomed up beside her.

He had been there all the time, going to and fro with his houseman and registrar, making sure that the children were recovering, but Daisy had been too occupied to see him. Now he took the matter smoothly into his own hands.

'A most unfortunate thing to happen; luckily, none of the children is seriously affected.' He glanced down at the wan-faced small boy clutching his mother's hand. 'This little chap will be fine in a couple of days—Sister has told you what to do, I expect? This young lady is an assistant at the nursery school and is not to be blamed in any way. The matter will be investigated by the proper authorities but it is evident that the cause was either in the cooking or in the food. I suggest that you take the matter up with the principal of the school.'

Daisy, listening to this, reflected that he had a pleasant voice, deep and unhurried and just now with a hint of steel in it. Which might have accounted for the ungracious apology she received before the small boy was borne away.

'The last one?' asked the doctor.

'Yes. Only I'm not sure if I'm supposed to stay—there are the children who are to remain here for the night; their mothers are here but they might want to ask questions—the children's clothes and so on.'

'What's the telephone number of this nursery school?'

She told him, too tired to bother about why he wanted to

know. She would have liked to go home but first she would have to go back and get her bike and very likely Mrs Gower-Jones would want a detailed account of what had transpired at the hospital. She yawned, and choked on it as Dr Seymour said from behind her, 'Mrs Gower-Jones is coming here—she should have been here in the first place. You will go home.' It was a statement, not a suggestion and he turned on his heel and then paused. 'How?'

'I have my bike at the school.' She hesitated. 'And my purse and things.'

'They'll be there in the morning; you can fetch them. The place will be closed as a nursery school at least for the time being. Did you come like that?'

She frowned. 'Yes.'

'I'll drive you to your home. Come along.'

Daisy, a mild girl, said, 'No, thank you,' with something of a snap. But that was a waste of time.

'Don't be silly,' advised Dr Seymour, and he caught her by the arm and marched her briskly out of the hospital and stuffed her into the Rolls while she was still thinking of the dignified reply she wished to make. No girl liked to be told she was silly.

'Where to?'

'Wilton.'

'Where in Wilton?'

'If you put me down by the market square…'

He sighed. 'Where in Wilton?'

'Box Cottage—on the way to Burcombe. But I can easily walk…'

He didn't bother to answer as he drove through the city streets and along the main road to Wilton. Once there, within minutes, he turned left at the crossroads by the market. 'Left or right?' he asked.

'On the left—the last cottage in this row.'

He slowed the car and stopped, and to her surprise got out to open her door. He opened the little garden gate too, which gave her mother time to get to the door.

'Darling, whatever has happened? You said the children were ill—' Mrs Pelham took in Daisy's appearance. 'Are you ill too? You look as though you've been sick…'

'Not me, the children, Mother, and I'm quite all right.' Since the doctor was towering over her she remembered her manners and introduced him.

'Dr Seymour very kindly gave me a lift.'

'How very kind of you.' Her mother smiled charmingly at him. 'Do come in and have a cup of coffee.'

He saw the look on Daisy's face and his thin mouth twitched. 'I must get back to the hospital, I'm afraid; perhaps another time?'

'Any time,' said Mrs Pelham largely, ignoring Daisy's frown. 'Do you live in Wilton? I don't remember seeing your car…?'

'In Salisbury, but I have a sister living along the Wylye valley.'

'Well, we don't want to keep you. Thank you for bringing Daisy home.' Mrs Pelham offered a hand but Daisy didn't. She had seen his lifted eyebrows at her name; Daisy was a silly name and it probably amused him. She wished him goodbye in a cool voice, echoing her mother's thanks. She didn't like him; he was overbearing and had ridden roughshod over her objections to being given a lift. That she would still have been biking tiredly from Salisbury without his offer was something she chose to ignore.

'What a nice man,' observed her mother as they watched the car sliding away, back to the crossroads. 'How very kind of him to bring you home. You must tell us all about it, darling—' she wrinkled her nose '—but perhaps you'd like a bath first.'

When Daisy reached the nursery school in the morning she found Mrs Gower-Jones in a black mood. The cook had disappeared and the police were trying to trace her, she had had people inspecting her kitchen and asking questions and the school was to be closed until it had been thoroughly cleaned and inspected. A matter of some weeks, even months. 'So you can take a week's notice,' said Mrs Gower-Jones. 'I've seen the other girls too. Don't expect to come back here either; if and when I open again parents won't want to see any of you—they'll always suspect you.'

'I should have thought,' observed Daisy in a reasonable voice, 'that they would be more likely to suspect you, Mrs Gower-Jones. After all, you engaged the cook.'

Mrs Gower-Jones had always considered Daisy to be a quiet, easily put-upon girl; now she looked at her in amazement while her face slowly reddened. 'Well, really, Miss Pelham—how dare you say such a thing?'

'Well, it's true.' Daisy added without rancour, 'Anyway I wouldn't want to come back here to work; I'd feel as suspicious as the parents.'

'Leave at once,' said her employer, 'and don't expect a reference. I'll post on your cheque.'

'I'll wait while you write it, Mrs Gower-Jones,' said Daisy mildly.

She was already making plans as she cycled back to Wilton. She would have to get another job as soon as possible; her mother's pension wasn't enough to keep all three of them and Pamela had at least two more years at school. They paid the estate a very modest rent but there were still taxes and lighting and heating and food. They relied on Daisy's wages to pay for clothes and small extra comforts. There was never any money to save; her father had left a few hundred pounds in the bank but that was for a rainy day, never to be spent unless in dire emergency.

Back home, she explained everything to her mother, carefully keeping any note of anxiety out of her voice. They would be able to go on much as usual for a week or two and surely in that time she would find a job. It was a pity she wasn't trained for anything; she had gone to a good school because her father had been alive then and the fees had been found, although at the cost of holidays and small luxuries, and since she had done well the plan had been to send her to one of the minor universities, leading to a teaching post eventually. His death had been unexpected and premature; Daisy left the university after only a year there and came home to shoulder the responsibilities of the household and take the job at the nursery school.

Her mother reassured, she went out and bought the local paper and searched the jobs column. There was nothing; at least, there was plenty of work for anyone who understood computers and the like and there were several pigpersons wanted, for pig breeding flourished in her part of the world. It was a great pity that the tourist season would be over soon, otherwise she might have enquired if there was work for her in the tearooms at Wilton House. Tomorrow, she decided, she would go into Salisbury, visit the agencies and the job centre.

It was a bad time of year to find work, she was told; now if she had asked when the season started, no doubt there would have been something for her—a remark kindly meant but of little comfort to her.

By the end of the week her optimism was wearing thin although she preserved a composed front towards her mother and Pamela. She was sitting at her mother's writing desk answering an advertisement for a mother's help when someone knocked on the door. Pamela was in her room, deep in schoolwork; her mother was out shopping. Daisy went to answer it.

CHAPTER TWO

DAISY RECOGNISED THE person on the doorstep. 'Lady Thorley—please come in. The twins are all right?'

'Quite recovered,' said their mother. 'I wanted to talk to you…'

Daisy led the way into the small sitting-room, nicely furnished and with a bowl of roses on the Georgian circular table under the window, offered a chair and then sat down opposite her visitor, her hands folded quietly in her lap, composedly waiting to hear the reason for the visit. It would be something to do with the nursery school, she felt sure, some small garment missing…

'Are you out of a job?' Lady Thorley smiled. 'Forgive me for being nosy, but Mrs Gower-Jones tells me that she has closed the place down for some time at least.'

'Well, yes, she has, and we all had a week's notice…'

'Then if you are free, would you consider coming to us for a while? The twins—they're a handful, more than I can cope with, and they like you. If you hear of something better you would be free to go, but you would be a godsend. There must be other nursery schools, although I don't know of any. I thought that if you would come while I find a governess for them…only I don't want to be hurried over that—she will have to be someone rather special. Would you give it a try?'

'I could come each day?'

'Oh, yes. We're at Steeple Langford—about three miles from here. Is there a bus?'

'I have a bike.'

'You'll give it a try? Is half-past eight too early for you? Until five o'clock—that's a long day, I know, but you would have Saturday and Sunday.' She hesitated. 'And perhaps occasionally you would sleep in if we were about to go out for the evening? We have some good servants but I'd rather it was you.' And when Daisy hesitated she added, 'I don't know what you were paid by Mrs Gower-Jones but we would pay the usual rate.' She named a sum which sent Daisy's mousy eyebrows up. Twice the amount Mrs Gower-Jones had paid her; heaven-sent, although she felt bound to tell her visitor that it was more than she had earned at the nursery school.

'By the end of the week you will agree with me that you will have earned every penny. You have only had the twins for a few days, diluted with other children. Full-strength, as it were, they're formidable.' She smiled charmingly. 'You see, I'm not pretending that they're little angels. I love them dearly but because of that I'm not firm enough.'

'When would you like me to start?' asked Daisy. 'Only you'll want references.'

'Oh, never mind those,' said Lady Thorley breezily, 'Valentine told me that you were a sensible girl with an honest face and he's always right.'

Daisy blushed and Lady Thorley thought how pleasant it was to find a girl who still could, happily unaware that it wasn't a blush at all, just Daisy's temper, seldom roused, coming to the surface. Even if that was all he could think of to say about her, it would have been far better if he had kept quiet—honest and sensible indeed; what girl wanted to be called that?

For a moment she was tempted to change her mind and refuse the job, but then she remembered the marvellous wages… 'How kind,' she murmured, and agreed to cycle over to Steeple Langford the next morning.

Lady Thorley went presently and Daisy tore up her reply to the advertisement for a home help and then did cautious sums on the back of the writing paper. The job wouldn't last forever—a month, six weeks perhaps—but the money would take care of the phone bill and the gas and electricity as well. There would be enough left over for her mother to have a pair of good shoes ready for the winter, and Pamela to have another of the baggy sweaters she craved, and she herself—Daisy sucked the end of her pen—torn between high-heeled elegant shoes she would probably never have the chance to wear and a pair of sensible boots; last winter's pair had had their day and were beyond repair. She was still brooding over this when her mother and Pamela came back, and, much heartened by the news, Mrs Pelham fetched the bottle of sherry they hoarded for special occasions and they all had a glass. 'I mustn't forget Razor,' said Daisy. 'I'll get some of that luxury catfood he enjoys and perhaps a tin of sardines.'

The road along the Wylye was quiet, used mainly by local people, winding from one small village to the next one with glimpses of the river from time to time and plenty of trees. It was a splendid morning and Daisy cycled along it trying to guess what the job would turn out to be. Hard work, no doubt, but the money was good…

The Thorleys' house was on the further side of Steeple Langford, a roomy place typical of the area, with plenty of large windows, a veranda and a wide porch. It was surrounded by nicely laid-out grounds with plenty of trees and as she went up the short drive she could see ponies and a donkey in the small adjoining field.

The front door was opened as she reached it and the two children and a black Labrador dog spilled out noisily. Daisy got off her bike. 'Hello,' she said cheerfully, 'what's your dog's name?'

'Boots. Have you got a dog?' They had crowded round her, all three of them.

'No, though we had one when I was a little girl. We have a cat; he's called Razor.'

'Why?'

'He's very sharp…'

The twins hooted with mirth. 'May we see him?'

'Perhaps one day your mother will let you come and see him. We'll see.'

'Why do all grown-ups say "we'll see"?'

Daisy was saved from answering this by the appearance of Lady Thorley, wearing the kind of thin jersey dress that Daisy coveted.

'Good morning. May we call you Daisy? Come on inside and have a look round. We've just finished breakfast but there's coffee if you'd like it.'

Daisy declined the coffee, propped her bike against the porch and, with a twin on either side of her, went into the house.

It was as nice inside as it was out; comfortably furnished

with some good pieces, a great many comfortable chairs, flowers everywhere and a slight untidiness which one would expect in a house where there were children and dogs. The nursery was on the first floor overlooking the back lawn, a large room with a low shelf around its walls to accommodate the various toys the twins possessed. There was a low table too and small chairs and also a comfortable chair or two for grown-ups.

'They prefer to be out of doors,' said their mother. 'They're very energetic, I'm afraid. I'll show you the garden and then leave you, shall I?' She led the way downstairs again. 'The children have their milk about half-past ten and Jenny will bring your coffee at the same time. They have their lunch just after twelve, with me—and you, of course—and they have their tea at five o'clock before bed at six o'clock.' Lady Thorley hesitated. 'I'm sometimes out to lunch…' She looked doubtfully at Daisy.

'I'm sure Josh and Katie will keep me company when you are,' said Daisy matter-of-factly and watched their mother's face light up with relief.

'The children had a nanny until quite recently,' confided Lady Thorley. 'She—she was very strict.'

'I don't know if I'm strict or not,' said Daisy cheerfully. She beamed down at the children. 'We'll have to find out, won't we?'

She spent the rest of the morning in the garden with the twins and Boots, pausing only long enough to drink her coffee while they reluctantly drank their milk. At lunch they were difficult, picking at their food, casting sly glances at their mother as they spilt their drinks, kicked the rungs of their chairs and upset the salt cellar. Lady Thorley said helplessly, 'Darlings, do behave yourselves.' She spoke in a loving voice which held no authority at all and they took no notice of her.

'I wonder,' observed Daisy pleasantly, 'if it would be a good idea, Lady Thorley, if Josh and Katie were to have their lunch in the nursery for a few days—by themselves, of course…? I'll sit in the room with them, naturally.'

Lady Thorley caught Daisy's look. 'What a good idea,' she said enthusiastically. 'Why didn't I think of it before? We'll start tomorrow.'

The twins exchanged glances. 'Don't want to,' said Josh, and was echoed by Katie. They had stuck their small lower lips out, ready to be mutinous.

'Well,' said Daisy, 'if you really don't want to, will you eat your lunch like grown-up people with your mother and me?'

'You're strict…'

'Not a bit of it. While you're having your rest I'll read whatever story you want.'

It had seemed a long day, thought Daisy as she cycled back home, but she had enjoyed it. The twins were nice children, spoilt by their mother and probably too strictly brought up by the nanny. She began to plan a daily regime which might, at least in part, correct some of that. They were very bright for their age; she would have to win their confidence as well as their liking.

By the end of the week she felt reasonably sure that she had done that; the twins were about the naughtiest children she had had to deal with while she had worked for Mrs Gower-Jones, and so charming with their large blue eyes and innocent little faces that it was sometimes difficult to be firm, but they seemed to like her and since she ignored their small tantrums she felt that she was making progress. She liked the job too, and enjoyed the cycle ride each day and the long hours spent out of doors with the children. The weather was delightful too, dry and warm with no hint of autumn. Of course, the ride wouldn't be so nice in rain and wind, but she would be gone by then, although Lady Thorley hadn't mentioned the likelihood of a governess yet.

Lady Thorley was going out to lunch, Daisy remembered as she pedalled along the quiet road, and since it was such a fine day perhaps she and the twins could have a picnic in the garden; she was good friends with the cook and the elderly housemaid and surely between them they could concoct a picnic instead of the usual meal indoors.

The twins were waiting for her with faithful Boots and she went up to the nursery with them for an hour's playschool—Plasticine and wooden blocks, crayons and large sheets of scribbling paper—and they were tidying up when their mother came to say that she was going out to her lunch party and would be back by teatime. She looked elegant and pretty and Daisy had no doubt in her mind that her husband must adore her. The twins were kissed and told to be good, and Daisy was to be sure and ask for anything she might want. The three of them escorted her to the door and waved as she drove away in her smart little Mini, and Katie began to sniff sorrowfully.

'Who's coming to help get our picnic ready?' asked Daisy, and whisked the moppet out into the garden with Josh and Boots. 'Look, Cook's put a table ready; let's put the plates and knives and things on it and then we'll go to the kitchen and fetch the food.'

She was leading the way back to the garden, laden with a tray of dishes—hard-boiled eggs, bacon sandwiches, little sausages on sticks and a mushroom quiche—when she saw Dr Seymour sitting on the grass leaning against the table.

The children had seen him too; the dish of apples Josh had been carrying went tumbling to the ground and Katie, close behind him, dropped the plastic mugs she held as they galloped towards him with shrieks of delight. He uncoiled his vast person in one neat movement and received their onslaught with lazy good humour. 'May I stay to lunch?' he asked Daisy and, since he quite obviously intended to anyway, she said politely,

'Of course, Dr Seymour. Lady Thorley is out but she'll be back at teatime.' She put down her tray. 'I'll fetch the rest of the food...'

She started back to the house and found him beside her, trailed by the twins and Boots. 'Quite happy here?' he wanted to know.

'Yes, thank you.'

'Pleased to see me again?'

What an outrageous man, thought Daisy, and what a colossal conceit. She said pleasantly, 'Should I be, Dr Seymour?'

'Upon reflection, perhaps not.' They had reached the kitchen and found Cook, who had seen his car, cutting a mound of beef sandwiches. 'You'll be peckish, sir,' she said comfortably. 'Hard-boiled eggs and sausages on sticks aren't hardly fitting for a gentleman of your size, if you don't mind me saying it.'

He took a sandwich and bit into it. 'When have I ever disputed an opinion of yours, Mrs Betts? And if I can't finish them I'm sure Daisy will help me out.'

So she was Daisy, was she? And she had no intention of eating his beef sandwiches. She didn't say so although she gave him a chilly look.

It was impossible to remain chilly for long; the twins, on

their best behaviour because their favourite uncle was going to share their picnic, saw to that. The meal was an unqualified success; Josh ate everything he was offered and, since Katie always did as he did, the usual patient battle to get them to eat didn't take place; instead, the doctor kept them entertained with a mixture of mild teasing and ridiculous stories in the face of which it was impossible to remain stand-offish; indeed Daisy enjoyed herself and found herself forgetting how much she disapproved of him. That was until he remarked, as the last of the lemonade was being drunk, 'I hope Meg has got you on a long lease.'

She gave him a puzzled look. 'A long lease…?'

'It would seem to me that you have all the makings of a family nanny, handed down from one generation to another.'

Daisy, a mild-tempered girl, choked back rage. 'I have no intention of being anything of the sort.' Her pleasant voice held a decidedly acid note.

'No? Planning to get married?'

'No, and if I may say so, Dr Seymour, I must remind you that it's none of your business.'

'No, no, of course it isn't; put it down to idle curiosity.'

Josh, for nearly four years old, was very bright. 'You're not married either, Uncle Val; I know 'cos Mummy said it was high time and it was time you thought about it.'

His uncle ate a last sandwich. 'Mummy's quite right; I must think about it.'

Daisy began to collect up the remains of their meal. 'Everyone carry something,' ordered the doctor, 'and no dropping it on the way to the kitchen. What happens next?' He looked at Daisy.

'They rest for an hour—I read to them.'

'Oh, good. I could do with a nap myself. We can all fit

into the hammock easily enough—not you, of course, Daisy. What gem of literature are you reading at the moment?'

'Grimm's fairy-tales; they choose a different story each day.'

She wasn't sure how to reply to the doctor's remarks; she suspected that he was making fun of her, not unkindly but perhaps to amuse himself. Well, she had no intention of letting him annoy her. 'Perhaps you would like to choose?' she asked him as, the picnic cleared away, they crossed the lawn to where the hammock stood under the shade of the trees.

He arranged a padded chair for her before lying back in the hammock with the twins crushed on either side of him. '"Faithful John",' he told her promptly.

She opened the book. 'It's rather long,' she said doubtfully.

'I dare say we shall all be asleep long before you've finished.'

He closed his eyes and the children lay quietly; there was nothing for it but to begin.

He had been right; Josh dropped off first and then Katie, and since he hadn't opened his eyes she supposed that the doctor had gone to sleep too. She closed the book on its bookmark, kicked off her sandals and sat back against the cushions. They might sleep for half an hour and she had plenty to occupy her thoughts.

Dr Seymour opened one eye. He said very softly, 'You don't like me very much, do you, Daisy?'

She was taken by surprise, but Daisy being Daisy she gave his remark thoughtful consideration. Presently she said, 'I don't know anything about you, Dr Seymour.'

'An indisputable fact. You haven't answered my question.'

'Yes, I have—I don't know you well enough to know, do I?'

'No? Personally, I know if I like or dislike someone the moment I set eyes on them.'

He would have disliked her on sight, she reflected, remembering the cold stare at the traffic-lights in Wilton and the short shrift he had given her, almost knocking her off her bike. She said primly, 'Well, we're all different, aren't we?'

The mocking look he gave her sent the colour into her cheeks. The doctor, watching her lazily, decided that she wasn't as plain as he had thought.

The twins woke up presently and they played ball until their mother came back. The twins fell upon her with shrieks of delight, both talking at once. 'Val—how lovely to see you—I wanted to talk to you…' Seeing Daisy, she turned to her. 'Do go home, dear, you must be exhausted—I know I am after several hours of these two.' She unwound her children's arms from around her neck. 'Take Daisy to the gate, darlings, and then go to the kitchen and ask Mrs Betts if she would make a pot of tea for me.'

Daisy got to her feet, reflecting that Lady Thorley's airy dismissal had been both friendly and expected; she was the daily mother's help and was treated with more consideration than she had ever had with Mrs Gower-Jones. All the same, she wished that Dr Seymour hadn't been there.

Her goodnight was quietly said. 'I'll be here at half-past eight, Lady Thorley,' and she left them without further ado, taking the twins with her.

The doctor watched her go. 'What do you want to tell me, Meg?' he asked.

'Hugh phoned—such news—the man at the Hague is ill—jaundice or something—and he's to replace him until he's fit again. Hugh says there's a lovely flat we can have and he wants us to go there with him—he'll be home this evening but I wanted to ask your advice about the twins. I'll go with Hugh, of course, but what about them? I did wonder if they had better stay here with Daisy—that is if she would agree to come...'

'Why not take the children with you and Daisy as well?'

'Well, that would be marvellous—she's so good with them and they like her, but she might not want to come...'

'Why not ask her and find out? What does Hugh say?'

'He told me I could do whatever I thought was best as long as it won't upset the twins—going to live somewhere else—foreign too...'

'My dear girl, Holland is hardly darkest Africa, and it's only an hour away by plane.' He stood up. 'I must go back to town. You're quite satisfied with Daisy?'

'Oh, yes. How clever of you to tell me about her, Val. She's so sensible and kind—it's hard to find girls like her. Plain, of course—such a pity for she'd make a splendid wife.' She walked round the house to where his car was parked before the door. 'I suppose you wouldn't find the time to visit us while we're at the Hague?'

'Very likely—I'm lecturing at Leiden Medical School and there's a seminar for paediatricians in Utrecht—I'm not sure of the dates.' Lady Thorley tiptoed to kiss his cheek.

'Lovely. I'll talk to Daisy—better still I'll get Hugh to do that.'

'Why not? When does he go?'

'Two weeks—at least, he's to go as soon as possible; he thought it would take me two weeks to pack up and so on.' She stopped suddenly. 'Oh, what shall I do about Boots? We can't leave him here just with Mrs Betts...'

'I'll have him.' He glanced at his watch. 'I must go, my dear—give me a ring when you have things settled.'

Daisy, unaware of the future being mapped out for her, cycled home and thought about Dr Seymour. She wasn't sure if she liked him but she was fair enough to admit that that was because he was a difficult man to get to know. He was splendid with the children, probably he was an excellent paediatrician, but he was arrogant and, she suspected, used to having his own way. Moreover, he had this nasty habit of mocking her…

She was surprised to find Sir Hugh at home when she reached Steeple Langford the next morning. He was still young but he had a serious manner which made him seem older.

'If we might talk?' he suggested, coming to the nursery where the twins were running riot with the Plasticine under Daisy's tolerant eye.

Daisy's heart sank. He had come to tell her she was no longer needed, a governess had been found, and she was mentally putting her name down at several agencies in Salisbury when he went on. 'I'm about to be posted to Den Haag for a time; we wondered if you would consider coming with us to look after the children? I'm not sure for how long; I'm to fill in for a colleague who's on sick leave.'

'Me?' said Daisy.

'If you would. We're to take over an apartment in the residential part of the city, with a garden, I believe, and there are parks close by, so I'm told, and of course it is close to the sea.'

'I don't speak Dutch,' said Daisy.

He smiled faintly. 'Nor do I. I believe that almost everyone speaks English—there are certainly a good many English people living there—there would be other children for the twins to play with, and I'm sure there are young Englishwomen living there—you wouldn't be lonely.' When she hesitated he added, 'I'm told it will be for a month or six weeks.'

'If I might have time to talk to my mother? I could let you know in the morning if that would do?'

'Certainly, I shall be here for a good part of tomorrow.' He got up. 'My wife and I do so hope that you'll see your way to coming with us! You'll let me know in the morning?'

'Yes, Sir Hugh. For my part I should like to come, but I must tell my mother first.'

She thought about it a good deal during the day with mounting excitement; it would mean that she was sure of the job for at least another month besides the added pleasure of seeing something of another country. She would have to talk to Pam and make sure that she could cope with the various household demands. She wouldn't be able to add to the housekeeping money each week while she was away, but there was enough in the bank to cover them and she could pay that back when she eventually returned. All in all she was sure that everything could be arranged with the minimum of trouble for her mother and sister.

Her news was received with pleased surprise; there was no doubt at all, declared her mother, that they could manage very well while she was away. 'It's a marvellous opportunity,' said Mrs Pelham happily. 'Who knows who you will meet while you are there?' she added enthusiastically. 'Sir Hugh is something to do with the Foreign Office, isn't he? There must be clerks and people…'

Daisy said, 'Yes, Mother, I'm sure there are.' There was no harm in letting her mother daydream. Daisy, well aware of her commonplace features and retiring disposition, thought it unlikely that even the most lowly clerk would give her as much as a second glance.

Not a girl to give way to self-pity, she spent the evening combing through her wardrobe in search of suitable clothes. The result was meagre; it was Pamela who remembered the raspberry-red brocade curtains some aunt or other had bequeathed to their mother. They were almost new; they spread them out on the sitting-room floor and studied them. 'A skirt,' said Pamela. 'We'll get a good pattern, and Mother—there's that white crêpe de Chine blouse with the wide collar you never wear.'

'But will I need them?' asked Daisy doubtfully.

'Perhaps not, but you must have something, just in case you get asked out. There's your good suit and we can get your raincoat cleaned…'

So when Daisy saw Sir Hugh in the morning she told him that she would go to Den Haag with the twins, and was rather touched by his relief. His wife's relief was even more marked. 'I hardly slept,' she told Daisy, 'wondering what we should do if you decided not to come with us; Josh and Katie will be so happy. I should warn you that I shall have to be out a good deal—there's a lot of social life, Hugh tells me—you won't mind, will you?'

Daisy assured her that she didn't mind in the least and Lady Thorley gave a sigh of relief. 'You'll have a day off each week, of course, though I dare say it will have to be on different days, and an hour or two to yourself each day. Hugh wants us to go in ten days' time. We'll see to the travel arrangements, of course. There's just your luggage and passport.' She smiled widely. 'I think it's going to be great fun.'

Daisy agreed with her usual calm. Looking after the twins

wasn't exactly fun; she liked doing it but it was tiring and keeping the upper hand over two small children determined to be disobedient was taxing both to temper and patience. But she truly liked Lady Thorley, and the twins, naughty though they were, had stolen her affection.

It was impossible not to be excited as preparations got under way for their journey: clothes for the twins, their favourite toys carefully packed, and a good deal of over-time because their mother needed to go to London to shop for herself. Daisy assembled her own modest wardrobe, wrapped the crêpe de Chine blouse in tissue paper, dealt with the household bills and with Pamela's help made quite a good job of the skirt. Trying it on finally and eyeing it critically, she decided that anyone not knowing that it had been a curtain would never guess…

It wanted two days to their departure when Dr Seymour turned up again. Lady Thorley was packing and Daisy and the twins, housebound by a sudden bout of heavy rain, were in the nursery. He came in so silently that none of them was aware of him until he spoke in Daisy's ear.

'An artist as well as a nanny?' he wanted to know, studying the variety of drawings on the paper before her.

Her pencil faltered so that the rabbit's ear that she had been sketching didn't look in the least like an ear. She said evenly, 'Good afternoon, Dr Seymour,' and rubbed out the ear while Josh and Katie rushed at their uncle.

He pulled a chair up beside Daisy, picked up a pencil and added a moustache and beard to the rabbit.

'Ready to go?' he asked her.

'Yes, thank you. Would you like me to fetch Lady Thorley?'

'No. I came to see these two. Being good, are they?

Not turning your mousy locks grey or causing you to lose weight?'

How could he know that she detested her soft brown hair and was shy about her slightly plump person? A good thing she wouldn't see him for at least six weeks for she didn't like him.

'No,' said Daisy, 'they're good children.' Which wasn't in the least true but Katie, hearing it, flung her arms round her neck.

'We love Daisy; we think she is beautiful and kind like a princess in a fairy-tale waiting for the prince to come and rescue her.'

'And why not?' said her uncle idly, getting up from his chair. 'I'm going to see your mother but I'll say goodbye before I go.'

Josh climbed on to a chair beside her. 'Draw a bear,' he ordered. 'I'm going to be just like Uncle Val when I grow up.'

'So am I,' said Katie, and was told not to be a silly little girl by her brother. Threatened tears were averted by Daisy's embarking on a description of the party dress Katie, being a girl, would be able to wear when she was grown up.

Josh curled his small lip. 'Girls,' he said scornfully.

The doctor was still there when Daisy went home; she cycled past his car in the drive, unaware that he was watching her from the drawing-room window.

Two days later she said goodbye to her mother and Pamela, gave Razor a cuddle and went to the gate where Lady Thorley and the twins were waiting in their car. Her case was stowed in the boot and she got in the back with the children. They were strangely subdued and their mother said, 'Val came for Boots last night and they miss him—he's to stay with my brother while we're away.'

So Daisy spent a good part of their journey explaining how very much Boots would enjoy a holiday. 'And think of all the things you can tell him when we get back,' she pointed out.

'We wouldn't let anyone else have him, only Uncle Val,' said Katie tearfully.

'Well, of course not. He's family, isn't he? And Boots knows that he belongs to all the family as well as you two. You might send him a postcard from Holland…'

A suggestion which did much to cheer the children up.

Sir Hugh had made sure that his family need have no worries on their journey. They were met at Gatwick, the car was garaged and they were guided through the business of checking tickets, baggage and Customs and seen safely aboard the plane. The children were a little peevish by now and Daisy was relieved to see lemonade and biscuits and, for herself, coffee.

Lady Thorley was on the other side of the aisle and the first-class compartment was only half-full; Daisy drank her coffee while the twins munched and swallowed, grateful for the short respite. Afterwards there were comics to be looked at and the excitement of visiting the toilets, small enough at the best of times but needing a good deal of side-stepping and squeezing, much to the delight of the children.

By then the plane was coming in to land, something the twins weren't quite sure if they liked or not. Daisy wasn't sure if she liked it or not herself.

They were met by a well turned-out chauffeur at Schiphol and shepherded through Customs and into a gleaming, rather old-fashioned car and driven away. A little over an hour's drive, the chauffeur told them, joining the stream of traffic.

The twins, one on each side of their mother, on the back

seat, stared out of the windows and had little to say beyond excited 'oh's and 'ah's. Daisy, sitting beside the chauffeur, gazed her fill too; she mustn't miss anything for she had promised to write every detail to her mother.

Presently the car left the busy streets around the airport and picked up speed along the motorway. There wasn't much to see here—occasional patches of quiet meadows, but it seemed to her that there were a great many factories lining the road and she felt vague disappointment. Not for long, however; soon the factories dwindled and died away to be replaced by trees and charming houses, set well back from the road which in turn gave way to the outskirts of the city.

The streets were busy here and the chauffeur had to slow down, so that she had a chance to look around her. It looked delightful—old gabled houses, canals, imposing buildings, a splendid place to explore on her free days... They left the heart of the city, driving down a straight road with parks on either side and then large, solid houses, set well apart from each other, before they turned off into a side-road, wide and tree-lined. There were blocks of modern flats on either side and here and there town mansions in their own grounds. Halfway down they stopped before the wide entrance of a solid red-brick block of flats and the chauffeur got out, opened their doors and led the way across the pavement as a concierge came hurrying to meet them.

'I do hope,' said Lady Thorley, 'that someone has put the kettle on; we need a cup of tea.' She smiled at Daisy, 'You must be tired; I know I am.'

Daisy had the twins by the hand, dancing with excitement. She thought it unlikely that she would have time to be tired until they were given their tea and put to bed, but that didn't worry her. 'I'd love one,' she said cheerfully.

CHAPTER THREE

THE CONCIERGE LED them inside, across a wide hall to an ornate lift. She was a tall, bony woman with a hooked nose and a cast in one eye and the twins stared at her with growing delight. 'Is—is she a—?' began Josh.

'No, dear,' began Daisy before he could utter the word, 'this is the lady who looks after these flats…'

'Juffrouw Smit.' She ushered them into the lift which took them to the first floor. The landing was as wide as the hall below with a door on either side, one of which she now opened. 'The apartment,' she announced, and ushered them inside.

The flat was large, with lofty ceilings, large windows and a balcony overlooking a sizeable garden. There was a staircase at one end of it leading to the garden and Juffrouw Smit waved a generous arm. 'It is yours, the garden.'

'Oh, how nice,' said Lady Thorley uncertainly. 'The people in the flat below?'

Juffrouw Smit shrugged. 'A very small apartment; he is but a clerk.'

Daisy peered over the balcony balustrade. There were

iron railings separating the flat from the garden; it seemed hard on its occupant.

It was obvious that Juffrouw Smit was preparing another speech in her very basic English. 'The cook and the serving maid wait in the kitchen.'

She led the way through two handsome reception-rooms, a small sitting-room and down a short passage and opened a door.

The kitchen was a good size and, as far as Daisy could see at a glance, well equipped. There were two women there, stoutly built and well past their first youth, with pleasant round faces and white aprons over dark dresses. They smiled and nodded, shook hands and said, 'Welcome,' several times. The elder of them pointed to herself. 'Mien,' she said and then pointed to her companion and said, 'Corrie—we speak English a little and understand.'

She beamed at everyone. 'I make tea? I make good English tea…'

'Oh, splendid,' said Lady Thorley. 'Please—in the sitting-room?' She turned to Juffrouw Smit. 'Thank you for your help.'

'At your service, Lady Thorley. I will help at any time.'

She stalked away and Lady Thorley said, 'Well, we'd better go to the sitting-room and have tea and then we can get unpacked. Hugh will be here soon. Daisy, I shall leave you to see about the children's suppers and get them to bed. I must say this is rather a nice flat. You like your room?'

Daisy had had no time to more than glance at it; it was next to the children's room and what she supposed would be the play-room while they were there. There was a bathroom too; all were tucked away at the end of a passage at one end of the flat. She said now, 'It seemed very nice and the twins' room is a nice size.'

'Oh, good.' They were all in the sitting-room now, a comfortably furnished room obviously meant for family use, and Lady Thorley was leafing through the little pile of envelopes on the small desk under the window. 'Heavens, invitations already; I only hope I've brought the right clothes with me...'

They had their tea while the children drank their milk and presently Daisy took them with her to do the unpacking, a lengthy business as they wanted to help, and by the time it was done and she had put away her own modest wardrobe it was almost bedtime for them. There was no sign of Lady Thorley although there was a distant murmur of voices from the other end of the flat. Daisy, with a twin on either hand, found her way to the kitchen.

Mien was at a table putting the finishing touches to a salad.

'Could the children have supper?' Daisy asked.

'You tell, I make,' said Mien obligingly.

'Milk?' She glanced at the twins who were scowling horribly. 'Buttered toast?' she suggested. 'Coddled eggs? Yoghurt?'

She was rewarded by Josh's glare. 'Noodles—buttered noodles?' Daisy asked hopefully and saw Mien nod. 'These I have, with buttered toast and a special sauce. In fifteen minutes, miss, it will be brought to you in the play-room.'

Daisy heaved a sigh of relief. Mien's English was excellent; her accent was terrible but who cared about that? She smiled widely at the cook, went back to the children's room and got them ready for bed. They had had their baths and were cosily wrapped in their dressing-gowns when their supper was put before them.

The play-room had a door on to the balcony; moreover it

boasted a piano, several small comfortable chairs and several shelves and cupboards. The children were hungry and the noodles were almost finished when their parents came in.

'Daisy, how clever of you. The children look at home already. How did you make Cook understand?'

'She speaks good English and is so helpful. The children are ready for bed when they've finished their supper; I thought an early night…'

'Quite right. As soon as you've tucked them up come to the sitting-room and we will have dinner.' The Thorleys stayed for a while, talking to the children, and presently went away, leaving Daisy to coax them to their beds. They were disposed to be fretful but she tucked them in firmly, picked up a book and sat between their beds until they slept and then went away to tidy herself for dinner.

Her room was small but comfortably furnished and the bathroom she was to share with the twins was more than adequate. She did her face and hair, changed her dress and went along to the sitting-room.

'We thought we would dine here this evening,' said Lady Thorley, 'as it's just the three of us. Hugh says that we shall entertain a lot, Daisy, so you won't mind if you have your dinner in the play-room from time to time?'

'Not at all,' said Daisy. 'I'm quite happy to have it there every evening. It's near the children if they should wake, too.'

Lady Thorley looked relieved. 'You wouldn't mind? You will have lunch with me, of course, unless there are guests. Now, we have to decide your free time too.'

Of which there was none, it seemed, during the day, although she was free to take the children out to the beach at Scheveningen whenever she wished. There was a car with a driver she might use if Lady Thorley wasn't free to drive them, and there was a park close by where she would meet other English girls and could chat while the children played together. 'You must have one day a week to yourself,' declared Lady Thorley. 'One of Hugh's colleagues has a nanny who is free on Wednesdays and he suggests that his wife and I should join forces and take it in turns to spend the day at each other's houses with all the children. If you would get the children up and dressed I'll see to their breakfasts and there is no need for you to come back until late evening.' She added apologetically, 'I know that compared with other jobs, you won't get much free time, but you can arrange your days to suit yourself, as long as I know where you are. The children will love the beach… Oh, and some Sundays we'll take the children out and you will be able to go to church…'

'Thank you, that sounds fine, Lady Thorley, and I'll let you know each day where we shall be going. The twins love to walk and there'll be a lot to see.'

She drank her coffee and excused herself on the plea that she would like to write home…

'There's a phone in the lobby leading off the hall,' said Sir Hugh. 'Telephone your mother now and there won't be such an urgent need to write at once.'

It was a temptation to have a good gossip with her mother and Pamela but she confined her news to the fact that they had arrived safely and that everything was quite perfect, promised to write as soon as possible and took herself off to bed.

The Thorleys were still in the sitting-room with the door half-open. As she went past, Lady Thorley's rather high voice reached her clearly. 'Val's coming over quite soon. There's heaps of room for him to stay here; we must invite some people to meet him…'

Daisy, getting ready for bed, allowed her thoughts to wander. She wasn't sure if she wanted to meet Dr Seymour again; on the other hand she had to admit that she found him interesting. Not, she reflected, that she was likely to have much to do with him even if he was a guest in the flat; she could see that any social life she might see would be from the outside looking in. Not that she minded, she told herself stoutly and, being a sensible girl, went to sleep at once.

The next day was largely taken up with finding their way around. They went into the garden after breakfast and then walked to the nearby park, although there wasn't time to do more than give it a brief visit before they went back to have their lunch with Lady Thorley; and, since they were nicely tired by now, the twins consented to lie down for a while, giving Daisy a chance to get her letter home started. In the afternoon they went out again, this time to watch the trams at the end of the road. These went to Scheveningen and back and Daisy decided that going to the beach by tram might be much more fun than driving there in a car. She would have to ask Sir Hugh if that was allowed. Tucking the children in that evening, she considered that their first day had been quite successful. The twins were taking everything in their stride, Mien produced exactly the right food for them and Corrie hadn't seemed to mind the extra work when Daisy had asked if she might have her dinner in the play-room. Perhaps there had been a nanny before her and it was the normal thing to do.

They spent most of the next day at Scheveningen, driven there by a morose man from the British embassy and collected by him during the afternoon. Daisy's request that they might use the trams had been received by Sir Hugh with sympathy, but he wished to take advice from his colleagues first… All the same, they had a lovely day. The sand stretched as far as the eye could see in either direction and there was a great deal of it. They built sandcastles, paddled in the rather chilly water and ate a splendid lunch of sandwiches and buns and potato crisps and went very willingly to bed when they were home again. Lady Thorley had joined them for nursery tea. 'Such a busy day,' she had declared. 'I would have liked to be on the beach with you. You must be tired, Daisy. We're going out to dinner this evening, but when you have had yours, do watch television in the sitting-room or go into the garden for an hour.'

It was a splendid evening, the first hint of autumn in its creeping dusk and faint chill, much too nice to sit and watch an indifferent TV programme which she couldn't understand anyway. The twins already asleep and her dinner eaten, Daisy pulled a cardigan around her shoulders and went down the staircase to the garden. The sun had set but the wide sky reflected its rays still and the garden, carefully tended, smelled faintly of lavender and pinks with the faintest whiff of roses along the end wall. She wandered along its length and then back again to be brought up short by a voice from behind the iron railings before the ground floor apartment.

'I saw you yesterday but you had the children with you.' A cheerful face peered at her through the bars. 'Philip Keynes—I live here. It's a very small flat but I'm a clerk at the embassy and on my own. It's nice to have someone in the flat above… Are you a daughter?'

'Me? No. I'm a temporary nanny—Daisy Pelham—just until they can find a governess for Josh and Katie.'

They faced each other through the bars, liking what they saw.

'You're not lonely?' he asked.

'No, no, I don't have time; the twins keep me busy all day.'

'You get time off?'

'Not during the day and in the evening Sir Hugh and Lady Thorley get asked out a good deal, I believe.'

'But you get a free day?'

'Oh, yes—Wednesdays. There's a lot to see here, isn't there? I hope I stay long enough to see everything...'

He said diffidently, 'I'd be glad to show you round if you'd like that; I can always get an afternoon off. Next Wednesday perhaps?'

'Well, that would be nice...'

He heard the doubt in her voice. 'Sir Hugh knows me...' He grinned suddenly. 'I mean, I'll get him to introduce us properly if you like.'

Daisy laughed. 'No need. I would be glad of someone to show me round the Hague.'

'Good. I'll be free at half-past twelve. Do you think you could meet me? There's a brown café just across the street from the Bijenkorf—that's the big department store in the shopping street—you can't miss it.'

'Yes, of course. I must go and make sure that the children are all right.'

She bade him goodnight and went back up the stairs to the balcony where she paused to look down into the garden. It was somehow comforting to see the reflection of a lamp from his sitting-room window.

During the next few days she met some other English girls when she took the twins to the park. They were friendly, giving her useful tips—where to find the nearest hairdresser, the best shops to go to for humdrum things like toothpaste and tights, the cafés which served the cheapest food. They wanted to know if she had a boyfriend and gave her faintly pitying looks when she said that no, she hadn't. They considered that she was badly treated when it came to time off, too. 'You should have at least two evenings a week as well as a whole day; some of us get weekends…'

'I wouldn't know what to do with them,' said Daisy, 'and anyway I'm only here until Lady Thorley finds a governess.'

They smiled at her with faint patronage. A plain little thing, they told each other when she had left them.

Wednesday came with pleasing swiftness. Daisy had seen very little of Lady Thorley for there was a constant stream of visitors and she was out a good deal. True to her promise, she came to the play-room in good time for the children's breakfast this morning. 'I asked Corrie to take a tray to your room,' she told Daisy, 'and you go just as soon as you like. Will you be out late this evening?'

Daisy thought it unlikely; Philip Keynes hadn't mentioned any kind of evening entertainment. 'I don't think so, not this evening. Some of the girls I met in the park suggested that we might all go to a cinema on Wednesday evening but I expect I'll come back once the shops have shut.'

'Then I'll ask Mien to leave a tray for you in the kitchen. Have a pleasant day, Daisy; we shall miss you.'

Daisy gobbled her breakfast as she got ready to go out. She was a little excited; she had a week's pay in her purse and the prospect of a morning's window-shopping and then the unknown pleasures of the afternoon. She boarded a tram at the end of the road, thankful that it was a cool day so that the good suit didn't look out of place.

The shops were absorbing; she gazed into elegant boutique windows, shuddering at the prices, had coffee and spent the rest of her morning in de Bijenkorf, rather like a small Selfridges and more suited to her pocket. Not that she bought much but it was fun to go round the departments deciding what she would take home as presents, and at half-past twelve she crossed the road to the brown café and found Philip Keynes waiting for her.

She had felt a little shy of meeting him again but there had been no need; he was friendly, full of enthusiasm at the idea of showing her round the Hague, but it was a casual friendliness which quickly put her at her ease. He came from Bristol, he told her, and knew her home town quite well. Over coffee and *kaas broodjes* they talked about the West Country and its pleasures. 'I don't care much for cities,' he told her, 'but this is a good job and once I'm promoted I'll get a posting back home. What about you, Daisy? Do you want to travel before you settle down?'

'Not really. I'm glad I've had the chance to come here but when I get back home I'll find a local job.'

They didn't waste too much time over their lunch. He had the afternoon planned and kept to it. They visited the Ridderzaal and after that the Mauritshuis with its famous paintings. Daisy would have liked to have lingered there but she was urged on; the Kloosterkerk was a must, he told her; never mind that they could spend only a short time there—she would know where to go when next she went exploring and from there there was a glimpse of the eighteenth-century Kneuterdijk Palace. They stopped for tea then, this time in a café in Noordeinde, and it was as they emerged from it that Daisy came face to face with Dr Seymour. The pavements were crowded with people hurrying home from work, and since they were going in opposite directions it seemed unlikely that he had recognised her, but all the same she had been surprised at the sudden delight she had felt at the sight of him, instantly followed by the hope that she wouldn't meet him while he was in Holland. A good thing, she reflected, that she dined alone each evening; there would be no chance of meeting him if he came to see his sister…

She was recalled to her present whereabouts by her companion. 'I say, will it be all right if I put you on a tram? I've got to get to one of these official gatherings at the embassy. It's been a delightful afternoon; we must do it again.' He added anxiously, 'You hadn't any plans for this evening?'

'No, and I said I'd be back some time after tea, I've all kinds of odd jobs I want to do.' She saw the relief in his nice face. 'And you don't need to come with me to the tram; I know which one to catch.'

He wouldn't hear of that; they walked through the narrow streets together and he actually saw her on to a tram which would take her to the end of the road where the Thorleys were living. It was still early evening, but she had letters to write and her hair to wash and an hour or so just sitting with a book would be pleasant. She told herself this as she wished him goodbye, doubtful if he would repeat his invitation; she thought that she was probably rather a dull companion… All the same she had enjoyed the afternoon and she thanked him nicely for it and was surprised when he said, 'I meant it when I said we must do it again. A cinema, perhaps?'

'I'd like that.' She nipped on to the tram and was borne away at high speed down the Scheveningenscheweg, to get out at her stop and walk the short distance to the house.

The concierge admitted her with a muttered 'good evening' and Daisy, ignoring the lift, skipped up the stairs to the Thorleys' apartment and rang the bell. Corrie opened the door, bade her a cheerful hello and told her, in her peculiar English, that her dinner was ready whenever she liked to have it. Daisy thanked her and crossed the hall, to be stopped by Lady Thorley's voice from the half-open door of the drawing-room.

'Daisy?' she called. 'Come in here and tell us if you've had a nice day.'

The drawing-room was a grand room, rather over-furnished in a handsome way. Daisy crossed the parquet floor to the group of people sitting together at the far end by the open windows. She was halfway there when she saw that Dr Seymour was there too, standing leaning against the wall, a drink in his hand. There was a woman sitting there, a strikingly handsome woman in her early thirties and dressed in the kind of clothes Daisy, not given to envy, envied now.

'You know Dr Seymour already,' said Lady Thorley in her friendly way, 'and this is Mevrouw van Taal.'

Daisy said, 'How do you do?' and wished the doctor a good evening.

'You enjoyed your day?' Sir Hugh wanted to know. 'The Hague is a most interesting city. Of course you would have enjoyed it more if you had had a guide...'

Daisy glanced at the doctor. He was looking at her and smiling, a rather nasty little smile, she considered. So he had seen her after all. It was on the tip of her tongue to tell him that she had spent most of her day with Philip Keynes, but that might sound boastful and besides, he might not like that. She agreed quietly that it was indeed a most interesting city and it would take several days to explore it thoroughly.

There was a little silence and the *mevrouw* said in a sugary voice in faultless English, 'Well, I suppose if you have nothing better to do it passes the time.'

'Most agreeably,' said Daisy. 'Goodnight, Lady Thorley, Sir Hugh.' She smiled in the general direction of the doctor and Mevrouw van Taal and walked tidily out of the room, shutting the door gently behind her.

'I wish him joy of her,' she muttered as she went to her room.

The twins were asleep; she wondered what sort of a day their mother had had—she would hear in the morning, no doubt; in the meanwhile she would enjoy her dinner. She had been only a few minutes in the play-room when Corrie came in with a tray. Cold lettuce soup with a swirl of cream in its delectable greenness, chicken *à la* king, asparagus and game chips and a chocolate mousse to finish. Coffee too, brought by Corrie just as she had polished off the last of the mousse. Really, she thought, life couldn't be more pleasant. The unbidden thought that she was lonely crossed her mind, to be dismissed at once. It would have surprised her if she had heard the doctor, sitting at the dinner-table, waving away the chocolate mousse in favour of some cheese. 'Does Daisy not have her meals with you?' he asked idly.

'We almost always have lunch together—the two of us and the children. Of course Daisy could dine with us if she wished but she thought it would be better if she stayed in the play-room in case the children should wake.'

Lady Thorley sounded apologetic and then frowned when Mevrouw van Taal spoke. 'Well, one would hardly expect the nanny to dine, would one? Besides, it is likely that she has no suitable clothes. They have a garish taste in cheap clothes, these au pairs and nannies.'

Dr Seymour's face was inscrutable. He said mildly, 'One could hardly accuse Daisy of being garish.' He thought of the times he had seen her; mousy would be a more appropriate word, and that terrible plastic mackintosh…

The conversation became general after that and presently

Mevrouw van Taal declared that she would really have to go home, smiling at the doctor as she said it. 'If someone would call a taxi?' she asked. 'Since my dear husband died I have not dared to drive the car.'

The doctor rose to his feet at once. 'Allow me to drive you back,' he said; his voice held nothing but social politeness. 'I have to go back to the hospital.'

An offer which Mevrouw van Taal accepted with rather too girlish pleasure.

Unaware that the doctor was spending the night at the apartment, Daisy slept peacefully; she still slept when he went down into the garden very early in the morning. There was a decidedly autumnal chill in the air but it was going to be another fine day. He strolled around and presently became aware that there was someone watching him—the occupier of the downstairs flat, leaning against the wall, behind the railings.

The doctor caught his eye, wished him good morning and was sure that he had seen him before—with Daisy yesterday afternoon. 'Are you not allowed to share the garden?' he enquired pleasantly. He held out a large well cared-for hand and thrust it through the railings. 'Valentine Seymour—Lady Thorley's brother—over here for a few days. I saw you yesterday with Daisy.'

Philip shook hands. 'Philip Keynes—I'm a clerk at the embassy. Yes, I showed Daisy something of the Hague. She's nanny to the children, but of course you know that.'

'Yes. She must have been glad of your company; it's hard to find one's way around a strange city.' The doctor leaned up against the railings. 'Have you been here long?'

'Almost a year; I'm hoping for promotion so that I can go back home! You're not at the embassy, are you?'

'No, no. I'm a paediatrician; I'm over here lecturing and seeing one or two patients that they've lined up for me. I live in London, but I have beds at Salisbury and at Southampton.' He glanced at his watch. 'I must go—I have to be in Utrecht soon after nine o'clock. I dare say we shall meet again.'

He went back upstairs to the balcony just as the twins, dressed and released to let off steam before breakfast, tore on to the balcony, screaming with delight at seeing him and followed at a more sedate pace by Daisy.

She stopped at the sight of him, uttered good morning in a small cool voice and added, 'They must have their breakfast.'

'So must I; shall I have it with you?'

He had spoken to the children and their shouts had drowned anything she might have wanted to say. Not that he would have taken any notice. He went into the play-room with them and found Corrie there, putting boiled eggs into egg-cups. She received the news that he was breakfasting with his nephew and niece with smiling nods, laid another place at the table and went away to get more eggs and toast. She came back presently with a plate of ham and cheese, a basket of rolls and croissants and a very large pot of coffee.

Daisy sat the children down, tied their bibs and poured cereal and milk into their bowls while the doctor leaned against a wall, watching, before pulling out her chair for her and seating himself opposite.

Daisy, pouring coffee and beakers of milk, had to admit to herself that he was good with children. They were, she suspected, a little in awe of him, and upon reflection she supposed that she was too but she found herself at ease and laughing with the children over the outrageous stories he was telling them. Daisy stopped abruptly at his quiet, 'You should laugh more often, Daisy, it turns you into a pretty girl.'

She went very pink. 'If that's meant to be a compliment I can do without it, Dr Seymour.'

'No, no, you mustn't misunderstand me; I was merely stating a fact.'

He spoke mildly and she felt a fool, her face reddening at his assured smile.

He passed his cup for more coffee. 'I had a talk with young Keynes—a sound young man—pity he's caged up behind those iron railings. Did you enjoy your afternoon with him, Daisy?'

'Yes, he knows where everything is…how did you know?'

'Well, I saw you, didn't I? Besides, I asked him this morning.'

Her small nose quivered with annoyance. Before she could speak he added, 'None of my business, is it? How do you like being a nanny?'

She said sedately, 'Very much, Doctor.' She got up to wipe the twins' small mouths and untie their bibs. 'And now if you will excuse us…?'

'Being put in my place, am I?' He got up too, tossed the children into the air, promised them sweets next time he came and made for the door, to turn and come back to where Daisy was standing, lift her firm little chin in his hand and stare down at her, his eyes, half hidden by their lids, studying her face.

'Kiss Daisy goodbye,' shrieked Katie, who, being female, was romantic even at four years old.

'Not this time,' said her uncle, and went unhurriedly from the room.

Daisy swallowed all the things she would have liked to utter; the twins were remarkably sharp for their age and they might repeat them to their mother and father. She urged the children along to the bathroom to wash teeth, faces and hands, vowing silently that if she saw Dr Seymour again she would run a mile, or at least go as quickly as possible in the opposite direction. Perhaps there would be no need to do that; hopefully he would be going back to England soon.

It was with relief that she heard Lady Thorley tell her that her brother had gone to Utrecht; she wouldn't have felt that relief, though, if Lady Thorley had added that he would be with them again that evening.

She spent the day on the beach with the children; there wouldn't be many more days in which to do that, she reflected. There was a distinct nip of autumn in the air now; October wasn't more than a few days away and already the beach kiosks and little seaside shops selling buckets and spades and postcards were putting up their shutters. Then it would be the park and, should they still be there, carefully planned hours to be spent in the play-room. She doubted, though, if she would be called upon to do that; long before then she would be back in Wilton, and if a governess had been found she would be looking for another job.

She took the children home in time for tea, and they had it with their mother in the play-room, and, much to Daisy's astonishment, Lady Thorley asked her if she would dine with them that evening. 'Just us,' she said. 'It will be nice to have a quiet evening. There's a reception tomorrow evening so we shall be out again—you've been very good and patient, Daisy, staying with the children; I'm sure I don't know what we should have done without you. Mrs Perry was telling me about Katwijk-aan-Zee—it's no distance away and she says it's so much nicer than Scheveningen—I thought I might drive you and the children there before it gets too chilly. I don't think I can spare the time to stay all day, but I could pick you up during the afternoon.'

Daisy agreed because she saw that Lady Thorley expected her to. One of the girls she had met in the park had told her it was a nice little seaside town and it would make a change.

She put the children to bed, read to them until they were sleepy and then changed into the blouse and skirt, did her face and hair with rather more care than usual and went on to the balcony to wait for the dinner-gong. It had been another fine day, now fading into a golden dusk, and the garden below looked inviting. She leaned on the balustrade and wondered if she had time to go down there, and decided against it just as Dr Seymour ranged himself alongside her.

He ignored her gasp of surprise. 'A delightful evening,' he observed pleasantly. 'There's a great deal of wide sky in Holland, isn't there?'

'Haven't you gone back to England yet?' asked Daisy, not bothering with the sky.

'Now that's the kind of encouraging remark I suppose I should have expected from you, Daisy.'

He turned his head to smile at her and she thought how very good-looking he was and so very large. 'You surprised me,' she told him.

'I'm relieved to hear that.' He smiled and this time it was kind. 'You're looking very smart this evening—Margaret tells me that you're dining with us.'

He had seen the beautifully washed and pressed blouse, certainly not new and decidedly out of date, and the skirt—a pretty colour which suited her and made, unless he was much mistaken, from what looked suspiciously like a curtain…

'Yes, Lady Thorley invited me, but perhaps now you're here—I mean, if she didn't know you were coming…'

'Oh, but she did—it will be an opportunity to talk about the twins; they seem very happy and they're fond of you.'

'They're very nice children.' She couldn't think of anything else to say, so that the faint sound of the gong came as a relief.

They went down together and he waited for her while she went to take a quick look at the twins, and, to her surprise, once they were downstairs sipping sherry before they went in to dinner, she forgot to feel shy, happy to find that Lady Thorley was wearing a blouse and skirt too—rather different from her own—oyster satin with a filmy black skirt and a jewelled belt. All the same Daisy felt at ease because she was wearing the right clothes.

They dined splendidly at a table covered with white damask, shining silver and gleaming glass; lobster bisque, guinea fowl with sautéd potatoes, artichokes and asparagus followed by profiteroles with a great deal of cream, all nicely helped along with a white Bordeaux and then a sweet white wine she didn't much like to go with the pudding. There was brandy served with the coffee but she declined that. It seemed to her that nannies shouldn't do that; anyway, she wasn't sure that she would like brandy. She had maintained her part in the conversation very well and, since she was a good listener, Sir Hugh declared after she had said goodnight and gone upstairs that she had been a much more interesting table companion than Mevrouw van Taal. 'Nice manners too,' he observed. 'Do you agree, Val?'

'Oh, indeed, you have found yourselves a treasure—if a temporary one.'

'That reminds me,' said his sister, 'I was talking to Mrs

Ross today—her husband's been posted to Brussels and her governess wants to go back to England. It seems she's a marvellous woman, splendid with small children and able to give lessons until they're old enough for school. Would it be a good idea if I found out a bit more about her? Personal recommendation is so much better than advertising.'

'That sounds promising,' Sir Hugh agreed. 'Make quick work of it, darling—I'll be here for another month at the outside; this paragon could take over when we get back home.' He paused. 'I'll be sorry to see Daisy go.'

'So shall I; she's so nice and gentle and kind. She should get a good job, though; I'll give her a splendid reference.'

To all of which conversation the doctor listened without saying a word; and, as for Daisy, blissfully unaware of what the future held in store for her, she put her head upon the pillow and went to sleep.

CHAPTER FOUR

DAISY WOKE WITH a pleasant feeling of excitement which, upon investigation, and to her surprise, was due to the fact that she would see the doctor again. She expected him to come and say hello to the twins—perhaps stay to breakfast—but there was no sign of him, nor did Lady Thorley mention him when she came to wish her children good morning after that meal. It wasn't until lunchtime, after she had taken the twins for a walk in the Scheveningse Bos, where there was plenty of open space in which they could tire themselves out, that Lady Thorley mentioned that her brother had gone back to England. 'He works too hard,' she complained. 'I tell him that he should marry, but he says he has no time for that. Such nonsense; one day he'll fall in love and then he'll find the time.'

As long as he didn't fall in love with someone like Mevrouw van Taal, reflected Daisy, and wondered why she disliked the idea so much; after all, she still wasn't sure if she liked him and he was surely old and wise enough to take care of himself.

The days unrolled themselves smoothly, each one rather like the last, until it was Wednesday again and Daisy, released from her duties, took the tram into the Hague. She had seen Philip Keynes on the previous evening and he had arranged to meet her at four o'clock for tea and then take her to the cinema. She was looking forward to it and now that she had some money in her pocket she would spend the morning looking for something for her mother and Pamela. Coffee first, she thought happily, as the tram deposited her at the stop nearest to the Bijenkorf.

She found a silver brooch for her mother and a silk scarf for her sister, both costing rather more than she could afford, so that her lunch was sparse, but in any case, she reminded herself, eating took up precious time and she planned to spend the afternoon, map in hand, getting some idea of the town. She lingered for some time along the Korte Vijverberg and the Lange Vijverberg, admiring the old houses with their variety of gabled roofs, and from there she walked to Lange Voorhout, pleasantly broad and tree-lined with its small palaces and embassies and luxurious Hotel des Indes. It must be pleasant working in such surroundings, she decided, thinking of Philip, even in the capacity of a clerk. She looked her fill at the patrician houses around her—a far cry from her own home; the thought of it made her feel homesick for a moment; it would be nice to see her mother and Pam again, but not just yet. Each week she was adding to her small nest-egg; a month, six weeks even, would allow her to put by more money than she had earned in months of work at the nursery school.

She strolled back to the café where she found Philip waiting for her. His pleasure at seeing her added to her enjoyment of her day and he was an easy person to talk to. They drank their tea and ate the rich creamcakes so temptingly displayed and then made their way to the cinema.

It was a good film and there was time for a quick cup of coffee before they boarded the tram for home. Saying goodnight in the entrance to the flats, Daisy reflected that she hadn't enjoyed herself so much for a long time. Philip was the kind of man she would like to marry: easy to get on with, not given to sarcastic remarks and quite lacking in arrogance—unlike Dr Seymour, the sight of whose well-tailored appearance caused her instant annoyance.

She went indoors, spent ten minutes with the Thorleys describing her day and then went to her room, wondering if it was too late for her to get some supper. Tea had been delicious and the coffee after the cinema equally so but her insides were hollow.

She hadn't been in her room five minutes before Mien tapped on the door, bearing a tray. Soup in a pipkin, ham and a salad and coffee in a Thermos jug. A most satisfactory end to her day, she thought, gobbling her supper and then, after a last look at the twins, tumbling into her bed.

The weather changed, a mean wind blew and there was persistent rain. The twins reacted as might have been expected—tantrums, a refusal to do anything asked of them and a steady demand to go to the beach.

Lady Thorley finally gave way to their persistent small rages. 'Could you bear to go with them?' she asked Daisy. 'Perhaps if they went just once and got soaked they wouldn't want to go again—just for an hour or two?'

So Daisy buttoned them into their small mackintoshes, tied their hoods securely, stuffed their feet into wellies and then got into her plastic mac, tucking her hair under its unbecoming hood. They took a tram to the promenade and then, with buckets and spades, went down to the beach. Deserted, of course, and in a way Daisy liked it. The sea was rough and coldly grey and the wide sky was equally grey with the sandy shore below stretching away on either side as far as the eye could see. Lonely and magnificent and a bit frightening…

Daisy dispelled such a fanciful thought and got on to her knees the better to help build the sandcastle under Josh's shouted instructions.

They were to go back home for lunch, Lady Thorley had said, but there was time enough to build a dozen sandcastles. Daisy, fashioning a wall around the last of them, was startled by Katie's piercing shriek. The two children, shouting with delight, were hurtling up the beach towards Dr Seymour, making his leisurely way towards them. She got to her feet then, dusting the sand off her damp knees, looking just about as unglamorous as it was possible to look; the hood, never flattering, had slipped sideways so that a good deal of damp hair had escaped and her face was as damp as her knees.

She watched him coming towards her, a twin on either hand, wished him a good morning and stood quietly under his scrutiny, aware that she looked an absolute fright and hating him for it.

He smiled at her. 'Hello, Daisy, what marvellous sandcastles—I haven't made one for half a lifetime.' Unnoticing of the drizzle, he squatted down to inspect their work, fashioned a drawbridge, added an imposing tower, invited Daisy to admire them and got to his feet.

'Want a lift back?' he wanted to know. 'It's a bit early for lunch, but you'll all need a wipe down first, won't you?' His glance swept over Daisy and she lifted her chin. If he dared to smile… But he didn't. They went back up the beach to the promenade with the children happily hopping and skipping between them, making so much noise that there was no need to talk. A good thing, for she could think of nothing at all to say.

The Rolls was at the kerb and sitting in it was Mevrouw van Taal.

'You know each other, don't you?' observed the doctor easily as he stuffed the children into the back of the car. 'Hop in between them, Daisy.'

Mevrouw turned an elegant shoulder to look at them. 'What a very strange way in which to spend the morning,' she said acidly, 'but of course I suppose it doesn't matter to you when you do not need to bother with your appearance.'

Daisy thought of several things to say and uttered none of them; it was the twins who yelled rudely at her, protesting that the beach in the rain was the nicest thing they knew of, a sentiment echoed by their uncle, who had got into the car, taken a quick look at Daisy's outraged face and smoothly taken the conversation into his own hands, so that the twins, hushed by Daisy, subsided, allowing him to carry on a desultory exchange of remarks with Mevrouw van Taal. When they arrived at the house she whisked them upstairs to be washed and tidied for their lunch, and they were so pleased with the idea of their uncle having lunch with them that they forgot all about Mevrouw van Taal. But, when they were led into the dining-room, faced with the sight of that lady sitting by their uncle, sipping sherry, their small faces puckered into scowls.

'Why—?' began Josh, and was hushed by Daisy.

'Tell Mummy about the castles we built this morning,' she urged.

He went obediently but his lower lip was thrust out in an ominous manner. It was Katie who spoke in her shrill voice. 'I thought Uncle Val was having lunch with us, not with her,' she observed.

'Well, we are all having lunch together,' observed Daisy. 'Do tell Daddy about that crab you found.' She caught the doctor's eye and saw that he was laughing silently. Let him, she thought savagely, and looked away from his mocking glance.

Mien came to the door then to announce that lunch was ready, which was a good thing—the children had a look on their faces which boded no good. She prayed silently that they would behave themselves at table.

The prayer wasn't answered; it was unfortunate that Mevrouw van Taal was seated opposite them, and Daisy, sitting between them, knew without looking that they had fixed their large blue eyes upon her and at any moment would say something outrageous…

'Which reminds me,' said Dr Seymour apropos of nothing at all, 'I have something for you two—you may have it after lunch if your mother says you may, on condition that you're extra-good.'

Daisy let out a relieved breath and then drew it in again sharply when the doctor winked at her from a bland face. Really, the man was simply impossible. She busied herself attending to the children and was thankful that they were behaving like small angels. Their father paused in the middle of a sentence to ask if they were sickening for something. 'You must have performed a miracle on them, Daisy,' he said kindly. 'Let us hope…' he caught his wife's eye '…that it lasts,' he ended tamely. He had forgotten for the moment that Daisy hadn't been told that the new governess would be taking over very shortly—something which would have to be broken to the children at the proper time, which wasn't now.

Mevrouw van Taal could be charming in the right company. Daisy had to admire her—she had good looks, the right clothes and a helpless-little-girl manner which Daisy felt simply certain would appeal to any man. She was an amusing talker too; Daisy allowed her rather high-pitched voice to go over her head while she thought about the doctor. Was he here for a long stay, she wondered, or a lightning visit? She frowned; it was no concern of hers anyway, only it would be nice to know…

The twins were allowed down from the table once the pudding had been eaten; they kissed their parents, stared stonily at Mevrouw van Taal as they muttered what Daisy hoped was a polite goodbye.

'Run along with Daisy, darlings,' begged their mother. 'We'll have coffee in the drawing-room, shall we?' she said to the others.

Dr Seymour got up to open the door and bent his massive person to whisper to Josh, 'Wait in the hall; I'll be out in a moment.'

He went back into the room, leaving the door half-open so that Mevrouw van Taal's voice was very audible to Daisy, waiting at the foot of the stairs with the twins.

'Charming children,' she declared, 'and so well behaved. That girl—their nanny—is the quiet sort, isn't she? Plain with it too.' She gave a tinkle of laughter. 'Let us hope she is as quiet and kind when she is alone with the children…' Daisy, rigid with rage, heard the Thorleys protest as the woman went on, 'Oh, I didn't mean to upset you, I'm sure she is a very good young woman, but one does hear such tales.'

'Not about Daisy.' It was the doctor, speaking in such a cold voice that Daisy shivered. 'I'm sure you meant no harm,

Rena, but it is perhaps a little unwise to give an opinion of someone of whom you know nothing, is it not?'

He came into the hall a moment later, shutting the door behind him.

'I'm sorry if you heard that; I'm sure Mevrouw van Taal meant nothing personal.'

'I don't care what she means,' said Daisy in a stony voice. 'Pray don't bother to make excuses for her. If you would be good enough to give the children their present I can take them upstairs so that I may be discussed at your ease.'

'Spitfire,' said Dr Seymour mildly and added, 'You have very lovely eyes.'

'Ah—you forget, a plain face…'

'We'll discuss that some time.' He smiled very kindly at her and she felt tears crowding her throat, which made her crosser than ever.

'There's a small box on the hall table,' he told the children. 'Will you fetch it, Josh?'

It was actually quite a big box; he opened it and took out two smaller boxes and gave them to the children. 'Not to be opened until you're lying on your beds.' He bent down and kissed their excited faces and then, in an afterthought, kissed Daisy too.

'I'm going away directly,' he told her. 'You'll be glad, won't you?'

'Yes,' said Daisy, not meaning it. She urged the twins upstairs and didn't look back.

The boxes contained musical boxes, the sort which, when wound, displayed a group of dancing figures on their lids. The twins were enchanted with them and quite forgot to be difficult about taking their afternoon nap, so that Daisy found herself with nothing to do until they woke again.

It was still raining and she turned her back on the dismal weather, got out her pen and writing pad and began a letter to her mother, anxious to occupy her thoughts with something other than dwelling on the kiss Dr Seymour had given her. It was exactly the same kind of kiss as those he had bestowed upon his small relations, and she hoped that it hadn't been bestowed in pity; she hoped too, with quite unnecessary fervour, that he would be gone by the time she went downstairs with the children again.

Fate always answered the wrong prayers; there was no sign of him when the children went down to have tea with their mother; moreover he was already on his way back to England, Lady Thorley told her. 'He will be back, though, for a few days shortly,' she continued, 'some meeting or other in Leiden.'

All memories of the summer were being washed away by a persistent fine rain, and the twins' high spirits, because they were largely confined to indoors, were rapidly turning to fits of sulks and displays of childish rage. Daisy took them out each day despite the wind and rain and the three of them, swathed in mackintoshes and hoods and sensible shoes, went to the park, empty of people now, where they ran races and then went home, sopping-wet and tired, but by the afternoon their energy was firmly restored, and Daisy was glad when it was bedtime and she could tuck them up. Of course, they were reluctant to sleep and she read to them until she was hoarse…

It rained on her day off too, which was a pity, for Philip had borrowed a friend's car and had promised to drive her to Apeldoorn then down to Arnhem through the Hoge Veluwe National Park and then back to the Hague. All the same they went, making light of the weather, and Philip, who prided himself on the knowledge he had of the Dutch countryside, took pains to point out everything interesting in sight. Even in the rain Apeldoorn was pleasant; they had their soup and a roll in a small café on the edge of the town and then set off for Arnhem. The road ran through wooded country and stretches of heath, the villages were small and infrequent and here and there they caught glimpses of large villas half-hidden by trees, and when they reached Arnhem he took her round the open-air museum where Holland's way of life was portrayed by farms, windmills and houses from a bygone age. Despite the rain, Daisy would have lingered for hours but it was quite some distance back to the Hague and they simply had to have tea…

Back at the house they parted like old friends. 'I'll get the car next week,' Philip promised, 'and we'll go north to Alkmaar and Leeuwarden. You're not going back home yet, are you?'

'No, I don't think so yet; I heard Sir Hugh saying that he expected to be here for another month or even longer.'

'Good. I'll see you next week.' She rang the bell and watched him get into the car to drive it back to his friend's flat. It had been a lovely day and Philip was an undemanding companion, always ready to agree with her suggestions. He would make a nice brother, she thought, as Mien opened the door and she went inside.

Mien took her wet things and nodded her head upstairs where small cross voices could be heard. 'It is good that you are back. Lady Thorley is weary. The children…' She raised her hands and rolled her eyes up to the ceiling.

Daisy sped upstairs and found Lady Thorley attempting to get the twins quiet. They were bellowing and screaming and quite out of hand but they paused long enough to shout at Daisy.

'If you're quiet,' said Daisy, 'I'll tell you where I've been today, so say goodnight to Mummy and lie down, there's dears.'

Lady Thorley gave her a thankful look, kissed them and went to the door. 'I'll tell Mien to send you up a tray in half an hour, Daisy.' She asked belatedly, 'You had a nice day?'

'Delightful, thank you, better than yours.'

Lady Thorley made a face. 'They need a dragon to look after them. I'll say goodnight, and thank you, Daisy.'

Getting ready for bed a few hours later, Daisy prayed once more, this time for fine weather; much more of the twins' naughtiness would make even her stout heart quail; at least out of doors they tired themselves out.

This time her prayers were answered; the really heavy rain ceased and although the wind was chilly and the sky overcast at least they could get out. Three days passed in comparative peace and on the fourth morning, just as they had finished their breakfast, Dr Seymour walked into the play-room.

The twins were delighted to see him and, although she wouldn't admit it to herself, Daisy was too. Disentangling himself from the twins' embrace, he addressed himself to her. 'I'll keep an eye on these two—Margaret would like you to go down to the sitting-room; she wants to talk to you.'

There had been some talk of buying warmer clothes for the children; Daisy, nipping smartly along the passage, rehearsed in her head the various garments which would be necessary.

Lady Thorley was at the breakfast table and Sir Hugh

was still there too. Daisy, her mind engaged in the choice of Chilprufe as against Ladybird vests, wished them both good morning and, when bidden to sit, sat.

'We wanted to talk to you,' began Lady Thorley, and looked at her husband, who coughed and said,

'Er—well, it's like this, Daisy…' and coughed again. 'You know, of course, that we engaged you on a temporary basis; indeed, we had intended that you should stay with us until we returned to England in a few weeks' time. However, a colleague of mine is being posted and the governess he employs for his children does not wish to stay with them but wants to return to England. We thought at first that she might take over from you when we go back there but it would make it much easier for everyone concerned if she were to come straight to us here. We think that if she were to join us here in two days' time you might spend a day with her—show her the ropes—and return to England on the following day. We will, of course, arrange your journey and, needless to say, a very good reference.'

Daisy said in a polite voice, 'That seems a very sensible arrangement, Sir Hugh. I'm glad you've found a governess; it's so much better to have someone recommended, isn't it?'

She heard herself uttering the words she felt sure her companions wished to hear while inwardly she fought unhappy surprise. She had felt secure at least for another month, which had been silly of her, and she was quite unprepared for such a sudden decision on the part of the Thorleys. Something of her thoughts must have shown on her face for Lady Thorley said quickly, 'You do understand that we have never been less than absolutely satisfied with you, Daisy. You've been splendid with the twins; I don't know how I would have managed without you…'

'I've enjoyed looking after them, Lady Thorley. If there's nothing else I'll go and get the children ready for their walk.' Daisy got up. 'I expect you know that Dr Seymour is with the twins?'

'Yes. He's due at the hospital this afternoon; he'll be going back home some time this evening.' Lady Thorley smiled at Daisy. 'Run along, then; if I don't see you at lunch, I'll be here in good time for the twins' tea.'

The doctor was sitting on the table, the breakfast things pushed to one side, and the children were beside him; the three heads were close together but they looked up as she went in.

'If you go to the hall,' said the doctor, 'you might find something in the umbrella stand by the door; if you do, take it to your father and mother and ask if you may have it.'

When they had scampered off he got off the table and went to stand before her. 'Surprised?' he asked.

'You knew? That I'm going back to England?'

'Yes. Hugh asked me what I thought about it some time ago when he first heard of this governess. I think it's a splendid idea; they need a female sergeant major to look after them. You're a splendid nanny, I should suppose, but you're too kind and forgiving, my dear; they'll be twisting you round their thumbs in a few months.'

'That's an unkind remark to make,' said Daisy coldly, 'but I suppose only to be expected of you. I know your opinion of me is low…' She added with a snap, 'Not that I care about that.' She drew a sustaining breath. 'I shall be sorry to leave the twins but nothing will give me greater pleasure than the thought that I need never see you again.' She went to the door. 'Now if you will excuse me, Dr Seymour, I will go to the children.' Her hand on the doorknob, she turned to look at him over her shoulder. 'I do hope Mevrouw van Taal manages to catch you; you deserve her.'

She didn't exactly sweep out of the room—she was too small for that—but she managed a dignified exit.

The doctor stood there where she had left him, the outrage on his face slowly giving way to a wide grin.

Daisy buttoned the children into their outdoor things and took them for their walk. She would have liked time to sit down and think about the turn of events; she had known that the job was temporary but she had expected to have a longer warning of its finish so that she could have made plans about getting work when she got home. Now there would be no time to do that and although she had saved up almost all of her wages it might be weeks before she found another job. There was no time to worry about that now, though; the twins, intent on reaching the park to see if any of their small friends were also there, hurried her along, both talking at once, leaving her no time at all for her own thoughts. Which was just as well.

Nothing was to be said to the children until the new governess arrived; Daisy, carrying on with their usual routine during the next two days, wondered if they would like her. Dr Seymour had described her as a sergeant major… She wished she could stop thinking about him; he had gone as swiftly as he had come, and presumably he was back in England. She reminded herself that she had no wish to see him ever again and, once the children were in their beds, began to get her clothes ready to pack.

The sergeant major arrived after breakfast as Daisy was arranging painting books and paints on the play-room table; the dull morning had made it easy to persuade the twins that a walk later in the day would be a better idea so that when their mother and the new governess came into the room they were engaged in quarrelling amicably together as to who should have the bigger paintbox.

Daisy put a jar of water in the centre of the table out of harm's way, smiled at Lady Thorley and said good morning to her companion. The woman was a good deal older than herself, tall and thin and good-looking, but she looked kind and when Lady Thorley said, 'This is Amy Thompson, Daisy,' she held out her hand and gave Daisy a firm handshake.

The children had come to stand by Daisy, eyeing the stranger with suspicion; it was their mother who said coaxingly, 'Come and say hello to Miss Thompson; she's going to spend the day with us…'

'Why?' asked Josh and then, urged by Daisy, offered a small hand.

'Well,' began his mother, 'Miss Thompson is going to live with us and be your governess; you're going to have lessons at home, which will be much more fun than going to school…'

Katie shook hands too, eyeing the newcomer. 'We'd rather keep Daisy,' she observed.

Josh's bottom lip was thrust forward in an ominous manner and Daisy said quickly, 'The thing is, my dears, I do have to go home and live with my mother and sister…'

Katie burst into tears and Josh flung himself on to the floor, where he lay kicking and shouting. Daisy got down beside him. 'Look, Josh, we'll still see each other; I live very close to your home, you know—perhaps Miss Thompson will invite me to tea sometimes and allow you both to come and see Razor.'

He opened an eye. 'Promise?'

Daisy glanced at Miss Thompson who nodded and smiled. 'Promise,' said Daisy, 'and now if you will get up and Katie will stop crying we can have some fun showing Miss Thompson where everything is and what you wear when you go out and just how you like your eggs boiled. She will really depend on you both for a little while, just as I had to when I first came to look after you.'

It took time to coax the children to calm down, something they did unwillingly, but Miss Thompson was a veteran at the job; by lunchtime they were on good terms with her, with only the occasional suspicious look. She went away at teatime with the assurance that she would return the following morning.

With Josh and Katie in bed, Daisy packed, washed her hair, checked the contents of her handbag and went downstairs to dine with the Thorleys. Sir Hugh gave her her ticket. 'One of the drivers will take you to Schiphol,' he told her. 'We thought if you took the late morning flight—Miss Thompson will be here at ten o'clock, and it might be easier if you go shortly afterwards, in case the children…'

He paused, and Daisy said, 'Yes, of course, I quite understand.'

'You'll go home by train? You'll find travelling expenses in that envelope—you'll have to go up to London from Gatwick unless you can get a bus to Basingstoke.'

'Either way will be easy,' said Daisy; she sounded as though she knew what she was talking about although she had only the vaguest idea about the train service to Salisbury from London; but there were bound to be several and she would be at Gatwick by one o'clock at the latest.

Sir Hugh said thankfully, 'Oh, good, it should be quite simple. Do telephone your mother if you wish to…'

She decided against that; she wasn't sure what time she would get home and her mother would worry. They went in to dinner and she joined in the conversation in her quiet way, all the while not quite believing that in twenty-four hours' time she would be home again and out of a job once more.

She hated leaving the twins; she was quite sure that Miss Thompson would be kind as well as seeing to their education, but all the same it was a wrench and all the harder since she had to keep a cheerful face on things when she said goodbye. It was a wet morning; the last she saw of them was two small faces pressed against the play-room windows. She waved until the car turned into the street, and since the driver was disinclined for conversation she spent the journey to the airport musing over a choice of jobs. Another nanny's post perhaps? Or a mother's help? Failing those, how about working in a shop? But wouldn't she have to know something about selling things? How did one start? she wondered. She was still wondering when they reached Schiphol and the driver fetched her case from the boot and carried it to the desk for her. She thanked him, gave him a tip and joined the queue of passengers being processed towards their various flights.

The flight was uneventful; she collected her case from the carousel, went through Customs and to the entrance, borne along on a stream of people intent on getting home as quickly as possible. There were taxis there and, some distance away, a bus. She picked up her case, to have it taken from her at the same time as Dr Seymour said quietly. 'The car's over here.'

She turned round and gaped up at him. 'That's my case,'

she told him sharply. 'And I'm not going by car; there's a bus…' She drew breath. 'How did you get here, and why?'

'How you do chatter.' He took her arm. 'I'm on my way back to Salisbury. Margaret rang me this morning and mentioned that you would be on this flight; it seemed only good sense to collect you on my way.'

They had reached the car and he had opened the door and stuffed her inside and put her case in the boot; now he got in beside her. She was still thinking of something to say as, with the minimum of fuss, he drove away from the airport.

'Had a good trip?' he asked casually.

'Yes. Thank you.' She had remembered that she had never wanted to see him again and she sounded waspish.

'Still peeved?'

Hateful man. 'I don't know what you mean, and please don't feel that you have to—to entertain me with conversation; I have no wish to come with you. Probably you mean it kindly but I thought I had made it clear that I didn't want to see you again…'

They were away from the airport and the big car surged silently forward.

'Yes, yes, I know that, and if you're bent on keeping to your rigid principles I won't say another word; you can sit there and pretend I'm not here.'

And he didn't. They went down the M3 at a spanking pace, slowed to go through Salisbury and ten minutes later slowed again as they reached Wilton. He stopped outside her home, got out, opened her door, fetched her case and banged the knocker on the door.

'Thank you for the lift,' said Daisy. 'Would you like a cup of coffee or—or something?' She looked as far as his tie and then gave him a quick glance. He was looking down at her, an eyebrow raised to mock her.

'My dear Daisy, is this an olive-branch?' He turned to the door as it opened and Mrs Pelham gave a small shriek of delight.

'Daisy, darling—how lovely.'

She looked enquiringly at the doctor and Daisy said, 'Hello, Mother. This is Dr Seymour, who kindly brought me home…'

'That's twice,' said her mother, and smiled at him. 'Come in and have a cup of tea.'

'I should have liked that, Mrs Pelham, but I've an appointment.'

Mrs Pelham nodded sympathetically. 'Well, of course, you doctors don't have much time to spare, do you?'

He had nice manners; his goodbyes weren't to be faulted but the eyes he rested upon Daisy were as cold and hard as granite.

They waited until the Rolls had reached the end of the street before they went indoors.

'Such a lovely surprise,' said her mother. 'I thought you wouldn't be home for another few weeks, dear.'

'Well, so did I, Mother, but there was a governess who'd been with friends of the Thorleys and she's taken over the twins.'

'Well, I'll put on the kettle and you shall tell me all about it. Pam will be home soon; she will be pleased.'

Mrs Pelham led the way into the kitchen. 'That nice doctor driving you back like that. Did he meet you at the airport?'

'He was on his way to Salisbury and the Thorleys did tell him which flight I'd be on.'

'Now that is what I call kind; you must have had a delightful journey together.'

Daisy took off her jacket. 'Oh, yes, we did, indeed we did.' She uttered the lie so heartily that she almost believed it herself.

CHAPTER FIVE

PAMELA CAME HOME when Daisy was halfway through the account of her stay in Holland, so she would have to begin all over again, but before she had a chance to start her sister said, 'Do tell; this Philip you wrote about, is he nice? Will you see him again?'

'Perhaps, if he comes home on leave and he hasn't forgotten me. He had planned to take me to the north of Holland but I've come home instead—I only had a few minutes in which to say goodbye.'

Her mother said, 'There, I knew you'd meet someone nice.'

'He was just a friend, Mother; I think he felt lonely and he enjoyed showing me round the Hague.'

Her mother looked disappointed. 'Yes, well, dear...did you meet anyone else while you were there?'

Daisy refilled the teapot from the kettle. 'Friends of the Thorleys—there are a lot of English people living there—and Dr Seymour; he's abroad a great deal and he came to see them while I was there.'

'He didn't bring you all the way home?'

'No, I told you, he was on his way from London to Salisbury and Lady Thorley had told him I would be coming back on the late morning flight.'

'So kind,' commented her mother. 'It's lovely to have you home, Daisy.' She glanced at Pamela. 'We've managed quite well, I think.'

'I knew you would. I've almost all of my wages; I'll go to the bank tomorrow and pay them in.'

'Yes, dear. Now I'm going to get us a nice supper while you unpack.'

It was much later, after Pam had gone to bed and her mother was sitting contentedly knitting, that Daisy took a look at the housekeeping purse and then leafed through the chequebook. Even in those few weeks while she had been away the money seemed to have melted away alarmingly; she would have to start looking for a job as soon as possible.

She spent a couple of days at home, sorting out the small problems her mother had, paying one or two bills which had been overlooked, catching up with the local news and tidying the garden. After the weekend, she promised herself, she would start looking for a job.

There was nothing in the local paper on Saturday so she cycled into Salisbury on Monday morning, bought all the magazines which advertised work and visited two agencies. Neither of them had anything for her; there was, it seemed, no demand for mother's helps, nannies or unqualified kindergarten teachers. 'Now if you had simple typing and shorthand,' suggested the brisk lady at the second agency Daisy went to, 'I could offer you several good jobs. I suppose you haven't had any experience in a shop? There's a good opening for an experienced sales girl in a fancy goods shop.'

Daisy shook her head; she wasn't sure what fancy goods were anyway, and the lady gave her a scornful look. 'Well, dear, all I can suggest is that you take a course in something and then try again—there's always domestic work or work for early morning office cleaners…'

It might even come to that, thought Daisy. How fortunate it was that there was a little money in the bank, enough to keep them all for several weeks, although the uneasy thought that she would have to order coal for the winter very soon haunted her… There was no point in getting pessimistic, she told herself; after all, she had only just started to look for work.

She spent the week applying for various jobs she found in the magazines but they were few and none of the advertisers bothered to answer her applications. So she sat with Razor on her lap, writing an advert to put in the local paper, and had to admit that her skills were too limited to attract more than the casual eye. All the same, she sent it off and went along to the job centre.

There wasn't anything there, either; it seemed that she was unemployed. But things could have been worse; the local bakery needed part-time help—Friday mornings and Saturday afternoons for two weeks only. It was quite hard work and she didn't get on very well with the till but the money was a godsend, little though it was. She received her wages for the last time and started to clear up in the shop before she went home. The manageress was totalling the day's takings and was disposed to be friendly.

'Well, you've not done too badly, love,' she observed, 'though I can see it's not quite your cup of tea; still, anything's better than having no work, isn't it?'

Daisy, wiping down the counter, agreed. 'I've liked working here. I dare say something will turn up soon.'

However, it didn't, and September was nudging its way

into October. Daisy ordered the coal; paying for it left a hole in the bank account, a hole which would have to be filled. She cycled to Salisbury again and tried the two agencies once more; the first one had nothing at all, the second offered her work as a mother's help in a family of six children living on a farm at Old Sarum; she would have to live in and the wages were low. Daisy said that she would think about it and despite her lack of money went and had a cup of coffee. If only something would happen, she reflected as she drank it.

It was as well that she was unaware that Dr Seymour was drinking coffee too—in her mother's kitchen. He had called, he told Mrs Pelham, on the spur of the moment. 'I know my sister will want to know if Daisy has found a good job and I shall be seeing her shortly.'

Mrs Pelham gave him a second cup of coffee and offered biscuits. 'Daisy's gone to Salisbury to see those two agencies again; there's nothing, you know, and you have no idea how difficult it is to find work, and the dear child isn't trained for anything—you see, my husband died and there was such a lot to see to and I'm not very businesslike and then we found that there wasn't enough money so she took that job with Mrs Gower-Jones—it was just enough with my pension.'

'So Daisy has no work yet?'

'Well, she helped out at the local bakery for two weeks, just for two half-days a week.' Mrs Pelham paused. 'I really don't know why I'm bothering you with all this…'

'Perhaps I can be of help. I happen to know that the hospital is short of ward orderlies—not domestics but they help with all the small tasks so that the nurses have more time for their own work.' And since Mrs Pelham was looking bewildered he explained, 'Helping with the meals, tidying beds, arranging flowers and so on. I believe that the hours are reasonable and the pay is adequate; at least it might tide her over until she finds something more to her taste.'

'She wouldn't need any training?' asked Mrs Pelham eagerly.

He said gently, 'No, just common sense and kindness, and she has both.'

'I'll tell her the moment she gets in...'

'Why not? But I think it might be a good idea if you don't mention that I've been to see you or that I've told you of the job; I think Daisy might resent anything which smacks of charity and it might seem like that to her. Could you not say that you've heard of work at the hospital from some friend or acquaintance?'

'Well, yes, I can do that; we know a great many people in the town—I could have heard about it from a dozen people. And I see what you mean about not telling Daisy that you called and told me about it; she is a dear girl but very independent.'

They had another cup of coffee together and parted on the best of terms and Mrs Pelham sat down and rehearsed what she would say to Daisy when she got home, pausing to regret that the doctor seemed to have no interest in Daisy; his voice had been impersonal when he had talked of her, and why should it have been otherwise? Daisy was no beauty and she had a way of saying exactly what she thought which could be disconcerting; perhaps she had annoyed him in some way, in which case it was kind of him to put himself to the trouble of finding her a job and in all probability he was only doing what his sister had asked him to do.

Daisy, despondent at her lack of success, listened eagerly

to her mother's news when she returned home. 'I met Mrs Grenville—remember her, dear? She lives somewhere in Salisbury. She was at the market and we got chatting. She told me that they need these orderlies at the hospital; they're going to advertise but if you went along you might stand a chance before it gets into the paper.'

'I'll go in the morning; I can at least apply if there really are vacancies.'

It wasn't until she woke up in the middle of the night that she remembered Dr Seymour worked at the hospital. Unfortunate, she thought sleepily, but that was a small hindrance compared with the possibility of a secure job.

She telephoned the hospital the next morning and was told that yes, applicants were to be interviewed for several vacancies for ward orderlies and if she cared to present herself at two o'clock that day, bringing with her two references, she would be seen some time during the afternoon.

It was rather daunting to find that she was one of many and one of the last to be interviewed.

She hadn't much chance of getting a job, she reflected, answering the questions the severe woman behind the desk was asking her, unaware that the severe lady had been discreetly told that, should a Miss Daisy Pelham present herself for an interview, Dr Seymour would vouch for her personally. Thoroughly reliable, hard-working and trustworthy, he had said, previously employed by his sister and leaving only because the children had grown too old for a nanny.

The severe lady did not mention this for the simple reason that she had been told not to; she merely told Daisy that she would be notified if she was successful.

'I'm not very hopeful,' said Daisy as she had supper with

her mother and sister that evening. 'There were dozens of us there and most of them looked frightfully efficient.'

'We'll have to wait and see,' sighed her mother placidly.

They didn't have to wait long; there was a letter the next morning confirming her appointment as a ward orderly, starting on the following Monday. She was to report for work at half-past eight each morning except for Saturdays and Sundays, but she would be expected to work one weekend in four. The wages were adequate; there would be no money to spare but they would be solvent. They had a rather excited breakfast and Pamela said, 'I'm glad you've got a job, Daisy, but you're not to stay a ward orderly a day longer than you must—if something better turns up… Will the work be rather beastly? Cleaning up after patients and fetching and carrying for the nurses?'

'It will be interesting,' said Daisy stoutly.

When she presented herself in a wrap-around pink overall on Monday morning she really found it more than interesting—thoroughly bewildering. She was to work on Women's Medical with another orderly, a woman in her thirties, who, Daisy quickly discovered, did her work with a kind of dogged thoroughness, disregarding the occupants of the beds—indeed, they might as well have been empty for all the notice she took of them. Daisy, friendly by nature, smiled at the patients, moved their glasses of water where they could reach them, picked up their knitting dropped on the floor and unreachable, and exchanged magazines and papers.

'You'll never get your work done while you waste your time with them,' observed Mrs Brett sourly. 'Just you collect up them empty cups and take them out to the kitchen. The trolley's on the landing.'

So Daisy collected cups, wiped locker-tops, collected

water jugs and ran errands for Sister, who, beyond asking her her name and telling her to do whatever Mrs Brett told her to do, had had nothing more to say to her. Mrs Brett, relishing her superiority, told her to do a great deal: carry round the trays at lunchtime, help frail elderlies to the loo, change sheets in the beds of those who had had unfortunate accidents and hurry with bowls to those who felt sick. It was all very muddled and Daisy wasn't sure if she was going to like it; Mrs Brett was far too bossy and the nurses were too busy to see it…

She was sent to the canteen for her lunch at half-past twelve and was much more cheered to find several girls of her own age at the table, orderlies like herself and prepared to be friendly, and when she told them where she was working a comfortably plump girl with a pleasant country accent observed kindly that it was hard luck having to work with Mrs Brett, who had been at the hospital for a long time and behaved as though she ran the place. 'A pity that once you get a ward you stay on it, though you might be lucky and get moved.'

Daisy went back for the afternoon's work feeling more cheerful; it was, after all, her first day and probably Mrs Brett would be nicer when they got to know each other. Mrs Brett, however, wasn't disposed to be friendly; indeed if anything she became more sharp-tongued as the afternoon wore on. Daisy, her day's work done, went home and presented a cheerful face to her mother and sister; the work was interesting, she was sure she was going to like it, and to her mother's enquiry as to whether she had met any of the doctors on the ward she said no, not yet, not wishing to disappoint her parent with the fact that the doctors, even the young housemen, didn't so much as cast a glance in her direction and weren't likely to either; an orderly was a domestic after all.

By the end of the week she had come to the conclusion that Mrs Brett, for all her bossiness, wasn't organised; there was a great deal of time wasted over their various jobs and far too much to-ing and fro-ing. Besides, she didn't much like the way Mrs Brett tossed knives, spoons and forks on to the patients' beds ready for their meals, so that some of the less agile patients had to wait until someone bringing their lunch- or tea-tray scooped them up and handed them over. Daisy knew better than to say anything and, uncaring of Mrs Brett's cross voice, nipped around arranging things within reach, and tidily too, and when Mrs Brett wasn't looking cutting up food and filling water glasses. She got the sharp edge of her colleague's tongue several times a day but she ignored that. One day, she promised herself, she would tell Mrs Brett just what she thought of her. It was a great pity that she was allowed to do more or less what she liked on the ward but to Sister she presented an appearance of hard-working efficiency, ready with the tea-tray when that lady sat down in her office to do the paperwork and running errands for the nurses. The patients didn't like her; indeed, some of the elderlies who depended on a helping hand were a little afraid of her.

Daisy, going home at the end of the first week with her pay packet in her pocket, decided that even if she didn't much like being an orderly the job provided her family's bread and butter and gave her the chance to help some of the patients.

'Have you seen anything of Dr Seymour?' her mother asked that evening.

'Him?' Daisy had washed her hair and was winding an

elaborate turban around her head. 'No, but he works in London as well, you know. Probably he only comes to Salisbury when he's needed.'

'A pity, but at least you'll see something of the Thorleys when they come back, won't you?'

'I expect so. I promised the children I'd go and see them.'

She had been happy with Josh and Katie, she reflected and, despite the fact that she never wanted to see Dr Seymour again, she had been unable to forget him. He would have forgotten her already, of course.

Halfway through the next week she met him face to face on her way back from her lunch; there was no one else in sight and she debated whether to stop and speak to him—a wasted exercise for he gave her a wintry smile, nodded briefly and walked past her. She stood, watching him go out of sight; she still wasn't sure just how important he was; if the young housemen ignored the domestic staff, she supposed that the more senior medical staff were hardly aware of any but the senior nursing staff. All the same, he could have said something—hello would have done…

Gobbling bread and butter and drinking strong tea with some of the other orderlies during her brief tea break, she suddenly realised that they were talking about him.

'Marvellous with the kids,' said a voice, 'a pity we don't see more of him; comes twice a week for his outpatients and ward-rounds; ever so polite too—says good morning as affable as you like, more than some I know…'

There was general laughter. 'Well, what do you expect? No one's going to look twice at the likes of us. He's different, though—a real gent.'

'Married, is 'e?' asked one of the girls.

'Well, I don't know him well enough to ask…' There was

a good deal of good-natured laughter as they got up to go back to their wards.

It must be that he didn't like her, reflected Daisy, hurrying along corridors and up stairs; if he had said good morning to the other girls, why couldn't he have done the same to her? She had quite overlooked the fact that she told him in no uncertain terms that she had no wish to see him again.

That afternoon, when she was cycling home after work, the Rolls whispered past her. The doctor was looking straight ahead and there was a good deal of traffic on the road; he wouldn't have seen her. All the same, she wished most unreasonably that he had at least lifted a hand in salute.

When she got home her mother said in a pleased voice, 'Lady Thorley phoned, love. They came back today and the children want to see you. I told her you were only free at the weekends—she said she'd ring again.' She glanced at Daisy's face. 'You've had a horrid day, haven't you? Come and sit down; I'll have supper on the table in no time. It'll be nice for you to have an outing and go and see those children again—she said that they still miss you.'

Lady Thorley phoned after supper; the children were well and getting on famously with Miss Thompson but they did want to see her again. Daisy agreed to go to tea on Saturday and was relieved and at the same time disappointed to be told that Lady Thorley would be on her own. 'Hugh won't be home until Sunday—we can have a nice gossip and I know Miss Thompson will be glad to see you again.'

Daisy put down the phone; the doctor would have got back to London by then, of course. A good thing too, she muttered to Razor as she gave him his supper.

She woke to rain on Saturday morning, not that she minded overmuch; for two days she was free of Mrs Brett's grumbling voice. She got the breakfast, saw Pamela off to spend the day with friends, made a shopping-list with her mother and walked to the centre of Wilton; doled out carefully, there was money enough to buy all the right sort of food; she visited the butcher, the grocer and the post office, bought bread still warm from the oven, and carried the lot home, had coffee with her mother and, since there were only the two of them, settled on soup and bread and cheese for lunch. While her mother got them ready, she went up to her room and changed into a navy blue jersey dress she had bought in the January sales. It was elegant, well cut and well made, and it fitted her nicely, but the colour did nothing for her. A well-meaning friend had once told her in the kindest possible way that unless a girl was pretty enough to warrant a second look it was wise to wear clothes which didn't draw attention to herself. Daisy, aware of her shortcomings, had taken her advice. Besides, one didn't get tired of neutral colours; at least, in theory one didn't. That she was heartily sick of them was something she never admitted to herself.

The twins would have been happy to see her wearing an old sack; they gave her a rapturous welcome and the welcome from Lady Thorley and Miss Thompson was equally warm. There was a good deal of talking before everyone settled down—Lady Thorley to go back to her drawing-room and Miss Thompson and the children, taking Daisy with them, to the nursery where she was shown the twins' latest craze. They had discovered the joys of Plasticine, which they had not been so keen on when Daisy had looked after them—not just small quantities of it, but large lumps which they were modelling into a variety of large and obscure objects.

'I'm no good at making things,' confessed Miss Thompson as they sat down at the table. 'I can just about manage a dog or a cat but Josh wants a model of Buckingham Palace.' She handed Daisy a hefty lump. 'They tell me that you're very good at making things...'

So Daisy embarked on the royal building while the twins, their tongues hanging out with their efforts, started on their various versions of the Queen and Prince Philip, all the while talking non-stop. Presently Miss Thompson said quietly, 'Daisy, I've some letters to post; would you mind very much if I go now? Josh and Katie are happy with you—if it weren't raining so hard we could all have gone...' Daisy didn't mind. At Josh's request she had stopped her modelling to make a drawing of Razor and she had no worries about keeping the children amused. The village post office wasn't too far away; Miss Thompson would be back in plenty of time for tea. Daisy glanced at the clock; she had promised to be home as soon after six o'clock as possible, but that was three hours away.

One drawing of Razor wasn't enough; she embarked upon a series of this splendid animal, handing over each sketch for the children to colour, Katie in her favourite pink, Josh with large spots and stripes. It was a good thing that Razor, a dignified animal, wasn't there to see.

She was putting the finishing touches to Razor's fine whiskers when she heard the twins give a kind of whispered shout, but before she could look up two large, cool hands covered her eyes.

'Guess who?' asked a voice she had done her best to forget.

There was no need for her to reply—the twins were shouting with delight, 'You don't know, do you, Daisy? You must guess—we'll help you...'

She should have been feeling annoyance but instead she felt a pleasant tingling from the touch of his hands and a distinct thrill at the sound of his voice. Which simply would not do. Besides, the children would be disappointed.

'Father Christmas?' she suggested, a remark hailed by peals of laughter from Josh.

'Silly Daisy, it's not Christmas yet,' and,

'Two more guesses,' said Katie.

'Mr Cummins?' She had heard all about him from the twins; he had been in the nursery all day repairing the central heating.

'One more,' shouted Josh.

'Dr Seymour.' Her voice was quite steady.

'You mean Uncle Val. You've guessed; now you don't have to pay a forfeit.'

'What a pity,' remarked the doctor and dropped his hands to let them rest on Daisy's shoulders, which she found even more unsettling. 'I don't mind being taken for Father Christmas but I'm not so sure about this unknown Mr Cummins.'

'The plumber,' said Daisy and wished he would take his hands away.

However, he didn't; indeed he began to stroke the back of her neck with a thumb, which, although wholly delightful, she soon put a stop to by getting up quickly; and, since she had no idea what she was going to do next, it was a relief when Miss Thompson, followed by Lady Thorley, came into the room.

'Shall we all have tea here?' asked Lady Thorley, and didn't wait for an answer.

'I'll tell Cook,' said Miss Thompson, leaving Daisy to clear the table of the lumps of Plasticine, fend off Boots's delighted caperings and find a cloth for the table. The doctor, sitting with a twin on either knee, listened to his sister's idle talk and watched Daisy.

Tea was noisy, cheerful and leisurely, and Daisy, despite the doctor's unsettling presence, enjoyed herself so much that she forgot the time, and, her eye lighting on the clock, she saw that it was already past six o'clock.

She caught Lady Thorley's eye. 'I really have to go,' she said. 'I said I'd be home by six…' She lifted Boots's great head off her lap and stood up as the twins raised a roar of protest. 'Look,' she told them, 'if your mother and Miss Thompson will allow it, you can come and have tea with me and meet Razor.'

'When?' asked Josh.

'Any Saturday.' She paused. 'No, not next Saturday; I have to work that day.'

She began her goodbyes, long-drawn-out on the part of the children, brisk and friendly from Miss Thompson, and was politely cool towards the doctor.

'I'll see you to the door,' Lady Thorley said comfortably and they went down the hall, lingering for a moment while Daisy got into her plastic mac and uttered suitable thanks. She had her hand on the doorknob when the doctor joined them, took her hand off the knob and opened the door.

'Ready?' he asked briskly, and to his sister said, 'I'll be back shortly, Meg.'

Daisy swept out into the porch, then found her voice. 'My bike's here—I'm cycling home—I can't leave it here, I need it…'

He had opened the car door and she found herself inside without quite knowing how she had got there. 'Your bike will be delivered to you at the latest by tomorrow afternoon, so stop fussing.'

He got inside the car, fastened her seat belt as well as his own and made no effort to start the car.

'Enjoying your new job?' he asked.

She said peevishly, 'Oh, so you did see me the other day—you looked at me as though I weren't there. Thank you, I quite like the work; I like the patients too…'

'But?'

His voice was beguilingly encouraging and for a moment she forgot that she wanted nothing more to do with him. 'Mrs Brett—the other orderly—she's been there a long time and she's a bit set in her ways; I suppose she's seen so many patients she doesn't really notice them any more.'

'And what do you intend to do about that?'

'Me? Nothing. I've only been there for a few weeks and I want to keep the job; and besides, who am I to criticise her? Only I can see that the patients can reach their water jugs and cut up their meat and pick up their knitting.' She stopped and went a bright pink. 'That sounds priggish; I can't think why I'm telling you about it—it's not important.'

He said casually, 'Why not get a transfer to another ward?'

'Orderlies are sent to a ward and stay on it until they're moved somewhere else.' She stared ahead of her. 'I think we're called ancillary workers but we're domestics. When are you going back to London?'

The sound which escaped his lips might have been a chuckle. 'Very shortly; that's a relief, isn't it? We shan't need to ignore each other if we should meet at the hospital.'

There didn't seem to be a reply to that.

He drove her home then, carrying on the kind of conversation which meant nothing at all but sounded pleasant. He got out when they reached her home, opened her door and held the gate as she went through it.

She thanked him as he shut it behind her, making it obvious that if she had invited him in he would have refused anyway, so she wished him goodbye and went into the house.

'Is that you, darling?' called her mother from the kitchen. 'Are you very wet?'

'I got a lift,' said Daisy, getting out of the hated mac, 'and my bike will be brought back some time tomorrow.'

'Who brought you back?' Her mother had poked her head round the door to ask.

'Dr Seymour came to tea and brought me back.' She added quite unnecessarily, 'It's raining.'

Her mother gave her a thoughtful look. 'Yes, dear. I've started supper.' She opened the door wider. 'But I thought you might like to make the pie—all those apples and they won't keep.'

Daisy, rolling pastry ten minutes later, wondered if Dr Seymour was staying with his sister, and if not where was he? He must live somewhere. In London? He worked there too, didn't he? Perhaps he had a house there as well as living in Salisbury; but perhaps he didn't live there either.

She frowned, reminding herself that she had no interest in him.

Much refreshed by a weekend at home, Daisy went back to work on Monday, full of good resolves: not to allow Mrs Brett to annoy her, to carry out her orders even if she found them unnecessary—locker-tops didn't need to be washed twice a day, whereas water jugs, sitting empty, needed to be filled… She bade her superior good morning and had a grunted reply, followed by a stern request to get on with the cleaning since it was the consultant's round, 'And don't you hang around wasting time picking up knitting and such like, and see that the ten o'clock drinks trolley is on time; I don't want no 'itch.'

Daisy didn't want a hitch either; all the same she contrived to unpick a row of knitting and take two lots of hair curlers out while Mrs Brett had gone to have her coffee.

Her hopes of a better relationship between herself and Mrs Brett came to nothing; it seemed that she couldn't please that lady. Whatever she did was found fault with, and as the week progressed it was apparent that Mrs Brett had decided not to like her and nothing Daisy could do would alter that. They parted company on Friday evening with Mrs Brett full of foreboding as to how Daisy was going to manage over the weekend.

'You'll get no 'elp,' she warned her. 'You'll 'ave ter work for two, and lord knows what I'll find when I gets 'ere on Monday morning.'

Daisy said, 'Yes, Mrs Brett,' and 'Goodnight, Mrs Brett,' and cycled home, the prospect of two days without her surly companion quite a pleasing one.

Without that lady breathing down her neck every ten minutes or so, Daisy found herself enjoying her work; she had common sense, speed and a kind nature that, she discovered for herself, was what her job was all about. No one bothered her; she got on with her chores and found time to satisfy the needs of those patients who were not in a fit state to look after themselves. She went off duty on the Saturday evening feeling pleased with herself even though her feet ached abominably.

Sunday was even better, for Sister wasn't on duty until one o'clock and there was a general air of leisure on the ward so that there was time to listen to titbits of news read aloud by those patients who had the Sunday papers and pause to help with the odd crossword puzzle. She went down to the canteen feeling that life was quite fun after all.

She was going off duty that evening, crossing the main entrance hall, inconspicuous in her good suit, when she saw Dr Seymour watching her from one corner. He was talking to one of the house doctors, staring at her over the man's shoulder. She looked away at once and whisked herself out of the door and over to the bicycle racks and presently pedalled home as though the furies were after her, but no Rolls-Royce sped past her, and she arrived home out of breath and feeling foolish. What, she asked herself, had she expected him to do? Speak to her? Open the door for her? A thin-lipped smile perhaps?

She was free all day on Monday, a splendid opportunity to help her mother around the little house, tidy the garden before the weather worsened and change the library books. As she biked to work on Tuesday morning she allowed herself to wonder if she would see the doctor.

Scrambling into the pink overall in the small room the orderlies used, she was accosted by one of them. 'Lucky you,' said the girl, 'you're being sent to Children's—Irma told me—it's on the board outside. You'd better look for yourself.'

'Me?' said Daisy. 'But I thought you never got moved…'

'Someone off sick, I dare say—make the best of it, Daisy, it's the best ward in the whole place.'

There, sure enough, was her name—to report to the children's unit forthwith. She skipped along corridors and in and out of swing doors with a light heart; no more Mrs Brett… She was opening the last of the swing doors when she remembered that Dr Seymour was a consultant paediatrician.

CHAPTER SIX

AFTER THE QUIETNESS of the women's medical ward, the children's unit gave forth a steady roar of sound: shrill cries, shrieks, babies crying and cheerful voices, accompanied by background music just loud enough to weld the whole into a cheerful din. Daisy paused just inside the doors, not sure where to go; there were doors on either side of the wide hall leading to the ward. She supposed she should report to Sister…

A very pretty young woman put her head round one of the doors. 'Our new orderly?' she asked in a friendly voice. 'Come in here, will you, and I'll give you a few ideas…?'

Sister Carter was as unlike Sister on Women's Medical as chalk was from cheese. Not much older than Daisy, with curly hair framing a delightful face, she looked good enough to eat. Daisy, bidden to sit, sat and said politely, 'Good morning, Sister. I'm the orderly; my name's Daisy.'

'Nice—the children will love it.' She glanced at a folder on her desk. 'I see you've been working in a nursery school, just the kind of person we need here.' She smiled at Daisy. 'Lots of dirty work, though.'

'I don't mind that, Sister.'

'Good. Come and meet Maisie—our other orderly.'

Maisie was on her hands and knees clearing up a toddler's breakfast porridge which had been hurled away in a fit of childish pique. She came upright, beaming from a round and cheerful face. ''E's at it again, Sister,' she observed without rancour.

'Naughty boy,' said sister. 'Maisie, here is Daisy, your new partner.'

''Ello, love, am I glad to see you—one pair of 'ands don't go far with this lot.' She looked Daisy over in a friendly way. 'Like kids?'

'Yes,' said Daisy.

'You and me'll get on fine,' declared Maisie. ''Elp me clear the breakfast things and I'll tell you what's what as we go.'

Daisy had never been so content; the ward was a happy place despite the sick children in it and she had spent the day clearing up messes, sorting clean linen and bagging mountains of soiled sheets and small garments, going to and fro with meals, making Sister's coffee and listening carefully to Maisie's advice. Maisie was a treasure with a heart of gold and endless patience. The nurses were nice too; she might not be one of them but she had been made to feel that she was part of the team. Daisy blessed the unknown authority who had seen fit to send her to the children's unit. Going down to her short tea break, she wondered who it was.

The unknown authority was sitting in Sister Carter's office, going over his small patients' case-sheets and drinking strong tea from a mug. Presently he glanced up. 'The new orderly—she'll settle down?'

'Daisy? Oh, yes, sir. A nice little thing. You recommended her, didn't you? Not quite our usual sort of girl but she has a way with the children and our Maisie assures me that she's a good worker. She's at tea—did you want to see her?'

'No. My sister employed her as nanny to her children and she needed to have a job near home. Now, what are we going to do with baby George? He had better have another X-ray. I have to go back to town this evening but I'll speak to Dr Dowling before I go—I shall be away for the rest of this week.' He got up to go. 'Thanks for the tea.' As he went through the door he saw Daisy's pink-clad person disappearing into the ward.

It was late evening when he left the hospital and drove himself through the city, through the medieval gates of the cathedral close and parked before his house. It was a very old house, but like many of its neighbours had a Georgian front with an important pillared door and a charming transom over it. He let himself in and was met in the hall by a tall, bony woman of uncertain years, whose sharp-nosed face lighted up at the sight of him.

'There you are, sir. And there's your dinner waiting for you, and eat it you must before you go to London… I've packed your case and there's messages for you—' She was interrupted by a deep-throated barking. 'That's Belle, in the garden with all the doors shut, but she knows it's you.'

'Sorry I'm late, Mrs Trump. Give me five minutes, will you? Thanks for packing my bag; I'll join Belle for a moment—I could do with some fresh air.'

The doctor opened a door at the back of the square hall and went into a fair-sized walled garden behind the house, to be greeted with ecstasy by a golden Labrador. He bent to fondle her ears and then strolled round the small garden still bright with autumn flowers until his housekeeper called from the door and they both went inside to the dining-room, its walls panelled, the mahogany table and sideboard gleaming with polished age, silver and glass gleaming in the soft light of the wall-sconces. He ate his solitary, deliciously cooked meal without waste of time, had coffee at the table and, accompanied by Belle, went to his study to collect up those papers he wished to take with him. It was a pleasant room at the back of the house, its walls lined with books, its leather chairs large. His desk was large too, every inch of it taken up with case-sheets, folders and a mass of reading matter. It looked a splendid muddle but he put his hand on what he wanted without hesitation, put it into his briefcase and went up to his room to fetch his bag.

Downstairs again, he went through the door beside the graceful little staircase and found Mrs Trump loading the dishwasher. He let Belle into the garden and addressed himself to his housekeeper.

'I'll be away for the best part of the week,' he told her. 'I'll ring you later.' He smiled at her. 'Take care of yourself.' He whistled to Belle and presently got into his car and drove himself away. It would be late by the time he got to London but the drive would give him time to think. Rather against his will he found he was thinking about Daisy.

Daisy was thinking about him too. She had been on tenterhooks all day expecting to see him on the ward, but there had been no sign of him, nor had his name been mentioned. 'And a good thing too,' she muttered to herself. 'The less we see of each other the better; he unsettles me.'

Luckily, when she got home her thoughts were happily diverted by a letter from Philip, home on leave in Bristol and asking if he might drive down to Wilton and see her. A day out together, he suggested in his neat handwriting, or failing that could they meet for a meal? If she would like that could she phone him and perhaps something could be arranged.

Her mother and Pamela, apprised of the contents of the letter, were enthusiastic. 'Phone him now,' urged Pamela. 'You're free this weekend, aren't you? Well, say you'll spend the day with him. Wear the good suit. Debenhams have got a sale on; see if you can get a top to go with it—one of those silk ones, you know, short sleeves and a plain neck; you can borrow Mother's pearls...'

Philip sounded pleased when she phoned. Saturday, he suggested with flattering eagerness. They could drive out into the country and have lunch. He assured her that he was looking forward to seeing her again and to exchanging their news. Daisy put down the receiver feeling a faint glow of pleasure.

Before she slept that night she lay thinking about Philip; it would be nice to see him again—he was a very pleasant companion and they got on well together, which thought somehow reminded her that she and the doctor didn't get on well at all. Surprisingly, it wasn't Philip in her sleepy thoughts, but Dr Seymour, his handsome face vivid under her eyelids.

Naturally enough, she saw no sign of him during that week. There were a number of children under his care and a youngish man with a friendly face came each day to see them. Daisy, cleaning the bathrooms with Maisie, asked who he was.

''E's Dr Dowling, registrar to Dr Seymour—keeps 'is eye on the kids when 'is nibs isn't here.' Maisie gave her a sidelong glance. 'Got a boyfriend, 'ave you, Daisy?'

'Me? No...'

'Go on with you, a nice girl like you.'

Daisy thought of Philip. 'Well, it's true, though I'm going out on Saturday with someone I met a little while ago in Holland. Just for lunch.'

'Holland, eh? Been to foreign parts, 'ave you? I've always fancied a bit of travel meself. Is 'e a Dutchman, then?'

'No, he just works there; he's on holiday.'

Maisie was mopping the floor. 'Our Dr Seymour, 'e goes over to Holland once in a while—very clever, 'e is, with the kids. Tells other doctors what to do.'

That sounded like him all right, thought Daisy, arranging the tooth-mugs in a neat line on their appointed shelf. She squashed an impulse to talk about him and instead suggested that she should go to the kitchen and get the trolley ready for the dinners. 'Unless there's something you'd like me to do first, Maisie?'

'You run along, Daisy, and get started, then, and lay up a tray for Sister at the same time, will you? She likes her pot of tea after her own dinner.'

Saturday came at last. Daisy got up early and dressed carefully. She had found a plain silk top to go with the suit, very plain, round-necked and short-sleeved, but if they were to go to the kind of restaurant where she would be expected to take off her jacket it would pass muster. The pearls gave it a touch of class, or so she hoped. Carefully swathed in one of her mother's aprons, she got the breakfast, saw to Razor's food and sat down with her mother and Pamela to boiled eggs and bread and butter.

'Let's hope you get a smashing lunch,' said Pam with her mouth full. 'Any idea where you're going?'

'Not the faintest. If he hasn't been to Salisbury before I dare say he'll want to look round the cathedral.'

Pamela looked horrified. 'But that's not romantic.'

'I'm not expecting romance,' said Daisy. She had the ridiculous idea that if it were Dr Seymour and not Philip it would have been romantic in a coal hole. She frowned; really she was allowing the most absurd ideas to run through her head. She helped clear the table, made the beds and did her hair again and then went downstairs to wait for Philip.

He arrived punctually, greeted her with pleasure, drank the coffee her mother had ready and led the way out to his car. It was a small, elderly model, bright red and nice but noisy. Daisy got in happily enough. Philip had no wish to see the cathedral; instead he had planned a trip down towards the coast, through Fordingbridge and Ringwood. A friend of his had said that there was a good pub in Brockenhurst where they could have lunch. 'We could go on to Beaulieu but I don't suppose there would be time for that; I have to get back this evening.'

'Yes, of course; come home to tea, though.'

They were almost on the outskirts of Salisbury when the doctor, driving the other way, passed them. Neither of them noticed the Rolls slide past them but he, even in the few seconds allowed him, had a clear view of them both laughing.

Less than ten minutes later he drew up before her home, got out and banged the knocker. Mrs Pelham came to the door, beaming a welcome.

'How very nice to see you again!' she exclaimed. 'Did you want to see Daisy about something? Such a pity you've just missed her.' She opened the door wider. 'Do come in and have a cup of coffee; I've just made some.'

'That,' said the doctor at his most urbane, 'would be delightful. I'm on my way to see my sister.'

Mrs Pelham looked past him. 'Is that a dog in the car? Yours? Bring him in, do. Razor won't mind.'

'Her name's Belle; she's very mild. You're sure—er—Razor won't mind?'

'Our cat. He has a keen brain, so Daisy says, but he's bone-idle.'

They sat over their coffee, with Belle at her master's feet and Razor sitting on the corner of the mantelpiece for safety's sake, and since the doctor was at his most charming Mrs Pelham told him all about Philip coming to take Daisy out. 'All the way from Bristol,' she observed. 'They've gone down towards the coast—I told Daisy to bring him back for tea. He seemed a nice young man.'

'Indeed, yes,' agreed the doctor, at his most amiable. 'I met him while I was at the Hague—a sound young man.' He put down his coffee-cup. 'I must be on my way.'

It was only as he was at the door saying goodbye that he asked casually, 'Daisy is happy at the hospital?'

Mrs Pelham said happily, 'Oh, yes, and now she's been moved on to the children's ward—your ward?—I dare say you'll see her.' She hesitated. 'But of course she's an orderly; I don't suppose you talk to them.'

He said gravely, 'Well, I don't have much contact with anyone outside the medical or nursing profession. I must look out for her, though.'

'Yes, do,' said Mrs Pelham. 'I'm sure she'll be delighted to see you again.'

He agreed pleasantly, reflecting that delight was the last thing he expected to see on Daisy's face.

In the car, he assured himself that it was because Daisy was so unwilling to like him that he found her so often on his mind. She appeared to have got herself a possible husband too. There was nothing wrong with young Philip; he would be an ideal husband in many ways, reliable and hard-working with little time for romantic nonsense. 'Well, if that's what she wants…' he muttered so savagely that Belle lifted an enquiring ear.

It might have been a relief to the doctor's feelings if he had known that Daisy had never once thought of Philip as a husband. If she had had a brother she would have liked him to be just like Philip—easygoing and cheerful, a good companion. She was enjoying herself enormously; there was a great deal to talk about, mostly about his work in the Hague and his hopes for the future, and at Brockenhurst they had found the pub without difficulty and had a ploughman's lunch, and presently drove on to Lymington, parked the car on Quay Hill and walked the length of the High Street and then down to the shore to look at the sea.

'We must do this again,' said Philip as he drove back later. 'I've got two weeks. Are you free every weekend?'

'I have to work every fourth weekend. That'll be in two weeks' time—I've been sent to another ward and the off duty's different.'

'I'm going to Cheshire to spend next weekend with friends and I'll be gone before you get your next free weekend. Could I come and see you at the hospital?'

'Heavens no. I mean, not just like that—I suppose if something really urgent happened and someone needed to see me about something.' Daisy shook her neat head firmly. 'Otherwise not.'

'I'll be home for a few days for Christmas; we must see each other then.'

He gave her a brotherly grin and she said, 'Yes, that will be nice.'

They had a splendid tea with her mother and Pamela, and Mrs Pelham, if she hoped for signs of a romance, was very disappointed; nothing could have been more prosaic than Daisy's manner towards Philip, and he, thought Mrs Pelham sadly, was behaving like a brother.

He left soon after tea, unknowingly passing the doctor's Rolls once more in one of Wilton's narrow streets, happily unaware of the frowning scrutiny that gentleman gave him as they slowed, going in opposite directions. The doctor had spent several hours in his sister's company, had a civil conversation with his brother-in-law, obligingly played a rousing game of snakes and ladders with his nephew and niece and had pleaded an evening engagement as soon as he decently could, and now he was driving himself back to his house in the close. He had a consultation at the hospital on Monday morning and there was no point in going back to London. He had no engagement; at the back of his mind had been the tentative idea that it might be pleasant to take Daisy out to dinner and use his powers of persuasion to stir up her interest, even liking, for him. Only an idea and a foolish one, he told himself and greeted his housekeeper with tight-lipped civility so that she went back to the kitchen to cook an extra-splendid meal. 'To take his mind off things,' she explained to Belle, who was eating her supper under the kitchen table.

She might just as well have served him slabs of cardboard although he complimented her upon the good food as he went to his study, where he sat, Belle at his feet, doing absolutely nothing but think about Daisy.

It was a waste of time thinking about the girl, he reasoned; cold facts proved that. She had disliked him on sight, and she had even told him so, hadn't she? He was far too old for her and he was quite sure that if she were to discover that it was through his good offices that she had got work at the hospital she would quite likely throw up the job at once. As far as he knew, she had never discovered that it was he who had asked his sister to take her on as a nanny, nor did she know why she had been moved to the children's ward or who had arranged that. He hoped she never would. What had started as a kindly act towards a girl who had intrigued him had become an overwhelming desire to make life as easy as possible for her.

He went up to bed at last, long after midnight, resolved to put her out of his mind. There was more than enough to occupy it; he had his work, more than he could cope with sometimes, many friends and family; he would find himself a wife and settle down. The doctor, a man with a brilliant brain, a fund of knowledge and priding himself on his logical outlook on life, had no idea how foolish that resolve was.

As for Daisy, she had enjoyed her day. They had reminisced about the Hague, and she had listened to Philip's light-hearted criticism of his job, pointing out in a sisterly fashion that however dull it might be at the moment it could lead to an interesting post.

'Well paid too, I shouldn't wonder,' she had added.

'Oh, yes,' he had agreed. 'I don't do too badly now. They like married men for the more senior jobs, though the thing is to get promotion and find a wife at the same time.'

They had laughed together quite unselfconsciously about it.

She had settled down nicely on the children's ward; it was hard work and at times extremely messy but Sister Carter was a happy person and the ward and its staff took their ambience from her; the nurses were treated fairly and if there were any small crises—and there very often were—and it was necessary for them to work over their normal hours, she worked with them. Daisy, going about her lowly tasks, wished that she could be a ward sister. She was happy enough, however; she was on good terms with the nurses and Maisie and the children had accepted her as a familiar face.

The week went by without a glimpse of Dr Seymour and she didn't know whether to be pleased or vexed when she went back after the following weekend to hear from Maisie that he had been to the ward several times during the weekend but had now returned to London.

As casually as she could, Daisy asked, 'Does he only come at weekends?'

'Lord bless you, no—'e comes when there's something needs sorting out, too much for 'is registrar; 'e comes regular like, for 'is rounds and out-patients and that. Busy man, 'e is.'

It was her turn to work at the weekend and she couldn't entirely suppress a feeling of expectancy as she cycled to work. Maisie had said that the doctor sometimes visited on a Saturday or Sunday and there was a chance that he might as there were several ill children on the ward…

There was no sign of him on Saturday; the registrar had been to the ward several times, obviously worried about some of the children, and Sister, who was on duty for the weekend, had spent a long time at their cotsides. Daisy longed to know what was the matter with them and if Sister hadn't been so busy she would have asked. As it was, she was busy herself, managing to do Maisie's work as well as her own. Sunday was just as hectic too but in the early evening the children seemed better and the ward was quiet. Daisy could hear the distant continuous murmur of visitors on the floors below; in another hour she would be going home… She picked up the tray of tea she was taking to Sister's office and, pausing at its door, came face to face with Philip.

He said breezily, 'Hello, is this where Sister lives? I've come to see you—I'm sure she won't mind just for a few minutes; I brought a friend down from home to visit his granny—she's had an operation.'

'You can't...' began Daisy, but it was too late; he had tapped on the door and she heard Sister's nice voice telling whoever it was to come in.

Afterwards she tried to understand what had happened. Sister had looked up from her desk and she and Philip had just stared at each other; they looked as though they had just discovered something they had been searching for all their lives and for the moment she had been quite sure that neither of them had any idea of where they were or what they were doing. She had waited for a moment for someone to say something and then put the tray down on Sister's desk. Sister had moved then and so had Philip.

Philip spoke first. 'I brought someone to visit and I wondered if I might have a few minutes with Daisy—we met in Holland.' He held out a hand. 'Philip Keynes...'

Sister blushed. 'Beryl Carter. You're a friend of Daisy? It's not really allowed to visit staff, but since you're here...'

'It's not at all important,' said Philip, summarily dismissing Daisy from his mind and life without a second's thought, so that Daisy slipped away and fetched another cup and saucer. She was in time to hear Sister say,

'Do sit down, Mr Keynes; have you come far?'

Daisy had never quite believed in falling in love at first sight, but now she knew better. They would make a nice pair, she reflected as she helped a hard-pressed nurse to change cotsheets. Philip would have to get a larger place in which to live, of course—if he had a wife he might get his promotion. She was deep in speculative thought when Sister came to the ward door.

Philip was standing by the swing doors, ready to leave. He said in a bemused kind of voice, 'I say, Daisy, I'm so glad I came to see you.' Then when she agreed pleasantly he went on, 'She's got a day off tomorrow; I'm coming to take her out for the day…'

'What a splendid idea,' said Daisy. 'I'm sure you'll have a lovely time. She's so very nice, Philip.'

'Nice? She's an angel—I knew it the moment I set eyes on her.'

He was, she saw, about to embark on a detailed description of Sister Carter's charms. Daisy cut him short in a kindly way. 'Good for you; I must go. Let me know what happens next, won't you?'

She went back into the ward; there was still almost an hour before she was free to go home.

Sister was in the ward checking one of the ill children when Dr Seymour came quietly in. Daisy, going down the ward with an armful of nappies for one of the nurses, slithered to a halt when he came towards her. He gave her a cold look and she wondered why; she hadn't expected a smile but his eyes were like grey steel. Naturally enough, if she had but known, for he had seen Philip leaving the ward only seconds before he himself entered it. The young man hadn't seen him; indeed, he was in such a state of euphoria that he was in no shape to see anything or anyone. The doctor, his face impassive, entered the ward in a rage.

He was still there when it was time for Daisy to go off duty. She bade Sister goodnight, and whisked herself away. It was a pity that she was free the next day—Dr Seymour might still be at the hospital, although, if he was going to look at her like that, perhaps it was just as well that she wasn't going to be there. She frowned; the last time they had met they had been quite friendly in a guarded sort of way. She shook off a vague regret and fell to planning what she would do with her free day.

It was nice to have a day at home, to potter round the garden, help her mother around the house; do some shopping. After supper she sat down at her mother's desk and carefully checked their finances. There was very little in the bank but at least they were paying the bills as they came in and putting by a little each week into what she called their 'sinking fund', which really meant schoolbooks for Pamela, and for having shoes mended and what she hoped would be a winter coat for her mother. She went back to work on the Tuesday morning feeling that life wasn't too bad; a few months' steady work and it would be even better; further ahead than that she didn't care to look. The thought of being an orderly for the rest of her working days made her feel unhappy.

She was cleaning out the older children's lockers by their small beds when Dr Seymour came in. Sister was with him; so was Staff Nurse, his registrar, a young houseman and one or two persons hovering on the fringe whom Daisy couldn't identify. He brought with him an air of self-assurance nicely timed with a kindly, avuncular manner—very reassuring to his patients, reflected Daisy, getting off her knees and melting discreetly into the nearest sluice-room. Maisie had dinned it into her on her first day that orderlies kept off the wards when the consultants did a round.

Maisie was having her coffee break and the sluice-room was pristine; Daisy wedged herself near the door and watched the small procession on its way round the cots. It was a leisurely round; Dr Seymour spent a long time with each occupant, sometimes sitting on the cotside with a toddler on his knee. He had a way with children, Daisy admitted, making them chuckle and undisturbed when they bawled.

The group moved round the ward and crossed over to the other side to where the older children were and Daisy, getting careless, opened the sluice-room door a little wider just as the doctor came to a halt and looked up, straight across the ward and at her. His look was impassive so why did she have the feeling that he was laughing behind that blandness? She stared back, not sure whether to shut the door or melt into the sluice-room out of sight, or perhaps stay well out of sight where she was.

The problem was solved for her, for he moved away, his head bent to hear what Sister was saying.

She had been at home for half an hour that evening when the doorknocker was soundly rapped. Pamela was in her room doing her homework, her mother was making a shopping-list and said vaguely, 'The door, dear,' so Daisy, spooning Razor's supper into his saucer, put the tin down and went to see who it was.

Dr Seymour stood on the doorstep and at her startled, 'Oh, it's you,' wasted no time on polite preliminaries.

'I should like a word,' he told her, and since he expected to be invited in she stood on one side.

'Come in, Dr Seymour.' Her voice was tart for she saw no reason to be anything else. Why he should want to come and see her was a mystery—surely if she had needed a reprimand for something she had done wrong on the ward it should be Sister who administered it?

She opened the sitting-room door but he brushed past her. 'You're in the kitchen?' he said, and before she could answer he had stalked in, to wish her surprised mother good evening with just the right degree of apologetic charm.

Mrs Pelham put down her pencil. 'Dr Seymour—how nice. Do you want to talk to Daisy? I'll make a cup of coffee.' She smiled at him in her gentle way. 'Do sit down.'

He sat, refusing the coffee at the same time. 'I've come to ask a favour of Daisy.' Since she was still standing just inside the door, he got up again. Lovely manners, reflected Mrs Pelham and told Daisy quite sharply to sit down. It would be easier to talk to him sitting down; he loomed rather large on his feet…

'My sister asked me to come and see you; she's unable to leave the children. Miss Thompson has had to go home to look after her sick mother and she thinks that I can explain matters more easily than if she spoke to you on the telephone. She and her husband have to attend some function or other next Saturday evening. There is no one she cares to leave the children with; she'll have to take them with her. She hopes that if you're free you might be persuaded to go with her and look after them—just for Saturday and Sunday. They'll take you up in the car and bring you back, of course.' He looked at Daisy. 'Of course we realise that it is an imposition; you have little enough free time. But the children like you and Meg trusts you, Daisy.'

Daisy opened her mouth to say no and then closed it again. After all, he was only passing on a message from his sister; it was really nothing to do with him, and Lady Thorley had been very kind to her. She glanced at her mother who smiled faintly at her. 'Why not, dear?' asked her parent. 'It will be a nice little change for you, and Lady Thorley has always been so kind to you.'

Daisy still hesitated, though; indeed she might have refused if Pamela, hearing voices, hadn't come down to see who had called. Her hello was casually friendly. 'I bet you want to borrow Daisy,' she said, and pulled up a chair to the table. 'Do tell. What is it this time? Measles?'

The doctor laughed. 'Nothing to do with me; I'm only the bearer of a message. My sister wants Daisy to go with her and the children to London for the weekend—their governess has had to go home for a few days.'

'Good idea; will you drive her up?'

'I—no, no. I shan't be here. My sister would fetch Daisy if she's willing to go.'

'Of course she'll go,' said Pamela, 'won't you, Daisy?'

Daisy, unable to think of any reason to refuse, said that yes, she would.

He got up to go presently, saying all the right things before going to the door with Daisy. As she opened it he asked carelessly, 'Have you seen any more of young Philip?'

He gave her a friendly smile and she quite forgot that she had no wish to be friendly too. 'Oh, yes, he came to see me the other evening; he met Sister Carter, though.' She forgot for the moment to whom she was speaking. 'It was really very strange—I mean, they just looked at each other as though they had known each other all their lives. I've never believed in love at first sight, but now I do.'

She glanced at him and saw the little smile and felt her cheeks grow hot. 'Goodnight, Dr Seymour,' she said coldly and opened the door wide.

His, 'Goodnight, Daisy,' was uttered with great civility and he said nothing else. She stood at the door, keeping still and not looking as he got into his car, and as he drove away closed it with deliberate quiet. Otherwise she would have banged it as hard as she was able; she had made a fool of herself talking to him like that. He would be sitting in his car, smiling that nasty little smile…her face was scarlet at the thought.

The doctor was indeed smiling, a slow, tender smile which made him look years younger. He drove to his sister's house, whistling softly under his breath, and Belle, sensing that he found life very much to his satisfaction, sat on the back seat and thumped her tail happily.

CHAPTER SEVEN

THERE WAS NO sign of the doctor when Daisy went to work in the morning and she wasn't sure whether to be relieved or disappointed. Dr Dowling did a ward-round with the housemen and staff nurse, since Sister Carter had a day off—out with Philip, no doubt of that. Daisy wondered where they would go—somewhere romantic, she hoped. Maisie, bustling up and down the ward, gave her opinion that Sister was far too pretty to be stuck in a hospital. 'Ought to 'ave a 'ome of her own with kids.' She gave a hoarse chuckle. 'And that won't be no trouble to 'er—she's 'ad enough practice 'ere.'

At home, Daisy combed through her wardrobe again. She supposed it didn't really matter what she wore when she went to London, and it was only for two days anyway. It would have to be the good suit once again; she could travel in a blouse and take the silk top, spare undies and night things and her small collection of make-up. They could all go easily enough into the roomy shoulder-bag, which would leave her arms free for the twins.

'You don't suppose you might get asked out?' asked her mother hopefully.

'No, love. I shall be with the twins while the Thorleys go to this banquet or whatever it is. I dare say I shall take them for a walk in the morning and we'll come back here in the afternoon. I shall enjoy the trip there and back,' added Daisy in her sensible way.

'Where will you stay?'

'Don't know. In a hotel, perhaps, or they may even have a flat or house in London—that's the most likely, I should think.'

'It sounds rather dull to me,' observed Mrs Pelham. If Daisy agreed with her parent she didn't say so.

Sister Carter was on duty the next morning, starry-eyed and looking prettier than ever. During the morning she sent for Daisy to go to her office, and when she tapped on the door and was bidden to enter she was told to sit down.

Daisy sat composedly while she beat her brains trying to remember if she had done something worthy of a talking-to. So it was all the more surprising when Sister Carter said cheerfully, 'Philip was telling me about you yesterday. You really shouldn't be an orderly, you know, Daisy. Can't you train as a nurse?'

It was so unexpected that Daisy didn't answer at once. When she did her voice was as quiet as usual. 'I think I might like to do that, Sister, but until my sister is through school I do need to have a job; a student nurse's pay wouldn't be quite enough...besides, I—I need to live at home.'

'For how long would that be?' asked Sister Carter kindly.

'Another three years. There would still be plenty of time for me to train as a nurse—I'm twenty-two—I wouldn't be too old...'

She was uttering a pipe-dream—her mother couldn't be

left alone and Pamela would be miles away at some university, but there was no need to burden Sister with that.

'A pity. Still, there doesn't seem to be anything we can do about it at present, does there? As long as you're happy here?'

'I am—very happy, Sister.' That at least was true, thought Daisy.

'Well, we'll have to see,' said Sister Carter vaguely. She smiled suddenly. 'I don't suppose I'll be here in three years' time, but I'll make sure that you have a special splendid reference when I go.'

She hesitated. 'Did you have no opportunity to train for anything, Daisy?'

'No, my father died.'

'I'm sorry. Anyway, you can count on me if ever you see the chance to start training.'

Back in the ward, bagging the endless nappies, Daisy thought it unlikely.

Saturday came, bringing with it chilly blue skies and a sunshine without much warmth. Just the right weather for the suit, decided Daisy, getting up early.

Lady Thorley arrived late, explaining worriedly that the twins had been troublesome at the last minute. 'If you wouldn't mind sitting in the back with them, Daisy?' she asked. 'They're cross because we haven't brought Boots with us.' She added hopefully, 'They usually listen to you.'

At first they weren't disposed to listen to anyone, even Daisy whom they liked, but presently they decided to be good and the rest of the journey was made in comparative harmony. All the same Daisy was relieved to see the outskirts of London closing in around them; there was so much more to see and the children, rather excited now, were kept busy pointing out everything which caught their eye. Daisy was excited too although she appeared serene enough, as Lady Thorley drove along Millbank and the Victoria Embankment until she turned off at Northumberland Avenue, skirted Trafalgar Square and turned into Pall Mall, and after that Daisy was lost—she didn't know London well; all she knew was that they had crossed Piccadilly and were driving through streets of dignified mansions opening out from time to time into quiet squares encircling a railed-off garden. Very pleasant to sit there under the trees on the wooden seats, thought Daisy, and indeed there were small children and mothers and nursemaids doing just that. Living in such surroundings it would be hard to remember that the busy London streets were close by.

Lady Thorley drove past another square and turned into a tree-lined street where the houses were smaller, although to Daisy's eyes they looked of a handsome size, and presently stopped halfway down the terrace.

'Well, here we are,' Lady Thorley observed. She looked over her shoulder to the twins. 'You've both been very good—are you tired, Daisy?'

'Not in the least, Lady Thorley. Would you like me to see to the cases or mind the children?'

'The children, please; Trim will take the bags inside.'

The house door had opened and an elderly man, very spry, crossed the pavement.

'Trim, how nice to see you again. Will you see to the luggage for us? This is Miss Daisy Pelham who has kindly come with me to look after the children.'

Trim greeted her with dignity, exchanged a more boisterous greeting with the children and took the car keys from

Lady Thorley. 'Nice to see you again, my lady,' he said. 'Mrs Trim will be waiting for you.'

The door opened on to a small vestibule which in turn led to a long wide hall. Daisy, following Lady Thorley indoors, saw that the house was a good deal larger than it appeared to be from the outside but she had little time to look around her. Advancing to meet them was a stout middle-aged woman with improbable black hair and eyes to match. She had a round face which crinkled nicely when she smiled and the children rushed towards her with shouts of delight.

'There, my darlings—you've grown, I declare.' She embraced them and swept towards Lady Thorley. 'Welcome, my lady. Your usual room and I've put Miss Pelham next to the children.' She turned a beady eye on Daisy and smiled largely. 'You'll be wanting to see to them. If you, my lady, would go to the drawing-room while I show Miss Pelham their rooms? There will be coffee in a few minutes and lunch is at one o'clock.'

She bustled Daisy and the children up the elegant staircase at one side of the hall, along a narrow passage and into a room at its end. 'The children usually sleep here.'

It was a large room with two beds and white furniture geared to suit a small person and a big window overlooking a surprisingly long, narrow garden at the back of the house. 'You will be here, Miss Pelham.' The housekeeper opened a door and Daisy walked past her into a charming room, the bed and dressing-table in maplewood, a comfortable little chair by the window and a matching tallboy against one wall. The bedspread and curtains were in a faint pink and the carpet underfoot was a deep cream and very soft.

'The bathroom is here,' said Mrs Trim, throwing open another door, 'if you won't mind sharing it with the children.'

Daisy nodded wordlessly and Mrs Trim trotted to the door. 'You'll want your coffee. It'll be downstairs in the drawing-room; the twins know where that is.'

Left with the children, Daisy made haste to see to their wants, brush their hair, apply handkerchiefs to small noses, and urge them to good manners when they went downstairs while she tidied her already neat head, powdered her prosaic nose and added lipstick. That done, she led the way downstairs again. In the hall she said, 'Josh, dear, which is the drawing-room?'

He took her hand and the three of them opened the door to which he led them. Lady Thorley was sitting there comfortably by a small fire in a handsome Adam fireplace but for the moment Daisy only had eyes for the room. It was of a comfortable size, its bow window overlooking the street and it was furnished with what she recognised as antiques. Beautiful cabinets, lamp tables, a long sofa table and in one corner a long-case clock was tick-tocking in a soothing monotone. The chairs were large, upholstered in wine-red velvet, and there were two sofas, one each side of the fireplace.

'There you are,' said Lady Thorley. 'Daisy, come and have some coffee; you must be parched. Josh, Katie, Mrs Trim has made some lemonade especially for you. Sit down by Daisy and drink it up.'

Over coffee Lady Thorley voiced her plans for the evening. 'This banquet is at nine o'clock but there's a reception first and that's at eight o'clock. We shall have to leave here about a quarter past seven. Would you see that the children have their suppers and go to bed? Mrs Trim will have a meal ready for you about eight o'clock. We shall be very late back so go to bed when you want to. In the morning would you give the twins their breakfasts and have yours at the same time and perhaps take them for a walk for half an hour or so? I expect lunch will be at one o'clock and we'll leave about three o'clock. Hugh's coming back with us, so he'll drive, thank goodness.'

Daisy took a sip of coffee. It was delicious. 'Very well, Lady Thorley. I could have supper with the children if that would be more convenient.'

'No, no. You deserve an hour or two of peace and quiet. Trim will look after you.' She glanced at the clock. 'Lunch must be almost ready.'

She looked across at the children, one each side of Daisy, drinking their lemonade with deceptive meekness. 'Now you must behave nicely at table…'

'If they don't,' said the doctor from the door, 'I shall throw them into the garden—not you, of course, Daisy.'

He strolled into the room, kissed his sister's offered cheek, suffered an excited onslaught from his nephew and niece and wished Daisy a bland good-day. 'You had a good trip?' he asked. 'Hugh should be here at any minute; I'll tell Trim to serve lunch ten minutes after he gets here—that will give us time for a glass of sherry.'

Daisy hadn't uttered a sound. She was surprised and delighted and at the same time puzzled; he had spoken as though he owned the place…

He caught her eye. 'Welcome to my home, Daisy,' he said and smiled with such charm that she blinked her lovely eyes and went pink.

'You've gone all red,' said Josh but before his mother could reprimand him Sir Hugh joined them and in the general hubbub and the handing of drinks Daisy was able to regain her normal colour and during lunch she was far too busy seeing that the children ate their meal and behaved themselves to feel self-conscious. The doctor's manners were impeccable; whenever possible he included her in their conversation but beyond polite answers she took little part in it, which gave her the chance to look around.

The dining-room was behind the drawing-room, overlooking the back garden. Here again was a bay window with a door leading to a covered veranda. The walls were panelled and hung with paintings, mostly portraits, and the table and sideboard were mahogany of the Regency period. The table had been decked with a damask cloth, crested silver and crystal glasses. The soup was served in Worcester plates, as was the ragout of chicken, and, as a concession to the children's presence, the trifle, with glacé cherries and whipped cream. The twins spooned their portions up without any urging and were bidden by their uncle to sit still while Daisy had her coffee. She didn't linger over it; she felt sure that the three of them had plenty to talk about. She excused herself, removed the children from the table and bore them off upstairs where they were prevailed upon to lie on their beds while she told them a story. They were asleep within ten minutes, looking like two cherubs, leaving her to sit by the window with nothing to do. Presently, lacking anything to keep her awake, she closed her eyes and dozed off.

She woke to find the doctor sitting on Josh's bed, a twin on either side of him. All three of them were watching her with unnerving intensity.

'You were snoring,' said Josh.

'I never snore,' declared Daisy indignantly, very conscious of being at a total disadvantage.

'No, no, of course you don't.' The doctor was at his most soothing. 'Josh, no gentleman ever tells a lady that she snores—it's bad manners.'

Daisy sat very upright. 'I'm sorry I went to sleep…'

'No need to be sorry. I expect you were up early and two hours or more of these children, mewed up in a car, is sufficient to make anyone doze off. But we're glad you're awake. We wondered if you would like to come with us—we're going to take a quick look at the zoo.' He glanced at his watch. 'It's not yet three o'clock—we could have an hour there and come back for a late tea.'

He didn't wait for her to agree. 'If you could get these two ready, and yourself, of course, and come downstairs in ten minutes or so, I'll have the car outside.'

He had gone before she had said a word.

For once the twins were both quick and helpful; with a minute to spare they were downstairs in the hall where they found the doctor talking to his sister.

'Splendid, you're ready. Meg, we'll be back around five o'clock—tell Mrs Trim to have tea ready for the children, will you? Ask for yours when you want it.'

He ushered his party outside, shovelled the children into the car and told Daisy to get in beside him. 'A pity Belle can't come too…'

'Oh, is she here? I haven't seen her.'

'She has been with me all the morning—she's in the garden now; you'll see her when we get back.'

The streets were comparatively empty, and the distance wasn't great; beyond the excited chatter of the twins, little was said. Once there, they lost no time in deciding what had to be seen in the time they had.

'Snakes and scorpions, sharks and man-eating tigers,' demanded Josh, to be instantly contradicted by his twin.

'Bears and elephants,' she demanded, 'and a camel.'

'Well, I dare say we shall have time to see all of them, provided you don't hang around too long. Let's get the snakes and scorpions over first, shall we?'

Daisy, annoyed at the high-handed way in which the doctor had arranged her afternoon without so much as a by your leave, found her annoyance melting in the face of the children's happy faces and his whole-hearted enthusiasm for the afternoon's entertainment. The snakes and scorpions duly shivered over, the bears admired, the camels marvelled at, there was time to have a ride on an elephant. The twins weren't faint-hearted; they needed no one with them, they assured their uncle and Daisy watched the great beast with its burden of small people plod away.

'They'll be all right,' she breathed anxiously. 'They're so small, though…'

'Well, of course they're small; they're children, aren't they?' The doctor sounded testy. 'Do you suppose I should allow them to go unless I was quite certain they would come to no harm?'

'Well, no,' said Daisy placatingly, 'I'm sure you wouldn't.'

He looked down at her. 'How's the job going?'

'Very well, thank you.' She considered telling him that Sister Carter had mentioned her training to be a nurse, but decided not to—it might sound a bit boastful.

'I suppose you won't be there long,' he said airily, a remark which sent her into instant panic.

'Oh, why not? Aren't I suitable? I know I'm not as quick as Maisie…'

'Suitable? Oh, you're that all right. I was merely uttering my thoughts aloud.'

He said no more, leaving her to wish that he would keep his thoughts to himself.

The children came back then and there was no chance to ask him what he had meant. With the promise that they should come again next time they came to London, the twins were stowed in the car and, with a silent Daisy beside him, the doctor drove back to his house. It was a crisp winter evening and Daisy thought longingly of tea and was delighted to find that Mrs Trim, mindful of the twins' bedtime, had set out a splendid meal in a small room at the back of the house. It was a very cosy room, with a bright fire burning, plenty of bookshelves and comfortable chairs as well as the round table loaded with the twins' favourite food, a pot of tea for Daisy and a dish of little cakes.

Lady Thorley joined them for a moment. 'I'm just off to dress,' she told Daisy. 'We shall have to leave in an hour or so—you'll be all right? I know Val has told the Trims to look after you. We shall be late back, I expect.'

She embraced her children. 'I'll come back and tuck you up before we go,' she promised, 'and so will Daddy.'

The children were nicely tired and, after a splendid meal, sleepy. Daisy led them away upstairs, undressed them, and urged them, rather reluctantly, to their baths. They were emerging from these noisy and damp activities, the twins with shining faces and smelling of the best kind of soap, and Daisy dishevelled and damp, when their parents and the doctor came to say goodnight. Lady Thorley, in sequinned black chiffon, looked superb, as did Sir Hugh in his white tie and tails, but it was the doctor who stole the show; he wore his evening clothes with ease and elegance, his broad shoulders enhancing the inspired cut of his coat, the very size of him meriting a second or even third glance. Daisy took one look and turned her head away because he was watching her with that small smile which she found so disconcerting. There was no need to look at him again; she was fully occupied in keeping the twins from embracing their mother too fervently.

'If you get into your beds,' she suggested in her calm fashion, 'I dare say everyone will kiss you goodnight.' She added artfully, 'And there'll still be time for another chapter of *The Rose and the Ring*.' This was a book to which they were passionately devoted and which Lady Thorley had had the presence of mind to bring with her.

Soothed by their favourite story, the children presently slept and Daisy went down to the quiet dining-room and found Trim waiting for her.

'A glass of sherry, miss—little Josh and Katie can wear you out.' When Daisy hesitated he added, 'The doctor said you should have a glass before your dinner, miss.'

'Oh, did he?' asked Daisy. 'How kind of him. In that case I'd like one.'

Presently Trim led her to the table. At the sight of the damask and silver and crystal, for all the world as though the table had been decked out for a dinner-party, Daisy exclaimed, 'Oh, but you shouldn't have gone to all this trouble! I could have had something on a tray.'

'The doctor wished it, miss,' said Trim, 'and I must add it is a pleasure for us. Mrs Trim has cooked a meal which she hoped you will enjoy.'

He disappeared and returned presently with vichyssoise soup, and Daisy's small nose wrinkled at its delicious aroma. It tasted good too—this wasn't something out of a tin, it was the real thing, made with cream and eggs and chicken stock nicely mingled with the creamed leeks. It was followed by a perfectly grilled sole, sautéd potatoes and braised celery, and when Trim offered her white wine she accepted, quite carried away by the unexpectedness of it all.

'Mrs Trim's special sweet,' murmured Trim, removing her empty plate and offering a chestnut soufflé with chocolate cream, 'and I shall serve your coffee in the drawing-room, Miss Pelham.'

When she hesitated again he added, 'The doctor hoped that you would keep Belle company for a little while.'

'Well, just for a short time,' said Daisy, 'and do please thank Mrs Trim for that delicious meal.'

Belle was delighted to see her and accompanied her on a tour of the room. There was a lot to see: fine porcelain and silver in their display cabinets and a great many paintings, mostly portraits. She supposed that they were of the doctor's ancestors, for several of them had his dark hair and heavy-lidded eyes, even the suspicion of the smile which made her feel so uneasy.

An hour passed quickly and when the case clock chimed a tinkling half-hour she bade Belle goodnight and went into the hall. Should she go to bed without telling Trim? she wondered. Would he mind if she went in search of him through the baize door at the end of the hall? As if in answer to her problem Trim appeared silently from the dining-room, asked if there was anything she required, wished her goodnight and informed her in a fatherly way that should the children wish to get up early either he or Mrs Trim would be about in the kitchen should they require a drink of milk before their breakfast.

Daisy thanked him, wished him goodnight and went to

her room. The twins were fast asleep; she bathed in peace, got into her own deliciously comfortable bed and closed her eyes. Before she dozed off she wondered what the doctor was doing and whom he might be with. Some lovely young woman, she thought forlornly, dressed with the same expensive taste as Lady Thorley. She was too tired to wonder why the thought made her unhappy.

She was wakened by the twins who had climbed on to her bed and were whispering into her ear, urging her to wake up. 'We want to go into the garden with Belle,' Josh explained.

Daisy sat up in bed, tossing back her mousy curtain of hair. 'Isn't it a bit early? Wouldn't it be nice if you got under the eiderdown and I read a bit more of *The Rose and the Ring*?'

Katie liked the idea but Josh thrust out his lower lip and shook his head. 'I want to go into the garden...'

'So you shall presently, love, but it's only just after six o'clock; it isn't even quite light...'

'Belle wants to go too.' He fixed her with a very determined eye. 'We're going home today and she won't see us again.'

'Oh, I'm sure she will; your uncle often goes to see you. You stay here with Katie like a good boy and I'll fetch your book.'

The house was pleasantly warm and the carpet was soft under her bare feet when she got out of bed and went in search of the book—a matter of a minute or so, but when she got back Josh wasn't there.

'Josh says he's going out into the garden,' said Katie. 'I think I'll go too.'

'We'll all go,' said Daisy desperately, 'only give me time

to get some shoes on his feet and his dressing-gown on. Stay there, darling—I promise we'll all go if you do.'

Katie had made a tent of the eiderdown and was prepared to stay. Daisy flew out of the room and down the stairs, guided by the murmur of Josh's voice, to be halted at the bottom step by the doctor's voice. He was leaning over the banisters watching her with interest.

'Good morning, Daisy,' he observed in the mildest of voices. 'A pleasant surprise so early in the day…'

'Oh, be quiet, do,' said Daisy waspishly. 'Josh is going into the garden and he's only in his nightclothes…' It was borne in upon her that she was in a like state and she wasn't wearing sturdy winceyette pyjamas.

The doctor had come down the stairs, wearing a rather splendid dressing-gown and soft slippers. He hadn't been told to be quiet for a very long time and certainly not by a small girl in her nightie; he found it intriguing. He said, with a glance which reassured her that he hadn't even noticed what she was wearing, 'I'll get him out of the kitchen and bring him back to you. Get the pair of them dressed and we'll all go into the garden.'

Daisy was already halfway up the stairs but she turned round to whisper fiercely, 'But aren't you tired? Don't you want to go back to bed?'

'Yes to both questions. Just do as I say, there's a good girl.'

She opened her mouth to tell him that she wasn't his good girl but thought better of it and he went on down the hall to the baize door.

Katie was delighted as Daisy told her of the prospect of a walk in the garden with her uncle. 'I'll dress you in a minute,' declared Daisy, tearing into her clothes, washing her face and cleaning her teeth and tugging a comb through her hair. She looked a fright but at least she was decent… Katie, for once, was only too glad to be dressed too; Daisy was fastening her shoes when the doctor, bearing a tray of tea and two mugs, closely followed by Josh and Belle, appeared silently at the door.

He had them all organised within minutes. The children were to drink their milk and Josh was to get into his clothes as far as he was able, 'And Daisy and I are going to enjoy a cup of tea.'

Belle had got on to the bed beside Katie and since the doctor didn't seem to mind Daisy said nothing but meekly took the cup of tea she was offered and drank it.

'Put on something warm,' advised the doctor, finishing his tea. 'I'll be with you in ten minutes.'

Daisy still said nothing; it was hardly an occasion for aimless conversation and she was feeling shy because of the inadequacies of her nightie. The doctor took his vast person silently away and she set about rearranging Josh's clothes in the right order—jersey back to front, shoes on the wrong feet and childish hair standing up in spiky tufts all over his small head.

She had time to tie her hair back before the doctor returned and they all crept downstairs and, with Belle in close company, out into the garden through the kitchen door. It was chilly with a hint of frost still in the air but the sun had almost risen by now and the birds were singing. No one, thought Daisy, would know that they were in the heart of London, standing in the quietness.

She wasn't allowed to stand for long. The doctor took her arm and urged her along the flag-stoned path between a wide border—herbaceous in the summer? wondered Daisy, being whisked briskly past—and a strip of lawn which took up the whole of the centre of the garden. The path disappeared behind shrubs and ornamental trees, ending in a charming little rustic hut with an arched door and tiny windows on either side of it.

'The witch's house,' explained the doctor as the children tumbled inside. He pushed her gently before him and then followed her so that they were a bit crowded. There were benches built along its walls and he sat her down and then folded his great size into the space beside her. The children had no intention of sitting; they were exploring the little place as they always did, finding plates in a shallow opening in the wall. Everything was taken down, examined and put back again until presently Josh came to stand by Daisy.

'She's a good witch,' he explained; 'she's kind to animals and children and if she casts a spell it's a nice one.'

'She sounds a very good sort of witch; does she have her meals here?'

Josh, carried away on childish imagination and with Katie playing dutiful chorus, went into some detail while the doctor watched Daisy's face. It was alight with interest and the practical suggestions she offered as regards the witch's diet showed that she was entering whole-heartedly into the children's world. He sat back, enjoying himself.

Presently he said, 'We'd better go back for our breakfasts.' So the children put everything neatly back in place and they all went back into the garden, out of the shrubs and the small trees, on to a similar path on the opposite side of the lawn with an identical flowerbed against one high brick wall. The sun was up now but held little warmth and the children danced to and fro with Belle weaving between them.

'You have a very charming garden,' said Daisy, for something to say.

'A bonus in London. The house has been in the family for many years—George the Fourth's time, I believe, and in those days gardens were considered small. Be that as it may, it's secluded and quiet.'

She took the children upstairs to wash their glowing little faces, brush their hair and tidy them for breakfast, a meal they shared with the doctor and their father. Lady Thorley was having hers in bed.

The two children, perched each side of Daisy, ate their meal in an exemplary fashion, calling forth praise from their parent. 'We're going home directly after lunch,' he told them. 'What do you want to do this morning?'

'A ride on the top of a bus,' said Josh, as usual speaking for Katie as well as himself, and when neither gentleman reacted with enthusiasm to his suggestion it was Daisy who said,

'Oh, what a splendid idea. If you tell us which bus to catch and what time we're to be back here…'

She was disappointed that the doctor had made no offer to go with them. Their father, she guessed, would want to remain with his wife, but surely the doctor could have spared an hour or so…

'There's a sightseeing bus goes from Trafalgar Square—I'll drop you off,' said the doctor casually. 'I won't be able to pick you up when you get back but take a taxi, Daisy.' He glanced at her. 'Have you enough money?'

She flushed. Somehow he had made her sound like a servant.

'I've no idea what it will cost, but I don't expect I have.'

Sir Hugh took out his wallet, found some notes and handed them over. 'That should cover it. If you're short, we can settle with the cab when you get back.'

The two men sat back, looking as though they had settled the matter to their satisfaction, and since the children were getting restless Daisy excused herself and them and took them upstairs to get them ready for their trip. Ten minutes later, without seeing anyone, the three of them left the house. The doctor had said he would give them a lift to the bus, but she hadn't believed him; it shouldn't be too difficult to find a bus stop and get to Trafalgar Square.

He was leaning against the car's gleaming side, obviously waiting for them. Belle was already on the back seat and the children lost no time in joining her; unlike Daisy, they had had no doubt in their minds that if their uncle had said he would do something it would be done.

The doctor opened the car door. 'You didn't believe me, did you?' He sounded mildly mocking as she went pink.

'Well, no. You must have got home very late in the night and you were up early this morning.'

He had got in beside her. 'And how very worthwhile that was,' he observed softly. And she, remembering, blushed.

An episode to be forgotten, she told herself as the three of them sat perched on the top deck of the bus and she pointed out the House of Commons, Westminster Abbey, Buckingham Palace, the Tower of London and all the other sights on the route. The children looked when bidden but like all small children were far more interested in the people on the pavements and the other traffic. Culturally, the trip hadn't been very successful although they had enjoyed every minute of it and at lunch they gave colourful accounts of people they had seen: the policeman, the horse guards, several ambulances, flashing blue lights and racing through the traffic, plenty of policemen on motorbikes, and a small crowd surrounding a man who had fallen down in the street. Their sharp eyes had missed nothing.

'Did you see Buckingham Palace?' asked their father.

'Where's that?' asked Josh.

'Anyway, they enjoyed their morning,' said their mother comfortably.

The doctor had little to say; only when his sister put a low-voiced question to him did Daisy realise that he had been at the hospital. He would be glad to see the back of them, she reflected. She stole a look at him and decided that he looked tired; the twins, as she knew to her cost, could be exhausting and they had begun their day very early.

She repacked their bags after lunch, dressed the children in their outdoor things once more and collected her own possessions while the Thorleys stowed everything in the boot and made their farewells. No mention was made of the doctor returning to Salisbury; he took leave of them cheerfully on his doorstep, his hand on Belle's collar, and his polite, 'It was a pleasure,' was the only answer Daisy got to her thank-you speech.

She got into the car between the twins, telling herself that she never wished to see him again.

CHAPTER EIGHT

THE TWINS WERE peevish and inclined to quarrel and Daisy breathed a sigh of relief as Sir Hugh drew up before her home. She bade the twins a brisk goodbye, assuring them that they would see each other again, responded suitably to Sir Hugh's thanks and Lady Thorley's heartfelt gratitude and got out of the car.

'We will keep in touch,' declared Lady Thorley. 'We won't stop now—the twins…'

'I quite understand, Lady Thorley.' Daisy saw ominous signs of temper in the children's small faces and felt sympathy for their mother. They would be a handful by bedtime. She went through the gate and watched the car drive away and then went indoors.

There was no one at home, only Razor, who lifted a welcoming head and went to sleep again. Her mother, said the note on the table, had gone to church and Pamela was spending the day with her best friend and wouldn't be back until eight o'clock. Daisy took her bag upstairs, took her coat off and then made herself a cup of tea and laid the table for supper. Her mother would have had nothing much to eat since Pam hadn't been at home; she poked her nose into the fridge and set about gathering the ingredients for a Spanish omelette.

'You're back,' said Mrs Pelham, letting herself in half an hour later. 'Darling, I couldn't remember when you said you'd be home so I thought I'd go to Evensong. Have you been in long?'

She sniffed the air. 'Something nice for supper? What a dear you are; what would I do without you?'

Over the meal Daisy told her about her weekend; it didn't amount to much when all was said and done and her mother listened eagerly. 'Dr Seymour seems such a kind man; tell me some more about his home—it sounds lovely.'

Pamela came in presently, wanting to talk about her day with her friend and for the moment the doctor and his house were forgotten; only later, as Daisy got ready for bed, she allowed her thoughts to dwell on him.

She didn't see him until the end of the next day. She had been to tea and when she returned to the ward he was there, standing halfway down it talking to his registrar and Sister. His back was towards her, his hands in his pockets, crushing his long white coat, looming head and shoulders above his companions. Daisy paused just inside the door, staring at his vast back; she didn't know why, but she was sure that he was bone-weary although there was no sign of that, and she had a great urge to do something about it—a sensation which welled up inside her and left her feeling breathless, and what breath she had left her entirely when he turned his head and looked at her. She knew what the feeling was then. It was love, catching her unawares, and it couldn't have been at a more awkward or inappropriate time, nor could she have been more surprised. She wanted to smile with the sheer delight of it but his look was grave and thoughtful, reminding her that just for a moment she had imagined herself in a fool's paradise, so that she looked away and hurried down the ward to the far end to where she could see Maisie stuffing the day's dirty laundry into sacks. She felt terrible; a quiet corner, preferably in the dark with the door locked, where she could have a good weep in comfort, would have been just the thing. As it was she picked up an empty sack and began on the cotsheets.

Maisie didn't pause in her work. 'What's eating you?' she wanted to know. 'Look as though you've 'ad a nasty dream—white as them sheets, you are.'

'I'm fine,' declared Daisy. 'I've a bit of a headache…'

''Eadaches is useful things sometimes,' said Maisie. 'Make an 'andy excuse. Dr Seymour's back. Looks tired, 'e does too. All this to-ing and fro-ing don't do 'im no good. Can't think why he wants ter do it—'e's got 'is nice 'ouse in the close—what more could a body want?'

'Oh, I didn't know he lived in Salisbury as well as London.'

'Got a posh 'ouse there too, so I've heard. Not that I grudge 'im that. Does a lot of good, 'e does.' Maisie tied the strings of the last sack. 'I think 'e's gone—good. We'll get rid of this lot and go 'ome.'

Leaving the hospital presently, Daisy peered cautiously around her; there was no sign of the Rolls-Royce, nor its owner. The doctor had parked it behind the hospital and was standing at a ward window, watching her. He grinned tiredly, for she was craning her neck in all directions before getting on to her bike and pedalling way out into the busy street. He had wanted to walk down the ward and take her in his arms but even if that had been possible he was sure that she was still not quite certain of her feelings.

He turned away from the window and dismissed her from his mind.

As for Daisy, she cycled back home, her head in the clouds; it was one thing to find herself in love and quite another thing wondering what to do about it. Common sense dictated that to find work which would take her as far away as possible from the doctor was the thing to do but the very thought of not seeing him again sent such a strong shudder through her person that she wobbled dangerously on her bike. On the other hand, would she be able to bear seeing him at the hospital? Not speaking to him, of course, not even smiling, and probably in the course of time he would marry…

She wheeled her bike through the gate and into the garden shed behind the house and went in to find her mother rolling pastry.

Her, 'Hello, darling,' was cheerful. 'Pasties for supper and the gas bill came this morning, not nearly as much as we expected. I must say life is much easier now that you've got this job. You should be doing something better, I know—perhaps later on…'

Daisy kissed her mother, took off her outdoor things and gave Razor his supper. She said cheerfully, 'That's great about the gas bill. I'll pay it as I go to work—put it through the door; it'll save postage.'

'Had a nice day, dear?' asked Mrs Pelham.

Daisy gave the answer expected of her and reflected that unless she could find a job as secure with the same wages as she now had she would have to stay at the hospital. She would talk to Pam and see if she would look for a part-time job during the Christmas holidays. If only they could save a little money…

'You're very quiet, love,' observed her mother. 'Perhaps you're tired?'

It was Pamela, while they were washing up the supper things, who asked, 'What's up, Daisy? Is that job awful? Shall I leave at the end of term and get a job? It's so unfair that you should have to keep us going.'

'Don't you dare suggest such a thing—another couple of years and you'll be well on the way to a career and then it'll be your turn. And the job's not bad at all; in fact I quite enjoy it—the children are fun and the nurses are friendly.'

'Yes? All the same, you look different. Are you sorry about Philip?'

'Heavens, no. I liked him but that was all. He and Sister are so exactly suited to each other. I'm hoping to hear any day now that they're engaged.'

Pamela piled the plates neatly. 'All the same, there's something.'

Daisy wiped the bowl and wrung out the dishcloth. 'There's some money to spare—the gas bill's much less than we reckoned. There's the end-of-term disco…would you like something to wear?'

'No—you have it.'

'Shall we take Mother to Salisbury next Saturday and let her choose?'

'Is it enough for a dress?'

'Afraid not—a blouse from Marks and Spencer, or some slippers—hers are worn out…'

'OK,' said Pamela wistfully. 'Do you suppose there'll ever be enough money for us to go into a shop and buy something without looking at the price ticket?'

Daisy had picked up Razor and he lay across her shoulder, purring. 'Well, of course—just give me time to find a millionaire and marry him.'

Pamela laughed with her but she looked at her thoughtfully at the same time; Daisy's laugh had sounded a little hollow.

There was no Maisie when Daisy came to work the next morning. 'It's not like her,' commented Sister. 'I've never known her miss a day. I hope she's not ill—she's not on the phone.'

It was Staff Nurse who said, 'Probably she's overslept or been to a party...'

As the day wore on there was still no sign of her. Towards the late afternoon Sister sought out Daisy.

'I've got Maisie's address—I ought to go and see her myself but Philip's coming this evening.'

Daisy looked at the pretty worried face and said at once, 'I'll go on my way home, Sister. Probably it's nothing to worry about. I've got my bike and it won't take me long.' At Sister's relieved sigh she asked, 'Where does she live?'

It wasn't far out of her way—one of the little streets she passed each day turning off Fisherton Street. 'If I could ring my mother and tell her that I'll be home later?'

'Yes, yes, of course. Daisy, I'm so grateful.'

Maisie lived in a row of terraced houses at the very end of a narrow street, dwindling into a kind of no man's land of abandoned houses, old sheds and broken-down fences. She leaned her bike against dusty iron railings and thumped a dirty brass knocker.

She had to wait before someone came to the door—a young woman with her hair in pink plastic rollers, in a T-shirt and leggings and with a grubby baby under her arm.

'Good evening,' began Daisy politely and remembered

that she had no idea what Maisie's surname was. 'I've called to see Maisie—she does live here?'

'Course she does. Miss Watts. Front room upstairs. 'Aven't seen her all day.'

The narrow hall was dark, so were the stairs. There were three doors on the small dark landing; Daisy knocked on the one facing the street and when no one answered tried the handle. The door opened under her touch and she found herself in a small room, surprisingly light and airy and smelling strongly of furniture polish.

'Maisie?' Daisy crossed the room to the bed along one wall where Maisie was sitting up against her pillows; she looked flushed and ill and took no notice of Daisy. There was a tabby cat curled up beside her and a small, scruffy dog on her feet. The dog growled as Daisy bent over Maisie and bared elderly teeth but Daisy was too concerned at the sight of Maisie to worry about that.

'Maisie,' she said urgently, 'what's the matter? Do you hurt anywhere? Did you fall down?'

Maisie opened her eyes. 'Pain in me chest,' she mumbled. She put out a hand and touched the cat. 'Look after 'em, Daisy...'

A doctor, thought Daisy, or better still get her to hospital where everyone knew her. 'And the animals...they need their suppers,' muttered Maisie.

There was a curtained-off alcove where Maisie had her kitchen; Daisy found cat and dog food kept there, piled it into bowls, filled a dish with water and gave Maisie a drink. 'I'm going to get a doctor,' she told her. 'I must go away for a little while and phone. I'll be back.'

There was a phone box further up the street and she rang the children's ward because she wasn't sure what else to do and since Maisie worked there surely someone would get her into hospital.

Sister was still on duty; Daisy didn't waste words. 'Sister, I'm so glad it's you. Maisie's ill. She has a pain in her chest; she looks awful. What shall I do?'

'Stay with her, Daisy; I'll get an ambulance organised as quickly as I can. Has she had a doctor?'

'No, I don't think so…' She rang off and hurried back, to find Maisie lying exactly as she had left her. The dog and cat had eaten their food and got back beside her, and Daisy rather warily picked up one of Maisie's limp, sweaty hands and found her pulse. It was very rapid and faint and Maisie seemed to be asleep even though from time to time she coughed painfully.

Daisy pulled up a chair, wiped Maisie's hot face with a damp cloth and sat down to wait. Sister would send help but it might take at least ten minutes, perhaps longer than that, before an ambulance arrived. Perhaps she should have dialled 999 first…

The door behind her opened quietly and she turned round; if it was the young woman who had let her in she might know who Maisie's doctor was.

Dr Seymour came hurriedly into the room. 'I was with Sister when you phoned,' he said in his calm voice which instantly soothed her worst fears. 'The ambulance is on its way. Has Maisie a doctor?'

'I don't know. There's a woman downstairs who let me in; she might know.'

'Don't bother. We can sort that out later.' He was bending over Maisie, taking her pulse, talking gently to her and getting a mumbled response.

'You're going to be all right, Maisie,' he assured her with

calm matter-of-factness. 'You're going to hospital presently and we'll look after you.'

Maisie opened her eyes and caught at his arm. 'Milly and Whiskers—' she stopped to cough '—I can't leave 'em.'

'I'll take them home with me until you're well again.'

'Promise.' Her eyes sought Daisy. 'You 'eard what 'e said, Daisy? They're all I've got…'

'Don't worry, Maisie; if Dr Seymour says he will look after them, he will. All you have to do is get well again.'

The ambulance came then and after a brief delay while the doctor took the cat and dog out to his car and shut them in Maisie was borne away to hospital. The doctor had gone down with the ambulancemen and presently as she tidied the room and stripped the bed of its bedclothes Daisy heard it drive away. The room needed to be cleaned and there was food in the cupboard which would have to be either given or thrown away and she had better see the woman downstairs and then lock the door.

The doctor came soundlessly into the room. 'Maisie will go to the women's medical ward—virus pneumonia—I've warned them.' He looked round the room. 'We must do better than this when she's well again. Leave it all now, Daisy. I'll see that someone comes in in the morning to clear up. Perhaps you'll be good enough to come with me and give a hand with those animals?'

'My bike's here. And where are they to go?'

'To my house, of course. God knows what Belle will say when she sees them.' He took the key from the door. 'Come along, there's nothing more you can do here.'

He ushered her out on to the landing, locked the door and followed her downstairs, to knock on the nearest door. The young woman opened it, eyeing him with a slow smile. 'Got rid of 'er, 'ave you? Poor cow...'

'Miss Watts,' said the doctor evenly, 'has been taken to hospital; she is a much liked member of the staff there. We're taking her cat and dog with us and will care for them and in the morning someone will come and clear out Miss Watts's room. One more thing—is there someone here capable of riding a bicycle to Wilton? This young lady will be going back there by car later but she'll need the bike in the morning.'

He put a hand in his pocket and took out a note.

'Me 'usband'll do it—give us the address.'

The doctor was writing in his notebook and tore out the page. 'Your husband...he's here?'

A young man came to the door. 'OK, I 'eard it all. I'll ride the bike back—I've 'ad an 'ard day's work too.'

'Perhaps this will compensate for that,' said the doctor, handing over the note and the address. 'It's very good of you and I'm much obliged.'

'A doctor, are you?'

'Yes, indeed I am.'

The man laughed. 'A good idea to keep on the right side of the medics; you never know.'

'Be sure if ever you or yours should need our attention, you shall have the best there is,' said the doctor gravely and bade the pair of them goodnight before ushering Daisy out to the car.

The animals were sitting on a blanket on the back seat, looking utterly forlorn, and the sight of them was just too much for Daisy. Two tears trickled down her cheeks as she sat rigidly staring ahead of her while the doctor drove back into the heart of Salisbury and in through the entrance to the cathedral close. She hadn't said a word; she was beyond words—everything had happened so quickly and she seemed no longer capable of doing anything for herself.

The doctor hadn't spoken either although she knew he had seen the tears, but as he drew up before the house he handed her a beautifully laundered handkerchief, and waited while she mopped her face. Without looking at her he said in a matter-of-fact voice, 'Will you carry the cat? We'll take them straight to the kitchen and see if Mrs Trump can find them some food; Maisie has obviously cared for them but I suspect that she hasn't felt up to feeding them since she fell ill.'

Daisy said in a watery voice, 'I gave them something—Maisie was so worried about them.'

'Very sensible.' His manner was nicely detached and the brief glance he gave her was somehow reassuring. Perhaps she didn't look quite as frightful as she felt.

He got out of the car, opened her door and reached for the cat. It wriggled half-heartedly as Daisy took it in her arms and the dog, tucked under the doctor's arm, made no sound although it quivered. 'Poor little beast,' said the doctor and fished in his pocket for his keys.

His housekeeper came through the baize door as they went in and he said at once, 'Good evening, Mrs Trump. We have two lodgers to keep Belle company for a few days. Their owner is ill.'

Mrs Trump's sharp nose quivered but she said in the mildest of voices, 'I dare say they'll want a bite to eat, sir…?'

She glanced at Daisy, standing tidily beside the doctor, and he said, 'And this is Miss Daisy Pelham whose sensible help led to the patient being admitted to the hospital.' He swept Daisy forward, a great arm on her shoulders.

'Daisy, this is Mrs Trump, my housekeeper and long-standing friend.'

Daisy offered a hand and smiled and Mrs Trump smiled back, shook the hand firmly and asked, 'What about your dinner, sir?'

'Oh—stretch it for two if you can, Mrs Trump. Miss Pelham will be dining here before I take her home.'

A piece of high-handedness which Daisy had her mouth open to censure, to be stopped by his casually friendly, 'You will, won't you, Daisy? We must discuss what's to be done with Maisie. You shall telephone your mother in just a moment.'

He took the cat from her with the remark that he would only be a moment, and went through the baize door followed by his housekeeper, to return almost immediately, which gave her no time to gather together her scattered wits.

'Let me have your jacket.' He unbuttoned it and threw it over a chair before she could speak. 'Now come into the drawing-room and phone your mother.'

His large gentle hand propelled her through the door and into a room which took her breath away. There were tall windows and a door leading to the garden at the back and a wide arch opposite leading to the dining-room at the front of the house. There was a brisk fire burning in a burnished steel grate with a massive sofa on either side of it and a satinwood sofa table behind each of them. The walls were hung with burgundy silk and the ceiling was strapwork. There was a William and Mary winged settee by the window with a tripod table with a piecrust edge beside it and above a hanging cabinet with a delicate lyre pattern. At the other end of the room was a small grand piano, several winged armchairs grouped around a Regency library table and in the corner a wrought-iron stand holding a great bowl of chrysanthemums.

Daisy revolved slowly, taking it all in. 'What a very beautiful room,' she observed. 'Your London house is grand and beautiful too but this is like home...'

'As indeed it is.' He picked up the phone and dialled her home number and handed it to her, walked to the door to let Belle in from the garden and stood there with his back to her.

'Mother,' said Daisy and waited patiently while Mrs Pelham asked a great many agitated questions. 'No, I'm quite all right; Dr Seymour will bring me back presently. Yes, I know a man brought my bike home—I shall need it tomorrow. I'll explain when I get home; I'm quite all right—really. Now bye.' She hung up and the doctor came back from the window and offered her a seat on one of the sofas. He sat down opposite her with Belle's great head on his shoes.

'I'll drive you home when we've had dinner,' he told her. 'I'll take a look at Maisie later on once she has been settled in bed and tomorrow I'll get Dr Walker to look her over. If it is virus pneumonia—and I'm sure that it is—she can have a course of antibiotics and a week or ten days in hospital and then some sick leave. But you must agree with me that some other place must be found for her. That room was terrible.'

'It was spotlessly clean,' said Daisy. 'Bed-sitting rooms cost an awful lot of money, you know.'

He got up and went to a side-table with a tray of drinks on it. 'Will you have a glass of sherry?' He turned to smile at her. 'You look as though you could do with it.'

She felt her cheeks grow hot; she must look awful, hair anyhow and probably a red nose from crying. 'Thank you,' she said primly, and he hid a smile.

'I'll ask around; I'm sure there must be somewhere more

suitable than her present room. You don't know if the furniture is hers?'

'No, I don't, but I think perhaps it is, because it was all so beautifully polished…' She sipped her sherry. 'What about Milly and Whiskers?'

'Oh, they can stay here. Mrs Trump has a heart of gold, Belle will be delighted to mother them and they can enjoy the garden.'

'But you're not always here.' She wished she hadn't said that because he smiled and didn't reply and that made her feel as though she had been nosy. The silence went on for a little too long and she was racking her brains for a suitable remark when Mrs Trump came to tell them that she had put the soup on the table. 'Those two poor creatures are asleep in front of the Aga,' she told them. 'Fair worn out, they are.'

The table was decked with the same elegance as that of his house in London; the doctor seated her, took his own chair at the head of the table and politely offered salt and pepper. They weren't needed; Mrs Trump was quite obviously the kind of cook whose food needed nothing added. The soup, served in Worcester china, was a creamy blend of leeks and potato with a hint of sorrel; Daisy, who cooked very nicely but of necessity dealt with the plainest of food, supped it with delight and wondered what would come next.

The plates were removed and the doctor engaged her in small talk and offered her white wine. Fish or chicken, she decided, agreeing pleasantly that Salisbury was a lovely city. It was roast duck, something she had never tasted before and it was delicious. She had known about the orange sauce but there was a delicious tang to it as well; if ever she had the chance, which wasn't likely, she would ask Mrs Trump what it was…

It was followed by castle puddings, served with a custard so rich that it must have been made almost entirely from cream. She refused a second helping and said rather shyly, 'That was the most delicious meal I've ever tasted.'

'Mrs Trump is a splendid cook and I must agree with you—what's the food like at the hospital?'

'Really very good—of course, cooking for several hundred people can't be the same as cooking for one, can it?' She thought for a moment. 'Besides, it's cabbage and mince and boiled potatoes, though we do get fish on Fridays and sometimes roast meat.'

She stopped then, afraid that she was boring him. 'If you don't mind I think I should go home...'

The doctor hadn't been bored; he had been sitting there, watching her nice face, listening to her pretty voice and thinking how delightful she looked sitting at his table, but he allowed none of this to show.

'Coffee? We'll have it in the drawing-room, take a quick look at Maisie's animals and then I'll drive you back.'

Daisy had had a long day; her eyelids dropped as she drank her coffee and the doctor bent forward gently and took the cup and saucer from her. She looked exactly right, sitting there in a corner of the sofa. Her small nose shone, the lipstick had long since worn off and her hair needed a good brush; moreover her gentle mouth had dropped very slightly open so that what sounded very like a whispered snore issued from it. Nevertheless her small person had an endearing charm. He touched her shoulder gently and she opened her eyes.

'I went to sleep,' said Daisy prosaically. 'I'm so sorry—it was the wine and the sherry. Whatever must you think of me?'

She sat up very straight and the doctor decided not to answer that. Instead he said soothingly, 'You must be tired. I'll take you home—are you on duty in the morning?'

'Yes. Please may I see the animals before we go so that I can tell Maisie how well cared-for they are?'

'Of course. We'll go now.'

Milly and Whiskers were curled up in front of the Aga in the kitchen—an apartment which Daisy considered to be every woman's dream. They eyed their visitors warily for a moment but Daisy got down on her knees and stroked their elderly heads and mumbled comfortingly and they closed their eyes again. 'I'll take care of them, don't you worry,' Mrs Trump assured her.

The doctor drove Daisy back in a comfortable silence, got out and knocked on her door, assured Mrs Pelham that there was nothing to worry about and wished Daisy goodnight.

She put out her hand. 'You've been awfully kind, sir. Thank you for my dinner and for seeing to the animals. Will Maisie be all right?'

'Yes. I can promise you that. Goodnight, Daisy.'

He had gone and she went indoors and sleepily told her mother and Pamela what had happened. It was Pamela who told her to go to bed. 'You're tired out, aren't you, Daisy? And I suppose you've got to go to work in the morning?' When Daisy nodded she added, 'Do go to bed now—I'll see to laying the table for breakfast and feeding Razor. You would have thought they would have given you a day off…'

'Well, if Maisie's not there there's only me,' said Daisy and went thankfully to her bed.

She went to see Maisie the following morning during her coffee break. Feeling a good deal more self-possessed than on the occasion of her first visit to the women's medical ward, she tapped on Sister's door.

That lady said grudgingly, 'Ah, Daisy. I've been instructed to allow you to visit Maisie whenever it's convenient.' She lowered her head over the papers on her desk. 'She's at the end of the ward.'

Daisy met Mrs Brett halfway down the ward. 'And what are you doing here?' demanded her erstwhile colleague.

'Visiting,' said Daisy sweetly and walked past.

Maisie was sitting up in bed, looking a lot better than she had done the evening before. All the same, she was a shadow of her former cheerful self.

'Hello, Maisie,' said Daisy cheerfully, 'you look better already. I may come and see you whenever I have the time. I thought you'd like to know that Milly and Whiskers are fine. Dr Seymour's housekeeper is such a nice person and I'm sure she'll look after them.'

Maisie nodded her head. ''E came ter see me last night. I wasn't feeling too good but 'e said 'e'd look after 'em. What about me room?'

'Dr Seymour told me that he'd see about it so I shouldn't worry about it. Is there anything you want?'

'Me nighties and me 'andbag.'

'I'll get them for you this evening as I go home. Will it be all right if I bring them in the morning?'

'Yes, ducks.'

The unbidden thought crossed Daisy's mind as she left the ward that it would have been nice to see the doctor, but there was no sign of him. She went back to her work, doing her best to do Maisie's share as well and a little to her surprise getting some willing help from the nurses. All the same she was tired when she finished work for the day and got on her bike. It wasn't until she was knocking on the door of the house where Maisie had been living that she remembered that the doctor had locked the door of her room and probably there wasn't another key. She would have to ask the young woman if there was another one.

There was no need. 'Go on up,' said the young woman wearily, 'the door's open. Any more of you, are there? I don't aim to be opening the door all night.'

Daisy murmured apologetically and went up the stairs and opened Maisie's door. The doctor was there, sitting in one of the chairs, doing nothing.

'Oh,' said Daisy, aware of a rush of feeling at the sight of him. 'I didn't know—that is, Maisie asked me to get her handbag, only when I got here I remembered that I hadn't a key…'

He had got to his feet and took the key out of his pocket. 'I went to see her this afternoon and she told me and since I have the key I thought I'd better come along with it. By the way, Mrs Trump tells me that one of her friends is a widow living in Churchfields Road. She wants to let part of her house; I thought we might go along and see her. Tomorrow evening?'

'Me?'

He was lounging against the back of a shabby armchair, watching her. 'I feel certain that you know better than I what kind of a place Maisie would like.'

'Does she know? I mean, will she mind?'

'I suggested that it might be nice for her to move from this place, somewhere where there was a garden for Milly and Whiskers. She'll be in hospital for ten days; if we could get her settled before then she could go there and have some sick leave.' She was surprised when he said unexpectedly, 'How are you managing, Daisy?'

'Me? Oh, fine, thank you; the nurses are being marvellous and I believe there's someone coming to help part-time until Maisie's back.' He nodded and she went on, 'Don't let me keep you; if you'd let me have the key…'

'Anxious to be rid of me?' he said, but he said it kindly and smiled so that she found herself smiling back. 'Pack up whatever she needs and I'll take them back with me.'

She had found a large plastic bag and was collecting things from the chest of drawers; she put in all the things she thought Maisie might want and laid the handbag on top. 'But you haven't got the car here.'

'Ten minutes' walk.' He took the bag from her and opened the door. Locking it behind him, he said, 'I'll be outside tomorrow evening. We'll go in the car for I have an engagement later on. Leave your bike at the hospital—you can come in by bus in the morning?'

'Yes.' She had followed him down the stairs and the young woman poked her head out of a door and demanded to know how many more times they intended coming. 'The rent's paid until the end of the week—I shall let the room unless I get it by Saturday.'

'The furniture is Miss Watts's?'

'Yes, but not the carpet or the lights. Moving out, is she? I shan't be sorry—her and her animals. Don't know why I've put up with them all this time.'

'Someone will come here tomorrow to remove the furniture. Perhaps you would be good enough to be present when that is done. Good evening to you.'

He propelled Daisy out on to the pavement and the door banged shut behind them. 'You're never to come here alone,

Daisy,' said the doctor firmly. 'I'll attend to whatever has to be done. Now get on your bike and go home.'

He waited while she unlocked the bicycle. 'Goodnight, Daisy.' His kiss was unexpected so that she almost fell off her bike. She muttered something and pedalled away from him at a furious rate. She heard him laugh as she went.

CHAPTER NINE

DAISY WORRIED ABOUT that laugh all the way home. What had there been to laugh about? Did she look comical on a bike? Had she said something silly? With an effort she dismissed it from her mind. His kiss was harder to dismiss but then by the time she had reached her home she had convinced herself that it had been a casual gesture of kindness, rather like patting a dog or stroking a cat. She wheeled her bike into the shed and went in through the kitchen door.

Pamela was at the kitchen table, doing her homework, and her mother came from the sitting-room as she took off her jacket.

'Darling—you're so late again, I was getting worried.'

'I'll be late for the next few days, until we get some help instead of Maisie, Mother. I had to go to Maisie's room and get something for her.'

'You never went all the way back to the hospital?'

'No, Dr Seymour was there; he took it back for me.'

She saw the pleased speculation on her mother's face and sighed soundlessly; her parent was indulging in daydreams again. Such hopeless ones too.

'What a kind man he is and you see quite a lot of him, don't you, love?'

'No,' said Daisy matter-of-factly, 'only if it's something to do with Maisie. He's asked me to go and look at a room to rent for her—she can't possibly go back to that awful place. I thought I'd go tomorrow after work.'

She wasn't going to mention Dr Seymour again; it would only add fuel to the daydreams.

Pamela was watching her thoughtfully. 'Lady Thorley phoned. She's asked you to go to tea on Saturday. I said you'd give her a ring.'

'Then I'd better phone her now…'

'Your supper's in the oven; I'll have it ready when you've done that.' Her mother peered anxiously at the cottage pie. 'We've had ours.'

'It's Miss Thompson's birthday—we thought we would give her a tea party. I'll come for you about three o'clock,' said Lady Thorley when Daisy duly phoned her. She had taken it for granted that Daisy would go and she agreed readily. It would be nice to see the twins again, and the proposed shopping trip to Salisbury with her mother and Pamela could wait.

She left the ward half an hour later than usual the next day—there was still no help and she had tried her best to do the work of two. Besides, she had gone to see Maisie in her dinner-hour, which had meant gobbling down Monday's mince and carrots and missing the pudding. She was in no mood to go anywhere but she had promised the doctor, and she wasn't a girl to break a promise lightly.

He was standing by the entrance, talking to the senior consultant physician, but they broke off their conversation to watch her cross the hall. Both gentlemen greeted her politely and the other man wandered away, leaving Dr Seymour to urge her through the door and into the car.

'Busy day?' he wanted to know.

'Yes,' said Daisy baldly.

'You've seen Maisie?'

'Yes. She's better, isn't she?'

'Yes. You went in your dinner-hour?'

'Yes.' Daisy felt that her conversation hardly sparkled but she was too tired to bother.

'You're bound to be hungry.' He picked up the car phone. 'Mrs Pelham, I'm just taking Daisy to look at rooms for Maisie—I dare say you know about that?' He was silent for a moment and Daisy wriggled with embarrassment; her mother would be explaining that her dear daughter, while mentioning that she would be late, hadn't said that he would be with her.

Dr Seymour's voice took on the soothing tones so effective with his small patients. 'I'll bring her back in the car, Mrs Pelham, you've no need to worry.'

He put the phone down and started the car without speaking and Daisy looked out of the window and wished that she were anywhere but there.

The drive was a short one; the quiet street he stopped in was lined with neat terraced houses with front gardens and well-kept front doors. He got out of the car and opened her door, remarking easily, 'This looks more like Maisie, doesn't it? We shall see…'

The door was opened the moment he knocked and the plump middle-aged woman said at once, 'Dr Seymour? Mrs Trump told me. Come on in.'

She looked enquiringly at Daisy, and the doctor said, 'This

is Miss Pelham, who works with Miss Watts—I thought that perhaps she might know better than I…?'

He smiled gently and Mrs King smiled back. 'Of course.'

She nodded at Daisy in a friendly fashion and led the way into her house. The room they were shown into was exactly right, thought Daisy, and a door at its end led into a small conservatory which opened out on to quite a long garden, well-fenced. There was a gas fire and a very small gas cooker and a washbasin in one corner.

'Before my husband died he was ill for quite a long time, so we had this room specially done for him—there's a shower-room at the end of the hall. I never use it so it could go with the room. She's got her own furniture?'

The doctor had gone to look at the conservatory; obviously he expected Daisy to arrange things. 'Yes, she has. She has a dog and a cat too, both used to living indoors. You wouldn't mind?'

'As long as they don't bother me. A good dog would be quite nice to have—I'm a bit nervous, especially at night.'

'It's a very nice room,' said Daisy. 'I'm not sure if Maisie could afford it…'

'At the hospital, isn't she? Mrs Trump told me what she earned. Would she consider…?' She paused and then mentioned a sum a good deal less than Daisy had expected.

'I should think she could manage that. Could I let you know tomorrow? I shan't see her until then.'

The doctor didn't turn his head. 'Never mind that, Daisy. Would a month's rent in advance be acceptable?'

Driving back to Wilton presently, Daisy asked, 'Wasn't that a bit high-handed, Dr Seymour? How do you know that Maisie will like the room?'

He said placidly, 'If you were Maisie, would you like the place?'

'Oh, yes…'

'There's your answer.'

He stopped the car outside her home and got out to open her door.

'Thank you for bringing me home,' she told him and opened the gate.

'Your mother asked me if I would like a cup of coffee,' he said at his most placid, giving the knocker a brisk tattoo.

Pamela opened the door. 'Come on in,' she invited; she stood aside to allow him to pass her. 'The coffee's ready and Mother's bursting with curiosity.'

Her mother had got out the best china and there was a plate of mince pies on the table. The doctor took off his jacket and sat down, very much at his ease, answering Mrs Pelham's questions with every appearance of pleasure. Anyone looking at them sitting around the table, thought Daisy, would have considered him to be an old friend of the family.

Presently he got up to go and somehow it was Daisy who saw him to the door. 'I'll see Maisie in the morning but I'd be glad if you'd visit her if you can spare the time, convince her that she'll have a comfortable home and that it'll be much better for Milly and Whiskers. Once she has agreed I'll arrange to have her furniture moved in.'

'Very well,' said Daisy sedately, anxious to appear detached but willing. It was disconcerting when he patted her on the shoulder in an avuncular manner and observed that she was a good girl before bidding her a brisk goodnight and getting into his car and driving away.

'Such a delightful man,' declared her mother, collecting

the coffee-cups. 'Supper's all ready. Do you suppose he enjoyed the mince pies?'

'Well, he ate almost all of them, so he must have done,' said Pamela. 'It's hard to think of him as a well-known man in his own particular field of medicine.'

Daisy turned to stare. 'Whatever makes you say that?' she asked.

'Well, he is, you know. I looked him up in the medical *Who's Who*. He's got a string of letters after his name and there's a whole lot about him.' She peeped at Daisy. 'Aren't you interested?'

'Not really,' said Daisy mendaciously.

Maisie was sitting up in bed looking better when Daisy went to see her during her lunchtime the next day, and there was no need to persuade her to do anything; the doctor had been to see her and everything was what she termed hunky-dory.

'Bless the pair of you,' declared Maisie, 'going to all that trouble; me and Milly and Whiskers are that grateful. Me own shower too and a bit of garden. I'm ter go 'ome in a week and just take things easy, like. 'Ow are yer getting on, ducks?'

'Just fine, Maisie. We've been promised part-time help for a day or two and the ward isn't busy.'

'Yer looking peaky. Working too 'ard, I'll be bound. P'raps you'll get a bit of an 'oliday when I get back.'

Daisy went back to the ward and started on the endless chores, glad of something to occupy her thoughts. At the end of the day when she went to tell Sister that she was ready to go, that young lady greeted her with the news that she and Philip were engaged. 'I'm going to tell everyone tomorrow morning, but I wanted you to know first, Daisy. Philip and I hope you'll come to our wedding.'

Daisy offered suitable congratulations, admired the diamond ring, hanging on a gold chain round Sister's neck under her uniform, and went off home. She was glad about Philip and Sister Carter; they would make a splendid pair. She must remember to write and congratulate him. It was to be hoped that someone as nice as Sister Carter would take over the ward; surely Dr Seymour would have a say in the matter?

She hadn't seen him that day and she guessed that he was back in London; indeed as she was leaving the hospital at the end of the day the hall porter handed her a letter addressed in an almost unreadable scrawl. It was from the doctor and very brief and to the point. Would she be so good as to go to Maisie's new home and make sure that everything was suitably arranged? It took a few minutes to decipher and it ended as abruptly as it had begun, with his initials.

'Written with the wrong end of a feather and with his eyes shut,' said Daisy to the empty hallway. All the same she tucked the missive safely away until she could put it under her pillow when she went to bed that night.

She could find no fault when she went to Maisie's new home that evening. It had been furnished with care, Maisie's bits and pieces polished, the bed made up. There was nothing for her to do but compliment her new landlady on the care which she had lavished upon her new lodger's room.

'Me and Mrs Trump,' she was told. 'Dr Seymour said as we were to make it as home-like as possible.' She beamed at Daisy. 'He's a real gentleman.'

Daisy had to work on Sunday for there was no one to relieve her but she was free on Saturday and she cycled to

Lady Thorley's house in the afternoon. She had taken pains with her face and her hair, telling herself that since it was a birthday tea party it behoved her to make the best of her appearance. It was a pity that Lady Thorley had phoned in the morning to say that the car was being serviced and could she find her own way, but it was dry even if it was cold and she could wear her good shoes… And if at the back of her mind she was hoping that the doctor would be there she wasn't going to admit it.

He wasn't there. She was greeted rapturously by the twins, more soberly by Lady Thorley and their governess and informed that Sir Hugh wouldn't be home until evening. 'And Valentine, of course, is still in London—probably catching up on his social life.'

Despite her disappointment, Daisy enjoyed her afternoon; tea was a splendid meal and the birthday cake was magnificent and she had been led away to look at the presents, the best of which, Miss Thompson assured her, were a bead necklace threaded by Katie and a cardboard box containing Josh's model of Belle in Plasticine. These needed to be admired at some length before Miss Thompson, asked what she would like to do since it was her birthday, diplomatically opted for a rousing game of snakes and ladders.

Daisy, promising to return in the not too distant future, went home a few hours later.

Salisbury was quiet when she went to work the next morning—a few people either going or coming from church, an infrequent car and several workers like herself. Even the hospital seemed quiet as she went up to the ward after changing into her pink pinny in the cloakroom used by the orderlies.

It wasn't quiet in the ward, of course. Most of the children were convalescing and making a fine racket, and since Sister had a weekend off and Staff Nurse was in charge they were noisier than usual; Staff Nurse was a splendid nurse but she lacked Sister's authority.

Daisy plunged into her day's routine, buoyed up by the news that there would be help in the morning. During her lunch break she went along to see Maisie and found her sitting by her bed, looking almost her old self.

'Can't wait ter get out of 'ere,' she confided to Daisy. 'The nurses are all right but that Sister—she's an old dragon. I wouldn't work 'ere for a fortune.'

'Well, you won't have to,' said Daisy. 'Sister can't wait to get you back.' She glanced at her watch. 'I must go—we all miss you, Maisie, really we do.'

Maisie looked pleased. 'Go on with you. Mrs Trump came ter see me yesterday—nice of 'er, weren't it? Thought I might like ter know about Milly and Whiskers. Very 'appy, she says.' She added wistfully, 'I'll be glad ter see them…'

'They'll be glad to see you too, Maisie, and it won't be long now. You're all going to be so happy…'

The children were unruly that afternoon; mothers and fathers had come and they had become over-excited. They were allowed to visit any day they liked, of course, but the fathers were mostly at work and most of the mothers had other children or jobs, so Sunday afternoons saw an influx of mothers and fathers who stayed for the children's tea, so that they wouldn't eat, because they were excited or, worse, ate too much of the various biscuits and sweets which should have been handed over and very often weren't.

The last reluctant parent was ushered out finally and the nurses set about getting the children washed and ready for supper and bedtime, Daisy trotting to and fro with clean sheets, collecting up used bedlinen and bagging it, carrying mugs and plates out to the kitchen where an impatient maid, doing double duty since it was a Sunday, waited to wash up.

Stacking mugs and wiping down trays, Daisy became aware of a distant rumble. It wasn't thunder; it sounded like a vast crowd all talking at once but a long way off.

'Kids on the rampage,' said the maid crossly when Daisy mentioned it. And presently when the noise got nearer Staff Nurse made the same remark.

'A protest march or a rally, I dare say, marching through the town. Daisy, will you go down to the dispensary and get that Dettol Sister ordered? It didn't come up this morning and Night Nurse might need some during the night.' She picked up her pen to start the report. 'I've only got Nurse Stevens on and she's still feeding baby Price.'

Daisy made her way down two flights of stairs and along several corridors; most of the wards were at the back of the hospital and it was suppertime, early on Sundays. There was a pleasant smell of cooking as she nipped along, and her small nose twitched. As usual she had cut short her midday meal in order to have more time to spend with Maisie and now she was empty.

The dispenser on duty was on the point of going home and grumbled a good deal as he handed over the bottle. 'I don't know what this place is coming to,' he observed to no one in particular so that Daisy felt it unnecessary to answer him. She bade him goodnight and started on her way back.

It would be quicker if she used the main staircase from the entrance hall—strictly forbidden but there was no one around and it would save quite a few corridors. She reached the entrance hall, aware that the noise of a lot of people was growing louder by the minute; they sounded rather out of hand too. It was to be hoped that they would go past the hospital quickly.

She had her foot on the bottom stair when she realised that they weren't going past; the shouts and yells were very close now—they must be in the forecourt. Even as she thought it the double doors were flung open and a dozen or more youths came through them. They were laughing and shouting and ripe for mischief and she looked towards the porter's lodge. There was always someone on duty there; they could telephone for help—get the police…

It was apparent to her after a moment that there wasn't anyone there. The corridors on either side of her were empty, the rooms which led out of them would be empty too—the consultant's room, Matron's office, the hospital secretary's, and on the other side the committee room which took up almost all of one side of the corridor.

The youths had hesitated at the sight of her but now they were dribbling in, two and three at a time. Some of them had what looked to her like clubs and one of them, bolder than the others, was chipping the bust of a long-dead consultant of the hospital; he was the first in a row and Daisy felt sick at the idea of the damage he could cause. He had a knife; she shook with fright—she was terrified of knives. Her mouth had gone dry too and she clasped her hands in front of her to stop them trembling; all the same she stayed where she was.

'Go away at once,' she called in a voice which wobbled alarmingly; 'this is a hospital…'

The hooligans hooted with raucous laughter. 'An' you're the matron?' yelled someone. 'Try and stop us…' Those behind surged forward and the leaders came nearer, taking a swipe at a second bust, this time of the hospital's founder, as they did so.

Daisy had put the Dettol bottle down when she had turned to see what the commotion was; now she picked it up and held it clasped in both hands in front of her. It wasn't exactly a weapon but if she threw it… First she tried again; rage had swallowed at least part of her fear. 'Get out,' she bawled, 'you louts. The police will be here any moment now.'

This was greeted by jeers and bad language, a good deal of which she didn't understand, which was a good thing, although she had an idea that it was unprintable.

The lout who had been swiping at the marble busts edged nearer and her shaking hands tightened on the bottle…

A great arm encircled her waist and lifted her gently, to push her with equal gentleness behind Dr Seymour's vast back.

'Just in time,' said the doctor placidly. 'I do believe you were going to waste a bottle of Dettol.'

Daisy got her breath back. 'Valentine,' she muttered before she had stopped to think, and heaven alone knew what she might have said next if he hadn't said in a quite ordinary voice,

'Get help, my darling, and ring the police, just in case they don't already know…'

'They'll kill you,' said Daisy into the fine cloth of his jacket. 'I'm not going to leave you…'

'Do as I say, Daisy, run along.'

There was no gainsaying that voice; she turned and flew up the staircase and tore along the corridor until she reached the men's medical ward.

The charge nurse at the other end of the long ward looked up as she raced down its length.

'Mr Soames—there's a mob of hooligans in the hall; Dr Seymour's there, he needs help, and I'm to ring the police.'

Mr Soames was already walking up the ward, beckoning two male nurses to follow as he went. 'Ring the police then the porter's room and the housemen's flat. The numbers are by the phone on my desk.' He paused for a moment by a student nurse. 'You're in charge until we get back.'

He opened the ward doors and Daisy heard Dr Seymour's voice quite clearly. It wasn't particularly loud but it sounded authoritative and very calm. She went into Mr Soames's office and dialled 999. The police were already on their way, she was told; she hung up and dialled the porters' room and then the housemen's flat and a few minutes later heard feet thundering down the staircase. She still had the bottle of Dettol with her; she picked it up and carried it carefully up another flight of stairs to the children's ward and gave it to Staff Nurse.

'There's a frightful racket going on,' said that young lady, 'and you've been ages, Daisy.'

'Some hooligans broke into the hospital, Staff.' For the life of her she couldn't say any more, only stared at the other girl from a white face.

'A cup of tea,' said Staff. 'Sit yourself down. Did you get caught up in it?' When she nodded Staff added, 'A good thing it's time for you to go off duty.' She fetched the tea. 'Sit there for a bit—it must have been upsetting.' She eyed Daisy's ashen face and decided that she would have to wait to find out what was happening. There was a good deal of noise now, loud men's voices and heavy feet tramping around, luckily not so close as to disturb the children.

Daisy drank her tea. Everything had happened rather fast and she was terribly bewildered, but one thing she remembered with clarity. She had called the doctor Valentine and he had called her his darling. 'Get help, my darling,' he had said, but perhaps he had said that just to make her listen…

The phone rang and she supposed she had better answer it.

'Stay where you are until I come for you,' said the doctor in her ear. 'In the children's ward?'

'Yes.' She suddenly wanted to cry.

The phone went dead and she sat down again and presently Staff Nurse came back to write the report.

'Feeling better?' she asked kindly. 'Dr Cowie was in the ward just now; he said they'd cleared those louts away. You were very brave, Daisy, standing there all alone, telling them to go away. Weren't you scared?'

'I've never been so frightened in my life before; I think I would have run away if Dr Seymour hadn't come.'

'He said you were magnificent.' Staff glanced at Daisy's face. 'If it had been me I'd have cut and run.'

'I was too frightened,' said Daisy. 'I don't suppose I could have moved.' She smiled at the other girl, who reflected that Sister had been right—Daisy wasn't the usual sort of orderly; she wondered why she had taken the job…

The door opened and Dr Seymour walked in unhurriedly. 'Get your coat,' he told Daisy, 'I'll take you home. Feel all right now?'

Daisy frowned; he had made it sound as though she had had the screaming hysterics. 'I'm perfectly all right, thank you, Doctor.'

'Good. I'll be in the entrance hall in five minutes.' He held the door open for her and she bade Staff Nurse goodnight and went past him, her chin lifted.

In the car she asked presently, 'What happened to all those hooligans?'

'The police carted some of them off, the rest ran away. Very few of them were locals.'

His voice was casual; he couldn't have been more impersonal. She felt too discouraged to say anything else. As he stopped outside her home she made haste to get out, to be stopped by his hand on the door. 'Not so fast. I'm coming in.'

'There's no need,' she assured him but that was a waste of breath; he got out, opened her door and urged her through the gate as the door opened.

Before she could say a word her mother said, 'Oh, my dear—are you all right? What a dreadful thing to have happened—were you very frightened? And how can I ever thank you, Dr Seymour, for rescuing her as you did?'

'Hardly a rescue, Mrs Pelham.' He had pushed Daisy gently ahead of him so that they were all standing in the little hall. 'I happened to be passing—I'm sure Daisy would have coped very well on her own.'

'Well, of course, she's a very sensible girl,' agreed her mother. 'Nevertheless, I do thank you.' She hesitated. 'I dare say you're a busy man, but if you would like a cup of coffee…?'

'That would be delightful.'

Daisy hadn't said a word; he still had a hand on her shoulder, and now he turned her round, unbuttoned her coat and took it off, pulled the gloves from her hands and propelled her briskly into the kitchen where he sat her down in a chair, took a chair himself and fell into cheerful conversation with Pamela. It wasn't until Mrs Pelham had handed round the coffee and offered cake that Pamela asked, 'Were you scared, Daisy?'

Daisy put her cup down carefully, burst into tears and

darted out of the room. Mrs Pelham looked alarmed, Pamela surprised and the doctor undisturbed.

'No, Mrs Pelham, leave her alone for a while. She'll be all right but she had a nasty shock and the reaction has set in. She was remarkably brave—you would have been very proud of her. Tomorrow she'll be quite herself again; bed is the best place for her now and perhaps a warm drink before she sleeps.' He added kindly, 'You mustn't worry.'

Mrs Pelham said faintly, 'She's such a dear girl…'

'Indeed she is,' agreed the doctor, and something in his voice made Pamela stare at him.

'Are you in love with her?' she asked, and ignored her mother's shocked indrawn breath.

'Oh, yes,' said the doctor blandly and smiled at Pamela. 'I must go. The coffee was delicious, Mrs Pelham.' He said his goodbyes and Pamela went to the door with him.

'I won't tell,' she told him. He smiled then and dropped a kiss on her cheek before he went away.

He had been quite right, of course; Daisy slept like a baby all night, ate her breakfast and cycled to work, quite restored to her normal sensible self. She felt ashamed of her outburst in front of the doctor and as soon as she saw him she would apologise. It was a great pity that she had called him Valentine to his face like that, but he would surely realise that she had been upset at the time. She rehearsed a neat little speech as she cycled and presented herself in the ward nicely primed.

It wasn't until the end of the day that Sister mentioned in Daisy's hearing that he had gone to Holland. 'Lectures or something,' she explained to Staff Nurse. 'He does get around, doesn't he? I should have loved to see him telling those louts where they could go…'

Daisy, collecting the sheets and listening with both ears, wondered forlornly if she would see him again.

Sooner than she expected. It was two days later as she was collecting the children's mugs after their morning milk that one of the nurses told her that she was wanted in Sister's office. Daisy put down her tray, twitched her pink pinny into neatness and knocked on the office door, and when there was no answer poked her head round it. Her eyes met Dr Seymour's steady gaze and since she could hardly withdraw without saying something she said, 'Oh, I'm sorry, sir, I was told to come here but Sister isn't…' She tailed off, not sure what to say next, anxious to be gone even though her heart was beating a tattoo at the sight of him.

'No, she isn't,' agreed the doctor calmly. 'Come in, Daisy.'

He got up from the chair behind the desk, closed the door behind her. 'Do sit down,' he said and when she shook her head came to stand so close to her that all she could see was an expanse of dark grey superfine wool waistcoat. She counted the buttons and lifted her gaze sufficiently to study his tie—a very fine one, silk and vaguely striped. Italian, no doubt. Higher than that she refused to look while she strove to remember the speech she had rehearsed so carefully.

'I had no idea,' said the doctor at last, 'that courting a young lady could be fraught with so many difficulties. Why is it, I wonder, that I'm able to diagnose acute anterior poliomyelitis, measles, hydrocephalus, intersusception, inflamed adenoids, the common cold…and yet I find myself unable to find the right words?'

He was smiling down at her and she said with a little gasp, 'Oh, do be careful what you're saying; you might regret it—I dare say you're very tired or something.' She added urgently, 'I'm the orderly…'

His laughter rumbled. 'Oh, no, you're not, you're Daisy, my Daisy, the most darling girl in the world and so hard to pin down. I'm in love with you, my darling, have been since the first moment I set eyes on you…'

She looked up into his face then. 'But you never…' she began.

'You'd made up your mind that we didn't like each other, hadn't you? You are, my dearest heart, pigheaded at times.' He made that sound like a compliment. 'It seemed that I needed to be circumspect.' He wrapped great arms around her. 'You called me Valentine,' he reminded her, 'and you wanted to stay with me. You looked at me with those lovely grey eyes and I knew then that whatever you said it would make no difference, that you loved me too.'

'But I'm an…' began Daisy, and then added, 'Yes, I do love you.'

She didn't finish because he kissed her then. Presently he said, 'You'll marry me, my little love? And soon.'

She lifted her face from his shoulder. 'I have to give a week's notice.'

'Rubbish. I'll deal with that at once.'

'But you can't…'

'Oh, yes, I can and I will. You'll leave this evening.' He kissed her gently, 'My love, leave everything to me.'

She smiled mistily. 'I must go, Valentine—the milk-mugs…'

He kissed her once more and opened the door for her. 'I can't believe it's true,' she told him. 'What will everyone say?'

He caught her hand and held it for a moment. 'We'll ask them at our wedding. I'll be waiting outside for you this evening, my darling.' He smiled. 'The end of my waiting.'

Daisy nodded, her head full of glimpses of a delightful future. She stood on tiptoe and kissed his cheek and whisked herself away, back to her tray of mugs. But not for long.

* * * * *

Keep reading for an excerpt of
Rafael's Proposal
by Kim Lawrence.
Find it in the
Valentine's Day Collection 2025 anthology,
out now!

CHAPTER ONE

THE DOOR OF the lift was just closing when Maggie Coe slipped in.

'I've been trying to catch you all day, Rafe!' she cried breathlessly. 'I want to run something by you.'

Rafael Ransome didn't consider a lift a suitable place to conduct business conversations, especially when he was on his way home after working twelve hours straight to persuade the intransigent CEO of an ailing electronics company that awarding himself and the senior management team a fifty-per-cent pay rise while simultaneously laying off production staff wasn't the best strategy to ensure the long-term future of the firm!

Ninety-nine out of a hundred people would have been able to deduce his feelings from the discouraging expression on his striking dark features, but Maggie Coe was not one of the ninety-nine.

Rafe ran a hand over the dark stubble on his normally clean-shaven jaw and grimaced. Her tunnel vision made Maggie an asset professionally, but it was a real pain in the rear when all you wanted was a hot shower and a cold drink.

'It looks like you have me for the next sixty seconds.' Coincidentally the same time, according to his disapproving mother, of his longest *relationship* to date.

Despite the shaky start, about thirty seconds into her pitch Maggie had his full attention.

'So effectively all she'd be doing is sorting mail.' Typically Rafe cut to the chase. 'Is that right—?'

Maggie Coe nodded, too pleased with herself to note the steely tone of disapproval that had entered his deep voice. 'And licking the odd stamp,' she added with a smile of satisfaction.

She looked up with every expectation of seeing her boss looking dumbstruck with admiration that she'd come up with the perfect solution to a troublesome problem—the problem in question being Natalie Warner, a young woman who couldn't seem to get her priorities right.

They didn't need an employee who was going to turn up late if her child had a snuffle, even if she did always scrupulously make up that lost time and more. The fact that moreover she didn't complain when she was regularly allocated an unfair proportion of the tedious, boring tasks didn't cut any ice with Maggie. As far as she was concerned, if they tolerated such a *laissez-faire* attitude they were at risk of setting a dangerous precedent, and, as she had told Mr Ransome, before long everyone would be strolling in when it suited them.

In short, anarchy.

Even though she couldn't see his expression Maggie had no doubts that a man who valued efficiency as much as Rafael Ransome, and who furthermore was capable of being as ruthless as he deemed necessary to achieve it, shared her view.

The silent lift came to a halt at the required floor, but Rafe pressed a button to prevent the door opening and turned back to the woman beside him.

'Do you not feel that opening envelopes is a waste of someone with her qualifications?' he questioned his zealous subordinate mildly. Those who knew him best would not have been fooled by the casual tone, but Maggie was blissfully blind to any signs of danger in the cold eyes or in the nerve pulsating in his lean cheek.

'Well, I'm hoping she'll think so,' came the smart reply.

Rafael's eyes narrowed thoughtfully. Maggie was prone to seeing things in terms of black and white, but she was a normally fair-minded person. Her hostility for this young woman seemed almost personal, which wasn't like her.

Natalie Warner, he reflected grimly, seemed to have a knack for aggravating people. She had certainly got under his skin… not in a personal way, of course—he made it a rule never to mix business with pleasure. It was just he hated to see talent wasted and Natalie Warner had buckets of the stuff, even though she seemed determined not to use it.

'So you're hoping that she'll be humiliated and resign…?' A child could have seen exactly what Maggie's tactics were.

'That's her choice, but let's just say I wouldn't try and stop her.'

She sounded so complacent that it took Rafe several seconds to control the sharp flare of fury that washed over him. It was ironic that the person on whose behalf he felt so angry wouldn't have felt even slightly grateful if she'd known she had aroused his dormant protective instincts.

An image of a heart-shaped face floated in the air before his eyes, a rare distracted expression entered the densely blue—some said cold—eyes of the man who was famed for his single-minded focus. Natalie Warner barely reached his shoulder and looked as fragile as delicate china, but the likeness was highly deceptive. Any man whose chivalrous instincts were aroused by her appearance would be well advised to repress them unless he fancied an earful of abuse for his efforts—he'd seen her in action and had felt sympathy for the man foolish enough to imagine she needed any special favours.

Rafe admired independent, spunky females—*admired* but avoided involvement with. At this point in his life he wasn't into high-maintenance relationships. But Natalie Warner wasn't just self-reliant, she was the sort of prickly, pigheaded female who wouldn't have asked for a glass of water if she were on fire just to make a point.

'Have you considered that she could have a good case of constructive dismissal if she wanted to take it farther?'

Maggie quickly assured him she had covered this. 'Her job title will be the same, and there will be no drop in her salary. The content of her job would even be the same on paper.' The older woman shrugged. 'So she can't claim she's been demoted.'

'This is in fact a sideways move,' Rafael mused drily. 'Exactly.'

So much for the sisterhood he was always hearing about. 'It doesn't bother you that she's a single parent with a child?'

This time even Maggie couldn't miss the steel in his voice. She blanched as his long lashes lifted from the sharp angles of his razor-sharp slanting cheekbones to reveal disapproval glittering in his deep-set eyes.

'Bother me?' she echoed, evincing confusion while she did some fast thinking. It was becoming clear that, far from being pleased with her ingenuity, Rafe was inexplicably furious—in that quiet but devastating way he had. 'In what way?' she questioned, desperately trying to retain her composure in the face of the displeasure of a man she deeply admired and whose approval she craved.

'Don't play the innocent with me, Maggie,' he drawled, an expression of simmering impatience stamped on his classically handsome features.

'You say yourself that there's no room for sentimentality in the workplace,' she reminded him with a hint of desperation.

'I rather think you might be taking that quote out of context,' he returned drily.

Maggie flushed. 'So you want her to stay where she is?'

Do I...?

Ironically his life would be a lot more comfortable if he let Maggie install the distracting thorn in his side in some dark cupboard. He sighed; as tempting as it was, he couldn't let her do it. God, sometimes he wished he weren't a good guy.

'You will not hide Natalie Warner away in some Godforsaken back room, Maggie.' Firmly he spelt out his instructions so there would be no convenient misunderstandings. 'Neither will you move her anywhere without my *personal* say-so.' He saw the alert expression appear on Maggie's face and wished he had omitted the *'personal'*. The last thing he wanted was that sort of rumour starting up again.

A while after Natalie had started at Ransome it had come to his attention that there had been whispers that he'd been taking a particular interest in their smart new recruit. He blamed himself for not having foreseen his actions could have been interpreted that way—he knew all too well how people's minds worked.

He could still remember the hurt look of surprise on her face when she'd come to him excited by an idea she'd had, and he had cut her dead—he had made sure there had been plenty of people to witness the snub. It had been a case of being cruel to be kind. Even if the affair had been fictitious, the rumour that she had made it, not on talent, but because she was sleeping with the boss, would haunt a woman through her career.

'You will carry on treating her exactly the same way you do all the other trainees,' he elaborated quietly. 'Do I make myself clear—?' He lifted one brow questioningly and the woman beside him gulped and nodded.

Having made his point, he allowed the door to open and stood aside to let her pass. 'Incidentally,' he called after her, 'there's a meeting scheduled next month to discuss flexible working hours.' Or at least there would be once he'd asked his PA to organise it. 'You might like to ask around to see what the level of interest would be in a crèche.'

The last of Natalie's co-workers had left an hour earlier, laughingly predicting how many valentine's cards they would receive. 'Are you doing anything special, Nat?' asked the young woman who had just boasted that her boyfriend had booked them a table at a really swish restaurant—and was pretty sure he was going to propose.

'I'm going to a wedding,' Natalie explained.

'How romantic, getting married on Valentine's Day!' someone exclaimed enviously.

Then someone else asked the question Natalie had hoped they wouldn't.

'Anyone we know, Nat?'

'Mike, my ex-husband, is getting married to his girlfriend, Gabrielle Latimer…the actress.'

'Your *ex*!'

'Oh, God, she's *gorgeous*!' someone else breathed, only to be elbowed by the guy standing beside her.

'Personally,' someone else remarked, 'I don't think she'll age well—now, if she had *your* cheekbones, Nat…' Everyone looked at Natalie and nodded. 'And I read the other day she's had a boob job.'

Natalie smiled. She appreciated the loyal attempt to make her feel better but, like the others, she knew that when it came to looks she couldn't even compete in the same league as the younger girl.

Natalie would have actually preferred to spend Valentine's Day having root-canal work than attending the wedding of the century, but her daughter, Rose, who was to be a bridesmaid, had flatly refused to attend if Mummy wasn't there, too.

At least Luke would be there for moral support.

With a sigh she set about reducing the pile of paper on the desk. When half an hour later Luke Oliver put his good-looking blond head around the partition that separated her from the rest of the large office she had made good inroads into the backlog. 'You're working late, Luke,' she observed as the rest of his body followed suit.

'I'm not the only one—after Brownie points?' he teased lightly.

'There wouldn't be any point, would there?' Natalie felt guilty when Luke looked embarrassed by her dry observation. 'I'm making up for a late start,' she admitted hurriedly. 'Rose had another asthma attack last night.' Natalie pinned an upbeat smile on her face as Luke's good-looking face creased with sympathy. 'Fortunately I managed to get her an early appointment at the doctor's this morning, but they were running late and by the time I'd finally got her settled with Ruth it was almost eleven.'

'How is she?'

'She's loads better this morning, thanks.' Even so it had torn Natalie apart to leave her fragile-looking daughter. It was a guilt thing, of course. Rose had been more than happy to stay with Ruth, who doted on her and was more than capable to cope with any crisis.

'So now you're working twice as hard as everyone else to prove you don't expect any special favours just because you're a single mum,' Luke suggested perceptively.

Natalie gave a rueful smile and rotated her head to relieve the tension in her neck and shoulders. 'You know me so well, Luke.'

Luke's glance dropped to the delicate, clear-cut features lifted to him—features made nonetheless attractive by dark smudges of fatigue under the wide-spaced, darkly lashed hazel eyes and lines of strain around the wide, softly curving lips.

'Not as well as I'd like…' he sighed huskily.

Natalie's smile morphed into a wary frown as she registered the suggestive warmth in his expression; she'd thought they'd got past all that stuff. 'You know that I'm not…' she began wearily.

Luke sighed and held up his hand. 'Sorry, I know I said I wouldn't go there, Nat, but…' his attractive smile flashed out '…you might change your mind?'

'No, I won't change my mind.' Natalie hardened her heart against Luke's hurt puppy-dog look. 'And anyway, you know as well as I do that office romances never work.' She smiled to lessen her rejection. 'Besides, there's no room in my life for a man.' Or for that matter much for anything but work and sleep, and not too much of the latter when Rose wasn't well!

'Have you told little Rose yet about Mike moving to the States?'

Natalie rubbed the faint worried indentation between her feathery eyebrows and shook her head. 'Nope. I suppose I should before the wedding?' What am I doing asking a childless bachelor advice on child-rearing when I already know the answer? she thought begrudgingly. 'But I just don't know how she's going to react.' *Liar!* She knew Rose would react like any other five-year-old when she learnt the dad who spoilt her rotten every other weekend—when he turned up—was moving halfway around the world—*badly*!

Luke shifted uncomfortably. 'Actually it's about the wedding I wanted to have a word, Nat.'

His next words confirmed that the shiver of apprehension snaking down her spine was justified.

'I hate to do this to you, but Rafe has put me on the Ellis account; he's sending me to New York for a couple of weeks.' He tried to sound casual about this amazing opportunity and failed miserably.

'Congratulations.'

'Thanks, Nat. It should be you that's going, though.'

Natalie shook her head and pinned on a smile. Only a real cow would begrudge someone as nice and genuinely talented as Luke a break like this. 'You deserve it, Luke,' she assured him warmly.

'I'm afraid it means…'

'You won't be able to come to the wedding with me,' she completed, unable to totally disguise her dismay behind a sunny smile. 'That's fine, don't worry,' she added stoically.

She wasn't surprised that Luke had said yes; when Rafe *asked* hungry young executives like Luke they never said no. In fact, she brooded, people in general don't say no to him…*except me*. These days she didn't rate cosy chats with His Lordship, as the blue-blooded heir to a baronetcy was called—sometimes affectionately, sometimes not!—behind his back. Which just proves, she told herself wryly, that there is a bright side to having a career that's going nowhere.

On paper she and Luke had the same qualifications, they had even begun working at the top-notch management consulting firm within weeks of one another, but ten months on Luke had his own office and she was still sitting at the same desk doing routine stuff that she could have done asleep.

Things weren't likely to get better either. You didn't get offered a chance at Ransome twice and Natalie had, after much soul-searching, refused hers. Luke, who hadn't had to weigh his desire for promotion against the problems of child care, had not said no to his.

The rest, as they said, was history. She'd made her choice; she didn't consider herself a victim—lots of women managed to have high-flying careers and babies. Clearly she didn't have what it took.

'God, Nat, I'm really sorry.'

'It's not your fault,' Natalie soothed a guilty-looking Luke. 'It's *that* man,' she breathed, venom hardening her soft voice as she contemplated the grim prospect of attending the marriage of her ex to the glamorous Gabby without the support of a passable male to give the ego-bolstering illusion she had a well-rounded life. 'I don't suppose it even occurs to Rafael Ransome that some people actually have a life outside this place!'

'*Nat*, he's not that bad.'

'*Bad!* The man's a cold-blooded tyrant! I'm surprised he doesn't make us sign our contracts in blood,' she retorted with a resolute lack of objectivity. 'Forget all that stuff you read about him in the glossy supplements,' she advised Luke, imaginatively expanding her theme. 'He might have turned this place into one of the top management consulting firms in Europe virtually overnight—the success of the nineties…'

To Luke's amusement she proceeded to dismiss one of the

most spectacular financial successes of the decade with a disdainful sniff.

'And have every top company beating a path to his door, but I've always reckoned he was born in the wrong century.'

Luke looked amused. 'Sounds like you've given the subject some thought?'

'Not especially,' Natalie responded hurriedly. 'It's just obvious that underneath the designer suits—'

'You've not given that much thought either, I suppose.'

'Most certainly not!' Natalie denied, insulted by the suggestion she was in the habit of mentally undressing her boss.

'*Sure* you haven't. So what *do* you think goes on under his designer suits, Nat?'

'I think there lurks the soul of a feudal, your-fate-is-in-his-hands type of despot. I can just see him now grinding the odd handful of peasants into the ground.'

Her voice lost some of its crisp edge as an intrusive mental image to match her words flashed into her head. In her defence, Rafe Ransome, his well-developed muscular thighs covered by a pair of tight and most likely historically inaccurate breeches, was enough to put the odd weak quiver into the most objective of females' voices.

Unlike Natalie, most women were not normally objective about her employer's looks; his mingled genes—Italian on his mother's side and Scottish on his aristocratic father's side—had given the man an entirely unfair advantage in the looks stakes.

'Nat!'

Natalie was too caught up in her historical re-enactment to hear the note of warning. 'On his way to burn down his neighbours' castle and ravish the local maidens…'

Like the modern-day equivalent, his victims probably wouldn't have put up much of a fight, she thought, contemplating with disapproval the inability of her own sex to see beyond a darkly perfect face of fallen angel and an in-your-face sensuality.

It struck her as ironic, when you considered he was set to inherit a centuries-old title and the castle that went with it from his Scottish father, that Rafael Ransome, all six feet three of him—and most of it solid muscle—looked Latin from the top of his perfectly groomed glossy head to the tips of his expressive tapering fingers.

Even she, who wasn't into dark, dynamic, brooding types, had to admit that if you discounted his disconcertingly bright electric-blue eyes Rafael looked like most women's idealised image of a classic Mediterranean male. Dark luxuriant hair that gleamed blue-black in some lights, golden skin stretched tautly over high chiselled cheekbones, and a wide, sensually moulded mobile mouth…just thinking about the cruel contours caused a shudder to ripple through her body and she hadn't even got to his lean, athletic body!

'Natalie!'

It was Luke's strangled whisper that finally made her lift her unfocused angry eyes from the computer screen, filled by now with row after row of angry exclamation marks.

Oh, God!

Even before Natalie heard the inimical deep mocking drawl the back of her neck started to prickle and her stomach gave a sickly lurch. Why, she wondered despairingly, hadn't her selective internal radar, selective as in it only spookily zapped into life when His Lordship was in the vicinity, kicked in a few moments earlier?

Her wide eyes sent an agonised question to Luke, who almost imperceptibly nodded.

I must have done something really terrible in a previous life, she thought.